AGENT OF THE STATE

AGENT OF THE STATE

ROGER PEARCE

ISIS
LARGE PRINT
Oxford

First published in Great Britain 2012
by
Coronet, an imprint of Hodder & Stoughton

Published in Large Print 2013 by ISIS Publishing Ltd.,
7 Centremead, Osney Mead, Oxford OX2 0ES
by arrangement with
Hodder & Stoughton, An Hachette UK Company

CIP data is available for this title from the British Library

ISBN 978–0–7531–9182–8 (hb)
ISBN 978–0–7531–9183–5 (pb)

Printed and bound in Great Britain by
T. J. International Ltd., Padstow, Cornwall

For Maggie

Acknowledgements

To my agent Sonia Land, publisher Mark Booth, Charlotte Hardman and all the team at Coronet

To tell the truth is a duty: but it is a duty only in respect to one who has a right to the truth.

Benjamin Constant

Prologue

It is Wednesday, the last day of June 2005. London's workers read about the threat to aircraft as they trundle through the city's depths. Terrorists attack trains in Russia and Spain, but seem to ignore London's creaking Underground.

Detective Chief Inspector John Kerr is accompanying his daughter, Gabriella, to Heathrow for her flight home. Gabi is fifteen and lives with her mother. They take the Tube because Kerr's Alfa Romeo is in dock and he wants to buy Gabi lunch before she goes airside. She travels light, cabin baggage only, violin case and a small bag on wheels.

Shortly before eleven o'clock they board the half-empty, end carriage at Highbury and Islington, a few minutes' walk from Kerr's apartment. They rattle towards central London, Gabi listening to her iPod, Kerr half-reading *Metro*. In jeans, green polo shirt and suede loafers, Kerr is enjoying an away-day from the office but feels vaguely unsettled at being out of mobile contact until they emerge at Earl's Court.

The bomber boards their carriage at Euston, two stops down the line. Although there are plenty of seats, he loiters by the double doors. A little older than Gabi, he is strongly built, dark-skinned and clean-shaven, in jeans, trainers and a stained T-shirt with a long white scarf rolled around his neck. He is also wearing a rucksack, but this is not unusual or alarming.

No one is looking, including Gabi. Kerr notices him straight away, because nearly two decades of intelligence work in Special Branch have tuned his instincts. The young man's body language betrays him as he fidgets by the doors, hands bulging his pockets. He is muttering to himself, eyes flitting everywhere.

As they slow for Green Park station there is a loud *pop*. People look up in curiosity, not fear: they are unfamiliar with the sound of a detonator going off. But John Kerr has visited Israel and Sri Lanka to study suicide bombers, and to him the detonation is as obvious as a dog whistle. Everything snaps into focus as he forces Gabi to the floor and throws himself on top of her, the father using his body to shield his child before the main charge lacerates them.

But nothing happens. Kerr looks up. The man knows Kerr knows. He is panicking, struggling to free himself from his bomb as the doors open. He races from the carriage still wearing the rucksack, cannoning towards the exit sign with Kerr in hot pursuit.

The platform is clogged with tourists waiting to board the train. The bomber is fast. Kerr is just the right side of forty, but fit and athletic. He is half a carriage behind but makes up ground as he charges through the human funnel the bomber has created, yelling at people to get clear. Near the exit, the platform

2

supervisor half-heartedly blocks the man with the bat she uses to signal the driver, but he hurls her aside as if she were a child.

The station is deep and the escalator long. Kerr has done well along the platform but drops pace as they make for the surface, even though he attacks the steps two at a time. He has stopped shouting to conserve his energy but, at the half-way point, he is at least a dozen steps behind and losing the race. The bomber steals a glance back and looks surprised by Kerr's determination. Then, at the top, faced with several exits, he makes his fatal mistake. Vaulting the ticket barrier, he takes the underpass that will lead him to Green Park. But instead of choosing the sprint for freedom in open ground, he swings into the men's toilet, hoping his pursuer will take the wrong exit and leave him to escape in the confusion.

He is not fast enough for John Kerr. Leaping the barrier, as if on springs, Kerr has seen him. He reaches the entrance and assesses the scene in a split second: three men at the urinal; a couple of suits on the pick-up by the nearest cubicle doors, looking for a pre-lunch blowjob. At the dead end, his quarry.

Kerr's ID is superfluous. The men scatter, leaving him with the bomber. The young man bolts the door of the farthest cubicle, but Kerr defeats it in a single kick and has him round the throat before he can react. He forces him back on the toilet seat, crushing the rucksack against the cistern pipe, and lands punch after punch on his face. The bomber struggles hard, landing a couple of jabs in return. He is fighting back, which is

3

what Kerr wants: resistance means he does not have to stop. He can continue punishing the man who tried to murder his daughter.

Then, dragging the bomber out of the cubicle to the bank of washbasins, he smashes his face against the mirrored wall. A couple of punters enter, turn on their heels and hurry away. There will be no witnesses. The young man is groaning as the fight deserts him, but Kerr bangs his forehead again and again on a tap. He hears something give, bone, tissue, perhaps an eye, and the young man's blood flows as quickly as the water, spraying them both in diluted red.

The scarf is already rolled around the bomber's neck so Kerr pulls it tighter still, garrotting him, and hurls him back into the cubicle.

The cleaner has left his mop against the wall. Kerr snaps the handle in two and, with the free end and the scarf makes a tourniquet, twisting it until the man gives up the battle. Panting hard, Kerr leans down to look deep into his face. Yes, the left eye is seriously damaged, but he will not be needing it. Somewhere outside a young woman is screaming. The bomber's face slumps against his chest. "You tried to murder my daughter, you piece of shit." It is hard to tell if he is still conscious, but Kerr needs to tell him, anyway: "Here's where you belong."

He holds the tourniquet tight until the bomber is dead, lowers him face down to the floor and gently removes the rucksack. There is a bomb inside, a charred, inert plastic package of white powder. It has nails and screws for maximum damage, but is as dead

4

as its maker. Kerr pads to the entrance, pulls the iron gate shut and calls the office.

The bomb will excuse the murder. When they tell him, Kerr will shrug and walk away, uninterested in legal nicety. For him it is a case of vengeance.

Friday, 15 July 2005, is a time for blame-shifting, deck-clearing and defence-building. It is sixteen days after the murder and eight since the atrocity of 7/7. Counter-terrorism's Big Issue is its failure to prevent 7/7. Kerr's bomber was an associate of the main perpetrator, Mohammed Siddique Khan. It turns out he was from Batley in West Yorkshire and, like Khan, has security traces.

John Kerr had executed the man who, captured alive, could have led them to the London bombers before they left on their terrible mission.

In the late morning Kerr is summoned to the commissioner's private conference room "to meet some people". There are three civilians sitting around the table, but seven dirty coffee cups and plates, and the air is heavy with earlier heated exchanges. The biscuits have disappeared, along with the commissioner and his sidekicks. Kerr is unsurprised. There is no mileage in sitting alongside an employee who has murdered in cold blood. Probably no knighthood, either.

Kerr's interrogators introduce themselves as Beth, Hugh and Neil. They are white, middle class, surname-free and smiling, like talent-show hosts. The MI6 guy, Hugh, is an army retread, with streamlined collar and shiny shoes, straight off the parade ground.

The woman is skinny, with bleached, spiky hair and a butterfly tattoo on her neck. Kerr remembers that, after a secret intelligence briefing at Cheltenham seven or eight years ago, they shared a chicken Madras and got drunk on red wine. If Beth remembers it, she isn't saying. Years of dropping in on *jihadi* chit-chat have not been kind. She is thinner now, and the butterfly looks grounded for good.

When they are seated around the table, Kerr on his own facing the window, the boy from MI5 kicks off. Kerr is glad to find it is not to be an interrogation. They are all delighted that the attorney general has decided not to press charges. Really. They nod and flick on the smile switch again, sharing Kerr's joy that he will not be standing in the dock at the Old Bailey.

"There was no other option, was there," shrugs Kerr, "seeing as you covered the whole thing up?" The media has been silent about Kerr's interdiction, because no one told them about it. With the corpse and rucksack spirited away, the attempted bombing simply did not take place. The cover-up must have sounded a good idea right up until 7/7.

Neil is currently working police liaison. He wears wide braces and a watch with too many dials for a civil servant in charge of a desk. Since Kerr's last sighting, he has developed the beginnings of a goatee.

There is a bit more disarming preamble to show Kerr he is among friends, and they use his first name a lot, which puts him on red alert. Kerr's partners in the US State Department call it "time to decompress", but it does not work here and now because the atmosphere is stifling and Kerr has seen it all before.

Eventually it is Kerr who calls the meeting to order. He knows they want to ask him one question: why did you take the guy out when you should have arrested him? Arrest might have led them to the 7/7 bombers and prevented the attacks eight days later. It is a fair point. Kerr has thought about this.

Then Neil blows it by saying he understands: he can imagine what it's like to be facing that kind of threat. He says this to impress the others, as if he's just dropped in from hand-to-hand combat in Afghanistan. But it is a mistake, like telling a terminal-cancer patient you know how it feels. He wants to appear a man of the world, but Neil is really just another tosser from Thames House.

"John, we have to examine what you gleaned about this man. Explore if there's anything we could have done to prevent the attacks." When Neil says "we" he means John Kerr, of course. They want him to admit he found something out, then use it to hang him.

"You want to know if he shared his Facebook before I garrotted him?" asks Kerr, mildly.

"Not exactly," says Neil. "But he might . . . I dunno . . . did he shout something in the carriage before he ran off, for example? Or in the toilet before . . . you know? Any clues at all?"

"Did I torture him before I killed him, you mean? Abu Ghraib in the Gents at Green Park?"

Hugh evidently decides it is time to intervene. His neck is tighter against the collar and his eyes have become slits. He no longer looks decompressed. "Did you?"

"Did I fuck," says Kerr, which irritates them even more. "And the only clue was a rucksack full of fertiliser and shrapnel."

Kerr's statement of the bleeding obvious creates a lull while they regroup. The interview is going badly, for the subject is not showing the right level of contrition. Who would have expected him to come out fighting?

During the sparring match Beth has sat in silence, head down, doodling. Perhaps she's thinking she had a narrow escape all those years ago. "Your man was an associate of Khan, so probably knew their intentions," she says now, frowning at her rectangles and circles, "so why do you think he risked messing everything up for them?"

"You're the mind expert, Beth. You tell me," says Kerr, familiar. "Perhaps it was just good old vanity . . . you know, a compulsion to be first among the nutters. But he didn't tell me that, either. In case you're wondering."

"We're not, John. Honestly." Neil is back on track. "It's just that a lot of questions are going to be asked. We have to know if there's anything you think we could have done to prevent this atrocity."

"Well, it's obvious, isn't it? You should have gone public. Made people aware and warned them of the risk. In the end it's always the cover-up that gets you, Neil. You guys should know that by now."

"You know full well we had to avoid alarming the public unnecessarily."

8

"You kept it quiet because your office had just lowered the threat level."

"That's neither here nor there."

"Said there was no imminent threat."

"Whatever," says Neil, "we are where we are."

"Look, I have to live with what I've done. OK, seven-seven may have happened because I killed that bomber. That possibility will haunt me. But you have to live with the consequences because you kept it secret."

"And it has to stay that way."

"Does it?" This brings another pause. They are looking at him intently; even Beth has put down her pencil. And then, in a flash, all becomes clear. "You think I'm going to blow the whistle, don't you?" He laughs. "That's it, isn't it?"

"Not at all. We're in this together."

"Bullshit. You couldn't give a toss whether that young man said anything to me, only whether I'll hold the line. That's it, isn't it? So why don't you ask me up front?"

"Why did you do it?" snaps Hugh. It is a last-ditch attempt to subordinate him. "What made you murder a man in cold blood when you know you should have kept him alive?"

Kerr looks each of them in the eye. He knows they are not family people. "Ask me that when you have children."

Part One

CHAPTER
ONE

Thursday, 13 September 2012, 06.53, New Scotland Yard

Squeezing into the glass cubbyhole that passed for his office at the top of New Scotland Yard, John Kerr had to ease the door open with his left shoulder, Starbucks in one hand, encrypted laptop in the other, head tilted to clamp the BlackBerry to his ear. But the call from his deputy made him dump all that stuff and scramble for his firearm. It was a Glock 19 semi-automatic 9mm pistol, the lightweight weapon of choice for his surveillance teams. It should have been stored in the secure armoury next to the operations room but, against all the rules, he kept it in a locked cabinet inside his safe.

The call lasted less than half a minute. "Why didn't they tell us immediately?" Kerr demanded, then listened intently to the answer. "You're absolutely certain it's Melanie? Is she blown? Any demands yet? OK, Dodge, just get me the address of the stronghold."

When he bowled out, less than two minutes later, he was on the run, firearm concealed in the shoulder holster beneath his jacket, kicked by an adrenaline rush.

Thoughts accelerating ahead of his body, he calculated the threat. It was supposed to have been a routine job, short-term infiltration of a European gang of cocaine smugglers. Kerr had tasked Detective Sergeant Melanie Fleming as the undercover officer. She was to be the courier for the last leg of the importation, the cut-off between the importer and the UK receivers.

Kerr was operational head of the Covert Operations Unit. For decades his élite team had conducted the most secret work in Special Branch. There were three types of activity: surveillance, often armed and at close quarters; the recruitment and running of agents (or "covert human intelligence sources", as they were now officially termed); and "technical attack", the euphemism for bugging.

It was a wide remit, sensitive, political and risky, with always too much going on. Sometimes other departments "borrowed" his undercover operatives, which was what had happened with Melanie. Two days earlier he had offered her to the Anti-corruption Unit, the cops who investigate other cops. They were known as the "rubber-heelers" because you could never hear them coming. How could it have gone so wrong?

He punched the lift button. "Fucking amateurs," he muttered. The risk assessment from his opposite number had been crystal clear: in the event of compromise, there was a negligible risk of violence. That was his absolute, cast-iron assurance. Yet it seemed that, in the course of a single night, what had started as a regular sting operation had erupted into a siege, with Melanie as the hostage. Kerr had the lift to himself. The sit-rep was opaque and his mind a maelstrom of questions. The threat to Melanie had no up-side, but coldly, calmly, John Kerr knew exactly what he was going to do.

On the ground floor a cluster of female records staff crowded round the lift doors. He was working with them on a stronger system of human-source protection and found himself face to face with their head, a civil-service high flyer with stilettos to match her ambition. He felt her hand on his arm but kept moving. "Sorry, Jules, gotta crack on," he murmured. "Catch up with you later."

His phone vibrated and he took the call. "I'm going to the car now," he said, racing down the spiral staircase to dig out his Alfa Romeo 156T Spark from the Yard's cramped, subterranean garage. "Pick you up usual place."

He was still inserting the BlackBerry into the hands-free as he spun up the ramp, scattering another bunch of workers emerging from St James's Park Tube station. His Tetra radio mainset shared the glove compartment with a makeup bag Gabriella kept for emergencies when she stayed over. He switched it to Channel Five, the protected frequency used by his surveillance teams.

Accelerating into the thoroughfare he narrowly missed his commander's dark blue Toyota Prius as it crossed his path onto the Yard's forecourt. From the back seat Paula Weatherall lowered the window to glare at him. He knew the reason — one of the girls in

Registry had tipped him off. Weatherall had been studying the Met's summary of the inquest into Jean Charles de Menezes, the innocent Brazilian electrician shot dead by police two weeks after 7/7.

Among those criticised were Kerr's surveillance officers, who had followed him to the Tube. Believing Jean Charles was a suicide bomber, one operative had tried to arrest him in the Tube seconds before firearms officers had shot him. Afterwards Kerr had staunchly defended his bravery to the Met's top brass and anyone else who wanted a fight. His lone voice had set him apart as a maverick, but falling out with the bosses had never troubled him.

This morning, Paula Weatherall was having a working breakfast with the commissioner. Kerr knew that, too, because he made it his business to find out the hierarchy's significant diary fixtures. She looked ready to say something, but Kerr already had the blue Kojak light on the dash and squirted the siren to get her driver out of his way.

CHAPTER
TWO

Thursday, 13 September, 07.03, Victoria Street

Dodge was instantly recognisable from his bulk, at least two hundred and twenty pounds (which he regularly denied), the ruddy face beneath an unkempt shock of white hair, and the baggy grey suit that always looked like he slept in it. But it was the intelligence in his ice-blue eyes that drew everybody in. He was waiting at the corner of Victoria Street and Strutton Ground by the entrance to the market. Surprisingly agile, he jumped in while the Alfa was still moving, inputting the satnav as Kerr accelerated down towards Westminster and the Embankment.

"Head for Mare Street, Hackney." After three years in London, Dodge's Belfast accent was as hard as ever. "Stronghold's a Victorian house, converted ground-floor flat."

"It's all right, Dodge," said Kerr, switching off the device as the Alfa split the pack of vehicles trailing onto Parliament Square. "I've worked that ground a lot."

"Negotiators are in a junior school," said Dodge. "Same street."

The man Kerr had chosen to lead his undercover team was a former RUC agent runner in his early fifties. Everyone called him Dodge, irrespective of rank, but no one knew why. In another life he had survived an IRA assassination attempt near the border and moved his wife and daughter overnight twice, so they guessed it had something to do with that.

"How bad is it?"

Dodge steadied himself as Kerr slid round the square. "Two male hostage-takers." Dodge often claimed he had given up smoking, but the cough always gave him away. "Serious traces with Europol and heavy duty."

"Any demands yet? Threats against Mel?"

"Don't know."

"What's the firepower?"

"Shotgun and handgun. At least. Hostage-takers believed Turkish."

"Believed? For Christ's sake, Dodge."

"The tossers are only just giving us the full story." Despite the engine noise, as Kerr wove in low gear through the congestion around Parliament, Dodge's tone was conversational. He could have been out on a Sunday-afternoon drive with his family. "They took Melanie in the van on the dummy run to South Mimms services, showed her the handover spot in the lorry park, then straight back. Everything as planned."

"Did she let us know?"

"Coded text around midnight." Dodge was looking dead ahead. "She did everything right, John."

"Of course." Kerr knew Dodge was making a point. In the pub he was the life and soul, buying more than his share and sneaking outside for a guilty smoke. But in the field he was always deadly serious. Renowned for his meticulous attention to detail, he had never lost an agent yet.

"They drove back to the address," he said, "unloaded some gear, then all three went out for grub."

"What coverage did they have on them?"

"Uninterrupted mobile surveillance. That's what they're claiming, anyway. But we think they had a loss."

Kerr was accelerating hard now, racing east along the Embankment, with County Hall and the London Eye across the river to their right. "Uniforms gave them a pull as they were parking up on the way back," continued Dodge.

"Set-up or coincidence?"

"Everyone's insisting it was a routine stop. Whatever, the bad guys panicked, whacked a couple of shots at the patrol car and escaped into the stronghold. You know the rest."

Traffic was thinning so Kerr cut the siren. "No, Dodge," he said, "I bloody don't know." Melanie was thirty-four, but to Kerr she was like a daughter, the more so since his own daughter had stopped speaking to him. "How the fuck does Melanie suddenly become a hostage?"

"The uniforms were shitting themselves and got out of the way. But the driver saw them drag a female from the van. They were covering her with the shotgun. She was struggling hard, fighting."

"And the rubber-heelers didn't tell us our officer was compromised for, what, three hours?"

"Nearer five. 'Need to know'. Usual bullshit."

"With Melanie at the end of a shotgun? We subcontract our best and brightest because they can't do the job themselves, then they keep us out of the loop? Who the fuck do they think they are?" Kerr was silent for a second as he kicked through a clear space in the road, but he wasn't waiting for an answer. "Next time they can screw up with their own officers. I'm gonna crucify them."

Dodge looked at him. "I believe you."

Kerr had held misgivings about the role of the Anti-corruption Unit from the outset. They had the lead because this operation was complicated by the connection, somewhere along the line, to a corrupt police officer. The primary purpose of the infiltration was to identify and trap this individual. "How did Melanie get blown, Dodge? There's no way she would have slipped up. She's too good. Who betrayed her?"

"Perhaps no one. Maybe the patrol car spooked them and they're using her as a human shield. She may be their means of escape."

In covert ops there were no absolutes, only compromise, half-truths and missing pieces of the jigsaw. "What do we know about the informant they used for the intro?" said Kerr.

"Not much. Think they graded him B2."

"Which is probably an inflated write-up," said Kerr, "so he might have snitched on her."

"Our undercover officer compromised by the rubber-heelers' snout?" Dodge whistled. "Jesus. There's a strapline for the commissioner."

"And that's not the worst case, Dodge. What if something leaked to this bent cop and he sabotaged the whole thing?"

"Or her cover may be intact," said Dodge. "Let's go with what we know."

They turned north towards Hackney, using the siren again, and came head to head with a black Range Rover, double-parked and blocking the road. The driver was sitting behind the wheel with the engine running, a stocky, cigar-smoking cliché of stubble, dark glasses and bling. Complacent and unprepared, he simply shrugged when Kerr waved him out of the road, gesturing that his passenger was in one of the shops.

Kerr waited a couple of seconds with the siren going, then was out on the street, sprinting to the Range Rover. He had the driver's door open before the man could react. Jerking him out of the vehicle, he shoved him into the line of parked cars, leapt behind the wheel and reversed at speed into a potholed builders' yard. Dodge started to follow his boss out of the car, but too slow.

When the driver went to remonstrate, Kerr swung him into an armlock and threw him against a wall, so hard Dodge could see his face distorted against the rough brickwork, sunglasses crushed, cigar smoke curling up from the pavement. For a moment Kerr leant close, speaking urgently into the man's free ear, then walked calmly back to the Alfa, tossing the Range Rover keys into the gutter.

"Couldn't you just have asked him?" laughed Dodge, as Kerr accelerated away, checking his mirrors.

"Any witnesses?"

"Don't think so. But he'll complain."

Kerr glanced sideways and shook his head. "No, he won't."

"What did you say to him?"

"Doesn't matter." They came to a junction and Kerr fell silent as he negotiated a knot of traffic through the red light.

"You're all right. No one saw a thing."

"For all we know Melanie was compromised before she even got in the van." Kerr's voice was low, despondent. "This is my fault, Dodge."

There was nothing more to say. They drove on a couple of miles, Kerr deep in thought as he coursed through the traffic. Eventually Dodge looked at him again. "What are you going to do?"

"I'm gonna bring her back, of course." The Glock sat comfortably against Kerr's ribs.

CHAPTER
THREE

Thursday, 13 September, 07.36, Hackney

The stronghold was in Ferris Street, just south of London Fields. It stretched diagonally for half a mile between Hackney Road to the south and Mare Street to the east, with speed bumps every twenty metres. It was a mixed residential thoroughfare of crumbling council blocks alongside grand Victorian terraces converted into well-maintained private flats. Halfway down, the street made a gentle curve to pass beneath the railway line.

The hostage-takers were holed up in a ground-floor converted flat twenty metres west of the railway bridge. Three doors up from the target address there was a primary school. The cops had taken it over as their control post, filling the playground behind the blue metal railings with vehicles.

The whole area was eerily quiet, with nothing moving. Residents' cars remained parked on each side of the street, rush hour cancelled for the duration.

Local cops had diverted the traffic, sealing both ends of the street and setting up an inner cordon to create a sterile area within fifteen metres of the stronghold.

Residents had been evacuated from the nearest four houses each side of the target house, and from seven across the street. Most had gone to work, but about twenty rubberneckers loitered, a couple still in their nightclothes, on the safe side of the white tape. A pair of bored, hi-vis PCs, arms crossed, chewing gum, stood apart from them.

Kerr had cut the siren but everyone heard the engine racing as he swung into the street, and turned to watch. The cops stopped chewing and stiffened, evidently weighing the possibility of being mown down. He skidded to a halt over the police line and flashed his ID.

"DCI Kerr, SO15." Kerr still regarded himself as a Special Branch officer, although he wasn't allowed to use the term any more. These days, it was all policing by numbers. His élite unit now lay buried in a flow chart.

The younger and shorter of the cops took a step forward. His face was raw with acne scars and the oversized helmet sat low on his head, emphasising his squatness. He looked unimpressed as he bent down to check Kerr out. "Guv'nor says no one's to come through." There was a white flash of spearmint and Kerr felt a speck of saliva against his cheek. He could see the tape of the inner cordon thirty metres ahead and, just beyond it on the left side of the street, the school. He peered through the windscreen at a sniper on the roof opposite. "I need to speak with the negotiators right now."

"Sure you do." The cop stood upright and started chewing again, back in his comfort zone. A clipboard had appeared and he made a show of reading it. "But you're not cleared." The boy tried to stare Kerr down but stepped back with a snapped tape curling round his boots as the Alfa leapt forward. "Oi!" he called after Kerr.

Kerr parked on the nearside of the school, out of sight of the stronghold. He spotted a pair of snipers behind the garden walls across the street.

The primary school was a peeling mid-sixties block with large square windows and a flat roof. Kerr stepped out of the car and held up his ID to the snipers. He looked unofficial in his green-flecked jacket and grey trousers, but Dodge was wearing his suit, so he gestured to him to lead the way. At the school gate a PC was wielding another clipboard, but he was young and Dodge's fat swagger conveyed seniority.

The radio crackled with a message from the man on the outer cordon as Dodge introduced himself on the move, shovelling grit into his Belfast accent. "Negotiators are expecting us," he growled. Senior, experienced and battle-hardened. The PC pointed out the room as they slid past.

The negotiating cell was in the head teacher's office. Directions were unnecessary, as they had already taped their sign on the door. Dodge hung around outside to deter intruders and give Kerr time. Negotiators operate in pairs: one to negotiate, the other to signal ideas or reminders. Kerr eased the door open. He entered silently to find two detectives in shirtsleeves and headphones sitting at the cramped desk. They were hunched over the phone, which lay dead in the middle, as if their combined will might bring it back to life.

He didn't recognise either of them, which was good. "John Kerr, Anti-corruption Unit," he lied, offering his hand before they could react. He was expecting the secret Masonic hand-shake and they did not disappoint. "Just checking if you need any more from us."

Number One slanted his headphones and pointed to the whiteboard in the corner, used to record threats, demands and deadlines. Trendy waterproof coat slung over the back of his chair, he had gone for the tieless look, with the top buttons of his red check shirt undone and the sleeves tightly rolled to display tanned biceps. Pinned to the wall beside the board was a rough drawing of the stronghold: kitchen, bathroom, front room and bedroom. Communal front door, then a lobby with doors to the two flats. The one to the left led up the staircase, the other into the stronghold. No sign of any rear access. "Not unless you can add anything to that."

Top left on the white board were Europol mugshots and identities of the two perpetrators with their religion, Muslim, and a scrawled felt-tip summary of the convictions acquired in their rampage through Europe. Two were for armed robbery. Both were flagged as extremely violent, but it was the word "RAPE" that screamed out at Kerr. Under "hostage", where Melanie's cover name should have been, they had simply scribbled "FEMALE" followed by a question-mark. He needed answers quickly, but his voice was casual as he asked, "Anything happening?"

26

Number One nodded at the phone. "We've established contact three times. Guy on the left of the board slammed the phone down eleven minutes ago and we're waiting for him to get back."

"Any demands?"

"Breakfast is as far as they've got. They'll probably want a car to the airport by this afternoon. But they're going to prison or the mortuary." He was a young man trying to sound tough. The Lodge had sent a novice to bargain for Melanie's life, and this made Kerr angry.

"Are they all together in one space?" he asked.

"Snipers have a sighting in the front room."

"So, how soon will you raise them again?"

Junior glanced at his mate. "We're giving them time to reflect."

"Reflect?"

"Consider their options." Number Two was obviously the strategic thinker. In his early forties, he was wearing some sort of club tie over a white, short-sleeved shirt, his arms a mass of freckles and ginger hairs. His suit jacket hung neatly on an old wire hanger, like he was in for the duration. "No rush. We let them sweat for a bit. I sent out for some hot grub but the perps get nothing till they accept 'Merlin'. That's our code for . . ."

"The field phone. I know." Kerr's eyes darted back to the whiteboard. Underneath it a black attaché case held the instrument. Deployment of the phone into the stronghold was always an early objective in siege negotiation. It allowed secure, unbroken communication.

"That's our current negotiating position." He spoke like a salesman, and Kerr suppressed another surge of anger.

"What about release of the hostage? Doesn't that come first?"

"Negotiators negotiate," he said. "We don't make the decisions. It takes as long as it takes." Number Two was now playing the old sweat, veteran of a thousand sieges. Kerr wanted to punch his fat ginger face.

Instead, he took a deep breath and gestured to Melanie's non-person blank on the board. "Why the question-mark?"

"We're not sure about her."

"Sorry?"

"She may be an accomplice."

Kerr froze. Why had no one told them Melanie was one of the good guys? "Have they let you speak to her?"

"They may be using her to up the stakes," Number Two said, ignoring the question. "It's been done before. Until they're bundled up on the pavement we treat everyone as potential hostiles."

On the whiteboard Kerr took the felt tip and underlined "RAPE". "Doesn't this bother you?" he asked, struggling to keep his voice low.

"They've made no threats like that."

"But you should be negotiating her release — you know, in exchange for scrambled eggs on toast."

Number Two paused for a moment to stare up at Kerr. "Tell that to the co-ordinator," he said, then turned away. "You shouldn't be in the cell."

28

Kerr was staring at the wall again, memorising the room plan, calculating distances from the front door. "Ground floor, yeah?"

But then the phone rang again and they were making secret signs at each other, John Kerr forgotten.

CHAPTER
FOUR

Thursday, 13 September, 07.47, the stronghold

Through the glass double doors Kerr saw a PC arriving with breakfast on a tray: three Styrofoam takeaway boxes and cups from a local café. From that moment he acted through instinct. "Cheers," he said, holding the door open to take the tray from him, "perfect timing." He checked the contents: black coffee, congealed scrambled egg with sausage and bacon.

He exited the school and turned left towards the stronghold three doors away. There was the same unnatural quiet, but the whole street seemed to stiffen around him. Then the air was crackling with urgent walkie-talkie voices and he knew they were all talking about him. Snipers were visible now, a sprinkling of black spikes pointing at him as the uniforms tried to work out what was happening. Shadows were making frantic signs from the undergrowth, but he kept walking.

By the time he reached the stronghold he hadn't spilt a drop. Pause for a final memory check of the layout. At the communal front door he knocked, stood back a pace and waited, a quartet of rifles sizing up his back. Shouting in English drifted through the front-room bay window to Kerr's right and he guessed they were giving Number Two a hard time.

Then there was yelling in Turkish. Kerr was expecting an order to leave the tray and retreat, which would make things more difficult, but the door opened. The hallway to the right was narrow and dark, and one of the hostage-takers had the double-barrelled shotgun ready to fire. Perhaps the Turk was seeing a second prisoner, an easy civilian target, a lightweight with breakfast in his hands and "HOSTAGE" stamped across his forehead. He looked comfortable with his weapon, moving it like an extension of his body.

At times of uncontrollable anger or crisis, people talk about a red mist descending. For John Kerr, who had faced more extreme situations than most, it was different. Such scenes were always stark white, a big chill in which every object was frozen.

In a single photograph Kerr saw the finger curled round the trigger. He calculated his odds against the shaven-headed, overweight thug, unprotected in soiled vest and jockey shorts. In a second frame he sensed the half-open door into the front room two paces to his right and tracked the unseen second target's voice, placing him with the phone by the window. The door opened inwards and he could see Melanie's combat boots and untied lower legs. They stretched from an armchair in the corner to the left of the doorway, the rest of her body just out of sight. From the hallway he could reach her in three strides. Less than a second. The second thug would be distracted by the phone. "Breakfast?" enquired Kerr, the solicitous waiter. His target jerked the barrel, drawing Kerr forward. "Shall I leave it just here?"

"Inside." The guy beckoned.

Kerr stepped over the threshold into the hallway, using his foot to shut the door. The shotgun lowered as his target took a careful step back through the entrance to the stronghold, then leant forward to check the food. He looked at the forbidden meat and swore.

"Yeah, sorry about that." Kerr thrust the tray up and over him, three cups of coffee cascading over his shaven head, face, neck and shoulders. He yanked and twisted the shotgun barrel away from him as his victim bellowed in pain and rage, dropping forward to meet Kerr's knee jerking into his face and snapping his teeth. Then Kerr knocked the shotgun aside, took a step back and kicked him hard in the crotch. In two swift movements Kerr unholstered the Glock and pistol-whipped him. He fell silently.

Through the internal door, Melanie's legs had disappeared. Stepping over the shooter, Kerr charged into the front room, raising the Glock to fire as he came face to face with his second target. With the phone in one hand the Turk was raising the handgun with the other, but leaning back on a dining chair. Kerr instantly recognised the weapon. It was a long-barrel Smith & Wesson medium-frame .38-calibre revolver, and it was pointing right at him. Kerr's finger closed on the trigger for a rapid pair of shots. Then, in that split second, he realised why the target was leaning back. Face deathly pale, hair scraped back, Melanie was kneeling behind him. He recognised the faded denim jacket she

32

sometimes used for surveillance, then saw that her wrists were bound with tape but looped tightly around the Turk's neck, yanking his head back.

Before the thug could break free Kerr launched himself into the air, catching him square in the face with both heels. There was another crack, nose, teeth or cheekbone, as the chair tipped backwards, sending all three of them into a sprawling heap against the wall, Kerr's Glock spinning away from him. Kerr snatched the Turk's revolver and grabbed the man by the throat to keep his head still. The Smith & Wesson felt nice and solid, weightier than the Glock, so Kerr used the barrel to stab him in the eye. He screamed as blood spurted through his fingers and Kerr hit him again on the temple. "Hold onto him, Mel."

There was scuffling in the hallway as the first target came round, so Kerr re-holstered the Glock and turned back to batter him with his accomplice's revolver until he was unconscious again.

The landline was still connected and they could hear an urgent male voice. Kerr picked up the receiver. "This is John Kerr. We are safe. We are not under duress. Do not, repeat not, order any action until I give the all-clear." The voice at the other end was still going, but Kerr slammed the receiver down.

He checked both men, pulled Melanie clear and sat her on the sofa. "You all right?"

"What kept you?" She was grinning at him.

The phone was ringing again but he went to the kitchen for a knife and cut her bonds. "Where's the rest of the tape?"

Melanie searched under the sofa cushion for the roll of brown duct tape and bound the wrists and legs of her gently moaning captive while Kerr dragged the other man in from the lobby. "Better hurry up," said Melanie, taping his mouth to stop him moaning, "or this one's going to bleed to death."

They trussed up both men and left them at opposite sides of the room. Then Kerr disarmed the shotgun and the handgun and laid them on the kitchen drainer.

"Ready?" he said, when they were back in the hallway. "Let's go to work."

Kerr slowly opened the front door and held out his ID for all to see. As they made their walk down the street he held Melanie's arm. To the watching cops it could have been for support or restraint, and Kerr made it deliberately ambiguous. A couple of senior uniforms were waiting by the school to receive them. Kerr identified himself and told them where they could find the hostage-takers, weapons and ammunition. He didn't give Melanie a name, describing her as a source he needed to extricate immediately to avoid the media. Unimpressed, they ordered him to remain in the containment area for a "comprehensive debriefing".

"Understood. No problem," he conceded. Then he spotted an ambulance parked by his car. "Just need to get her checked out and make a couple of calls."

Armed police were swarming into the stronghold now. "Five minutes," ordered one of the uniforms, distracted. "Wait for us at Gold Command."

"What?"

"The caretaker's office."

"Of course." Kerr walked Melanie to the ambulance. He told her to look injured but all attention was directed at the strong-hold as they walked past the ambulance to the Alfa, where Dodge was waiting.

"Welcome back," he said, giving Melanie a bear hug and winking at his boss as he tossed him the car keys.

Kerr checked his BlackBerry as he and Melanie got into the car. "They're being a bit arsy, Dodge."

"So I'm staying here to cover, yeah?"

Kerr pushed the Alfa into 'Drive'. "Say I got called away."

"Great," said Dodge, deadpan. "That should calm them down."

Kerr turned round and drove slowly until he was clear of the cordon. At the end of the street he swung right into Hackney Road. "Thanks, John," said Melanie.

He flashed her a smile. "What went wrong?"

"Haven't the faintest. Nothing unusual, not a sign, until they got pulled. Then they went crazy, as if they'd suspected me of being a cop all along."

"Any signs before that?"

"No. They made a couple of calls on the way to South Mimms. In Turkish. The only English word I heard, kept hearing, was 'total'."

They paused while Kerr wove through the vehicles along Bishopsgate, heading for the City. Traffic was heavy, so he went left at Houndsditch, racing down towards Tower Hill.

"We'll get to the bottom of it. Do I get you checked out or is it straight home?"

"Not a scratch."

Channel Five erupted while Kerr was speaking. Melanie strained forward, touching his arm for him to pause. "That's my team," she said. "Something's up, John. We're needed in Lambeth." She listened intently, quite at ease in her lurching, braking, hyperactive workplace. "Bloody hell. It's Avon."

Kerr immediately pressed the horn to activate the siren, accelerating hard. "Ahmed Jibril. The sleeper," he said. Kerr was overseeing seven live surveillance operations, but Avon was always somewhere near the front of his mind.

"Whatever," said Melanie, flicking on the blue light. "Sounds like he just woke up."

They reached the river, the Tower flashing past to their left as they charged into Lower Thames Street. As they raced west beneath the underpass that would bring them onto the Embankment, a motorcycle pulled in behind them. It appeared from nowhere, headlight dead centre in Kerr's mirror, the growl from its powerful engine bouncing off the tunnel walls.

"Alpha from Red One."

Kerr spoke into the visor. "Go ahead, Jack."

"The Reds are short-handed. Can I have Mel back?" Despite the wind noise, Jack Langton's Geordie accent was as rich as if he had just ridden down from Newcastle.

Kerr shot out of the tunnel towards Temple. "What's your location?"

"Look in the mirror."

Kerr was doing seventy, but Langton's overtaking Suzuki GSX R1000 left him standing. Bike, rider and helmet were all black. Langton was Kerr's deputy and ran the surveillance teams on the ground. Opposite the Inns of Court Langton braked sharply to a stop in front of him, and Melanie already had the door half open. "Thanks again, John." She leant over to squeeze Kerr's arm. "You've got blood on your sleeve, by the way. And a bit of scrambled egg."

Langton already had the spare crash helmet and jacket ready as Melanie sprinted to him and climbed aboard, then a black-gloved hand lifted in acknowledgement and the radio crackled something as he and his partner roared away.

Part Two

CHAPTER
FIVE

Thursday, 13 September, 08.12, safe-house, Lambeth

Ahmed Jibril was the third terrorist to obtain his UK entry visa with the secret authority of the Home Office minister herself. All were *jihadis*, secret members of Al Qaeda, determined to re-establish itself after the execution of its leader, Osama bin Laden, by the hated Americans in May 2011. These three were dedicated to waging war against the United Kingdom. They were specially selected for this mission because Al Qaeda believed they were "clean skins", unknown to any Western security agency. Once past the immigration desk at Heathrow, they vanished without trace to the target cities of London, Manchester and Leeds, from whose alienated masses they spotted talent for military training in Pakistan and Afghanistan. Their holy mission was, of course, to prepare Al Qaeda cells for suicide atrocities.

Ahmed Jibril had entered the UK as a student of dentistry, with a perfectly forged offer of a place at Birkbeck College, University of London. His clean skin had become defiled because he had breached Al Qaeda's strict operational security. An unauthorised, unintelligible coded phone call lasting less than ten seconds to a contact in Lahore had been enough to suck him onto the Allies' global radar screen. GCHQ had tracked the signal, and MI6, the Secret Intelligence Service, had traced the body.

But he had only come to the notice of Kerr's team because the MI6 head of station in Yemen had owed his friend in London a favour and was a believer in doing the right thing.

On 9 September — a Sunday afternoon when the intelligence world was slumbering in the Home Counties — without getting clearance from Vauxhall Cross, Joe Allenby scanned a photograph with a Yemen Airways flight number to the old Special Branch office at Heathrow, a glorified broom cupboard hidden behind a one-way mirror at the front of Terminal 3's immigration hall. It gave Jibril's full name and date of birth, and the header was marked "STRICTLY PERSONAL" for the information of Detective Chief Inspector John Kerr. The picture was a ragged frame taken in the Yemeni capital, Sana'a, in the middle of the crowded medieval market-place. The image, blurry and skewed, had been snatched on a cheap digital camera by one of Allenby's secretaries playing tourist.

Late that night, while Jibril was in the air, Kerr's most trusted friend, Alan Fargo, had unearthed three top-secret "UK EYES ONLY" security traces linking Jibril to Al Qaeda. Fargo ran Room 1830, the Terrorism Research Unit, a square corner office on the Yard's south side, looking towards Battersea Power Station. Access was by swipe card and PIN, and heavily

42

restricted. Two sides extended six windows along from the corner, but the four highly vetted officers who shared the room with Fargo enjoyed no benefit from the view or natural light because the blinds were always closed.

Room 1830's primary purpose was to house a computer server known as Excalibur, which linked Fargo's office to databases in MI5, MI6 and GCHQ. The computer was a featureless, gunmetal-grey rectangle, taller than a man, a metre wide and deeper than Fargo's desk. It dominated the corner of Room 1830, to the right of the door, at the farthest point from the double-aspect windows. Government engineers from GCHQ had installed it shortly after 9/11, digging up Broadway outside the Yard one Sunday afternoon to connect the fibre-optic cabling from the street to the eighteenth floor.

Like a dangerous animal, Excalibur was completely enclosed by a metal cage and protected with an alarm. There were five terminals on desks around the room, but only Fargo was vetted to go near the server itself. As its keeper, he had his workstation between the door and the cage. Excalibur gave off a low, incessant hum, of which Fargo had long since ceased to be aware, and a heat that kept the temperature at a constant 75 degrees. Fargo's officers called their workplace "The Sauna", and no one ever wore a jacket.

Room 1830 was also the focus of intelligence about terrorist finance and cell-site analysis from mobile phones. People often described it as the beating heart of SO15, but Fargo downplayed its capability. The product depended upon the quality of the source intelligence: feed rubbish in, he was always warning in his Cornish burr, "and you get shite out".

Ahmed Mohammed Jibril, it seemed, had been born on 25 May 1981 in Karachi, Pakistan. In addition to the unauthorised mobile call, the results showed Jibril to have attended two training camps in Afghanistan, 04 and 05.

The target in Allenby's photograph was wearing a full beard, turban and calf-length white shirt. The man Kerr's surveillance officers later saw collect a single case from the baggage hall at Heathrow's Terminal 4 and walk swiftly to the Underground was contemporary and clean-shaven, dressed in faded jeans and Puffa jacket.

Apart from his one and only slip-up, Ahmed Jibril was to be highly professional. He stayed in a furnished bedsit, flat nine, on the top floor of a converted, double-fronted Victorian house in a narrow street of terraces between South Lambeth Road and Clapham Road, south of the Thames. On the Monday of his arrival from Yemen via Dubai he had taken the Tube direct from Heathrow, paying cash for a one-way ticket to Stockwell. There were no stop-offs along the way, no phone calls or emails, no indiscretions.

The change in appearance came as no surprise to the surveillance operatives, for the unexpected characterised their professional lives, as it had for generations of Special Branch officers before them. At the run-down letting agency across the road from Stockwell Underground station they watched him pick up the keys, a Yale and a Chubb, without paying any cash deposit, then followed him to the address. From the moment he had arrived in London Jibril had lived the life of a holy man during Ramadan. Or a terrorist who knew his every movement might be watched.

Whichever, his behaviour made life hard for the team trying to keep track of him. To keep pace with the enemy, counter-terrorism officers need a staple diet of raw intelligence. They relish CCTV, voice recordings, accommodation addresses, flat, garage and car rentals, cash deposits, credit and Oyster card records. They crave emails, Internet searches, mobile-phone calls, texts, Facebook, Twitter and other traces of social contact.

They follow a golden thread of interaction, for it is all they have. They can only guess where it will lead. It may snap at any time. And in the post-9/11 world the Islamic terrorist who operates alone is in a strong position.

From now on Ahmed Jibril would give them nothing. He appeared to have come to London with the express purpose of watching television. That was the other problem. Because the job was strictly need-to-know, Kerr's operatives covered their target with half a surveillance team, six officers, establishing an observation post in a block of council flats across the street. Jibril's sudden arrival had also meant there was no time to insert cameras and listening devices inside flat nine so they had to rely on a microphone Jack Langton attached to the external wall.

At eight in the morning on the first day, Jibril switched on the TV at high volume. Then, at exactly eleven o'clock, he crossed the busy junction by the Tube station and sauntered down Stockwell Road to make a show of checking out the fruit and veg on display outside the Indian general store.

On each short journey he crossed the road twice, wandered down a couple of one-way side-streets to check out the traffic, then doubled back, as if he had forgotten something. He always returned to his hideout by eleven forty-five. This was classic counter-surveillance, known to the watchers as "dry cleaning": they knew Jibril had no need to take the polluted air around Stockwell, except to lure them into the open. There were no other sightings, and the glow from the TV disappeared around ten in the evening.

Within seventy-two hours they had concluded that Ahmed Jibril was probably another neutral, ascetic loner, of long-term security interest but of no immediate significance. After talking it through with Kerr, Jack Langton reduced 24/7 coverage in the observation post to one officer, with three on the ground, and switched to other targets. Which, as it turned out, was probably what Jibril had guessed they would do.

So when at 08.12 on the fourth day, Thursday, 13 September, he walked swiftly out of the door, he took them by surprise. As he turned right, striding towards the Underground, he should have been just about waking up.

Tearing across Waterloo Bridge, Kerr spoke on the hands-free to Steve Gibb, the officer manning the observation post opposite Jibril's address. Gibb was a trooper in 22 Regiment SAS on secondment to Kerr's unit. Unassuming and inconspicuous, he was the smallest guy on the team, with the remains of a tan from a recent operation in Somalia. "What's the score, Steve?" said Kerr.

"It's the Yemen guy they slipped us under the counter, boss. He whizzed out of the house and off, off, off. Just as I was having a fucking leak." Gibb was a Glaswegian and sounded annoyed with himself, firing the words like bullets. "But I managed to get seven frames."

Kerr imagined Gibb using the SaniLav and trying to work the camera at the same time, probably getting piss all over his hands. "You did well to catch up. How many do we have assigned?"

"Half the Red team. Two vehicles and the rest on foot."

Kerr heard Melanie's voice again over the growl of Langton's motorcycle. "You can sign me on. Jack's dropping me off at the plot now."

"He's making a right, heading north up South Lambeth Road," said Gibb, "and walking like he means business. Red Three, do you receive?" Kerr heard a quiet voice bounce straight back to Gibb and the clunk of a car door as the surveillance operative got out to follow on foot.

"Yes, we have him."

Kerr split the traffic waiting on the south side of the bridge and called up Langton. "Jack, confirm our guys are armed?"

"Roger that," replied Langton. "Do we let him run?"

"Yeah, we stay with him," ordered Kerr. "Mel, let's have two of you on foot while I get back-up. Zulu, receiving, over?"

A soft burr came out of the ether: "Go ahead, John."

Kerr was relieved to hear Alan Fargo. After more than a decade of working counter-terrorism together, they often anticipated each other's thoughts, which meant they could cut the crap. "Al, I want you to go with a full ops-room set-up, just to be on the safe side."

"I already pressed the button."

Kerr was not surprised. He had guessed Fargo would be firing up state-of-the-art comms equipment in the operations room on the sixteenth floor of the Yard. Alan Fargo was that rare breed, a good field officer with an analyst's brain, as effective in the ops room as 1830. He was from Falmouth, non-flashy, cerebral and self-deprecating. But no one else could join the dots so quickly, which was why they all felt safe with him managing two key jobs.

"When do I break the news to Mr Ritchie?" asked Fargo.

Kerr heard voices and movement around Fargo and pictured the comms monitors taking their places in front of him and plugging in their headsets. "How much does he know?"

"No one above you knows anything about this," said Fargo. "Remember?"

"I'll take care of it," said Kerr, after a pause.

"John, I'm getting some good photographs from Steve Gibb coming through now." Fargo's voice faded and Kerr imagined him swinging round to check as the images rolled onto the two giant screens in the ops room. "I'll get them copied through to 1830."

"This is Mel. He's crossing the road and onto a bus, number eighty-eight, upper deck, heading south." There was a pause with the microphone open and Kerr heard Melanie's breathing quicken as she sprinted for the bus. "I'm on with him."

Jack Langton's voice came on the air as soon as Melanie closed her mike. "John, I'm pulling units from Leyton for support."

"I need him covered, so keep two units there. Where's the firearms back-up?"

"Camberwell," said Langton. "Reckon they can be on scene in seven."

"OK. Alan, who do we have for Gold?" Kerr heard a commotion in the ops room and several voices colliding with each other.

"Weatherall," said Fargo, softly. Everyone groaned.

CHAPTER
SIX

Thursday, 13 September, 08.39, Operations Room, New Scotland Yard

Commander Paula Weatherall polished her glasses as she took her place in the ops-room chair marked "Gold". She had come straight from her working breakfast in the commissioner's mess with the top man himself. He hosted breakfast for his senior officers on a rotational basis, interrogating them over muesli and fruit tea on their ideas for his Big Tent of top management. Some would ultimately be invited inside, others exiled to manage IT projects, youth justice and community-support officers. Success depended on image, hyperactivity and a culture of presenteeism. Prepared to make any sacrifice to get under canvas with the commissioner, Weatherall engineered more than her share of free breakfasts.

The moment Fargo's coded text came through she had excused herself with a private word to her boss. The timing was perfect, the whispered exchange suggesting privileged access and higher importance. The previous year the commissioner had promoted her from a uniform backwater to head the intelligence unit of SO15, Counter-terrorism Command, the forgettable new title for the organisation formerly known as Special Branch, in which John Kerr and his team had spent most of their careers. Weatherall calculated her new role was a springboard for even greater advancement. The government spin on Islamist atrocities was "Not if but when". Consequently, the fight against terror was heavily funded, great for the profile and practically unchallengeable. As Gold, Weatherall assumed complete operational responsibility for any action against Jibril the moment she took her seat.

The ops room was a rectangle four windows long and five paces wide, with workstations for Alan Fargo and the three comms specialists. The small adjacent office to the right had been converted into an observation room, separated by a glass partition. Fargo sat with his back to the door, opposite the windows. The two large TV screens were fixed to the left wall, with the comms staff facing them. The young man nearest the window was also responsible for processing surveillance stills and video onto both screens. Weatherall occupied a table at right angles to Fargo behind these experts, with her own radio link. Beside her were places for a couple of intelligence officers to add value from Room 1830. The room was not intended for the pair of uniformed, uninformed brass who had squeezed through the door in Weatherall's wake. The three monitors turned, horrified by the extraneous noise of the brass, then spun back, clutching their headsets closely to their ears in disgust.

"Sit-rep," demanded Weatherall. She used her normal speaking voice, for she was sitting closest to Fargo, with less than an arm's length separating them. Never slow to pull rank, she was shrewd enough to know that success this morning depended upon the bulky detective sergeant from Room 1830 and his wizard computer.

As he briefed her, Fargo indicated the photographs of Jibril and his address on the wall beside the TV screens. "Ahmed Mohammed Jibril, ma'am, code-named 'Avon', subject of investigation by the SIS station in Yemen, who passed him to us last Sunday because he was about to travel."

"And?" Weatherall was already looking pissed off.

"That's all we have, ma'am. At this stage."

Alice, the comms monitor, interrupted before Weatherall could reply, her blonde hair flicking round as she turned to face Fargo. Alice was a civilian officer, slim and single, a diligent expert the surveillance operatives trusted with their lives. She always occupied the seat nearest Fargo. "Still on the eighty-eight travelling south, into Stockwell Road towards Brixton Underground, junction with Clapham Road." Alice was rapidly working her desktop. "This route takes him down to Clapham Common. Melanie has him."

Fargo paused to acknowledge her. "Thanks, Alice." It was an unnecessary intervention, but Weatherall should already have known the background, and Fargo knew Alice was reasserting the priorities. "As I say, MI6 head of station gave us a heads-up and we picked him up at Terminal Four on Monday morning. He led us to a bedsit in Lambeth. We believe he may be here to contact or service an active cell."

"Why?" Weatherall was staring at the photograph of Jibril on the left TV screen.

"Because he's highly surveillance-conscious and disciplined, following a strict routine."

"Until today, apparently," said Weatherall, turning her attention to updated surveillance images scrolling through the other screen. "He's not carrying any bags. But he *is* wearing a quilted jacket, yes?"

"A Puffa jacket, correct."

"Loose fitting. And what can you tell me about that, about his intentions?"

"Well, to be honest, he did nothing unusual before he left the address."

Alice interjected again. "ETA for the firearms team three minutes, rendezvous point the builders' yard corner of Fentiman Road and Vauxhall Park."

"Thanks, Alice."

Suddenly there was video of Jibril on the right screen. "Did you have sight of him all the time?" asked Weatherall. "I mean continuously?"

"Not every second, no."

"Quite. And certainly not inside the flat while he was getting dressed. There's something around his waist, don't you agree, Brian?"

Weatherall turned to Brian Perkins, one of the two uniforms she had brought with her. Perkins was Silver, her rostered deputy. Weatherall was a firm believer in deputies: they provided a convenient ditch to shovel the blame into when things came unstuck. A superintendent in Public Order Branch, Perkins found himself sitting beside Weatherall because he was on call that day for any critical incident. Beside him was Bronze, last in the chain of command, a fresh-faced chief inspector from Colindale, who already wore the look of fall-guy-in-waiting. Perkins opted for safety. "Difficult to tell. It's a possibility."

Weatherall swung back to Fargo. "Why did no one brief me about this operation?"

"I can't say, ma'am."

"I saw Mr Kerr tearing off somewhere early this morning. He is aware, presumably?"

"Yes, ma'am. Definitely."

"So why isn't he here?"

"He's mobile."

"Who's in command on the ground?"

"Mobile and on the ground, ma'am."

"He's also supposed to be a manager. Tell him I want him in here."

In the confines of the room Fargo felt the explosion of breath on his cheek. "He was on the way back when we got the alert. Went straight to the plot."

"Then get him on the link."

Fargo turned to Alice, but she was already transmitting. "Alpha from Zulu, receiving, over?"

Kerr's voice crackled back: "Go ahead."

"I have Gold for you." Alice flicked the comms to speaker.

Kerr was cruising along Effra Road, parallel to Brixton Hill and a few hundred metres from the plot. Traffic

54

from the mainset crowded his thoughts because, in addition to Channel Five for the surveillance operation, he was also monitoring other Central units on Channel Eighteen as he awaited the call from the leader of the firearms teams, blue-lighting from their headquarters in the City. The Tactical Firearms Branch, known as CO19, had teams on standby 24/7. They were known as Trojans and used the call sign "Challenger". The Trojans responded to any incident involving a firearm or deadly weapon and were routinely called upon to assist in counter-terrorism operations.

Weatherall came through on Five. Her voice was brittle, several notes too high, leaking anxiety into the calm stream of surveillance messages. "What's going on down there? What are you doing there? Why the priority?"

The echo made Kerr cautious because it showed she was on the speaker. "Because of the provenance and the sourcing."

"But he's done nothing for three days."

Later, Fargo would tell Kerr of his astonishment at this. Weatherall had just suggested Jibril was carrying a bomb under his coat, but now she was suggesting he was low priority. Many of the new bosses camouflaged their inexperience by bullying the experts down the chain. "Aggressive indecision" was how Kerr described it.

Now Jack Langton's deep Geordie voice broke in: "Back-up three minutes from the plot."

"Received, confirm your units are carrying," said Kerr.

"Yup."

Kerr checked the time. The rest of the Red team, summoned by Langton to provide emergency support, had made it from Leyton in fourteen minutes. "Gold, I'll call you on the landline." Kerr pressed the speed dial without a pause. "Jack, do you have the location, over?"

"Still heading south on the eighty-eight towards Stockwell Underground, we have the bus in view. Melanie with him."

Kerr could hear Weatherall's insistent "Hello" on the mobile. He cut the mike and spoke into the hands-free, his brain automatically processing the operational traffic.

"Ma'am, this man's total inactivity is the reason we have to treat this as urgent. He's spent three days dry cleaning."

"What?"

"Being evasive, trying to draw out surveillance. This morning he broke the pattern and we believe he's out to do business."

"What do we know of his contacts?"

"Nothing. That's the point. That's why I'm heading this up."

"Your job as a manager is to be here in the ops room, briefing me."

Melanie's voice crackled into Channel Five. "He's off, off, off, and crossing the road. I'm with him, plus Red Three."

"Ma'am, can you stand by? I have to deal with this." Kerr cut the call without waiting for a reply. "Go ahead, Mel."

"He's seen a northbound bus and he's running hard for it, number two heading back towards Vauxhall station. He's going in the opposite direction. Now heading north, repeat north, towards Vauxhall. This guy is totally paranoid. I'm dropping off."

"All received. Jack, he's retracing his route, can your guys take this?"

"Red Four, I'm on it." Red Four was a young linguist, fluent in French and Arabic, who had just been accepted for a post in the international-liaison section. His mike stayed open as he sprinted for the bus. "He's going up . . . top deck . . . Shit, I need a mobile unit." They heard the officer banging on the door to the bus, and speaking to the driver. "Cheers, mate." Kerr realised he must have flashed his warrant card, not ideal for a surveillance officer. Then the breathless voice sank to a whisper: "I'm on."

"Good work," said Kerr, "and we need your exact location, so listen up, all units."

The voice murmured back against the traffic noise. On the crowded bus, Red Four would be just another Brixton schizo whispering to himself. "South Lambeth Road, junction Lansdowne Way, heading north."

"All units, I want containment around Kennington Lane, Nine Elms and Albert Embankment," said Kerr. "And Vauxhall Bridge in case he takes us over the river. If you think he's got his sights on Westminster, tell us. I don't want anyone being shy. Link man at this time is Red Four."

Kerr's vehicle filled with twelve voices organising themselves along the route in staccato bursts. There was no need for call signs from people who worked together twelve or even twenty-four hours a day because each knew the other like family. Kerr redialled. "You wanted background, ma'am. The MI6 head of station in Yemen gave him to us Sunday afternoon, on the hurry-up."

"Not through proper channels, you mean?"

"It was urgent because the target was about to travel."

"So without clearances, in other words."

Kerr felt a stab of vulnerability: Weatherall was already looking for a way out if things went wrong. She was on what Alan Fargo called the "scapegoat shoot", the survival sport of choice for any aspiring big cheese. Further down the line, Kerr calculated, he was going to need heavy-duty back-up from Joe Allenby in Yemen. For the present, he fell back on operational fundamentals: go with what you see. "I believe we need to develop this, ma'am," he said. "You're getting as much as me. He's all over the place, plus his erratic movements on the street over the past three days. It's either counter-surveillance or the guy's nuts. I go for the first. I believe he's going for a meet."

"Or to make an attack."

"No, there's been no preparation."

"But he's wearing something under that jacket," Weatherall said, performing another somersault. "There's something round his waist. Could be a bomb."

"No, I've checked with Steve Gibb in the observation post. Nothing abnormal about his clothing when he left the address. We need to let him run."

"And *I* have to minimise the risk."

Channel Eighteen came to life. "This is Challenger One. I have two Trojan units at the RVP in Fentiman Road. We're ready to deploy. Sit-rep, please."

"Thank you," said Kerr. "Change to Channel Five for current status. Subject is in South Lambeth Road north towards Vauxhall station." Kerr turned back to the phone. "Ma'am, the Trojan firearms teams are on standby at the rendezvous point and I need a moment to check this out for you . . . Melanie, Jack, any signs subject is carrying, over?"

"The way he sprinted across the road I'd say no way," said Melanie.

"This is Jack and I agree . . . stand by. All units, subject is off, off, off, and on foot. South Lambeth Road, still heading north, junction with . . . looks like Wyvil, repeat Wyvil, Road on the left, possibly going for Vauxhall Tube or Overground, Red Four remaining on the bus."

There was the growl of a motorcycle. "I'm covering from Vauxhall station and standing by," said Langton.

Kerr spoke into his mobile. "Did you get all that, ma'am?"

"Yes, and I'm not reassured, not at all. I want to know every movement."

Kerr's phone went dead, then Weatherall's voice crackled into Channel Five. "Any officer, this is Gold. How far is this man from Vauxhall station?"

"This is Jack. At the rate he's walking I estimate four minutes plus."

Kerr shook his head and spun the Alfa into Wandsworth Road.

In the ops room, Weatherall sat still, seemingly frozen with indecision. Then she turned to Fargo. "I'm going to need my Andromeda file."

"But he's not armed, ma'am," said Fargo, leaning forward and opening the drawer in her console, "and not carrying anything."

"Let me be the judge of that," said Weatherall, flicking through the pages. Andromeda was the police strategy for taking out a suicide bomber, a policy that, as an assistant commissioner had once quipped to an incredulous journalist, "does what it says on the tin". It changed the rules of engagement and was routinely described as a licence to kill. Police preferred "interdicting" to "taking out", and insisted on "incapacitate" in place of "kill". But in 2005 at Stockwell, less than a mile from the present operation, the tragedy of Jean Charles de Menezes had shown there could be only one outcome from such a strategy.

In horror, Fargo realised that Weatherall was seriously considering shooting their only lead. He felt the eyes of Alice and the two other comms operators on him, and knew they were all sharing his fear: the real risk of that catastrophe being repeated. Yet, to his side, Weatherall seemed blithely unaware of the implications. As she ran her finger down the menu of options, she might have been choosing a takeaway.

"What do you think, Brian?"

Perkins leant forward, elbows on the console, shirt stretched against his gut, and stared down at his desktop. Beside him, the boy of a chief inspector had rolled his chair back against the wall. Fargo could already hear the sound of shit being shovelled.

For the first time silence enveloped them all. It was the moment of truth. "Brian?"

Perkins was scratching the back of his hand. "I think we should stop him."

"Challenger One," said Weatherall, into the mike.

"Go ahead."

"I want you to . . ." she began, then hesitated. "I want you to . . . Don't let him get to the Underground."

"Gold from Challenger One, repeat, please. Are you directing Trojans to interdict, over?"

"I said he must not get onto the Tube."

"Gold, what are your orders?"

"It's perfectly clear," she said, "so do whatever is necessary."

"Roger that, we are mobile and have visual."

"Gold, no way." Kerr's voice crackled back immediately. "We need to let him run. It may not be the Tube. He may be taking the Overground. We have him contained and he's our only lead."

"All received, John. Stand by," said Fargo, on Weatherall's behalf, picking up on his friend's urgency. Fargo knew about John Kerr's involvement in the shooting of Jean Charles de Menezes at Stockwell, and was convinced the tragedy still troubled him. He also recalled Weatherall had studied the summary of the inquest into that terrible morning in 2005, which recorded Kerr's detailed evidence. He felt deeply for his friend as he waited for Weatherall's response. Could she be so lacking in wisdom as to override the judgement of the man who had actually been there?

Weatherall was looking to her right, but Perkins was examining his hand. Fargo counted seven seconds while she hesitated again and, as she lost control in a sea of ambiguity, he scrawled furiously, making sure he captured every word. "No. As you were, Challenger One," she finally blurted out. "I can't take the chance he may be a suicide bomber."

Kerr's voice hit the room like a punch. "This is John Kerr. All Trojan units, stay back. Repeat, stay back. Jack, Melanie, bump him."

CHAPTER
SEVEN

Thursday, 13 September, 08.44, South Lambeth Road

Good surveillance officers succeed because a credulous public brought up on a diet of TV spookery underestimates them. Their targets fail because fiction teaches them to look for people in distant shadows so they miss the blindingly obvious. Like the victims of a pickpocket, they ignore the student who sidles alongside, or appears next in line at the cashpoint, or sits opposite them in the café, immersed in a book.

Jibril was walking up South Lambeth Road, skirting Vauxhall Park, at full speed and on high alert. But the two surveillance operatives were quicker. Kerr's two-word command was sufficient. Jack Langton, still wearing his cracked motorcycle leathers, and Melanie converged on their target at a bus stop just past the park, three hundred metres south of Vauxhall station, within view of the "Underground" sign. The bus stop was crowded with morning commuters waiting for buses to Brixton, Stockwell and Clapham. About twenty of them thronged the width of the pavement between the bus shelter and a high brick wall, creating a natural choke point. By the time the operatives blocked Jibril's path, they had morphed into a young couple arguing violently about his unfaithfulness.

They knew the script by heart, and it worked every time. They left Jibril no option but to push against them. The moment he made contact, they turned on him, united in a torrent of abuse, and shoved him back into the crowd. Langton's heavy clothing gave them cover. Caught up in their decadent pushing and swearing, Jibril was unaware of the hand checking out his waist and upper body, and never heard the sniff of the explosives detector under his Puffa jacket. For all his training in the desert, he missed them both because he was too busy looking for spooks.

"This is Jack. He's clean."

"Received," said Kerr. "Gold, request you keep the Trojan units back in a holding position. We're in danger of compromise here, over."

Melanie's voice broke in. "This guy is in a serious hurry. Time to Vauxhall station, two minutes."

"Gold from Challenger One. We can take him in thirty seconds."

"No," snapped Kerr. "Gold, he's not, repeat, not carrying. Are you getting this?"

There was silence again in the ops room. From his chair, awaiting instructions, Fargo studied an exercise in paralysis as Weatherall and Perkins stared at each other. Perkins was an expert on safer neighbourhood teams. With a PhD researched in the job's time he liked to style himself "Doctor". This morning he looked like he would have settled for anonymity.

It was Fargo who broke the spell. "Ma'am, did you get that? Jibril is almost at the station." Fargo could recognise a fake and regarded them both with contempt. For all the bullshit and war stories, he knew their front-end experience amounted to a demo outside Marble Arch mosque and a couple of stabbings in north London.

Alice turned, too, her pale eyes darting between Fargo and Weatherall. "He's getting very close. We need a clear decision, Alan."

"What are your intentions, ma'am?" said Fargo.

Weatherall shot him a frozen look, and this time the scraping of the shovel filled the whole room. "Brian?"

"Your call, ma'am."

Weatherall turned back to the mike. "Withdraw the surveillance now." Her voice was quavering. "Challenger One, prepare to interdict."

"That's fucking crazy." Fargo and Alice winced as Kerr's voice exploded from the speaker a microsecond too soon. "Ma'am, subject is not, repeat, not carrying and if he's going somewhere interesting and they take him down we lose the lot. Are you getting this, over?"

Weatherall looked at Perkins again, but he was too busy scratching. In the past three minutes the marks on his hand had become red raw. "We can't take the risk," she said finally, and began reading from the checklist at the front of the file. "I am invoking Andromeda. Challenger One, I am passing you executive control at . . . oh-eight-forty-seven."

"No. No way. Cancel that." Kerr's voice bounced back again. "Look, he's practically at the station.

Remember Jean Charles. You can't risk the Trojans on the train again. But we can follow him wherever he goes, Tube or mainline, no problem. If you pull us off now you risk losing everything."

"That's enough. I've made my decision."

"All Red units, I'm calling Birdcage."

"Birdcage" was code for surveillance officers to close around the target while maintaining cover. It was a risky move, normally invoked in the closing seconds before arrest on the street, occasionally at gunpoint, in full view of the public. But this time it was different. The officers on the ground knew Kerr wanted them to provide a human shield against the Trojans, to sabotage the firearms operation. It was a direct breach of Weatherall's order, Kerr at his most subversive. "Report sightings of Trojans immediately," he added, before Weatherall could recover.

Langton's operatives immediately increased the pace around Jibril, their one-word acknowledgements echoing through the airwaves as they prepared to disappear into the railway system with their target. Then they saw Jibril make a detour left to walk beneath Vauxhall's vast iron railway bridge, a dark, echoing stretch of more than a hundred metres bordered by brick walls, the perfect place for a final exercise in dry cleaning. By the time the two blacked-out Range Rovers of CO19, Tactical Firearms Branch, whirred into the giant roundabout at Vauxhall, seven surveil-lance officers had assembled at the other end of the bridge, twenty metres from the station entrance, forming an invisible, protective bubble around Jibril.

"This is Mel. Trojan units approaching now."

"Received," said Kerr. "Challenger One from Kerr, urgent message. We have the target contained. Repeat. We have control of this and will maintain commentary. You need to hold back, over."

Weatherall was trying to say something to Kerr, but the head of the firearms teams beat her to it. "Alpha from Challenger One, negative to that. We are on scene and have visual. We're taking this from here. Withdraw your units now, over."

Jibril continued walking rapidly to the Tube, oblivious to the activity all around him.

"This is Mel, ten metres to the station."

"Challenger One from Alpha," said Kerr, "he's nearly at the entrance and I'm telling you to hold your fucking cowboys back. It's rush hour, for Christ's sake, a thousand witnesses. He's not, repeat, not carrying, and we can take him onto the train. We have to see where he leads us, so back off."

As he spoke, Birdcage tightened to a radius of three metres, with a couple of the Reds already loitering ahead in the station entrance.

"Trojan units from Challenger One. Attack attack attack!"

It was over in less than a minute. Both Range Rovers approached silently, taking a string of fifteen pedestrians by surprise as they drove the wrong way under the iron bridge and mounted the kerb right in front of them. At the same time Kerr's operatives tightened the circle around Jibril until they were practically advancing at arm's length.

In jeans, sweats and baseball caps, holsters strapped to the leg, with their Glock model 17 semi-automatic weapons already drawn, six Trojans steamed from the first vehicle. "This is Mel and they're attacking," was Melanie's last message, as the Trojans crashed through the circle of Reds and raced across the pavement, terrifying dozens of workers hurrying for the station. A pair of surveillance officers broke cover, signalling them to hold off, but the Trojans shoved them aside on the sprint to their target, already yelling at the tops of their voices: "Police! Stand still!"

The Trojans caught Jibril just inside the station entrance, dead opposite the crowded bus terminus, as he made a right and headed for the staircase leading down to the Tube network. They stopped the morning rush-hour commuters in their tracks as the first pair threw him to the ground. Crammed into the entrance, a dozen witnesses froze in open-mouthed horror as one Trojan held his weapon against Jibril's temple. Then they saw a lean figure in motorcycle leathers rush forward from the crowd and launch himself into the air to land on top of Jibril, completely covering his body and spoiling the officer's aim.

Before anyone could react Melanie swept in after him, shouting, "Police! Police!" and crouching protectively over Langton and Jibril as the Trojans piled in, pumped up, confused but ready to fire. They grabbed Melanie first, but Langton, still on top of Jibril, was already rolling over and shoving his ID up at them. "We told you, you stupid bastards," he was shouting, "we had him."

Sirens were coming from everywhere, but Jibril lay prone as one of the Trojans made a rapid body search. Their team leader stood over them while thirty commuters looked on from the station entrance, evidently stunned by the drama unfolding in front of them. Three Trojans roughly dragged Melanie and Langton aside and stood them against the station wall, then made a quick search and glared at Langton's ID.

The Trojan searching Jibril looked up and shook his head at his boss, just as Kerr appeared beside him. "Hi. I'm John Kerr," he said, nodding at Langton and Melanie, "and those two are mine."

The leader scowled back, ignoring Kerr's outstretched hand. "I'm gonna have you for this."

The second Trojan team appeared, carrying white forensic suits. Recovering from the shock, many of the commuters were taking photographs with their mobile phones, so the assault team carried Jibril to one side of the ticket hall as Langton and Melanie melted away. They drove one of the Range Rovers onto the pavement to block the entrance, then stood the prisoner on the middle of a giant sheet of plastic and methodically removed his clothes, placing each item in a separate evidence sack.

"So, are you going to tell her, or shall I?" Kerr asked the Trojans' leader, as they dressed Jibril in a white forensic coverall.

The team leader turned away and spoke into his mike. "Gold from Challenger One. Suspect is unarmed. We're taking him into Paddington Green."

Kerr was studying the gathering crowd, routinely spotting his own people. "Have to say," said Kerr, nodding at another pair of Trojans nearby carrying Benelli shotguns, "they look a bit disappointed."

"There was no need for your guys to jump in," said the team leader. "We weren't going to shoot him. No way."

Kerr watched a marked armed-response vehicle screech to a halt in front of the lead Range Rover and the crew recover Heckler & Koch 9mm automatics from the boot. "You sure about that?"

The firearms man glared back. "We couldn't afford to risk letting him run on the train," he said, instinctively checking his weapon.

"But we have to, mate," Kerr shot back, his head full of memories from 2005 and the torn body of Jean Charles de Menezes. "That's exactly what we have to do. It's why we're in this business. Bottom line is, he wasn't armed, not carrying a bomb. Perhaps you were gonna shoot him, perhaps not."

They watched the Trojans quick-cuff Jibril and lead him to the Range Rover.

For a moment Kerr was back in the toilets at Green Park station, smashing the young bomber's face against the mirror. "It's a fine line. And I'm not having a go, believe me. I've been there. A young man is dead because I overreacted."

70

"Oh, really?" The Trojan's voice was bitter with sarcasm. "And when was that, exactly?"

He was strangling the wannabe suicide bomber now, then Gabi was screaming at him, her eyes wide in disbelief at her father's violence. "Doesn't matter."

As he passed by, his face framed in white, Jibril looked hard at the firearms man. It was as if he had heard everything. "Doesn't like you much, does he?"

They carefully loaded Jibril into the vehicle and raced away. Uniformed cops were taping off the scene and a superintendent was coming their way.

In the ops room, they all heard the message that told Weatherall she had been wrong. Alice looked to Fargo for instructions, and Fargo turned to Weatherall. "Ma'am? Do you still want surveillance stood down?"

Weatherall put one hand to her mouth, and with the other slammed the Andromeda file back into the drawer. "Tell Mr Kerr I want to see him now."

"I think he's going to be pretty busy at the scene."

"No," she hissed, red-faced. "He's to return immediately and report to me in my office. That's an order. Understood?"

And with that, leaving chaos in her wake, she swept from the room.

CHAPTER
EIGHT

Thursday, 13 September, 09.13, Pepe's Place, Kennington

John Kerr's experience told him things were about to get bad. With countless witnesses and photographs showing cops apparently about to execute another unarmed man, the actions of Jack Langton, Melanie and the Trojans they had disrupted would soon come under the closest scrutiny.

Kerr had been here before. As surveillance leader when the Trojans had shot Jean Charles de Menezes at Stockwell, he still felt deep regret and a heavy burden of guilt, constantly asking himself if he could have done more to prevent such an unnecessary loss of life. But the tragedy had reinforced his views about the conduct of aggressive covert operations. He believed that the odds of fast-track bosses resolving a rapidly moving operation were slim, especially so many miles from the scene.

Serious operational business should be left to the other ranks covering the cold, noisy plot, not police-college clones with an eye on an extra paragraph for their résumé. You had to be able to feel the atmosphere, observe the target's body language, get close enough to touch him, then decide to interdict or let him run without sending a request up the line. That, for Kerr, was the lesson from the tragedy of Jean Charles; and it was the reason he had followed Jack Langton to the scene, rather than returning to brief Weatherall.

Today, as head of this surveillance operation, Kerr was convinced he had been right all along to argue that they should let Jibril run. Whatever the failures of command and control from the Yard, Langton's surveillance on the ground had been textbook, and he intended to prove it.

As soon as Kerr received Alan Fargo's message he called Weatherall's private office to say he would be unavailable until ten o'clock. Stalling her gave him just under an hour to brief Langton and Melanie before racing back to the Yard. They gathered in Pepe's Place, a greasy spoon in a side-street off Kennington Lane, one of their regular haunts.

Kerr had also called Justin Hine, his young technical guru, who drove up from Camberwell. Kerr needed Justin to analyse the data from Langton's explosives sniffer and interpret the surveillance photographs to confirm there had never been any indication that Jibril was wearing a bomb belt or vest.

Fargo managed to escape from the ops room and arrived last, just as Kerr was telling them to turn off their radios and mobiles.

Kerr's team was close, strong on friendship and easy on rank. They were part of a shrinking Special Branch core, experienced and tested, yet viewed with suspicion by the new SO15 imports from the boroughs, including Weatherall. Adrenaline was still flowing and, as Pepe brought over the bacon sandwiches and coffee, Melanie teased Langton, a human cannonball in his motorcycle leathers as he'd piled on top of Jibril. Langton, a divorced former sports teacher and motorcycle nut, reacted like she was paying him a compliment. "Yeah, and you couldn't wait to jump me, could you?"

Fargo was always tucking his shirt back in his trousers, and did so now as he squeezed behind the table. He winked at Mel. "Welcome back," he mouthed, to let her know he had heard about her ordeal in Hackney. The team was close enough for no one to ask her about her kidnap and violent escape, knowing she would talk about it in her own good time. Fargo was forty-three but single, living with his ageing mother in a maisonette in Edgware. There was a rumour of a sister with Down's syndrome, but Fargo never talked about her. He seesawed between starvation fish diets in 1830 and late-night fast-food binges, and this week he was overweight.

"Time to go back on the sardines, Al," said Justin, half his age and skinny, patting Fargo's stomach. But Fargo just signalled Pepe for another round.

When they were settled, Kerr told them to write down every single memory. The earlier the original notes from the field, the greater the credibility, so it was vital to make a record while memories were fresh. Trusting no one, Kerr concentrated solely on building a cast-iron cover over his team. In less than forty minutes they had emerged with a single coherent account, with times, places, people and events in the right order. When the mud-slinging started, he intended to ensure that his team was shielded by the facts, so he told Fargo to copy the ops-room log and his own notes made in the heat of battle and lock everything away in 1830. That was Kerr's first duty, well above taking a bollocking from the commander.

As Kerr was leaving, Langton told him he'd better stick Weatherall's diary down his trousers. That got everyone laughing, but they all wished him well, for John Kerr was their number-one guy, the leader who stayed on the plot, bought the grub and always took the hit for them.

Kerr arrived in Weatherall's outer office at 10.06. The PA and front of house was Donna, an immaculately groomed Jamaican in her fifties. Known as "the weathervane", because she signalled Weatherall's mood, she gave Kerr a thumbs-down from twenty paces, as soon as he rounded the lift lobby, distracting him with her glittering fingernails.

Donna had been around the Met for a long time, watching bosses come and go through a decade of casual racism into the crazily PC nineties. "You look like you've already been in a fight," she murmured, taking in Kerr's dishevelled appearance as he sailed through the office.

"Thanks a lot." He entered without knocking or breaking step, then winked as he closed the door on her.

"Morning, ma'am." Kerr knew Weatherall liked "ma'am" to rhyme with "palm," but only ever managed a short *a*.

"You're late," she snapped, glancing with disapproval at Kerr's stained jacket and tieless collar. He wondered if she knew about the siege in Hackney only a couple of hours earlier. The commander of SO15's intelligence unit had the best office in the Yard, a corner plot on the eighteenth floor with panoramic views of St James's Park and beyond. There were easy chairs and a long meeting table, but Weatherall saved these for her equals. To engage with the lower orders she remained behind her desk. Generations of Special Branch commanders had enjoyed the green-leather-inlaid oak desk once occupied by Viscount Trenchard, former Marshal of the RAF and Metropolitan Police Commissioner. But Trenchard's pride and joy had been dismantled alongside the Branch, replaced with a utilitarian rectangle of ash laminate.

Kerr took the chair beside Detective Chief Superintendent Bill Ritchie, head of operations and his immediate boss. Ritchie was forty-eight, with a full head of dark hair and a paunch just about held in check. Few people knew about his brush with prostate cancer eighteen months before. He was still married to his first wife, a primary-school teacher, with two grown-up children. A career Special Branch officer, he had joined the Met straight from school and would reach thirty years' pensionable service in a year. Ritchie had worked against every extremist group in the UK since the mid-eighties, eventually heading up the squads countering the IRA, domestic extremism and international terrorism. Everyone respected his impeccable operational record, and MI5 were always seeking his advice and judgement.

These days, as deputy to Weatherall, he looked distinguished in a dark, single-breasted suit, blue striped shirt and silk tie, but to Kerr he often appeared to be straining to get back on the plot. Since Weatherall's arrival he frequently had to act as a buffer between her and the guys on the ground, and his discomfort showed.

"How's it going, Bill?" said Kerr.

Ritchie's sideways look suggested there had already been complaints. "You tell me," he murmured.

Weatherall always tasked Donna to provide a litre bottle of water as soon as she arrived in the morning, and another after lunch. She was pouring from it now, and Kerr noticed it was already a third empty. Weatherall's TV, balanced awkwardly on the air-conditioning vent beside her desk, was switched to BBC24, with breaking news of Jibril's arrest.

"Give me one reason why I shouldn't suspend you right now," said Weatherall, without preamble. "Your officers were totally unprofessional. Again."

Kerr shot a glance at Ritchie, who appeared to be weighing his options. "But the Trojans were going to shoot him."

"To incapacitate him."

"They had a gun to his head, for Christ's sake."

Weatherall took a sip of water. "To arrest a terrorist suspect they believed could be armed and dangerous. My order was perfectly clear."

"Your order was clearly ambiguous. You ordered them not to let him get to the Tube." He felt Ritchie's shoe nudge his leg under the table, but he was on a roll. "We have your actual words," said Kerr, reading Alan Fargo's scribbled note. "You said, 'Don't let him get to the Underground.' What does that mean?"

"I'm not going to argue with you." Weatherall was speaking to Kerr, but aimed the glare at Ritchie. She held up a printed email, as if the irrefutable proof lay in her hand. "I've had the initial readout from the firearms team leader and it's quite clear your pair of mavericks compromised an armed operation."

"Well, he's talking bollocks. Jack Langton and Melanie Fleming saved that man's life." Kerr held out his hand. "Can I see it? Please?"

Weatherall returned the email to its folder.

"Bill, for Christ's sake," said Kerr, turning to Ritchie, "I was there. We told her Jibril was unarmed. He wasn't carrying any device, posed no threat to life."

"He wasn't on any agreed target list, either," said Ritchie quietly, "so I'll be asking why you deployed surveillance without authority."

Kerr exhaled. "Look, Joe Allenby gave him to us a few hours before Jibril boarded the plane for London. We're talking the head of station in Yemen here, Bill. A respected player. In one of the world's most volatile countries."

"So why did he send only you the tip-off? We select targets through the joint tasking group. With MI5, right here in the UK, not on the say-so of your mate on the other side of the world. That's what we're all signed up to. So why did Allenby throw away the rule book?"

Kerr had been asking himself the same thing, but kept his misgivings to himself. "It was a Sunday afternoon," he shrugged, "no one about in London, and no time to push this up through the Vauxhall Cross duty officer."

"So no agreement from MI5 either," interjected Weatherall, "who have the lead, in case you've forgotten."

This was indisputable. As the Security Service, MI5 was responsible for protecting the UK against threats to national security, with the Yard its major partner. Every second Tuesday in the month, they would meet Kerr, Langton and Dodge to prioritise security targets. If the two sides disagreed over what they called their "subjects of highest value", the MI5 lead trumped police partnership every time. Dodge's agent runners and Langton's watchers, the people who actually worked the streets, might rail against civil servants who rarely left the office, but MI5's primacy was the working reality.

Kerr held up his hands. "All right. I apologise for breaching the memorandum of bloody understanding, or whatever we call it these days, but we have to trust the man on the ground. Joe Allenby did the right thing to tip us off about Jibril and we proved he was clean. No doubt about it. It was a regular surveillance and people overreacted, simple as that. You gave the Trojans a green light to kill Jibril because you half thought he was a suicide bomber. Jack and I wanted to let him run because we knew he wasn't. Now we'll never find what he might have taken us to."

"And right now you need to back off again," interrupted Ritchie, as Weatherall shifted in her seat.

"Like I should have done when I took out the guy on the Tube who might have led us to the 7/7 bombers? Go on, say it."

"We don't need to go there."

"Yes, we do. Fair play, Bill. Tragic things can happen when you intervene too aggressively. No one knows that better than I do." He looked directly at Weatherall. "That was my fault, but at least I've learnt from it."

Kerr heard Ritchie clear his throat, as if he was gearing up to take charge. It gave him a pang of hope. With Ritchie at the helm things tended to work out all right.

"Ma'am, let me propose a way forward," said Ritchie. "These are experienced officers of integrity and talent. The last security assessment estimated five Al Qaeda cells in and around London. The number of active targets has rarely been higher and we suspect at least one bomb factory ready to blow." He held up his hands, as if conceding a point. "And, yes, I accept John may have made an error of judgement."

Kerr stayed silent. He knew Ritchie was playing politics. But if a slice of criticism was enough to keep Weatherall off their backs, then Kerr was big enough to take the hit.

80

"In total breach of our partnership with MI5." Weatherall glared.

"But in good faith," said Ritchie. "I'm simply advising that suspension now will destroy the morale of the surveillance officers we ask to do this dangerous work for us."

Kerr smiled to himself. Ritchie had worked counter-terrorism operations for ever. It was the best guidance Weatherall would get.

"I don't remember asking for your advice."

"It's my duty as head of operations to give it. I'm simply advising that you act with care. I need to study the Trojans' report and establish a clear timeline from our own officers."

"You can have it right now," said Kerr.

"We can rely on the Independent Police Complaints Commission to do that," Weatherall said.

"And that's my point," said Ritchie. "The IPCC are going to be all over us like a rash. We need a clear audit trail," he said, nodding at the folder, "and that email is exhibit one. I need to understand exactly what happened. This was a disrupted armed operation. Officers from different units fighting each other in the middle of the rush hour. Christ, it's probably already on YouTube. The IPCC will look at the whole decision-making process, top down, so we need to get this right."

"And you need to realise we're not dealing with the IRA here," Weatherall snapped, as the phone buzzed. "Everyone knows we face an unprecedented threat." She answered the phone and covered the mouthpiece.

"Times have changed, and you people don't seem to have noticed."

They had heard it all before. Weatherall belonged to the new breed of police bosses for whom page one in the Textbook on Terror was Al Qaeda, and 9/11 happened in Year Zero. To the generation with clear eyes and clean hands, Ritchie was a remnant of the old school.

"Thanks, Bill," murmured Kerr, while Weatherall was distracted.

"Do yourself a favour and button it."

The two men went back a long way. Two decades ago Ritchie had been Kerr's boss when he was deployed on a secret, long-term infiltration assignment. Ritchie's official title was "cover officer", and it meant he protected every aspect of Kerr's parallel lives as Special Branch officer and political extremist. In a way Ritchie, too, had led a double life. At debriefing sessions in safe-houses around London he was the friend who reassured and the chief who gave out the orders. Kerr would sometimes badmouth him as one part counsellor, three parts dictator, which suited Ritchie fine. From those hard-edged years had emerged a habit of plain speaking between them that transcended rank. These days it often troubled Kerr to see Ritchie morph from an effective operator into a politician; sometimes he had accused him of selling out, of receding into the pensioner's twilight zone. The two men would inevitably clash again, but this morning Kerr felt grateful to his mentor.

When Weatherall had finished the call she reached into her desk drawer and withdrew a policy file. It had a red cover and she held it forehead high like a sacrament. "We play by different rules, these days. You both know that."

Kerr got back first, this time too fast for Ritchie's nudging foot. "Yeah, like shooting an unarmed man in the head."

"I don't need you to tell me how to run a counter-terrorist operation, Chief Inspector," said Weatherall, letting the file drop to her desk. She looked from one to the other, her face red with anger. "Your job is to find this so-called bomb factory you keep telling me is out there."

"I think the suggestion is that Jibril might have taken us there," said Ritchie. As he delivered the killer blow, he was the height of reasonableness and looked her straight in the eye. "If it turns out Ahmed Jibril was our only link, you appear to have severed it."

Weatherall blinked. Lost for words, she turned up the volume on the TV. It was surreal, as if the presenter had been listening to their argument.

"In scenes reminiscent of the shooting of Jean Charles de Menezes at Stockwell Tube station in 2005, witnesses report seeing armed officers with weapons drawn aiming at the man's head, when two undercover police officers appeared to intervene to arrest him. A witness close to the police line says the two teams of officers appeared to be at odds in dealing with the incident. A spokesman from the Independent Police Complaints Commission said it has begun an independent investigation. Now we return to the scene for an update from Katy Bradley."

Weatherall stared at the screen, transfixed.

"So, are you content for me to review this, ma'am," Ritchie gestured at the TV, "before that lot really get started on us?"

Kerr spoke, not softly enough: "I can almost hear them hammering the nails in."

The gibe seemed to revive Weatherall. She swung to face Ritchie. "I haven't got time for this, so you'd better bring this officer back in line, Bill." She turned to Kerr. "And you need to get real, or get out."

The door flew open a nanosecond before the knock. Donna was followed by Melanie Fleming, still dressed in the combat pants and boots, T-shirt and denim jacket she had been wearing for her undercover operation in Hackney.

"Don't just crash in without . . ." began Weatherall.

"Melanie says this can't wait," interrupted Donna, as if she hadn't heard, then turned and left the room, closing the door behind her. Melanie approached the desk. "Ma'am, I need to speak with Mr Ritchie and Mr Kerr about the operation."

"And who are you?"

"DS Melanie Fleming, ma'am."

"Red Two," said Kerr, "works with Jack Langton."

"Then I'm surprised you have the nerve to show your face in here," Weatherall said, unscrewing the water bottle again.

"It's very urgent, ma'am. I'm here to pick up some equipment and I really need to get back to the plot. Jack's waiting for me."

"So let's all hear it."

84

Melanie looked at Kerr. "It's about Zoom in Leyton. Jack took a call in Pepe's. He went on the move about the time we were taking Jibril off the street. With a camera case and tripod."

"'Zoom'?" interrupted Weatherall. "Who the hell is that?"

"Osama bin Laden used him in Pakistan to produce his videos after nine/eleven," said Kerr, without taking his eyes off Melanie, "according to the Americans."

Ritchie looked at Weatherall. "I briefed you last week. They found his prints on the stuff taken from bin Laden's compound."

"We think he's on the way to make another one. Propaganda or suicide," said Melanie.

"How can you possibly know that?" said Weatherall.

"Al Qaeda don't do weddings," snapped Kerr.

"He caught the sixty-nine up Hoe Street to Walthamstow Central, then walked," said Melanie. "Jack's guys followed him to a block of flats off Fielding Road. Whole journey took him less than fifteen minutes. Sixth floor. Could be a safe-house or bomb factory. Jack and Justin are already on scene. I'm setting up the OP with Alan Fargo."

"Where?" said Kerr.

"We've commandeered a bus, actually, for now."

"You've what?" spluttered Weatherall.

Kerr guessed his team must have scrambled from Pepe's as soon as he'd left for the Yard. "What's the rendezvous point for surveillance?" he said, already halfway to the door.

"Jack's using the car park next to the health centre in Prospect Road."

"So let's move."

"Wait." Kerr turned to see Weatherall with water in full flow. She placed the bottle carefully on the desk. "Make sure you clear this with your MI5 counterpart. And if I invoke Andromeda again today I don't want one second of hesitation. Is that clear?"

Ritchie was already following Kerr, and positioned himself between Weatherall and Kerr's look of disbelief. "Let's go, John," he said quietly.

CHAPTER
NINE

By the time Kerr reached Walthamstow a light drizzle was falling and, although it was still mid-morning, the light was shut out by a bank of grey cloud. In his race to north-east London he felt a surge of relief that he had kept surveillance on the film-maker while Jack Langton was pulling units away to follow Ahmed Jibril.

In May 2011, when US Navy SEALs had stormed Osama bin Laden's compound in Karachi, Pakistan, they had recovered seven videos showing a younger bin Laden rehearsing his propaganda broadcasts, stumbling over his words through sometimes four or five takes. The same set of fingerprints was found on all the video casings, but this took the investigators no further forward: there was no match on any terrorism database.

It had fallen to CIA interrogators to extract more information from one of bin Laden's former couriers detained in Guantánamo. According to this prisoner, the man they wanted was in his late fifties, walked with the aid of a roughly hewn stick, and worked in a 7-Eleven in London, not far from a dog-racing track.

He was a producer of *jihadi* videos, but had never engaged in active service himself.

Three days before Ahmed Jibril's arrival in London, working on a radius from the site of the old Walthamstow Greyhound Stadium, closed since 2008, Alan Fargo's 1830 team traced the owner of the fingerprints to a vegetable store in Leyton, east London. They identified him as Fazal Shakir, a fifty-nine-year-old Pakistani raised in Karachi only a few streets from bin Laden's hiding place. He had lived undetected in London since escaping there in 2007.

MI5 wanted no action against Shakir until they had clearance from their Washington counterparts, but John Kerr had had him watched anyway. Jack Langton's operatives had tagged their target "Zoom" because of his skill with a camera and slow progress on the street. And because Kerr had followed his better judgement, there was now a real possibility that the ageing Pakistani would reveal the bomb factory they had been seeking for months.

The address he had led them to this morning was Barrington House in Walthamstow, to the south of the old dog stadium. Fielding Road ran east to west, with a cemetery to the north and a leisure centre at the western end near the junction with Blackhorse Road. It was a mix of residential and low-rise business premises, part industrial, mostly retail. Directly opposite Barrington House lay a tacky 1930s parade of shops with flats above. There were kebab, pizza and chicken joints, a pawnbroker, two bookmakers and a couple of shops offering best prices for gold and foreign-exchange currency.

The block itself was council-owned and twelve storeys high. Built in the 1950s, it was set back fifty metres from the road, separated by a rough stretch of treeless green with a fenced area to the left containing dilapidated swings, a broken slide and a "No Dogs" sign. To the casual observer the whole area looked barren. In Kerr's eyes it was a no man's land offering minimum cover for an assault from the front. He noted two worn tarmac footpaths crossing the green diagonally from Fielding Road and a narrow service road leading to a car park at the rear of the block.

Kerr had reached the scene from the Yard in seventeen minutes and parked up on a double yellow out of sight of the flats. Very soon the whole area would be sealed off but, for now, traffic was heavy, obstructed by the commandeered bus. Shoppers ran their local errands unaware they were in real danger of being shot or blown up on the street they had walked along for years.

Kerr grabbed his BlackBerry and sprinted along the front of the parade. The top deck of a London bus is not a bad site for a makeshift control post until the sourcing guys come up with something more permanent. Seven or eight disappointed passengers were still hanging around on the pavement, anticipating an imminent return to normal service, while the rat-faced, hi-vis-jacketed driver drew on his cigarette and shouted into his mobile.

Melanie had ridden pillion with Langton again, and Kerr found her on the top deck at the rear of the bus, already working with Alan Fargo. Already they had most of the comms up and running. Despite the cold, Fargo's face glowed red and his shirt was dark with sweat as he set up the remote surveillance and recording gear. He looked as though he had jogged all the way from Pepe's Place.

Kerr squeezed between them and peered through the side window. They were parked around a hundred and fifty metres from the building, half hidden by a beech tree. "So, what are we looking at?"

"Shakir went to 608," said Melanie, "halfway up. Couldn't be worse."

The block was covered with ugly grey cement cladding and had old-fashioned metal windows; the main entrance was a pair of double doors, dead centre, with a rough strip of tarmac along the front connecting the two diagonal paths and leading behind the block to the car park. There were no balconies. Kerr counted the windows from the ground. "The one with the dirty net curtains, yeah?"

"They're all disgusting," said Fargo, racing through the electronic voters' register, "and the adjacent flats are occupied, above and below."

Kerr stepped back and sat down to improve his line of sight. "Will the neighbours let us in to do some tech?"

"Mind your back, John." Kerr caught a whiff of old sweat as Fargo squeezed past. "This has been a no-go area for years."

90

"Let's phone them anyway, if you can find anyone who's still using a landline. Where's Justin?"

"Already in," said Melanie, tapping a small video screen. "Probably up to his ankles in used condoms and hypodermics by now."

"Assault teams?"

"Flexing their muscles," said Fargo, wiping his headphones. He waved a disinfectant swab in the direction of the rear window. Since catching an ear infection from headphones a decade ago, he had been fastidious. "RV point for the firearms teams is in Miller Road, supermarket car park."

"How the hell will they get in unseen?"

"They'll make the approach from the car park at the back — 608 only looks onto the front. Unless the targets leave the flat to check from the landing window, they have no visibility. And there's no way they'll risk that."

"There'll be another entrance direct from the car park?"

"Sure, but the Trojans are planning to snake round the front because it gives direct access to the stairs. Their leader wants a word, by the way." Fargo gestured for silence and spoke into his radio mike. "Go ahead, Justin."

Justin Hine, Kerr's technical whiz kid who had joined them at Pepe's, was lying prone on the floor of the living room in flat 708, directly above the target address. He lay completely still, stretched out on his stomach with his eyes closed.

The occupier, a Somali mother in *hijab* and veil, looked on from the doorway with her young son, trespassers in their own home. Justin had talked his way in less than three minutes earlier. The little boy, no more than five years old, crept up and tentatively prodded his thigh. Justin opened his eyes, removed one earpiece of the stethoscope he was using to detect signs of life in the flat below, and murmured into his throat mike, "At least three, possibly four males."

The little boy seemed to think Justin was speaking to him and looked up to his mother in bewilderment. Justin held a finger to his lips then carried on murmuring, confusing the kid even more. "Plus the TV on Al Jazeera, and they sound pretty worked up." He frowned and shook his head, as if disagreeing with someone, but this time the little boy retreated and clung to his mother's knees. "No, I can do something here. Switch on your screen and stand by."

Justin stood up, stretched, tucked his T-shirt into his jeans and made a tired face at Mum and her little boy. He knew she spoke hardly any English. At the front door a few minutes earlier she had simply stared at his woollen hat and rucksack as he had flashed his ID, winked at the little boy and eased himself into the hallway. Now he took their coats and gently ushered them from the flat to the lift lobby. Pressing the button for the ground floor, he listened to check that the lift was working. "You can come back in one hour," he said, holding up his index finger for the mother. He gave her elbow a reassuring squeeze, chucked the little boy under the chin, loped back to the flat and quietly shut their front door on them.

Back in the living room, he took from his bag a fibre-optic cable, a tiny TV screen and specially adapted drill. He pulled back the threadbare rug and calculated the exact central point of the room. Within thirty seconds, lying flat, he had silently drilled down five centimetres into the concrete floor. He replaced the bit and worked at the hole again, drilling until he reached the ten-centimetre marker. For the final stretch he used a device equipped with suction to prevent the tiniest fragment falling to the floor below.

Justin took his time but was inserting the fibre-optic cable inside three minutes of pulling back the rug. Within another forty seconds he was refining colour digital images on the miniature screen. He sat cross-legged, swivelling the cable to cover the room below. "OK, Al, we have a bomb factory, four up, two in their mid-twenties, English-speaking, Yorkshire accents. Number three is older, saying nothing yet. And the cameraman Shakir is setting up his equipment. You should be getting audio and video feed."

"Loud and clear."

"Workbench in the centre of the living room. Three devices minimum in plastic containers, fridge in the corner, possibly more stashed in there. Three rucksacks, half a dozen batteries, piles of white powder in a heavy plastic bag."

"How much?"

"Masses. Al, these boys are clean-shaven." This was significant, because suicide bombers shaved their faces and body hair immediately before blowing themselves up. Deprived of a proper burial, this was to ensure cleanliness when they entered Heaven.

"What's the stuff at the end of the bench?"

"Bottle of clear liquid — sulphuric acid, possibly." Justin strained his eyes. "Can't make out the label. Six, correction, seven plastic beakers, looks like a couple of eye-droppers beside them. There's a hacksaw and copper tubing for the detonators but can't see any wires to go with the batteries, not from here. Shakir, with his tripod et cetera, covering the wall to the left of the door. Three chairs. Sheets of A3 covered with felt tip. Al, this guy's even written the script for them. Bomb factory plus film set."

In their makeshift observation post, Kerr, Melanie and Fargo crowded round the monitor. Kerr grabbed the mike. "Justin, I want you out of there, do you hear me? I mean now."

"John?" said Melanie, quietly, tapping Kerr's arm. "We've got company."

Kerr turned to find the firearms team leader behind him and smiled with relief. "Hey, Jim," he said, grasping his hand, "am I glad to see you." Kerr and Jim Gallagher had worked many ops together over the years. Gallagher had arrived in complete silence, shrouded in black fatigues and ready for action, with CS canister, stun grenades, gas mask, quick cuffs, baton, and Glock 17 in the holster strapped to his thigh. Had he been in the jeans and sweatshirt he wore around the house, few would have guessed his job. A

94

Highlander in his early thirties, Gallagher was tall, blond, superfit and mildly spoken, and his youthful face belied the dangers confronting him every working day.

Kerr knew he was also ice cool. In 2005, the week after 7/7, Gallagher had co-ordinated three of the five firearms teams deployed to arrest *jihadis* planning a second wave of attacks in London. Because further attacks were believed to be imminent, his operations had been executed with very little notice to plan or recce, but had been faultless. Captured on TV and replayed constantly, the pictures showed the Trojans at their professional best.

Melanie cleared a space for Gallagher to study the screen.

"So, John, what crock of shit are you handing me this time?"

"See for yourself," said Melanie, activating the mike. "Justin, we're briefing Challenger One, so pan around again."

The picture moved jerkily as Kerr pointed at the screen. "Three targets in flat 608, plus one to record their suicide video. You can see the explosive mix here, at least three completed devices to pack into rucksacks."

Gallagher peered through the bus window, counting up the floors. "So, no chance to evacuate the building?"

"Not with safety," said Kerr, holding the headphones to Gallagher's ear. "They're really worked up, almost ready to hit the street. We don't have much time."

Gallagher listened intently. "I can't risk explosions in the block." He spoke calmly into his throat mike.

"Challenger Two, withdraw all units and await my instructions." Instinctively, he was checking his gear. "We'll have to regroup, and you should too, John. The uniforms have the cordons set up and you're about sixty metres too close. If this lot goes up you'll get hammered."

"There's no time," said Kerr.

"I reckon we'll have to take them out as soon as they move." As he spoke, Gallagher was already heading for the staircase, his body crackling with radio traffic. "Keep your heads down, guys," he said, as he pattered down the stairs. "It's going to get very noisy out there."

In flat 608, as Justin and the others watched and listened, the three Islamic terrorists moved about their bomb factory, preparing to make their video and head out for their target destinations. With the exception of Fazal Shakir, none had come to the notice of Room 1830. Sabri, their leader, was in his mid-thirties, a veteran of many training camps in Pakistan. His English was poor and he rarely spoke, but he was a legendary explosives and technical expert.

Daljit, husband and doting father of a young son, had lived in Bradford all his life and worked as an assistant manager in a supermarket. At twenty-four he was the same age as the third member of the group, Mahmoud, who had turned down a place at Leeds University to study chemistry and drifted through a series of dead-end jobs. The grandchildren of Pakistani immigrants and lifelong friends, they had become radicalised in their last year at the local comp and begun to worship at the same mosque until Sabri had ordered them to drop off the radar. Neither had ever travelled outside England, and none appeared to be acquainted with bin Laden's video producer.

Their bodies spiritually purified, they carefully packed the copper detonators with TATN for insertion into the mix of chapatti flour and hydrogen peroxide, while Shakir waited patiently by his camera. Except for the nails, which showed black through the plastic, they might have been preparing a meal.

They had placed each of the three rucksacks next to an improvised explosive device, IED, in a plastic box, ready to be packed inside. The bags already contained a map of the London Underground, one for each martyr. Apart from the workbench, fridge and large TV, there was no other furniture in any of the rooms, and nothing to distract on the walls. The flat was truly fit for purpose. None of the terrorists bothered with gloves and they knew their fingerprints would be on every surface. That was an up-side to suicide bombing: it did away with the necessity to conceal evidence.

Shakir turned down the volume on the TV. He was urging them to take their seats in front of the camera, but they ignored him. Mahmoud, agitated, checked his watch for the hundredth time. "Our brother is more than an hour late. Something bad has happened."

"He will come to us in good time," snapped Sabri. "We wait, as ordered."

The old Pakistani spoke for the first time: "And while he comes to you, brothers, you make your living wills."

Mahmoud glared at him. "Be silent!" He turned back to Sabri. "The cops may already have taken him down. We need the red dots now, brother. And the sequence. Then we must leave this place."

On the bus, this caused Kerr and Melanie to exchange a glance. "Red dots" was Al Qaeda code for London Underground stations. It suggested that, to maintain operational security and synchronise the attacks, another brother was to provide the station names and the exact timing for each explosion at the last possible moment. In Kerr's mind lay the conviction that the final link was Ahmed Jibril.

Sabri's harsh voice exploded with anger. "No. I told you. We wait as planned. We stay here until our brother gives us the targets." He looked at Shakir. "Old man, we are ready for you. You have the words for us to speak?"

"Everything is set," said Shakir, leaning on his stick as he checked his camera. "This is your legacy to the world. If you are careful, I need no more than three or four minutes."

Mahmoud stood between Sabri and the tripod. The younger man was fifteen centimetres taller than his leader and stretched his hand against his chest. "No. We have no time for words and pictures." He carefully removed a London Underground map from the nearest rucksack and slapped it on the workbench. "In the last hours of our lives we no longer need to fear you. So choose the targets for us now. Otherwise Daljit and I go alone."

"Mahmoud is right," said Daljit. "We need to move right now. If the cops already have our brother they will find us, too. It is time, *inshallah*."

"Are you getting this, guys?" murmured Justin, into his mike, from the flat above. "They're getting ready to roll." Then he saw Daljit run to the window, while Mahmoud, who had mixed the explosives, stayed at the workbench, checking the IED connections. As he worked, a speck of plaster dropped onto Mahmoud's hand and his eyes whipped to the ceiling.

Justin remained prone, capturing every movement on his monitor. He watched Daljit peer through the window and call to the others. Sabri joined him and they began to gesticulate excitedly. "Something's spooking them outside, Al," whispered Justin. "Who's moving around out there? You need to let the Trojans know. Alan, are you seeing this?" he said, into his throat mike.

He heard Fargo speak quietly and urgently. "Yeah, and we want you out of there right now. Christ, Justin, don't move. He's looking right at you." Justin and Fargo froze in their respective viewing points, mesmerised by the image on the screen as Mahmoud peered at the camera directly above him.

Justin lay completely still as the terrorist looked straight at him, keeping his voice to a whisper. "Wait, he's not sure."

Mahmoud gave a yell and Sabri joined him, leaving Daljit by the window. The two terrorists stared at the ceiling, suspicious but unsure, like brothers in some zany family snapshot. In the corner, Justin saw Shakir using the distraction to dismantle the tripod and pack away his camera.

"Trust me, Al," murmured Justin. "They'll never spot the hole, not enough to be certain." For a few seconds the two sides stared each other out in complete silence, as if testing who would blink first. Then Mahmoud spotted Shakir edging towards the door with his equipment and gave a shout. He seemed enraged that the old man should be trying to escape. Justin watched him leap across the room, strike Shakir hard in the face and drag him back, flinging him down by the workbench and snapping his walking stick. Suddenly Daljit yelled something from the window and Justin watched the other two bombers rush to join him.

Ice cool, Justin panned to follow them. "It's OK, we're clear. Where are the Trojans?" he said.

"Getting ready for the assault," said Fargo. "They're entering the building, Justin. You have to get out."

"And these boys must have seen them. It's really working them up."

Fargo again, urgent: "Listen, just stop fucking about and get your arse down here."

Then Kerr's voice was in his ear. "I already told you, Justin. Lock the cable so we have the best picture and get out of there. Call me on your mobile when you're clear."

"OK, but you have to hit them right now." Justin heard a sound and turned as the Somali mother reappeared, holding her little boy's hand. Justin got to

100

his feet and spoke gently to her. "I told you, it's not safe here. You have to go."

The mother pointed in the vague direction of the lift. "Not work."

Justin held his hands up, palms outstretched. "All right, I'll take care of you, but we have to be very quiet."

He checked the image on the monitor and secured the cable to capture the maximum coverage. Packing the rest of the kit into the rucksack, he spoke into his throat mike. "Al, I'm signing off. Seven-oh-eight is clear."

The little boy went up to Justin and took his hand. Justin heaved the rucksack on to his back, picked the child up and led them from the room. "Come, we'll use the stairs."

CHAPTER
TEN

Thursday, 13 September, 11.36, Fielding Road, Walthamstow

In the bomb factory directly below, Daljit watched through the window as the other two continued with the final preparations to their bombs. Then, as he leant out, he spotted Gallagher's firearms teams sneaking through the main door. "Sabri!" he yelled. "They are attacking! They are coming to kill us."

Their leader looked across from the table. "How many?"

"Too many. You must hurry, both of you, we have no more time."

Fargo's picture was imperfect, but Daljit's voice was loud and clear, so powerful that Fargo had to lift his headphones. He and Melanie crowded the screen as Kerr spoke to Gallagher: "Jim, do you still have the audio link? You have to hit them now."

Gallagher's voice was breathless. "Roger that, I'm with Team One, fourth floor," he panted, brushing past Justin and his charges, "forty seconds away."

* * *

Sabri helped Mahmoud and Daljit arm their devices and place them in the rucksacks while the old Pakistani cowered in the corner where he should have been filming their final message to the world. The bombers gave Osama bin Laden's film-maker a final look of contempt. This lame, sick man, who had once enjoyed access to the world's most famous *jihadi*, meant nothing to them. He belonged to the past. "Everything is finished," said Daljit, quietly.

When they were ready they held the rucksacks to their chests and shouted in unison, "We will take them with us, *inshallah*."

The trigger wire to Daljit's device became detached. "Wait! Wait!" His hands steady in the face of death, Mahmoud helped Daljit carefully reinsert the copper detonator.

The terrorists had their final moment of calm as Jim Gallagher and his first assault team assembled silently outside the door of flat 608.

"Are you ready?" said Sabri, sounding like a leader again, looking to each of his comrades.

They walked closer to the door and stood quietly for a moment, listening for movement outside. Then, as the door crashed open and the Trojans' stun grenades rolled across the floor, the cry went up in unison: "Allah is great! Allah is great!"

The grenades exploded in the same instant as the terrorist bombs, creating a blast that obliterated the senses and created a hell of ragged flesh, blood and fire. Gallagher had been the first across the threshold. He saw the terrorists were about to detonate their bombs, so charged into the room behind the grenades, firing his Heckler & Koch as he ran. From less than a metre he took the full force of Daljit's bomb. It tore away his helmet and every shred of clothing. The nails ripped his belly to shreds.

He landed on his back in the middle of the floor, firing his weapon until the magazine was empty, then looked down at the parts of his body that should have been in his stomach but were strewn haphazardly across his chest. His lower chest to his thighs was a mass of smoking, unrecognisable flesh. But the helmet had protected his head and face from the worst of the blast and he looked almost quizzically at the bright red blood pumping across his chest onto the floor.

Unthinkingly, Gallagher's number two had followed him. They were buddies at work and family friends outside, playing squash every week at Imber Court, one of the Met's sports clubs. Sabri's device seemed to have been destined for him, and he was charging at full speed when the blast hit. The bomb stripped him naked, too, scorching the front of his body and tearing away his left leg above the knee. A volley of nails ripped apart his torso, and a chair leg sliced into his face, tearing out his right cheekbone. Every wound was fatal, but none strong enough to kill him immediately.

His leg ricocheted off the wall and fell back on top of him, but he pushed it away as he crawled across to help Gallagher. In the last seconds before the shock killed them both, he weakly tried to replace Gallagher's intestines. To the end the two friends looked out for each other.

Sabri and Daljit were luckier. They destroyed themselves instantly, even before the rounds from Gallagher's carbine ripped into them, and took out Shakir as well. Sabri was decapitated, as is common with suicide bombers, his head shooting like a meteorite across the room and mashing itself against the wall. The blast pulverised their torsos, fusing their limbs and organs into a single, indistinguishable heap of flesh. Gallagher could see Daljit's head lying inches away, the eyes staring right through them in surprise. His last act was to pick it up by the hair and toss it aside, like a piece of trash.

With shock waves reverberating around them, a second pair of Trojans stormed into the room. Weapons cocked, torches lighting the way, they stood at the threshold searching fruitlessly for targets. Both men had witnessed bomb scenes before, but the sights and smells of flat 608 would never leave them. The room was dark as night and their gas masks protected them from the acrid smoke and dust, though the images were straight out of hell. The brightest light came not from their torches but from the flames shooting out of a gas pipe high in one corner, which had already set fire to the ceiling. From the other side of the room, water rushed down the walls in a torrent and a bloody pool lapped around their dead comrades, as if seeking out their bodies to cool them.

Then, with a rush, the Trojans saw daylight, which entered where the far wall should have been. As the smoke cleared, they felt another blast, this time of cold air. The scene outside was filled with flashing blue lights. They could see a double-decker bus in the distance, abandoned cars, and people racing towards them. It was as though they were looking through a giant picture window. In the deathly hush of the bomb factory, against the buzzing of their damaged eardrums, they heard strong voices shouting for them.

Their weapons found movement from the farthest corner. As the dust and smoke swirled away on the wind they saw a man balancing on the edge of the precipice, silhouetted against the clouds. He was standing with his rucksack still tight to his chest. Face lacerated and clothes in tatters, he had been wounded not by the energy of the bombs so much as his failure of courage. Hand out of sight behind the rucksack, he trembled in the cold as the Trojans' carbines arrested him in their sights. "Stand still!" the officers shouted, though neither had any intention of taking him alive.

They shot him as he tried to activate his bomb and launched himself into the air, crashing onto the roof of a police personnel carrier. His bomb detonated as dozens of officers in riot gear were streaming into the building. It stripped open the roof like a tin can to lacerate the driver, killing him instantly.

CHAPTER
ELEVEN

Thursday, 13 September, 11.47, Fielding Road, Walthamstow

Justin had reached the second floor on his descent with the Somali family when flat 608 exploded. He heard the snap of the stun grenade, then the much louder double crack of the terrorist bombs. The whole building shook violently. He threw the screaming mother and child onto the hard concrete stairs and flung himself on top of them, protecting them with his body just as a heavy chunk of ceiling plaster crashed onto his shoulders. With adrenaline keeping the pain away he picked up the little boy again and pulled the mother to her feet. Half dragging, half carrying her, he raced on with them down the staircase.

Five steps from the ground floor, with the open entrance door in view, their path was blocked by riot police storming the block. The surge of bodies overwhelmed them and almost certainly saved their lives: they were forced to stand to one side of the staircase as the bomber crashed onto the police personnel carrier. Seconds later Justin would have been running with them, past the vehicle, directly in line with the blast.

As they reached the ground, the bomb blew the heavy front doors three metres into the hallway as if they were pieces of cardboard. Because the three were pressed to the side of the entrance they escaped the full energy of the explosion. Ramming them into the corner of the stairwell, Justin enveloped mother and child with his body. A tornado scorched his face, then something struck his temple. He had the presence of mind to find his warrant card, then charged with them into the open, holding up his ID and yelling, "Police!" at every gun barrel he could see, shielding them from the devastation around the bombed vehicle and searching for a tree, a wall or a building to protect them from the next explosion.

With Melanie and Fargo in the bus, Kerr stared at the last images of the bomb factory. On the screen they saw Gallagher burst through the door and heard the staccato shots from his weapon before the pictures turned to snow. The building disintegrated a second before the shatterproof windows of the bus blew in. The shockwave tipped the vehicle so far they feared it would overturn. They crashed against the seats and partitions, then hurled themselves to the floor as the bus lurched the other way before righting itself. When they looked again, masonry and lethal shards of glass were still falling to the ground. Just as they thought the horror was over, they saw a man wearing a rucksack fall from the cavity. They felt the bus tip again, thrown sideways by the blast of his bomb.

"Dear God." Melanie was staring at the destruction. Smoke was pouring from the space where the wall had been, followed by flames spreading across the ceiling, fanned by the cold air. Dark clouds drifted on the wind, clogging their nostrils with the stench of burning. Then sirens rose with the dust and heat and screams as armoured carriers and ambulances tore past them, ignoring the cordons, racing to capture the perpetrators and search for signs of life.

"Anyone injured?" shouted Kerr, climbing to his feet, but Fargo was already scrambling for the radio, shouting for Justin on his bodyset. He tried twice, in vain.

"Call his mobile," yelled Kerr, as if he might yet save his officer by sheer force of will.

Fargo wanted to recover his kit, but Kerr ordered them off the bus into his car. The whole area was about to become a media circus, so he needed to get them clear. They were plastered with dust and debris, and Kerr's jacket was torn, but none would admit to any injuries.

Justin called as Kerr was driving them to the surveillance rendezvous point and gave his location.

In the health-centre car park Kerr told Fargo and Melanie to stay in the car while he briefed Langton's surveillance officers on the attack, then told them to scramble. He asked Langton to collect as much of Fargo's tech gear from the bus as he could, then wait for him at the Yard. Back in the car with Melanie and

Fargo, he parked at the perimeter of the cordon and found Justin among a crowd of walking wounded being shepherded to a fleet of ambulances stacked up in Hoe Street. Rucksack on his back, Justin held a little boy in one arm and comforted the child's hysterical mother with the other.

Kerr called to him as he helped them into an ambulance. "What happened to you?" he said, as they walked back to the car.

"I'm fine."

"Don't talk bollocks. None of us is fine."

Back at the Yard, Kerr asked Langton to have Justin checked out and arrange transport home for Melanie and Fargo. He caught Langton looking at him shrewdly. He knew his deputy was thinking about everything else that had tested him that morning. "How about you, John?" said Langton. "Are you OK?"

"Yeah. But there's something else I have to do."

The next call Kerr made was to the commander of the Trojans. Once the worst was confirmed, Kerr went with him to break the news to Jim Gallagher's widow at the neat three-bedroomed semi they had just bought in Croydon. Gallagher had a child of primary-school age from a previous marriage. His second wife of thirteen months was young, attractive and Muslim, and had just given birth to their son. Her name was Nandeeta, and she was the daughter of wealthy, high-caste immigrants from New Delhi. Kerr had met Nandeeta once before, and described how he had witnessed her husband's last moments. She listened to the story of Gallagher's heroism until they told her there were no remains to identify. Then she screamed that the terrorists had stolen her husband's soul.

With adrenaline flowing long after the endgame, detectives find different ways to wind down immediately after any dangerous operation. Like stand-ups buzzing after a late-night live performance, the young and unattached often prefer to hang out together, in the pub or briefing room, while battle-hardened veterans race home to make up for lost time with their families.

A few, like John Kerr, normally sociable and extrovert, prefer to reorient themselves alone. He arrived home shortly after four. His Islington apartment, on the top floor of a refurbished Victorian mansion block, had two bedrooms and a balcony overlooking Upper Street. It had a great view of the local market and Kerr had fallen in love with the place at first sight. Less flashy than the new-build apartments spreading out along the banks of the Thames, it retained masses of character, with high ceilings and ornate cornices. The style was contemporary, the décor neutral, and Kerr had changed scarcely a thing since moving in three years ago.

He could still taste the smoke and dust, and smell the burning. Waiting for the reaction to kick in, he poured a large brandy and opened the French windows onto the balcony. The light was failing, but the rain had lifted. Filling his lungs with cool air, he thought about the dead and injured. The body parts of four terrorists, two Trojans and a police driver were being laid out in mortuaries across London, as were those of four residents of the flats; they had been shredded by flying glass. The conviction that he could have prevented it filled him with sadness.

He knew the loss of life, of comrades and civilians, would have a profound effect on everybody. At such times, their immediate reactions might differ. But within hours, invariably, every single officer felt the same compulsion to return to work, to do something to mitigate the tragedy. Kerr discouraged this because he knew it made the families feel excluded, incapable of comforting or understanding their loved ones. Melanie, in particular, had been through hell in the past twenty-four hours, and badly needed to spend time with her husband and two young children. But whatever orders he and Jack Langton gave about rest and recuperation, Kerr was certain she would soon reappear at the Yard, alongside Alan Fargo, Justin and the others.

Back in the bedroom he dumped his clothes in the wash basket, threw his torn jacket aside and took a long shower. Collapsing on the sofa in his towelling robe, he switched on Sky News for the full story. The fleshy face of Derek Finch, counter-terrorism co-ordinator, filled the screen. Finch had a dual role. He was responsible for mounting national counter-terrorist investigations but, as overall head of SO15, he was also Paula Weatherall's boss. While Weatherall's officers worked invisibly behind the scenes to generate secret intelligence on extremist suspects, Finch's much larger team of detectives investigated terrorist crime. Through their forensic examination of bomb scenes, interrogation of terrorist prisoners and pursuit of leads anywhere in the world, his officers linked the evidential chain, working with Crown Prosecution Service lawyers to prepare the case for trial. Weatherall's job was to prevent the attack; but when the intelligence failed and the bombers got through, it was Finch's task to extract every speck of evidence from the scene and track down other conspirators to the farthest corners of the globe.

Kerr caught Finch in mid-flow, reciting dire warnings lifted from the current MI5 security assessment: ". . . all the indications are that we face a serious threat of further imminent attacks. It is a question not of 'if' but 'when'. I am urging the public not to panic but to remain vigilant and report anything suspicious . . ."

Kerr pressed "Mute" and checked his BlackBerry. All the messages were connected to the attacks. There was an email from his anxious parents, in Miami South Beach, who had just seen the news on the NBC breakfast show, and a text from Robyn, Gabi's mother. Robyn's text was as curt as ever: "gabi worried confirm ok".

Kerr felt a stab of pleasure that his daughter was asking after him. Gabi was now a music student. She shared a London flat with two other girls. She was staying for a couple of days with Robyn in Rome. His estrangement from his daughter more than half a decade before had deeply wounded him. Gabi was warm-hearted and kind, politically aware and always on

113

the side of the poor and downtrodden. That was the way Kerr and her mother had raised her.

Kerr sometimes felt their relationship had died alongside the boy he had strangled in the toilets at Green Park station in June 2005. Later that Wednesday, when he had tracked Gabi down and told her, she had been inconsolable, screaming that she hated his cold-blooded violence even more than the young man's bomb. "Why did you have to kill him, Dad? You're a fucking hypocrite, just like all the rest! And I so wanted you to be different," she had said, sobbing into his chest.

From the safety of her mother's flat in Rome, Gabi had ignored all his calls for more than three weeks. On Tuesday, 26 July, five days after the shooting of Jean Charles de Menezes, she had finally answered one. But it was only to blame him for not preventing the slaughter of an innocent man.

For nearly two years she had refused to visit him, though Kerr always kept the guest bedroom made up for her. When, finally, he had persuaded her to stay over again, they had circled each other warily, like an unhappy couple staying together for the sake of the children. Occasionally she would open up over a glass of wine, arguing passionately about the oppression of minorities around the world. And Kerr was always encouraging, not just to keep her close but because he truly believed she was right.

Then something had changed her. In the past two years she had dried up. Kerr knew she had become an activist in a couple of splinter groups working for peace in the Middle East, but he could never get her to talk about it.

Now he saw that Donna, Weatherall's PA, had also emailed. She had been trying to contact him all day. The rubber-heelers had been screaming for him, and Bill Ritchie needed confirmation the team was safe. He rang Fargo and Melanie. Both refused point-blank to go to hospital and insisted on coming in the next day. "This is a horrible time and I need to keep myself occupied," said Melanie, wide-awake and energised, her kidnap trauma shoved aside.

Suddenly Kerr felt shattered. He had been on high alert for more than ten hours without a break, fighting, tearing through the streets, protecting his team and arguing the toss with people who should have known better. He kept himself fit with late-night runs around the local streets behind the market, but now his muscles ached from the fight in the stronghold, and his heart from the terrible human loss.

Thinking back to the stand-off in Weatherall's office, he was also beginning to feel vulnerable. He called Ritchie, who took a while to pick up. His boss sounded strained, and Kerr guessed he must have a thousand things to do. He told him about his visit to Gallagher's widow and reassured him about Fargo, Melanie and Justin. "And I suppose everyone wants a piece of you, Bill," he said, trying to inject some lightness.

"Make sure they get themselves checked out," he retorted, "and yourself as well."

"I'm coming back in."

"No. You've done enough for today. My phone's still red hot with incoming from Hackney."

"And that makes you doubly pissed off, yeah?"

"Your hostage rescue put yourself and Melanie at unnecessary risk."

"If I hadn't she'd still be there now. Or dead."

"John, I need to get off the line. Watch some TV. Pour yourself a double and get an early night, whatever."

"We should meet tonight to get this sorted. You know, all that bollocks from the commander."

"Speak tomorrow."

"We never got this shit when Laura Mills was in charge."

"Mills never had to front a situation like Jibril."

"I was right to countermand her. Jibril would have led us to the bomb factory. You know it, Bill. It's exactly the point you made to Weatherall."

"John. Leave it."

"We could have followed him to the bomb factory and taken them all without loss of life. I feel bad about that, Bill. Don't you? It's all going to come out."

Kerr kept pressing him, but the longer he persisted the more Ritchie seemed to push back. "Let's wait and see," was all Kerr could get him to say.

When Ritchie eventually cut him off, Kerr brewed black coffee and made himself a ham and cheese omelette, a stomach-lining standby from bedsit days.

Then he dressed to return to the office.

CHAPTER
TWELVE

Thursday, 13 September, 18.45, Knightsbridge

The voice that had terrified a hundred victims retained its richness. He smiled and his eyes twinkled while he made his demand, as if he were doing the woman a favour.

"*Another* fast track, you say?" she said. "Harold, it's simply not possible. You know I can't do that again. It's too risky."

The man picked a speck of fabric from his lapel. "This is not a *request*, my dear. We all have to do things we find disagreeable." His voice was mellow, each rounded word chosen with purpose and enunciated with the assurance of one who enjoyed life at the top of society's pile. There was no trace of the poseur's drawl. When Harold spoke, resistance was futile. And whatever lay behind the eyes was harder than granite.

Immaculate in his dark suit and she in a low-cut, black cocktail dress that rode up when she crossed her legs, they sat in matching brown leather armchairs in a private room off the main hallway of a grand house in Knightsbridge. They were waiting for Harold's other party guests to arrive. For now, the house was silent, except for the ticking of the carriage clock on the mantelpiece. On one arm of each chair a line of high-grade cocaine lay on a strip of glass.

"You said they would leave me alone after Jibril?"

"This will be the last for a while. The requirement is for another student visa, my dear."

"To do what?"

"Only a sleeper. This lucky boy will disappear into the north until they decide to wake him." He held up a slip of paper. "Whatever, it's for our Turkish masters to know and for us to obey."

The woman was a minister in the Home Office and, in her late forties, at least a decade younger than Harold. She had a strong, pear-shaped body, with short fingers, brown hair in a bob and hard eyes that she somehow managed to soften for her TV appearances. She had come straight from the office, changing from her dark ministerial suit in one of the bedrooms. Later she would have to return to work to help manage the bombing crisis. She was high-powered and successful, but let Harold lean over and slowly ease the paper into the front of her dress.

"They have directed him to attend our embassy in Islamabad at ten o'clock next Tuesday morning, local time."

She transferred the paper to a zipped pocket deep inside her handbag. "Too soon. It'll set off alarm bells."

"He travels overnight on Sunday to Heathrow. Via Dubai."

"Harold, I can't do this."

118

"Neither of us has any choice, my dear, so you have to be imaginative." There was the sound of bolts being slid back as the Turkish assistants opened the front door. Automatically Harold glanced at his watch: twelve minutes to seven. He was the host, and was always punctual. "It's what politicians like you are good at. They do it for their nannies and lovers, don't they? Whenever they think they can get away with it?" The grandfather clock in the hallway, exactly ten minutes fast, was chiming the hour as they paused to snort the cocaine through rolled banknotes.

"Christ, you know how easily they can track these things."

"Relax. Just think of your husband and children. Of the things that matter to you." They heard laughter in the hallway from a couple of early arrivals. "There is another name on the paper I just gave you, an official who will contact your private office about an unconnected matter."

"And then we get the girl? That's the deal, right?" asked the woman.

He stood and moved behind her so that he could look down her dress. "They will deliver our English rose on Saturday. So you can relax, my dear. But now we should get ready. My guests will soon be arriving," he murmured, trailing his fingers around her throat and chin, making the hairs stiffen on the nape of her neck.

She arched back in the chair to meet his eyes and splayed her legs, the dress riding up to reveal lace stocking tops and the plump white flesh above. "In a minute. No more business, Harold," she said. "I need you to warm me up." He smiled. This was how she reacted whenever their masters made professional demands of her. Her pleading, almost childlike, never failed to arouse him. The drug kicked in, making her feel desirable. Leaning over, he slid his hand down her dress and cupped her breast. He had the hands of a much younger man, twisting her nipple until she winced, but instead of crying out she gripped his hand through the material, urging him on.

At two minutes to seven, one of the Turkish assistants smiled and nodded when he found the two middle-aged lovers sharing one armchair, mouths locked together, the man's fingers working hard between her legs. But by the time they joined the party at exactly seven, jacket buttoned, cleavage concealed by a silk scarf, they were respectable again, like a married couple who had just celebrated Evensong in the church across the street.

Friday, 14 September, 09.40 local time, Istanbul, Turkey.

Abdul Malik, Turkish entrepreneur and devout Muslim, was a thirty-five-year-old multi-millionaire who operated out of a modern office in downtown Istanbul. Handsome and respected, his love of expensively tailored suits and handmade shoes reflected his high position in Turkish society.

Malik's intelligence, dynamism and commercial instinct were exceptional. Through Malik Finance House, he laundered millions of dollars of *yesil sermaye*, "green money", withdrawn from the US by Saudi Arabia and other Gulf states after 9/11 and infiltrated into Turkey, often in suitcases. Through a second company, Malik Holdings, he reinvested the cash in automotive projects, petroleum, electronics, construction, shopping centres, and any other product likely to bring a healthy return. A Sunni Muslim, Abdul Malik was also exceptional by virtue of his quiet devotion to Islam.

He was a strong supporter of Turkey's ruling Justice and Development Party, the AKP, often accused of harbouring a hidden Islamist agenda on account of its deep roots in Turkey's religious communities and alleged links to banned Islamist parties. Since its victory in the 2007 elections Malik had prayed fervently that the AKP would inject strong religious values into its political programme. Years earlier the prospect of a clash between the AKP and Turkey's "deep state" of the army, judiciary and intelligence services had been real, and Malik would have welcomed it. He believed the new government should have turned the people back along a path of righteousness, following the will of Allah. Instead he had watched it race down the highways of infidel materialism in pursuit of the devil. To his dismay, the nation he had once loved was no better than the depraved and godless states of the European Union it had become so desperate to join.

To maintain the security of his *jihadi* operation in Britain, the tiny circle who knew about his work referred to Malik simply as the Director. His room was spacious and airy, with plenty of natural light. Working at a contemporary blond-wood desk with three slim computer screens, Malik operated the paperless office of any successful modern business in a thriving European city. In one corner was a water-cooler, in the other a printer with secure fax, and coasters on a coffee-table carried the Malik Holdings logo. An electronically operated safe housed the encrypted server Malik used for receiving emails and photographs from his associates in London.

He looked up as his partner entered the office, jacket slung over his shoulder, to brief him on the previous day's catastrophic events in London. Rashid Hussain, a Syrian, worked closely alongside Malik. Over a decade older than his partner, he was slim, with dark hair, recently cut. Like Malik, he wore the shirt of a successful businessman, with blue stripes and a starched white swept-back collar. But his face bore the mark of a fighter. A red scar, thin as a strand of cotton, ran from just below his left ear and across his cheek to disappear into his neatly trimmed moustache. For their secret business they spoke in English. "This matter of the arrest yesterday in London, it is serious, yes?"

Hussain slipped his jacket over the back of his chair, revealing a flash of pale blue silk lining, and shrugged. "No, it is nothing. Ahmed Jibril will tell the British police to screw themselves."

"How did they get to him?"

Hussain rolled back his chair, slid behind his desk opposite Malik and typed in three passwords. "Who knows? The boy's capture is regrettable but the hysteria in the British press shows the attack was a success."

"The woman who authorised his visa, is she contained?"

"She lives in fear, totally in our grip."

"You must be careful, Rashid."

The Syrian was checking his mobile phone for messages. "I directed Harold to create a firewall between her and the immigration office. The trail cannot lead back to us," he said. "Our operation is secure, believe me. I know about these things."

Rashid Hussain always spoke with confidence. Malik depended entirely on him to control his blackmail operation, but still had difficulty in accepting all of his judgements.

"Rashid, are you sure the intensive police activity around Jibril will not make us vulnerable? Can we still use him for the last phase?"

"The cops will be no problem," smiled Hussain, relaxed as ever. "The boy will be released. You have my promise."

They paused as one of the young women associates knocked and entered the office with the draft contract for a real-estate deal. Malik smiled at her as she turned to leave. "Give me a moment, please, Esra."

To conduct his legitimate commercial affairs Malik employed five graduates from the city's ancient university, including two women. They worked in an adjacent open-plan office, and the women wore the *hijab*. The door to his own office was secured by three locks and always alarmed at night.

He waited until the woman had closed the door behind her. "You are certain this allows us sufficient latitude for Operation English Rose?"

"The timing is perfect. The overseers will brief us for final clearance for the removal when they visit next week."

Malik pressed the buzzer to summon Esra. "We must return to this."

"I am telling you, Malik. We have the woman in our grasp. We will use English Rose to crush her. Then topple her government like a rotten tree."

CHAPTER
THIRTEEN

Friday, 14 September, 07.55, Room 1830

"I'm telling you, the databases are clear. Excalibur has been wiped. Everything on Jibril has disappeared." Fargo was taking it personally. Despite his promise to John Kerr that he would rest, he had obviously spent most of the night in 1830, searching his magic box. He was wearing a different crumpled shirt, probably a stand-by stuffed into his drawer for emergencies, but the same trousers, still flecked with dust and debris from the explosion. His damp hair showed he had used the shower next to the ops room, but he still looked wrecked and sweaty.

"Access denied, you mean?" said Justin.

"No," said Melanie, quietly. "I think he means destroyed."

Kerr's team were in what Fargo called the reading room, a tiny glass-screened area, with a single desk and computer terminal, squeezed into a corner of Room 1830. As soon as he had heard the alarming news from Fargo in the early hours, Kerr had decided to collect them together. Kerr, Langton, Melanie and Justin crowded round the small table while Fargo squatted on the airvent with the tower of Westminster Abbey looming behind him. Kerr had brought in double espressos from the sandwich bar in St James's Park station across the road from the Yard. When Fargo had immediately knocked his over, dousing his notes and spilling coffee into the airvent, the others had laughed and accused him of finally killing off the aircon.

"Let me show you." Fargo leant across Justin to type in the search. "Look, the old intelligence has gone, and if there's anything new we're not getting it."

"Since when?" said Langton.

"Since hours after his arrest. Or even minutes."

"Who put the block on?" said Melanie.

"Inter-agency politics," groaned Justin, shaking his head.

"Or something more sinister?" said Melanie.

They looked at Kerr, but he had done his thinking hours before and wanted their ideas. The pressure of their fast-moving surveillance operations meant Kerr's team spent most of their time together on the street, or in cold vehicles and freezing observation posts. Compared with that, Alan Fargo's cramped workstation was sheer luxury. Everyone was pretending this was just another day, but this morning they looked damaged. The gauze dressing visible beneath Justin's woollen hat was a reminder of his own narrow escape from death. Justin was a brilliant Durham University engineering graduate and held down the most sensitive job in SO15. But this morning he was in his jeans, T-shirt and baseball boots, and Melanie told him he looked just a kid.

Melanie had bruised her upper arm when she was thrown against the bus and Kerr saw her wince when Justin accidentally pressed against her. She had been the first to arrive after Fargo and looked all right, dressed for a normal shift at the office. Langton had winked at her and mouthed, "OK?" as he squeezed alongside. In jeans, polo shirt and motorcycle boots, he looked uncomfortable without his leathers, eager to return to the street.

"So, Joe Allenby gives us a terrorist from Yemen under the wire," continued Melanie. "Then somebody in London presses the button and the bad guy suddenly becomes a clean skin. What does that say to you?"

"Jibril is being brought into the UK by MI5 as, I dunno, some sort of Al Qaeda mole?" said Justin, frowning. "And whoever it is forgot to tell Joe Allenby. Isn't it inconceivable that MI5 wouldn't involve the man on the ground?"

Melanie gave a short laugh. "Five not speaking to Six, you mean? Come off it, Justin. We're talking serious power games here. And budgets, and sucking up to Number Ten."

"If Jibril was recruited in Yemen they'd need Joe to set the whole thing up," said Langton. "He would have known about it from day one, probably made the actual pitch."

"I still think it's completely possible MI5 would keep Joe in the dark," said Melanie. "Perhaps they were going to approach Jibril in London and we ruined the master plan by arresting him."

"OK, so who paid for his flight?" said Justin. "I say Joe would have to have been in the loop."

"That's the other piece of crap news," said Fargo. "Allenby has disappeared. I tried the MI6 office in Yemen last night but it was switched to voicemail. Closest I got was Vauxhall Cross. Night-duty officer blanked me."

They shot another glance at Kerr.

"So what about the intel?" asked Melanie.

Fargo shrugged. "Vauxhall wouldn't say."

"So, Jibril is either a terrorist or an agent. And if he's on our side everyone kept it from Joe, right? And now we're getting radio silence." Kerr was staying cool, but this concerned him as much as the interference with Excalibur. He needed cover from Allenby because he had defended himself to Weatherall and Ritchie solely on the basis of his friend's tip-off. "Remind us, Al," he said, "what was the info from Yemen? What were Allenby's exact words?"

"He scanned a handwritten message to our unit in Heathrow with Jibril's details, pic and flight number," said Fargo, wiping coffee from his notes. "Quote, 'This is to return a favour. Please forward urgently to JK. Take care and good hunting,' unquote."

Kerr was frowning. "I helped him last summer with an agent pitch at Terminal Four on the hurry-up, but that's nothing special."

"It was Sunday afternoon. Allenby had time on his hands." Justin shrugged.

"None of it makes sense," said Melanie, "because people like Allenby, working in a country as volatile as

Yemen, have a motive for everything. So let's not waste time on the cock-up theory."

"She's right, John," agreed Langton. "This has to be a calculated act. MI6 don't do return favours unless there's something in it for them. If Allenby short-circuited the normal reporting channels to London it was for a reason."

Kerr was beckoning to someone in the outer office. Detective Sergeant Karl Sergeyev, unfailingly correct, gave a courteous tap on the glass before squeezing round the door. Russian by birth, he was over six foot three, powerfully built and always immaculately dressed. This morning he was wearing a charcoal suit with white shirt and yellow tie. The cufflinks were gold, and the black shoes Italian. He took a long look at them all as they greeted him, and gave Melanie a special smile. "I heard about Hackney," he said, in his deep bass voice, the only person explicitly to mention her ordeal the day before. "I suppose you look pretty good, considering."

Justin reached out to test the wool of Sergeyev's jacket. "And nice of you to slum it with the lower orders." He shifted up to make room, but Karl joined Fargo on the airvent, carefully avoiding the pool of spilt coffee.

Karl Sergeyev worked the Rest of the World desk, just along the corridor from Room 1830. Known simply as ROW, it covered global political extremism apart from Al Qaeda, including counter-espionage. A natural intelligence officer, he was firmly plugged into London's *émigrè* community and seized every opportunity to cultivate visiting big cheeses from Eastern Europe. Karl was popular, the kind of guy everyone was happy to have alongside them. He was also attractive to women, a trait that, according to the rumour mill, was about to cost him his marriage.

"Looks like I'm a bit late, boss," he said, tapping Fargo's empty cup.

"Perfect timing," said Kerr. "You can imagine what I'm getting from my gang of conspiracy theorists. Anything happening on your radar?"

The others exchanged glances. At some stage during the night, Kerr had obviously briefed him on the whole story.

Karl slowly shook his head. "On my side everyone's got clean hands, these days. It's all about protocol and trade. With the focus on energy, of course. Cold War forgotten, relationship reset," he said. After sixteen years in the Branch his accent was as strong as ever, the sentences short and spare. "These are the days of co-operation. Joint investigations all over the place, especially against fraud and trafficking. Ambassadors taking tea with the commissioner. Multiple exchanges of criminal and political intelligence with us and other EU partners. Terrorism in the UK? None of the people I'm interested in would risk getting their hands that dirty. To me this looks straight Al Qaeda. Sorry, guys."

"That's fine, Karl. So let's concentrate on Jibril himself. Can you have a quiet recce at Paddington Green, Mel? See what they're up to?"

"I already called my contact. Uniform sergeant in the custody suite. There's something strange occurring there, too. Couple of MI5 girls pitched up almost as soon as Jibril. Plus a bloke he thinks must be from Joe Allenby's lot at Vauxhall Cross because the women don't seem to want him there."

"Probably arguing about who has the lead," said Langton. "But why would Five and Six want to muscle in on a UK police investigation? It's totally against protocol. Why isn't Finch telling them to fuck off?"

Melanie shrugged. "Whatever, between them they're trying to hijack the whole thing."

"I'll take a look at that," said Kerr.

"It's a bit pathetic, actually," continued Melanie, "and Jibril is staying dead silent, of course."

"Who's he got for his lawyer?"

"A woman no one's ever heard of. Julia Bakkour. Smart, polite and confident, like she's defending some hotshot City fraudster. Office in Manor Park, the smart end of East Ham. Wears a headscarf but she's Westernised and affluent, not one of your *pro bono* community-worker types. '*Jilbab* and jewels' is how my contact describes her. A real piece of work."

"Who called her?"

"No one seems to know. But I already did a look-up and Bakkour has no background in defending terrorists."

Kerr frowned. There was a well-known cadre of lawyers specialising in terrorism cases, so the sudden appearance of Bakkour on the scene was highly unusual. "Did Jibril ask for her?"

"Not according to my contact," said Melanie. "And there's no record of anyone instructing her. She appeared out of nowhere, apparently, pacing round Paddington Green front office almost as soon as they'd banged Jibril up."

"OK. Say thanks to your guy, Mel. And tell him to watch his back. I don't want him taking any more risks for us. Hold on, everyone." Through the window in the door he saw Bill Ritchie enter 1830, pick up the daily secret intelligence brief and head for the reading room. "Sit back," said Kerr, minimising the screen.

Ritchie paused as he spotted them, then put his head round the door. "What's new?"

"Just doing the welfare debrief," said Kerr, as Fargo covered his papers.

"Well done yesterday, folks." Kerr nodded at Karl, the outsider on this particular operation. "And you've all been for a med check, yes? Justin?"

"Yes, sir," said Melanie, lying for them all.

"Can you spare me a few minutes after this?" asked Kerr.

"Wall to wall meetings," replied Bill Ritchie. Kerr couldn't decide whether he was still pissed off with him. "Give me a call late this afternoon." Or perhaps he was hiding something.

When he was gone the team made faces at Kerr, as if he was in disgrace.

Kerr exhaled loudly, his mind made up. "So stuff them," he said, "we'll work this among ourselves. Let's find out how Ahmed Jibril got into the country. Can we track down his passport, check out his other possessions?"

"All embargoed by the investigators," said Melanie.

"What the hell does that mean?" Kerr felt a stab of anxiety. "Who says?"

"Detective Superintendent Metcalfe," said Melanie. "He's Finch's senior investigating officer for this job. Operation name 'Dragstone'. We're not allowed access while Jibril's being interviewed."

"Who says?"

"Orders from Finch himself, apparently."

"I'll see about that," said Kerr. "What about his safe-house? How soon will they finish the search?"

"Already gone," said Melanie. "Forensics were inside for less than two hours. If they recovered anything they're not sharing."

Justin seemed to understand even before Kerr turned to him. "Sure, boss," he said, "no worries. Want me to take a look tonight?"

Kerr smiled. "You and Jack wait till I get back to you."

"It's just one room in a run-down Victorian house," said Fargo.

"Anything on the history?"

"I've got the terrorist finance guys in 1830 working on it. Should have a result by tomorrow."

"Good. Make sure you copy all your notes from the ops room, Al, and lock the originals away." Kerr pushed his chair back. "Right now we need access to Jibril's passport, so I'm going downstairs to have a chat with Metcalfe. Thanks, guys. Try and take it easy today and let's catch up later."

Melanie stayed seated as the others began shuffling around her. "We've been talking about the possibility

Joe Allenby was out of the loop, made a mistake, whatever. That Jibril is an informant, under control. We arrested a good guy, and now people are trying to protect their asset without telling us."

"I don't buy that," said Langton. "What's an agent doing walking to a bomb factory? Meeting up with suicide bombers getting ready to blow themselves up? What kind of control is that? The man's a terrorist."

"Exactly. And I'm guessing the boss has already figured that out, too," said Melanie, tapping her pen on the desk. She looked at each of them in turn, ending with Kerr. "And if we're right about that, we have to face another possibility, don't we, John? Which you must have thought of. Am I going to say it, or will you?"

"Don't stop now," said Kerr.

"Well, it's obvious, isn't it? If Jibril is the bad bastard we think he is, we're prising off the lid on some gigantic cover-up."

Kerr nodded slowly. It was the possibility he had faced in the early hours, even before the news about the odd goings-on at Paddington Green. Now, as he felt their eyes on him, he was reassured. They were ahead of the game, their life experience as Special Branch officers allowing them to think the worst, and he found this liberating. He was already reaching for his BlackBerry, their collective energy bringing forward the call he had intended to make later that morning.

Bad people were slamming doors in his face, so he would find another way in. Kerr scrolled down through his contacts to "Kestrel", the work-name for his mole inside MI5. He speed-dialled and held up his hand as the voicemail kicked in. "It's eight-fifteen Friday morning and I need you to call me the minute you get this."

CHAPTER
FOURTEEN

Friday, 14 September, 10.26 local time, Istanbul, Turkey

When the office was quiet, Abdul Malik pushed his aviator glasses onto his forehead, carefully folded his shirt cuffs and leant forward in his slimline executive chair to scan the secret inbox. "So, let us move to business. Tell me every detail about our Foreign Office lawyer."

Rashid Hussain opened the folder he had been preparing for Malik. Then he rotated his chair and retied his shoelace. He wore highly polished Oxfords. The shoes and navy suit, almost as expensive as Malik's, had been purchased in London, a city Hussain had not felt safe to revisit for more than two decades. He crossed his legs, picking a speck of dust from his trousers, and rolled his chair closer to the desk. "His code name is Sandpiper, forty-seven years old, homosexual but married with two teenage children," he said, scrolling through the text. "Senior management and rising, and works in the main office in King Charles Street. All the detail is in the folder. I have the full profile with covering photograph." He checked the biographical details and background.

On his screen Malik studied the secret photograph of Sandpiper in a navy pinstripe suit, drinking a glass of champagne and laughing with a young man.

"There are two or three images I need to enhance, but the identifying features are good," said Hussain, clicking the "Forward" button again.

The digital photographs that flashed up on Malik's desktop showed Sandpiper naked and being sodomised by the same man. In five of the seven images his face was clearly identifiable. "And we have video, yes?" he asked.

"Yes. All the images are usable."

"How long has Harold known him?" he asked, scanning the text.

"From his days at Cambridge University."

"How many guests at the party?"

"Twelve, including two women, who were the first to occupy the bedrooms."

"The corruption of those whores knows no bounds," growled Malik, staring in disgust at the incriminating photographs. "And few infidels can match the depravity of Western foreign services."

He spoke from personal knowledge. During the nineties his own father had been posted to the Turkish consulate in London's Belgrave Square as third secretary, responsible for developing trade links. He had displaced the family from their comfortable home in Ankara to a government-owned apartment in Maida Vale, and a young Malik had gone to the London School of Economics to study for a BSc in international economics. In his youth he had been small and unprepossessing, with an adolescent's stringy moustache. But he was deeply thoughtful, with an intellectual horsepower that set him apart from most other LSE students.

The unworldly teenager had never been out of Turkey before, and the loud manners of Britain's capital had disoriented him. He was deeply offended by the drinking, drug-taking and promiscuity, the lack of modesty among the women and brashness of the men. When he watched television the whole of British society seemed depraved, and when protocol required that he and his elder sister attend the occasional reception at the consulate, he had realised with deep sadness that even his parents had been seduced by the excesses of the West.

By 1997, his final year at the LSE, Malik had emerged as the best in his class, on course for a first, and moved from his father's government apartment to a student flat in Herne Hill. He had had the smallest room at the very top of the rambling Victorian merchant's house, which he shared with three female and five male LSE undergraduates, including Dimitri, a third-year in labour economics.

Halfway through the new term Dimitri took him to a student party in Brixton where everyone was drinking and smoking cannabis. The students from his house were taking photographs of their friends having sex on the floor, often three at once, sometimes men with men. He went to find Dimitri to tell him he was going home, only to discover his fellow Turk having sex with an English girl in one of the bedrooms.

138

Late into the night, an English student, one of the most boorish offenders, had fallen to his death from the second-floor balcony. As everyone screamed and panicked around him, Abdul Malik had felt a quiet sense of justice. An hour before he had fallen, the victim had been kissing another man. Malik saw the tragedy as Allah's punishment for his decadence.

Back in the privacy of his loft room he had reached out for the Koran, which had opened at the story of the Fall of Adam. It was a moment of revelation. The accident was a sign. Here was a modern allegory of the wickedness of man through which Allah had spoken to him. From that night he had withdrawn from student social life into the shell of his private thoughts, studying the Koran and praying regularly. His housemates grew impatient with his shyness, which they misread as aloofness, and academic excellence, which made him a swot. They began to call him Shish Kebab, mocking his Turkish roots. The Turkish boy who should have protected him was especially vindictive, because he was a product of the age: Istanbul might be a cool city, they said, but boys with ambition sprinted across Turkey's cultural bridge to the West.

One night, as he was reading the Koran, his housemates had started throwing stones at his window. Peering through a chink in the curtain he had seen them crowding the pavement, drunk and shouting up at him. The men had been carrying takeaways and the women were passing round a bottle of vodka. When he had switched his light out he had heard them barge into the house, falling up the narrow stairs.

As he had trembled on the bed they had crashed through his locked door and stormed into his room. The noise had been unbearable. His most violent oppressor, a third-year physics student from the ground floor, had helped Dimitri tear away his duvet and hold him down on the bed. As he had screamed and struggled they had torn off his underpants and covered his genitals with chilli sauce. One of the women had masturbated him while they all chanted, "Shish Kebab! Shish Kebab!" at the tops of their voices. As he had endured the shame of his erection, another woman had poured vodka over his penis and sucked him until the chilli had made her throw up. They had let him cover his face with his hands and Dimitri had laid the Koran over the vomit, chilli and semen. It had been his first sexual experience.

The next day Dimitri had glared at him with contempt. A couple of the British guys had tried to laugh it off. None of it had mattered for, by the end of his second year, Malik's economics tutors were encouraging him to take a doctorate in econometric theory. By this time he had had few friends but a sound knowledge of the Koran. Then he had met a young Turkish woman studying chemical engineering. Her name was Jumaima and she was the only Turkish girl he knew to wear a *hijab* and dress modestly in jeans and dark tops, concealing her arms and breasts. They had begun to hang out around Edgware Road, searching for literature about Islam, and in restaurants behind Warren Street. She had taught him to embrace the

Wahhabi tradition and put into words his innermost feelings about the decadence of the West.

Jumaima's home was in Istanbul, where her father was a wealthy industrialist manufacturing agricultural machinery for export around Europe. When Malik had graduated with his predicted first-class honours degree, she had introduced him to her father and asked him to take Malik under his wing.

Malik had quickly shown commercial promise and helped Jumaima's father set up a combined finance house and export business. The young couple had married as soon as Jumaima graduated. He had bought a house in a prestigious area of Istanbul and, over the next decade, she had given him three healthy children. Malik had quickly become an entrepreneur to match his father-in-law, expanding his businesses to include chemical plants, property, cement, fertiliser, trucks and carpets.

When Malik's new family had encouraged him to invest in a property portfolio in London, alongside his other investments, he had searched for houses and apartments in the capital's wealthiest districts.

The two men worked in silence for twenty minutes, then Malik reopened the photographic folder and examined the images of Sandpiper again. "As for this high-flown pervert," he said, looking across at his partner, "when will you make the approach?"

"As soon as he takes the boy," replied Hussain, quick as a flash.

CHAPTER
FIFTEEN

Friday, 14 September, 08.30, SO15 investigations unit

Derek Finch's team was located three floors down from Weatherall's intelligence branch. Created in the seventies to investigate extremist crimes, the unit had become famous for its expertise in recovering forensic traces from bomb scenes and building the evidential case.

Avoiding the lift, Kerr walked to the end of the corridor and took the fire escape. He spotted Detective Superintendent Jim Metcalfe, Finch's senior investigating officer, the moment he entered the main office. He needed to find out exactly what Metcalfe had discovered about Ahmed Jibril, but knew he had a job on his hands. Resentful by nature, Metcalfe had regularly allowed skirmishes between the two sides of SO15 to spiral into civil war. Jacketless, dressed for action with tie loosened and double cuffs turned back, he looked as if he wanted to punch someone. For a second Kerr imagined him on the floor, being thrashed by Jack Langton.

"What are you doing here?" demanded Metcalfe, a Liverpudlian and champion of the get-your-retaliation-in-first philosophy. He was a leather-belt-and-loud-braces man, and both were too tight, drawing attention to his pot-belly. Close-cropped greying hair receding into a V accentuated his ferrety nose and made him appear permanently stressed. He was taller than Kerr and meaner-looking, and as they shook hands his close-set, hooded eyes leaked the hostility Kerr remembered from a decade ago. "Come to apologise for your surveillance fuck-up?"

"Nice to see you again, too," said Kerr.

"Welcome to the real police," Metcalfe whined.

Kerr said nothing. This was one of Metcalfe's standard gibes, a clumsy reminder that his investigators had a background in regular CID offices. About fifteen officers were working the phones and desktops designated to Holmes, the standardised national database for any major criminal investigation. They were mostly twenty-year men, paunchy, with ties loosened and shirt cuffs folded back, glasses perched on the ends of their noses. Kerr was surprised that they were already occupied in such routine work. The hours immediately following a terrorist arrest were crucial and the place should have been buzzing as they chased leads to track down other cells and disrupt further attacks.

Years ago, when detectives regularly drank at lunchtime, Special Branch officers had nicknamed investigators on this floor "the Bellies". These days the pub had mostly been abandoned for a sandwich at the desk, but the name had stuck. Among these middle-aged veterans Kerr detected a serious lack of energy, as if someone had told them the case was going nowhere.

"You've caused us a lot of grief," Metcalfe said.

Kerr smiled to himself as he remembered the Branch surveillance photographs showing Metcalfe naked in a suburban bedroom in west London, his white, humping arse filling the lens. Kerr had been a detective sergeant in Tech Ops at the time. The Branch team had assigned Metcalfe the code name Stubby, in recognition of his shrunken, post-coital dick.

Metcalfe was obviously going to keep him in the noisy squad office rather than take him back to his cubicle, so Kerr leant against a vacant desk. "Why are you blocking our access to Jibril's passport?" he asked evenly.

"Why did you put surveillance on a man who wasn't even on the SO15 tasking list?"

"We need to work together on this, Jim."

"You mean we need to cover your arse. No way. You screwed up, you find your own way out."

"As SO15. One command."

"Ah, I see. Your boss sent you down. Very corporate."

"Do you object to that?"

Metcalfe crossed his arms. "Letting you lot interfere in my investigation? Yeah, I do, actually."

"No," said Kerr, levelly. "I mean to women holding senior positions."

Their paths had not crossed since 1997. Kerr remembered Metcalfe as if it were yesterday. The Branch had been running an operation against an IRA active-service unit over from Dublin. The unwitting girlfriend of the main terrorist was a divorced special-needs teacher who had regularly entertained

144

Metcalfe at her neat three-bed semi, every move being captured by Branch cameras. And because she'd had special needs of her own, it had been his misfortune to be the married cop with whom she was two-timing the Irishman every Tuesday.

By discreetly warning him off, the Branch had probably saved Metcalfe's marriage and career, perhaps even his life. But he'd guessed what they must have seen and had never forgiven them for this humiliation.

"Thing is, Jim, I've got a nasty suspicion we're all working blind here. Did you recover anything interesting from the safe-house? Like a laptop?"

"Still searching," said Metcalfe.

"Of course," said Kerr, impassively, registering the lie. "Any idea when you'll be done?"

A shrug.

"So, what's happening at Paddington Green? His lawyer OK?"

"The usual."

"Anything juicy from the interviews?"

"Enough."

"When are you going to charge him?"

"You'll get what you need to know when I'm good and ready."

"Have to say, Jim, you're acting like a man who's been gagged. And that doesn't seem right."

A couple of detectives from the inquiry team were drifting past to eavesdrop, so Kerr led the way into Metcalfe's workstation, a rectangle separated from the main office by glass partitions. There was the usual "ego wall", with crests from American and European police forces, and the floor was littered with court-case papers. "Look, I'm offering to bring a couple of our officers down here to share the load."

Metcalfe sat behind his desk to regain the initiative. "What — the analyst geeks in 1830?" He smirked, logging on to his computer. "Don't think so."

"Someone from the terrorist finance side."

"Not necessary. It's all being progressed," Metcalfe said, looking vague, "through channels."

"Well, we're doing some work through our liaison in Pakistan to tie down the entry documentation," bluffed Kerr, "so we should compare notes."

Metcalfe looked up sharply. "That's a complete no-no."

"You what?" shot back Kerr, his antennae moving to action stations.

"Anything to do with visas and passports is actioned to us. I'm the officer in the case, and MI5 don't want Jibril's passport released outside my department."

"Why is that?"

"You don't ask MI5 why."

"Don't you?" Kerr waited for a couple of seconds, then gave up. "Right, here's our position. Alan Fargo in 1830 needs every scrap of information for the database, and if you won't co-operate we'll go to the Immigration Service and Home Office direct. We want to assist you on this, Jim . . ."

"It's 'sir' to you, Chief Inspector."

". . . to add value, so let's stop pissing about, shall we? We should be operating as a team, as one SO15, so

146

we can support you in the criminal investigation. We have to work in parallel."

Metcalfe screwed up his eyes as he scrolled down the screen. "We don't, actually. Things are different now. We're the ones with the need to know." He pressed "Print". "I have everything I require on there," he said, nodding at his desktop as the printer whirred to life. "MI5 are tasking us direct."

"I bet they are."

"And sometimes MI6."

"Congratulations."

"So here's something you can do to make yourself useful," Metcalfe sneered, holding out the printed sheet. "That's a list of current Islamic organisations." Kerr scanned the paper, which was an old schedule cut and pasted from MI5 research documents. "You can ignore Hizb-ut-Tahrir," said Metcalfe. "We've already got everything on those crazies. I want more on the Islamic Jihad Union, stuff like that. Mozzie bookshops in East Ham, Newham, Ealing, et cetera, et cetera. It'll give your people something to do." He sifted through his papers, located a thin booklet and threw it across the desk. Hands in pockets, Kerr let it drop to the floor. "Latest research from the Centre for Social Cohesion. I want anything about ragheads in London, local stuff. We'll cover the global ourselves."

"So tell them to Google." Kerr glanced through the glass. "I'll try again. How soon do you intend to charge Ahmed Jibril?"

"Who said anything about charging?"

Kerr laughed. "What? You're thinking of releasing him? After twenty-four hours in the bin?"

"We're looking at all the options."

"With MI5 looking over your shoulder in Paddington Green, feeding your boys the script, you mean? You've got to be joking." That Metcalfe might actually be contemplating releasing a terrorist back onto the streets had never occurred to Kerr. Senses at red alert, he stared at him in disbelief. Metcalfe's eyes showed a dangerous mix of arrogance and stupidity, and Kerr wondered if the ridiculous oaf even half realised he was being manipulated.

"OK, let me spell it out for you again," said Kerr. "We need an update on the investigation for 1830. A record of the information you've entered onto Holmes. So we can add the intelligence to strengthen the interviews."

"Well, you're not getting it, so tough." Metcalfe's phone rang and he picked up. "I'll take it out there," he answered, peering into the main office, where a detective was signalling through the glass. He brushed past Kerr. "Like I said, leave it to the real detectives and piss off back to the library."

Kerr waited until Metcalfe snatched the phone from the cop outside and went to the window. Kerr then moved quickly to the desktop. He searched Metcalfe's personal folders in the C drive until he found the record marked "Dragstone". He scrolled down to the folder marked "CHIL", short for "Current Holmes Investigative Leads", pressed "Forward" and typed in his own email address. Through the glass he saw the

DC tug his boss's arm and point. Kerr waited for Metcalfe to charge back into the office before tapping "Send".

"I'll fucking have you for that."

"Leaving your workstation unlocked is a serious breach of IT security, Jim," said Kerr, ruefully shaking his head.

"Who the fuck do you think you are?"

"I'm the unlucky guy who's seen your fat, naked, pimply arse," said Kerr, as he walked past Metcalfe. By the door he leant against the partition, legs and arms crossed, taking in Metcalfe's sudden look of realisation. The door was open and Kerr spoke within earshot of the main office. "And I'd really love to know how long it took you . . ."

"What?"

"Well, you've always been a bit of a twat," said Kerr, seeming genuinely curious, "but how many years did it take you to become such a sexist and racist prick?"

"Get out of my office," hissed Metcalfe, looking nervous for the first time.

"Nice to see you again, Jim," smiled Kerr, giving Metcalfe a casual wave on the way out, "or is it still Stubby?"

CHAPTER
SIXTEEN

2005, Istanbul, Turkey

Abdul Malik never doubted that Allah had brought Rashid Hussain into his world.

In 2005 he had begun developing business opportunities in Syria and visited Damascus in connection with the Turkey-Syria Interregional Co-operation Programme. One of the largest deals was a road-building scheme, which had brought Malik into contact with Syrian government officials. Hussain already knew about Malik's unhappy time in London, his religious conversion and burgeoning property interests. They shared a hatred of Britain that bordered on the fanatical.

Rashid Hussain was also a Sunni Muslim and an economist. Renowned for his interpersonal skills, Hussain found there was a chemistry between them and used all his weapons of charm and flattery. On the evening of his return to Istanbul he invited Malik to a private dinner at his home.

Over *bob chorba* and *tikvenik*, with garish cake for dessert, Hussain quietly evaluated his guest. He listened with care as Malik castigated the depravity,

150

greed and godlessness of the West, then reminded him that nations which rejected Allah were vulnerable from the devil within. "The British infidel is sexually dissolute, with no control over his base animal instincts," said Hussain, with a smile. "You have seen it with your own eyes, my friend, and I believe we share a similar view of life, a broken image of this godless world. We should speak again of these things."

By the time Hussain had manipulated an invitation to Malik's home for dinner the following week, he had thoroughly absorbed the business profile of his promising new partner. Towards the end of a convivial evening, as Jumaima served coffee, Hussain's conversation acquired a sharper edge. He questioned Malik about his property portfolio in London and the offshore companies holding the various titles. "You are an entrepreneur of great energy and business acumen who thinks on a grand scale." He smiled, eyes twinkling at Malik's plump wife, thinking that the photograph in his case file flattered her. "I believe I can help unleash the religious potential that lies deep within you."

"You overestimate me, Rashid. I am a humble businessman."

"On the contrary," purred Hussain. While Jumaima attended to them and the children slept upstairs, he delivered his carefully prepared pitch. Towards the end he leant across and took Malik's hand. "Listen to me," he said, with fierce intensity. "I believe you are an instrument of Allah, sent by him to work with us. I will assist you in acquiring a house for this work, a secret place, a club within a club as familiar and safe as Pall Mall."

"And who is this link man in London? The man you call Harold?" asked Malik. "I must know everything about him."

Hussain was smiling. "Harold is a British pervert of high birth and low morality, who belongs to me. He is willing and compliant, a creature for whom the demand is also the reward. A spider, who will entice these flies into your web. And tonight I present him to you as a gift, a weapon." He beamed, now gripping Malik's arm. "As your tarantula!"

Under Hussain's guidance, Malik hired two young men to enforce the operation in London for him, both former operatives in the MIT, the Turkish Secret Service. The first was twenty-eight, an intellectual who had come second in the highly competitive Turkish civil-service examination. His receding hairline, high forehead and round, wire-rimmed glasses gave him the look of a university lecturer rather than a spy. The MIT had trained him as a technical specialist and used him first to collaborate with the ISI, the Pakistani intelligence service, and then in secret operations against the Kurdistan Workers' Party, the PKK, on the border with Iraq. He viewed bomb-making as an art and was constantly seeking new ways to refine and increase the energy of his clever devices. His speciality was the destruction of cars, usually while the driver was still inside. Steering, brakes, tyres, fuel tanks, electrical circuitry: to the trained saboteur, cars offered limitless possibilities for booby traps.

152

The second recruit was a thirty-year-old interrogator, a muscle man of lesser intellect but equal passion, who in his youth had once served at Samsun, the military base in northern Turkey on the Black Sea coast.

Through his property company, Hussain leased a grand house in Knightsbridge, which Harold assured him would be suitable for the blackmail operation. As a fall-back for emergencies, he also acquired a slightly more modest property in Chiswick. When it was ready they all met in the reception room: Malik, Hussain, Harold and the pair of Turkish enforcers. Hussain turned to Harold, his recruiter and host. "I trust the house will be adequate for our purpose?" he said.

Elegant, extrovert and impeccably dressed in a wide-brimmed hat and British Warm overcoat, Harold tapped the floorboards with his umbrella. "Fine by me," he said. "I never say no to a good party."

CHAPTER
SEVENTEEN

Friday, 14 September, 08.47, Paula Weatherall's office

To manage each of the specialised covert functions for which he was responsible, John Kerr had to use different types of accommodation, although suitable buildings were hard to come by because of the highly unusual requirements. Jack Langton's surveillance teams worked out of a crumbling former fleet-sales office in Wandsworth. The heavily secured premises were spread above a row of shops that included an ironmonger, a kebab takeaway and an Afro-Caribbean hairdresser called Relax. The base was completely anonymous. Any burglar breaching the alarmed windows and door would have found a number of rolled-up sleeping bags on four single beds, two wooden tables with chairs, a couple of moth-eaten armchairs facing an old TV, a dozen mugs, coffee and sugar in the kitchen, and a wardrobe full of clothes for rapid changes of appearance. The walls were completely bare: there was no notice-board, calendar or other sign of officialdom. Beneath the block, and accessible only from a potholed service road to the rear, was an underground car park large enough to swallow the team's eclectic range of covert motorcycles and cars.

Reporting directly to Dodge, the unit's agent runners tasked and debriefed their sources in safe-houses, modest rented flats spread all over London and changed at regular intervals. These were more comfortable, with freshly made-up beds, pictures on the walls, decent TVs and sound systems, and modest working kitchens with food in the freezer. Dodge's handlers set great store by the homeliness of each flat. The previous year, when the Met's Estates Department insisted the flats be equipped with standard-issue furniture, they simply clubbed together from their own pockets and fitted them out independently. An agent compromised or falling under threat could be accommodated indefinitely while the team created a resettlement programme.

The hiding place for Justin Hine's technical engineers was a workshop built into a row of Victorian railway arches just west of Camberwell Green. The cover was a niche IT research business shared with a joiner's, a story that justified the metal doors, double locks, hi-tech alarm and irregular comings and goings.

The external appearance of damp and decay disguised the total makeover inside. The brightly lit interior was deceptively spacious, fifty feet by twenty, divided down the middle by an insulated glass partition with a central door. To protect the IT kit at the far end of the shop, the engineers maintained the temperature at a steady seventy-three degrees. In complete contrast, the two workbenches and lathe crammed into the

155

section nearest the door gave the place the look of a regular workshop, with drills, hammers, saws, screwdrivers and wood planes neatly laid out on the benches or hanging from the walls.

Justin's team made kit to order, drawing the designs from their own imagination. He always said they provided the full service. At the warm end of the shop they made their own housings for sensors, cameras and microphones, and dreamt up new methods to exploit computer hard drives and mobile-phone technology; at the other, two civilian carpenters, both in their sixties, built the furniture and adapted the fittings to conceal their secret devices. Alongside them, almost unnoticed, a middle-aged locksmith developed magic ways to defeat the most sophisticated entry systems.

The workship was heavily secured outside working hours, but disguised as a real business by an unmanned, partitioned reception area just inside the main door, with a small switchboard, a calendar from a communications company and marketing literature from various genuine IT outfits. Contact from the street was by buzzer and intercom, unsuspecting visitors soon redirected by Justin or one of his engineers. The adjacent businesses were a car body-repair shop, an MOT testing centre and a storage space for scrap metal. Some of the dangerous-looking men who ran them had heavy-duty criminal convictions.

Kerr would have preferred to hot-desk among his teams, but Weatherall insisted he base himself at the Yard, in an old storeroom at the far end of the open-plan office on the eighteenth floor, at the opposite corner from Room 1830. He had stolen a desk and a couple of chairs from the floor below and got Justin to fix a secure USB connection for his desktop, but it took three months to persuade Facilities to replace the walls with glass partitions. It soon became known as "the Fishbowl" because Kerr was always so visible.

Kerr was back at his desk inside three minutes of the bust-up with Metcalfe. Unlocking his computer, he forwarded the Dragstone folder to Alan Fargo with just one word, "Embed", the signal for Fargo to bury it out of reach in one of the top-secret 1830 databases.

Kestrel, his inside contact at MI5, had not returned his call. Such reluctance to get back to him never came as a surprise to Kerr, for their relationship had been fractious from the moment Kerr had approached him, almost three years earlier. Kestrel's reaction always followed the same pattern: denial, followed by resistance, protest and, finally, grudging co-operation. Kerr understood and tolerated Kestrel's brinkmanship, his need to perpetuate the fiction that he was still in control. He left him a second message, then worked back through his inbox while awaiting the inevitable call from Weatherall's PA. Donna rang in less than an hour. "Commander wants to see you now."

"Any idea what for?" he asked unnecessarily.

Donna's voice dropped to a whisper. "What the hell have you been up to now? They're steaming."

"They?" asked Kerr, deleting Dragstone from his email account and locking the screen.

"She's got the Bull with her, so wear your running shoes."

The atmosphere hit him as soon as he entered the office. Paula Weatherall was sitting in her usual place at the head of the conference table. Deputy Assistant Commissioner Derek Finch, overall head of Counterterrorism Command, had taken the chair at the opposite end. They sat three metres apart in hostile silence. It was bizarre.

Finch had progressed up the uniform ladder through brown-nosing, backstabbing and Freemasonry, forsaking the Lodge the moment serious rank came within his grasp. His teeth were a dazzling white, his hair jet black, and both looked unnatural. Kerr estimated he weighed in at around two hundred and fifty pounds. Television gave him another twenty and accentuated his heavy jowls, which pulled down the sides of his mouth to give him a look of unwavering disapproval. He was known as "the Bull" because of his propensity to charge at the slightest opportunity, often at the wrong target. Neither spoke to him, so Kerr elected for the chair midway down the table, just out of striking distance.

Finch was overdressed in his usual navy woollen pinstripe with red lining, matching tie and breast-pocket handkerchief, but to Kerr he always looked a sack of shit. Kerr pushed the chair back and crossed his legs. "Morning," he said, risking a smile and looking from one to the other.

Weatherall was still drawing breath as Finch fired the first shot. "My senior investigating officer just reported the theft of our investigation database."

"Jim Metcalfe and I had a conversation," Kerr shot straight back, "in which I offered to assist with Jibril. He declined, so I forwarded Dragstone for us to work on upstairs. I want our intelligence to add value to your investigation. That's all. You know, both sides of SO15 working together. I wasn't stealing anything."

"Theft and an integrity breach," blustered Finch, jowls shaking. "Totally out of bloody order."

"All right, sir," conceded Kerr, holding up his hands. "I acted hastily for the best motives and I apologise. I've already deleted it."

"But did you look at it?" Finch seemed even angrier than usual, as if Kerr was holding him back from the Friday early getaway.

"Didn't appear to be much in it, frankly. Which was a disappointment."

Finch glared at Weatherall. "I take it you didn't agree to his interference in my investigation? Or Bill Ritchie?"

"Of course not." Weatherall looked at Kerr accusingly. "You're supposed to be running my covert operations. Gathering intelligence. What the hell were you doing making a nuisance of yourself on the fifteenth floor?"

"Ma'am, yesterday you threatened to suspend me for the surveillance operation around Ahmed Jibril. I have to know that the actions of my officers were justified. The threat to the public is severe and all the indications are that Jibril is a terrorist, yet Jim Metcalfe hinted he might release him without charge." He gave a short laugh. "I mean, it's totally weird. Turn on the box and you get blanket coverage of the bomb scene, but nothing about Jibril since the Trojans tried to shoot him. Not a word or picture from any media outlet I can find. And no appearances from you, sir. Which is uncharacteristic." Kerr was genuinely surprised by the news blackout, which added to his unease around every aspect of the Jibril investigation. Finch's silence was especially perplexing, for the head of SO15 loved the media, especially TV. He gave hundreds of interviews, missing no opportunity to expand his public profile for a lucrative post-retirement role as tabloid commentator.

"Don't be impertinent," sneered Finch.

"I'm being curious. Everyone's back-pedalling with this guy and I'm just asking why."

Kerr suddenly sensed the focus shift from him. He felt Weatherall's foot lift from his throat as she turned to Finch in surprise. "Is that true?" she said. "Are you really thinking about a possible release after, what, less than twenty-four hours?"

"That's a matter for me."

"Quite. But as Gold in the ops room yesterday . . . I mean, I do have an interest here, Derek," she persisted.

Kerr was relieved that Weatherall's intervention had moved the meeting on from its original purpose, his own reprimand.

"The outcome of this case is for me to determine," said Finch, "with MI5."

"Well, I'm seeing the director-general on Tuesday," said Weatherall. "Our routine fortnightly catch-up. I imagine she'll raise Jibril, so I do need to be in the loop on this."

"No. Philippa and I had a working breakfast today. Take a step back, Paula. You don't need to know."

Kerr waited in vain for Weatherall to push back. She, like Finch, belonged to the country's golden circle of chief officers, and Kerr was astonished that Finch could be so offensive to a senior colleague. Mrs Bull must have a very tough time.

"I'll probably decide over the weekend," he blundered on, "in discussion with ministers."

"Politicians?" Kerr was unable to restrain himself. "You're consulting government about the conduct of a police operation? Who? Why?"

This was another red flag to Kerr. Finch's admission disturbed him as much as the interference of MI5 and MI6 in the interviews of Jibril at Paddington Green. Why should government ministers have any say in the conduct of a counter-terrorist investigation?

"Just stick to your job, Chief Inspector," said Finch.

"That's exactly what I was trying to do." Kerr was about to challenge the Bull about the wiping of the secret traces from Excalibur, but something about Finch's boast warned him to hold back.

"And keep away from things that are bigger than you." Finch glared, getting ready to charge again. With limited intelligence but an ego the size of Mars, Finch was known for his slavish subservience to the government of the day. The home secretary flattered him with lunch, called him by his first name and relied on his acquiescence to every assault on public freedom. "I don't want you anywhere near my investigation again."

"But Jibril was connected to the suicide bombers."

"I'll be the judge of that."

"We believe Ahmed Mohammed Jibril is a *jihadi* who intended to attack us. My officers disrupted him," continued Kerr, undeterred. "How can you be considering early release? Like I said, even the media are sleeping on the job. Has someone gagged them? Paddington Green is usually leaking like a sieve by now."

Notorious for cultivating London's crime reporters in exchange for a sympathetic press, Finch bridled. He turned to Weatherall. "Are you sure you didn't authorise him to go down there?"

"Certainly not," she said, with a glance at Kerr, embarrassed.

"Ritchie?"

"No."

Finch paused to pick a speck of fluff from his jacket. "All right, I'll leave it to you to deal with this internally," he said, smoothing his tie. Kerr recognised the signs and groaned inwardly. The Bull was preening himself prior to pulling rank. He leant towards Weatherall, his bloated gut pressing into the table. "Enlighten me, Paula. Is it normal for that man to address senior officers in this insubordinate way?" He spoke as if Kerr was invisible, eyes glinting at Weatherall across the divide. "Frankly, I'm surprised. And disappointed. When this is over we need to have a talk about how you run your department."

"No," interrupted Kerr, with a harsh laugh. "The Dragstone thing was my decision alone, because your

bloke was being so bloody obstinate and uncoopera-
tive." Weatherall looked startled but Kerr pressed home
the attack. "It had nothing to do with Commander
Weatherall."

"Shut it," was all Finch could say.

"And for what it's worth, I don't want you insulting
my boss in front of me." The Bull was getting excited
again, as if enraged by his own red tie. "It's
inappropriate," continued Kerr, "overbearing and
ignorant. She's trying to reform things, make us all
work together." Kerr was amazed to hear himself
defending the woman who had beaten him up twice in
as many days. "Christ, we're supposed to be protecting
the public, not fighting each other."

Nostrils flared, the Bull was practically snorting by
now. Kerr imagined his feet pawing at the carpet.

"Is that all you wanted?" Kerr asked quietly, looking
from one to the other.

Finch's state-of-the-art mobile was vibrating across
the table but he ignored it, his mouth gaping open.
"Get the fuck out," was all the deputy assistant
commissioner could come up with.

Kerr was unfazed. He had been a professional
intelligence officer for more than twenty years. Finch
was an over-promoted, accident-prone bully just
passing through. When he was ready he turned to
Weatherall. "Anything else, ma'am?"

"Not now," said his commander, quietly. "Just leave
us."

CHAPTER
EIGHTEEN

Friday, 14 September, 12.36, the Fishbowl

If Metcalfe's reaction had been disturbing, the Bull's display of aggression really set the alarm bells ringing in Kerr's head. He called his team to a crash meeting in his tiny office. He had already decided this would be their last meeting in the Fishbowl. If what he suspected was true, they would need to meet in secret from now on.

Melanie was the first to arrive, straight from a physio session at St Thomas's to ease the pain in her left arm and side. Kerr made coffee in a cafetière and sat with her quietly for a few moments, wanting to send her home to her family but needing her expertise. She looked drained — reaction to the trauma of her undercover ordeal had finally kicked in — but point-blank refused to take time out.

Justin loped in with a fresh dressing under his woollen hat, and Jack Langton, comfortable in his leathers again, had biked from a surveillance plot in Balham. Kerr shoved his desk into the middle of the room and they all squeezed around it. There were only four chairs, so Justin squatted against the door.

Kerr slid coffee mugs round the table. "OK, Al, what have we got?" he asked, pulling down the blinds and flicking on the lights.

Fargo had been researching non-stop in Room 1830. He had a printout of Dragstone, and spread this with his research notes on Kerr's desk. "This has to be the strangest case I've ever seen. Apart from the forensic recovery at the bomb scene, Metcalfe and the Bellies are making a lot of noise, charging about the place with so-called urgent enquiries, you know, everything action this day, but most of it's bullshit. The regular records are all 'no trace' for Jibril. DNA, Police National Computer, ports database, Inland Revenue, National Insurance, voters' registers. But he certainly didn't act like he was a stranger to London. We had sight of him for a long time, remember, at the airport, in the street, on the bus. Watched him pick up the keys from the letting agent. No paperwork or cash deposit. It was like they were waiting for him. If he's travelled or lived here before you'd expect him to throw up some kind of trace. But there's nothing."

"You're suggesting . . . what? Someone tampered with those records, too?" said Justin.

"I'm saying the *jihadi* Jack and I bumped at that bus stop yesterday has evaporated into some kind of non-person. Who knows? Anything's possible around this guy."

"What does Dragstone tell us about how he entered the country?" said Kerr.

Fargo studied his notes. "Again, very little recorded except his passport number."

"That's really unusual, surely?" said Justin.

"In a Terrorism Act investigation against a foreign national? I'd say unprecedented," said Fargo. "His solicitor says he came here to train as a dentist and, bingo, Metcalfe's boys find he has a place reserved for him next term at London Uni."

"And what's the role of Five and Six in all this?" said Langton. "Mel's contact tells us they each have a presence at Paddington Green, right? And Metcalfe brags to you about being tasked by both agencies. So MI6 must have known about Jibril right from the start. Which means Joe Allenby was working against his own organisation by tipping you off, John."

"And completely boshes any idea that this guy was infiltrated here as an agent," said Justin. "Ahmed Jibril on the side of the angels? Forget it."

"What does Dragstone have about his property, associates, that sort of thing?" said Kerr.

"Same as the security traces. Zilch. Property list shows a cloth bag and the clothes he was arrested in. Nothing from the search of the safe-house. No mobile to research. No computer to dismantle."

"So the belongings of a non-person, too, which is incredibly suspicious," said Justin, who had never known life without a keyboard.

"It comes down to this," said Fargo, who had already given Kerr the news. "We dealt with this guy on the ground. We think he's a bad bastard. The man banged up at Paddington Green is a *jihadi*. Full stop. Yet everything in Dragstone tells me they want an excuse to let him go, despite Five and Six crawling all over it."

166

"Or because of."

"Commander Weatherall refused to let Ahmed Jibril run, so now the man is going to walk," said Justin, mysteriously, from the floor.

"Time to get your head checked out again," said Melanie, giving him a gentle kick.

Kerr reached for Fargo's printouts. Everyone sat in silence for a while, watching him absorb the Dragstone material. "No personal profile to speak of," he said, after a few moments. "Hardly any confirmed antecedents. No interview record or details of the questions." He threw the notes aside. "So what do we know? We have a man we believe to be a terrorist, incriminated by Joe Allenby and the Excalibur traces, who used evasion techniques against you guys. Now Allenby has disappeared and the intelligence has been wiped." He was speaking rapidly, as if he'd rehearsed this in his head a hundred times. "Metcalfe is conducting the most pathetic non-investigation of all time. The Bull is consulting politicians about the suspected terrorist's imminent release and completely sidelining Weatherall."

Kerr sat silently again for a few moments. He was building up to something. Eventually he turned to Langton. "Tomorrow's Saturday," he said. "Are you up for a trip to east London, Jack? Manor Park?"

Langton understood immediately and his eyes widened. "You're asking me to burgle Julia Bakkour's office? Jibril's lawyer?" He uttered a laugh that could have been surprise or disbelief. "John, have you gone fucking nuts or what?"

"We need to know who instructed her and why," said Kerr.

"And I take it you mean without authority," continued Langton. "You know, a minor detail called the Regulation of Investigatory Powers Act."

"There's no way Weatherall will sign up under RIPA. Just a quick look. Shouldn't take more than ten minutes. Then straight round to Jibril's flat for the thorough search Metcalfe should have made."

"If I get caught we're all in the shit," said Langton, the man to whom risk was routine.

"That's right. All of us. I know." Kerr fell silent again, giving them time to absorb the implications. RIPA had been introduced in 2000 to control all cases of what Home Office lawyers termed "intrusive surveillance" by police and government agencies. It meant that every planned operation to follow, film, eavesdrop or infiltrate had to be specifically authorised. Any breach of the Act was career suicide.

"It's no problem," said Langton. "What exactly are we searching for here, John?"

"The truth," said Kerr, simply. That was the real reason he had called them together again, his plan beneath the wire. He already had it mapped out, and the scrum-down in the Fishbowl was his invitation to join him. As his team exchanged glances, it seemed to Kerr that they already knew. They acted like they were already alongside him; Melanie and Fargo might even be a couple of paces ahead.

He glanced at them in turn. A little more than twenty-four hours after the bombings, they all looked desperately tired. "Look, everyone," he said, after a few moments, "it's Friday afternoon and we're all knackered, so think carefully before you commit. You're right. We're looking at corruption and cover-up here, and I think it goes very deep. We can let it go, move on to the next job. Or we start lifting stones."

Justin laughed. "It's a no-brainer."

"The moment we disturb the ground the bad people are going to know. And when that happens, life gets very heavy for every one of us."

"I think you've already demonstrated that," said Melanie.

"You have to know that, guys. To be in no doubt before you commit. I mean, there's nothing career-enhancing in this." Kerr felt a sharp pang of guilt. The more he alienated his bosses, the greater his concerns for the officers loyal to him, and he knew he was placing them in a dilemma. All had good degrees and promising careers that he was asking them to jeopardise. With a master's in sports science from Loughborough, Jack Langton was a highly regarded detective inspector, newly married with a baby daughter. At thirty-nine, he would run for chief in a year or two. Melanie was married to a police officer, and had two young sons. As detective sergeants, she and Alan Fargo had everything to play for in SO15. At only twenty-six, Justin was a technical genius who had placed his life on the line to get the job done and rescue others, a walking example of unsung dedication.

Suddenly awkward, Kerr dropped his eyes and shuffled Fargo's notes on the desk. "Thing is," he said, after a pause, "you're all excellent officers with a lot to play for."

"What are you trying to say? Exactly," asked Melanie.

"That you can drop off at any time. However this turns out, no one's going to say thanks."

"Except you," she said.

"You're inviting us to join you off piste," said Langton, "so we'll drop in to Manor Park and Lambeth, and when it goes belly-up Justin can call you from the nick. You OK with that?"

Kerr chuckled. "Yeah, brilliant."

"And what crimes can Mel and I commit to sacrifice our dazzling careers?" asked Fargo.

"I want you to retrace Jibril's visa," said Kerr. "Follow it right back to Yemen or Pakistan or wherever. Find the Foreign Office person at the embassy who actually bloody interviewed him."

"I've already got a call in to Islamabad," said Melanie.

"All right. From now on we need to take special care about personal security. Assume we're all going to be hacked. I want you to leave each other loads of voicemails about regular jobs on the tasking list and any other diverting bullshit you can think of. We'll use separate encrypted mobiles exclusively for this operation. Can you get those for us, Justin?"

"No worries."

"And I'd like us to catch up on Sunday. That all right with everybody?"

Fargo and Justin nodded.

"I'm supposed to be playing footie in the morning," said Langton.

"And I've got my daughter's concert in the evening," added Kerr. "No way I'm going to miss it. Let's meet at three."

"Here?" asked Fargo.

"Not any more," replied Kerr, flicking open the blinds. A couple of officers were peering in, trying to see what was so important on a Friday afternoon. "My place. It's safer and I'll order in pizza."

As they drifted out, Kerr asked Melanie to stay behind.

"What's up?" she said.

"You know how inquisitive they get," he said, looking through the blinds, "and I'm going to need some more bodies if this kicks off. Tell the others I want everything kept absolutely tight, Mel. Strict mobile and email discipline. No outsiders." Through the glass a couple of officers acknowledged him, as if they knew he was picking a team. "Is Douggie Blain still with us?"

"Britbank made him a formal offer yesterday. Security and crisis management leader."

"How about Faz?"

"Race and diversity training," said Melanie, following his gaze through the glass, "and before you ask, Rula's going back to uni for a post-grad and Tony applied for Public Order Branch."

"People are so pissed off." He sighed. "I thought Faz already did his diversity last month."

"Failed."

"He was born in Lahore, for Christ's sake," said Kerr. "All right. But I want Karl on board."

"Rest of the World? You sure?" Melanie looked quizzical, but Kerr had his head down. "Are you going to brief Mr Ritchie, like he asked?"

"Not now. I've upset enough governors for one day."

"Yeah. I heard what happened upstairs, with Mr Finch."

"How?"

"Donna stopped me in the corridor."

"She wasn't there."

"Heard everything. She does something illegal to the commander's intercom, apparently. Thanks, anyway." She gestured into the main office. "Any of them will fly under the radar for you. You only have to ask."

CHAPTER
NINETEEN

Friday, 14 September, 13.38, Knightsbridge

From the moment his limousine swept out of the VIP lounge at Heathrow to his arrival at the embassy in Kensington Palace Gardens, Russian junior trade minister Anatoli Rigov made three calls on the mobile belonging to his driver, a bruiser in a shiny charcoal suit. Between the embassy and the Dorchester Hotel he made another two, and received two back. For all seven calls, Rigov spoke Russian. When he needed to communicate with his protection officer, he spoke through the driver, leaving him to translate to Karl. From his front passenger seat, Karl Sergeyev concluded that the cartoon figure behind the wheel doubled as a bodyguard. Probably a KGB retiree from the fag end of the Cold War, out of condition but still up for a fight in situations requiring no fancy footwork.

Unknown to his passengers, Karl had been brought up in Kazan and was still fluent in Russian. And he knew Boris's translation was rubbish.

The Russians had insisted on using their armoured Jag, which was so heavy it practically left ruts in the

173

tarmac all the way down the M4. The driver-cum-interpreter-cum-bodyguard shifted lanes, braked and swerved as if there was nothing else on the road.

"Three out of ten, Boris," murmured Karl, as they cut in front of a thirty-two-tonne artic. He couldn't believe the guy was actually called Boris. It had to be a joke. Christ, he'd stepped straight out of a James Bond movie. "Would it be easier if I speak in your language?" he asked, in perfect Russian, as they drew up outside the Dorchester. Boris swung round to his boss so sharply that the Jag almost wiped out the concierge's desk. Karl could read expressions, too. Although Rigov managed to maintain his fleshy mask, Karl could hear Boris's walnut-sized brain whirring as he rewound the journey's indiscretions.

Rigov recovered first. "Of course, my friend, why did you not say? What was your first name again? You are among friends."

Karl tried to look embarrassed. "It's Karl."

"And you are also Russian, I think?"

"Yes, and I apologise, but we are required to speak English for our initial meeting. It's protocol at the Yard."

Karl was lying, and knew that they knew it. He could have kicked off with some banter in their language and covered the usual émigré London-life crap the moment they arrived. Instead he had encouraged free speech by busying himself with the radio and ostentatious glancing in the passenger mirror. For Karl it was a routine liaison-protection trick, deceptive and productive: the visitors felt at home, and he got to hear what they were really up to.

Now he spoke Russian directly to the principal. "What time would you wish me to return, sir?"

But the reply came from Boris, in English. "Tonight the minister will rest here, in the hotel."

"But I understand Mr Rigov has an engagement this evening, a cocktail party?" pressed Karl, discreetly waving away the overdressed hotel flunkey on door-opening duty.

Rigov was smiling at him and his own English put Boris to shame. "Thank you, Karl, but that will not be required. Please tell your people at Scotland Yard I am very grateful."

"They will wish me to accompany you," persisted Karl, sticking with English.

"It is not necessary. This is an unscheduled addition to the programme, purely social." Rigov clapped his driver on the shoulder. "Boris here will take good care of me."

"I'm sorry, sir," said Karl, turning in his seat, "but with respect, my duty requires it. I understand the event is at ten o'clock in Knightsbridge?"

"Very well, but I hope you understand this is a private engagement."

To Boris, the interpreter, Karl spoke the order in Russian. "I will meet you here in Reception at twenty-one-thirty precisely." Boris looked round to his boss for support, but Karl was already out of the car and opening Rigov's door. "Enjoy your rest, sir."

"You have proved surprisingly attentive, Karl," said Rigov, as the concierge waved Boris into a parking bay, but the smile had disappeared.

Karl returned to the Yard for his evening meal but was back in the Dorchester's reception area ten minutes early. He waited until 21.33 and was not surprised they had tried to lose him. At Heathrow, Boris had given Karl the official embassy events schedule. Boris's copy had rested between them in the Jaguar and, as they had trundled from the airport towards London, Karl had memorised the extra-curricular events scrawled in Russian around the margins. Now he followed their trail around Marble Arch. He found the Jaguar parked round the corner with a few other limousines. Boris was leaning against the bonnet, having a smoke and texting. Karl parked farther down the street so that Boris would not see him, and waited until he was right in his face before surprising him in Russian.

"Zero out of ten for timekeeping."

Boris's oversized head jerked up in astonishment and he almost dropped his mobile. "What the fuck are you doing here?" When caught off-guard, before diplomacy could kick in, aggression came easily to Boris. "Piss off."

"Texting me, are you, Boris?" The bodyguard scrabbled at the phone, attempting to speed-dial, but Karl was already covering his hand. "It's OK, I'll see myself in."

Boris shoved Karl's hand away and seized his arm. "We already told you this is a private event," he hissed, "purely social."

"I'll just go and check he's OK and be right back," said Karl, removing the fat hand from his sleeve. "Then we can have a nice chat about life back home."

As he turned away, Karl sensed Boris make his move. "No! I told you!" Boris's meaty hands landed heavily on Karl's shoulders as he tried to turn him. Karl reacted instinctively. Spinning with the momentum, he took Boris with him, shoving him face first against the brick wall in an armlock.

"If I want you to speak, you pile of shit, I'll tell you," said Karl, into Boris's cauliflower ear, "so stay by the car and enjoy a cigarette. Make a move and I'll rip your bollocks off and shove them down your throat. Understood?" He reached into Boris's pocket. "And I'll take care of this for now," he said, removing the mobile. "Don't want a diplomatic incident, do we?"

The venue was a white stucco double-fronted house on three storeys, with broad stone steps leading up to the main entrance. A narrower flight went down to the basement, secured from the street by a black iron fence and gate; a tall wooden fence gave complete privacy from the side-street. Karl walked there first, out of sight from the main road, and checked the phone. He had given Boris no chance to lock it, so scrolled to the call log and rapidly recited the numbers into the recorder on his bodyset.

As he did so a dark red Audi A4 saloon caught his attention, parked a discreet distance from the house. It had the embedded registration-numeral leaf symbol on the upper left windscreen and specially toughened glass that, to the initiated, showed it belonged to a member of the Royal Family.

When he had everything he needed, Karl returned to Rigov's limousine and handed the phone back to Boris, as if he had changed his mind. "Wouldn't want to get you into trouble, big man." He smiled, calculating that Boris would never disclose the security breach to his boss.

The front door was unlocked, with no sign of security until Karl was inside the hallway. No wish to disturb the neighbours, he supposed. The noise hit him like an express train. It was definitely party time, and a heavy, ornate screen meant that he could hear but not see. So, private, too. The laughter and good-time voices screamed excess, while the sickly sweet smell of cannabis took him back to his student days at Kazan State University. Christ, you could get high just from standing in the hallway. No wonder Rigov's off-duty plans didn't include him.

There were two security men just inside the second set of doors. On liaison protections Karl generally fell back on the halting English of his early years in London and showed his warrant card only when absolutely necessary. He spoke on the move, giving his imitation of the driver with time on his hands and coffee in his bladder.

"I am with Mr Rigov," he said, heading in the general direction of the rumpus and pointing. "Rest room this way? Refreshments?" Blanking Karl's smile, the smaller of the two directed him down a spiral staircase to the basement.

He found himself in what was probably the old kitchen. There were already three or four drivers gathered around a flash coffee machine and water cooler, one still with Bluetooth bolted to his ear. Ex-Royal Military Police and Special Forces, he guessed, going to seed while they reminisced about better days. They fell silent for the split second it took them to sense he did not belong, then resumed their talk of good times in Africa and great limousines in London. There was no way in, so Karl settled by the American fridge in the corner of the room to the left of the staircase. As he reached in for a Diet Coke the room went quiet again.

"Excuse me, sir." The request was heavily accented because it came from Russia.

"Sure." Out of good manners, because the voice behind him belonged to a woman, Karl stepped back and held the door open. No, not Russian. The beautiful woman who stood before him was definitely from Romania — he could tell by the high cheekbones. Her skin was pale, with no trace of blusher, in beautiful contrast to the bright red lipstick; in the white light from the fridge it looked almost translucent.

"I need more champagne." Elegant and perfectly cool, she was smiling as she leant past him. Karl caught the scent of flowers, then glimpsed the dark valley between her breasts. Her fine chestnut hair shone with vitality, and he felt a sudden urge to release it from its sparkly clasp. He watched her reach inside for a bottle of Krug, then a Diet Coke. For a split second he imagined her naked, shaking her hair free.

She put the champagne on the counter, expertly popped the can and held it out to him, ignoring the gawpers but letting him know she had caught his eyes all over her body. This time she spoke in Russian. "I imagine you're having to drink this stuff, yes?"

"Only while on duty," murmured Karl.

"From Kazan, I think? You were born east of the Volga River, yes? Very special, you see, I could tell." She had intelligent green eyes, and they were smiling at him, too. "Already we know each other, wonderful, and you are come to save me. One moment."

She turned to the men behind her, their faces still fixed on the vision in basque and stockings. Shrugging, palms outstretched, she signalled the show was over. "Come, boys, you will have lots more important things to talk about. What would your wives say?" When she had finished staring them down she opened Karl's Coke for him, then leant against the fridge, her legs loosely crossed. "I know you are not with these voyeurs," she said quietly, her eyes flitting to the pin in Karl's lapel. "I say you are an officer, yes? Protection duty, it is obvious."

Karl said nothing.

She thrust out her hand, bracelet rattling. "Forgive me," she said. "My name is Olga, and it is very nice to meet you." She had long, manicured fingers and the grip was dry and firm. She held him a moment longer than was necessary, changing from party girl to poised business professional. Karl saw a woman who was intelligent and perfectly groomed, complete except for pencil skirt and jacket, and it completely disarmed him.

He had not visited Kazan for eight years, but Olga had made him think of home.

"Karl," he said.

She reached to the pin on his lapel. "And you are from Scotland Yard, I can see. Looking after the embassy man, I expect?"

"And you are having to keep him occupied?"

"I go nowhere near any of them." Olga nodded at the spiral staircase. Halfway down, demure in a lime green summer dress, stood a young girl. She had olive skin and, despite her makeup, much heavier than Olga's, looked in her mid-teens. She held onto the highly polished brass handrail with one foot on the higher step, as if ready to scamper back upstairs. "Tania and I are here to serve the drinks and be decorative," she continued. "Nothing more. Do we look ridiculous to you?"

Karl glanced at the staircase again. Rebuffed by Olga, the clutch of drivers had turned their eyes on the girl. They were smiling now, not leering, perhaps thinking she was young enough to be their daughter, but the attention seemed to intimidate her. "No," he said. "Quite the reverse."

He felt her shrewd eyes fixed on him. "May I?" she asked quietly, reaching for his Coke and taking a sip. "I tell you, they will send your man back to his hotel by midnight. Then you will be off duty." Karl sensed renewed interest from the direction of the coffee machine. "Tell me, Karl, what do you drink after work? Or do you go straight home to your wife?"

"Not exactly."

They gazed at each other silently, until she tore off a strip of kitchen roll and reached into his jacket for his pen. "I think you still like to drink vodka, for old times' sake?" She scribbled her mobile number, then held out the pen and paper to him. "The secret drink, which leaves no trace," she murmured. "Perfect for the man from Scotland Yard."

"Provided we are both off duty?"

Olga laughed. "Oh, how I love Tartar men. You always think you are a gift from God." She reached out and deftly stroked his cheek, then sighed and picked up the bottle of champagne. "Now I have to spread more sunshine, but only for a little longer," she said, lowering her voice again, as if their audience could suddenly understand every word. "Then we should enjoy life for ourselves."

With that, she shimmied from the room, blowing a kiss in the general direction of the water cooler.

In fact it was close to one-thirty when Anatoli Rigov finally detached himself from Karl outside his suite at the Dorchester. He did not go straight to bed but told Boris to await further instructions, then ordered a light supper and nightcap from room service. While he was waiting, he stood by the window overlooking Hyde Park, deep in thought. Rigov was a carefully calculating man, and the evening's unexpected turn of events had presented him with an opportunity. When he had worked out his plan he sank into one of the deep sofas and rang his most trusted associate in London, ordering him to test it for every possible contingency.

Within ten minutes, they had agreed the proposal was workable.

Rigov's next call, much briefer, was to the Russian ambassador, who made no complaint at being woken in the early hours. Before retiring to his four-poster bed, Rigov settled at the ornate desk and wrote a message on Dorchester notepaper, handing it to Boris for immediate delivery to the embassy in Kensington Palace Gardens. The ambassador was to have it translated into diplomatic language and sent to the Foreign and Commonwealth Office first thing on Saturday morning.

CHAPTER
TWENTY

Saturday dawned bright and fresh, a brief interlude of
blue sky and sunshine before the onset of winter as
Justin collected the dummy British Gas van from the
surveillance-vehicle hideout in Wandsworth. The van
was a fall-back, a contingency for urgent daytime
incursions involving occupants, and Justin hoped it
would prove unnecessary.

Julia Bakkour's law office formed part of a
handsome, three-storey Georgian terrace a stone's
throw from Wanstead Underground station in north-
east London. The terrace, fifty metres long, formed one
side of a quiet square overlooking a neatly mown green.
Residential houses, some divided into apartments,
shared the space with the offices of an architect, an
accountant and another law firm. A pollarded oak,
ringed by daffodils each spring, towered over the
tranquil green, and a traditional award-winning real-ale
pub nestled unobtrusively in the corner farthest from
the road.

The square was an idyllic middle-class enclave
cushioned by Wanstead Flats from the featureless urban

sprawl to the south. Access from the arterial road linking Leytonstone with Ilford was through a single narrow thoroughfare, with scarcely room for two cars to pass. It was a no-go area for heavy vehicles, with car parking strictly with permit only. Julia Bakkour had chosen well. Residents knew their neighbours, collected litter, used the dog-waste bins on the green and watched for anything suspicious. At the far end of the green an old woman in a fleece was trailing her arthritic terrier, plastic bag at the ready, and Justin could hear birdsong from the oak tree to his right. Private yet overlooked, the area was a perfect oasis for the surveillance conscious.

Sensing the old woman's eyes on him, Justin drove round the square in a slow recce before committing himself. He needed to check the layout, locate any CCTV and generally satisfy himself that the operation was viable. Bakkour's office was at number twenty-three but, with no name-plate, could have passed as a normal residence identical to the others along the terrace. A couple of cyclists were dismounting near the pub as he paused outside number thirty to take a call from Melanie, who confirmed that Julia Bakkour had arrived at Paddington Green with her laptop. Had she left it in the office, the intelligence opportunity would have been greater but he would have needed more time inside. While Melanie was speaking he assessed the challenge. He saw Yale and Banham locks protecting the door, and a standard domestic alarm on the wall. Conditions were difficult, but he had faced far worse.

As he parked outside Bakkour's address he clocked the illuminated desk lamp in the ground-floor office and a figure moving around inside. He swore beneath his breath, automatically pulling on his British Gas jacket. He checked his toolbox and fake laminated pass, then called Langton on the radio. "Someone's home, Jack."

"What about the building to the right?"

"Munro Investments. Looks unoccupied. Hard to say."

"I'll cover the neighbours while you do the business."

Justin drove fast to the house adjacent to the solicitors' offices, opened the rear doors of the van and activated the disguised canisters his engineers had developed for this type of operation. He rapidly cordoned off a section of the square with plastic tape as the air filled with the pungent smell of domestic gas and the dog walker retreated to her front door.

Jack Langton rode up a minute later on a marked police motorcycle, smart in the uniform of a conventional traffic PC, and took up position outside the front door to the right of the target address.

Justin rang the intercom. When a voice spoke, he replied, "Emergency gas engineer. Can you come to the door, please?" A dark-skinned man in white T-shirt and jeans opened the heavy door. He was mid-twenties with a black moustache, wire-rimmed glasses and a pencil wedged behind his ear. Leaning against the staircase was a bicycle, its tyre marks still damp on the carpet tiles. Justin held his pass in front of the young man's nose, but he scarcely glanced at it. "Sorry, mate. We've got a major leak. Need to evacuate you while we fix it."

"Where?" the man asked, wrinkling his nostrils and looking at Justin's tape. "Oh, smells serious."

"Neighbour." Justin's eyes flickered to the alarm pad just inside the door. It was new and conventional, but might complicate things.

"Health and safety, yes?"

Justin indicated the bike. "Anyone else in the building?"

"No. It's mine." That was good. Justin would not have to call on Langton's uniform for persuasion. The man was already picking his jacket off the hook and reaching in his pocket for the keys. "Just me on Saturday mornings."

"So get yourself a coffee, yeah?" Justin was already heading back to the van, a man with an emergency to handle. "Shouldn't take more than an hour. If the van's gone you're in the clear. And don't bother with the alarm," he called, making it sound like an afterthought. "Electrical charge could set things off."

Langton, loitering outside the neighbour's front door to demonstrate other engineers were already inside, gave Justin the all-clear as the young man ambled out of the square towards Wanstead station. Toolbox in hand, Justin trotted back to the offices. He defeated the Yale in less than thirty seconds. The Banham took ninety, and Langton covered him for both. On the ground floor a clump of office chairs in a waiting area faced an untidy reception desk. To the side were a small kitchen and washroom. The business area was on the first floor, converted to open plan with plain white walls and strip lighting, the staircase, with its original wooden banisters, ascending directly into the office.

Justin found five utilitarian oak desks heaped with documents, all in Arabic. There were more papers on wooden chairs around the room, and even piled on the floor. He spotted the wall safe in the corner while he was pulling on his gloves, a newish combination job. A half-full cup of coffee, still warm, marked out Saturday Boy's workstation.

Flitting around the other four he eventually found an envelope with Julia Bakkour's name beneath some sort of deed on the desk in the gloomiest corner next to the safe. The other stations had desktop computers but Bakkour's had only a docking unit for a laptop, which Justin assumed she must remove every time she left the office. Almost buried beneath the papers was a small gilt frame with a photograph of a boy and girl aged around five and seven. The two unlocked drawers contained stationery, cosmetics, a clump of business cards in a rubber band and a couple of practitioners' magazines, but nothing to catch his eye.

He took out his adapted Pentax Optio V10, switched on the desk lamp and photographed as many documents as he could, taking care to replace the papers exactly as he had found them. There were twelve business cards. He rapidly spread them on top of the desk to photograph them, then re-bound them in the same order. "You getting me, Jack?"

"Go."

"I've got most of the surface stuff. No laptop. I want to have a crack at the safe. OK?"

"I'm covering."

Justin already had his magnetic calibrating sensor locked over the combination dial. The safe was the type on which he regularly practised in the workshop at Camberwell and he estimated he would need five minutes. He did it in just under four. Documents crammed the two interior shelves, with nothing of obvious reference to Ahmed Jibril. On the top shelf was an A4 desk diary, also marked in Arabic. He turned back two days to Thursday, the morning of Jibril's arrest, and found an entry in script and numerals with a series of exclamation marks.

He almost confused the sound of a door being unlocked in the depths of the house with the shuffle of his Pentax as he grabbed shots of the diary. "What's happening, Jack?"

"All quiet. How long?"

"Stand by." Justin froze, screwing his eyes in concentration. There was the sound of a door gently being pushed shut, coming from the rear of the house. "Signs of life downstairs. He must have come back early. Rear door, from the golf course."

"I'll intercept him."

The back door must have been swollen with damp, for the lawyer took a while to completely close it. Then there was the sound of the key being turned again.

"No. I'll handle it." Justin estimated he had about twenty seconds. He repacked his bag and spun the combination in fifteen seconds, leaving the same numerals on the dial. He could hear footsteps and stole a look from the banisters. The lawyer was carrying a Starbucks cappuccino and texting as he slowly climbed the stairs. Justin retreated into the office and checked around him again. The open plan left him no place to hide except behind one of the desks. His hand reached over the gas meter in his jacket pocket and he prepared to talk his way out.

Then he heard the lawyer's mobile ring, a torrent of Arabic, and laughter. He took cover behind the safe as the young man walked past him into the office and peered through the window at Justin's van, then at Langton standing by his bike. He was laughing so much at his cleverness in deceiving the gasman that he slopped coffee over his shirt. The distraction gave Justin the perfect cover to sneak past in his fake uniform and pad downstairs, remembering to avoid the steps that had creaked on the way up.

He opened the front door an inch and paused, waiting for sounds of movement above him. When he heard the floorboards groan again and the sound of the chair rolling over the thin carpet he stepped outside, silently pulled the door shut and hugged the front wall until he reached the safety of Munro Investments and Jack Langton.

They were clear in three minutes, Langton riding off while Justin was still rolling up his tape, each sensing the young man's mocking eyes on them as they sped away to Lambeth.

CHAPTER
TWENTY-ONE

Saturday, 15 September, 12.17, Lambeth

They dropped off the cover vehicles at Wandsworth, changed and made mugs of instant coffee. Langton had already called Alan Fargo, waiting in 1830, and Justin had emailed the photographs even before the kettle boiled.

Before noon they were on the road again, heading for Lambeth and Ahmed Jibril's safe-house. Justin rode pillion on Langton's Suzuki, its high performance camouflaged by a scuffed and dented black chassis. Weaving through the Saturday shopping traffic they reached the rambling, three-storey Victorian house in less than fifteen minutes. This time Langton dropped Justin round the corner out of sight in the nearest side-street, then parked right outside the address.

The house was served by a communal front door reached by a short concrete path only five metres from the pavement. Speed bumps had done little to deter the constant flow of traffic using the street as a rat-run between Clapham Road and South Lambeth Road. Lining both sides of the street, once-grand houses had been converted into flats, interrupted by a launderette

191

and a shabby twenty-four-hour convenience store. Across the road from Jibril's safe-house, an ugly block of council flats dated back to the fifties and was in serious need of renovation. SAS secondee Steve Gibb had conducted the observation of Jibril from the tiny front bedroom of an uninhabitable flat on the top floor.

Langton dismounted, flipped up the visor and leant against the bike. He was just another courier checking a parcel against his job sheet, except that his attention was totally focused on the communal front door.

After a couple of minutes a girl appeared from the junction with South Lambeth Road and, absently searching for her key, turned into the path. She was wearing a sweatshirt and headscarf, and Langton saw the white iPod wire trailing into her jeans pocket. Immersed in the music, she only became aware of him when she unlocked the front door, which swung inwards of its own accord. "Cheers, love," he grunted, as prerecorded fake messages from a non-existent dispatcher crackled from his helmet, making any challenge pointless.

He placed the package on the mail shelf just inside the door, loitered while she went upstairs, and gave a double click as soon as she was out of sight. In less than twenty seconds Justin was inside the lobby, taking the stairs two at a time, and Langton was astride his bike again, gunning the engine to dissolve any second thoughts from the girl and cover Justin's ascent.

Flat nine was on the second floor at the top of the house and the locks were child's play. Justin already knew what to expect because the surveillance team had watched Jibril pick up the keys from the letting agent. There were only two flats on the landing, and no sound came from the door opposite Jibril's. He stepped inside, closed the door and stood on the threshold, perfectly still, acclimatising himself. The heavy curtains were closed, but even in the gloom he could see practically everything from the doorway. It was a bedsit, one half of the large converted attic, with the roof sloping from left to right. There was a small oak table with two chairs pulled clear of the window and a single bed against the left inner wall beside a chest of drawers. The only other item of furniture was an uncomfortable-looking armchair facing a small TV.

The tiny bathroom and shower lay directly ahead of him, but the kitchenette was no more than an alcove in the far corner, hidden by a dirty floral curtain. An ancient gas water heater hung above the stainless-steel sink and drainer, and a laminated shelf held a kettle, electric ring, tiny fridge and microwave.

The place looked as if Jibril had just left, with the bed unmade and clothes scattered on the armchair. A chipped dinner plate, knife and stained mug had been dumped in the sink, and the fridge was empty, except for an open carton of milk and the remains of the fruit and veg Jibril had bought from the stalls around Brixton on his mid-morning walks. The waste bin still contained the remains of his three days' occupancy. In the bathroom Justin found a toothbrush, a pair of nail scissors, shower gel, shampoo and a razor, with Jibril's towel draped over the shower rail.

There was enough for Justin to form two conclusions. Unless he was a suicide bomber, Jibril had intended to return to the address, which meant Langton's surveillance since his arrival at Heathrow had not been compromised. But it also showed there had been no effective police search or forensic recovery. Even for a place of this size, with no computer and very few items of property, Justin would have expected a comprehensive forensic examination to last at least forty-eight hours. There was no fingerprint dust or other sign that Metcalfe's people had been anywhere near the address.

Justin started his own examination in the kitchen. Citizens and criminals believed the kitchen was a good place to hide valuables or secrets because it was the place burglars and police checked last. He made his discovery within three minutes. The find was so significant he knew he could ignore the rest of the bedsit.

It was the dirt that gave Jibril away. Every hard surface was covered with dust, suggesting the flat had been unoccupied before Jibril's sudden arrival, and the kitchen work surfaces were covered with grease. Hands safe behind his back, Justin carefully studied every inch of space, concentrating on the areas behind the fridge, microwave and under the sink. Nothing had been disturbed for many months.

However, when he looked above the sink to study the water heater he noticed a scuff in the grease between the bracket and the wall, and a mark against the concave metal cover at the top of the unit. Around the cover there was a ridge of grease with a strip of clean metal above it less than a millimetre wide, showing it had recently been loosened or removed. It slipped off easily and, when he turned it over, Justin found a piece of paper smaller than a matchbook taped inside, marked "13 + ED-TA – 4" in ballpoint pen. He laid the cover on the work surface, photographed it and gently peeled back the tape. Carefully unfolding the paper, he used his torch to illuminate the jewel inside that was Ahmed Jibril's Sim card.

He was already speed-dialling as he rummaged around for an exhibits bag. In 1830 Fargo picked up straight away. "Listen, Al," said Justin, peering at his treasure trove, "you weren't thinking of an early night, were you?"

Justin's home was a one-bedroom flat on the first floor of a converted Edwardian house in Parsons Green. It was in a quiet side turning south of New King's Road, just a stone's throw to the north of Putney Bridge and close to Fulham Palace Road. He shared the flat with his girlfriend, a physiotherapist at Queen Mary's Hospital in Putney. Both were keen runners, spending Saturday and Sunday mornings along the riverbanks on both sides of the bridge. But Justin's favourite time to run was late evening, around eleven-thirty, just before bed. When work had been particularly stressful or demanding, as in recent days, he enjoyed a lone jog in the dark around the regular circuit on the side-streets north of Sands Park. The brief interlude at the end of the day, no more than fifteen minutes, helped him sleep and restored his energy.

On that Saturday evening he had a final brief call with Alan Fargo and changed into his tracksuit just before midnight, as his girlfriend got ready for bed. Alone with his iPod, he did not notice the Ford Thames van cruise past him in the opposite direction, and missed its approach as he accelerated into a twenty-second sprint along Broomhouse Lane, bordering Hurlingham Park. Even when he turned off into the street adjacent to his, he was unaware of anything threatening. The final stretch was along a little row of shops, a forty-second jog from his flat. There was a general store, a launderette between a couple of takeaways, and a drive at the far end led to an access road at the back. His assailants must have been waiting for him there, by the newsagent's, letting Justin come to them.

He was easing down, almost reaching for his doorkey when he ran into an obstruction that had not been there a second before. It was hard as concrete, and forced the breath out of him. Then he saw that the barrier was alive, its breath in the cool night air mixing with his own. There were two men, totally dressed in black, one about Justin's build wearing glasses, the other taller and much heavier. Winded, taken by surprise, incapable of resistance, he felt himself being dragged away from the safety of the lit street into the darkness of the access road.

When they were safely out of sight behind the shops the larger of the two punched him in the stomach and held a gloved hand over his mouth. His partner ripped away Justin's iPod, searched his pockets and removed his key. Justin never took his mobile on a run, and had no money on him. He thought this would anger them, but neither said a word. Their actions were co-ordinated and spare, as if they did this every night. The larger guy punched him again, creasing his body on the gravel. Then they were gone.

By the time Justin collected himself and reached the street, the men had disappeared. Checking himself over, he walked the final few metres to his flat and rang the bell. Apart from the punches and a graze to his thigh where they had dragged him along the gravel, he was unmarked. His girlfriend wanted him to dial 999, but he took a shower, then called his boss.

Kerr answered immediately, sounding alert, as if he was still working. Justin listened while he tried to persuade him to go to hospital, then, when that failed, fielded a bunch of rapid-fire questions. Kerr wanted to know everything. Had Justin seen anything suspicious during the day's searches? Any dodgy vehicles? What about the gap in between, when he and Jack had gone back to Wandsworth?

"It's probably just my bad luck, boss," said Justin, when he managed to get a word in. He tried to keep it light. "Street robbers. Or else a wacky couple who like dressing up and kicking the shit out of people."

"But they didn't, did they? Kick you, I mean, or really do you over. Was this a warning to back off? We have to consider you may have been targeted, Justin."

"How would they find out where I lived?"

"Followed you home today?"

"No way," said Justin. "I'd have spotted that."

"You didn't just now."

"Tonight I was a dopey bollocks, but it's been a long day. And can we just keep my rubbish personal security between ourselves? Please?"

There was a pause at the other end of the line. "Justin, could anybody outside the Yard have given them your address?"

"No one. Life is me, the girlfriend and the job." He laughed. "How sad is that?"

"So we may have a problem. Get some rest. We'll have another think tomorrow."

CHAPTER
TWENTY-TWO

Sunday, 16 September, 15.07, Kerr's apartment

The only person missing from the catch-up on Sunday afternoon at Kerr's home in Islington was Alan Fargo. They linked up with him on Skype because he was still awaiting some results and might need to access Excalibur.

Kerr's home was light and airy, with the original polished wooden floors stretching from front to back. It was another unusually warm autumn day so he opened the French windows onto the balcony, letting in the street sounds from three floors below. There were two en-suite double bedrooms to one side, and the kitchen was state-of-the-art. The walls were painted cream, hung with prints and original watercolours he had acquired on visits to Africa, the US and Rome. Over the limestone fireplace there was a nineteenth-century print of a crowded River Thames with a newly constructed Tower Bridge rising in the background. On the sideboard, in pride of place, stood a colour photograph of Gabriella on her graduation day.

There were two double sofas and an armchair, but everyone clustered round Kerr's laptop on the large glass dining-table so that Fargo could see them from his desk in 1830. His team looked refreshed in their weekend clothes. Kerr had a private word in the kitchen with Justin and was relieved to find he was uninjured and rested; in fact, Justin looked better than Fargo, who appeared pasty on screen, and Jack Langton, who had been scrambled in the early hours to assist MI5 with an urgent surveillance operation and had struggled to make his Sunday-morning football practice.

Relaxed in sweatshirt, white jeans and bare feet, Kerr took the pizza order and brewed coffee while Justin got Fargo to shift his position and joshed him that they needed a bigger screen.

"Right, everyone, brains in gear," said Kerr, once they were settled. He slid a single sheet of A4 onto the table. The code recovered from Jibril's safe-house was written on it in neat black felt tip: "13 + ED-TA − 4". "Let's assume Justin has found us some kind of operational instruction here. Worst case, it's an order for a second attack." He held up the paper for Fargo to see, then passed it around. "I want you to memorise it and share any thoughts as soon as you get them. Doesn't matter how bizarre, just tell me."

Fargo dived straight in, as if he and Kerr had already been bouncing a few ideas around. "Well, the date of the bombing was September the thirteenth," he said, "so it's plausible the 'thirteen' refers to that. In which case, as John says, this is some kind of *jihadi* timetable. We're right to take this very seriously. What the hell is 'ED-TA'? We have to unpick this as soon as. Like, by tonight."

200

"So every minute is of the essence, guys," said Kerr, automatically checking the date on his watch. "This is our absolute priority. Justin's found us a puzzle I want you to think about every second until we've solved it." He left the paper on the table and pushed round the coffee. "OK, Al. You were telling me the visit to the lawyer was also worthwhile."

"Absolutely. Hang on, I've got the translations and some research stuff." Shuffling his notes he inadvertently nudged the camera and they had to wait a few seconds while he adjusted it. "Sorry. Four lawyers in addition to Julia Bakkour. All first or second-generation Syrian. The firm does commercial work, matrimonial and property. Specialists in sharia, mainly the application of Islamic law to property and divorce cases here. No background whatsoever in terrorism cases. The note in her diary for last Thursday tells her to call the number written there urgently, underlined, and timing it ten-forty."

"Who from?"

"No name. Just the number."

"And?"

"Something odd about it," said Fargo, adjusting his glasses. "We're having trouble tracking it, which is interesting in itself. But the number also appears on the business cards Justin copied. It's assigned to an Omar Taleb."

"Address?"

"Just a name and profession underneath it. Attorney. No company or email address. Looks like one of those spook cards MI6 give out at drinks receptions."

"Which country?"

"Can't tell yet. But he's certainly not licensed to practise in the UK."

"So where?"

"I'm working on it."

"Any security traces?"

"Unidentifiable without more details."

"This has to be a good lead, Al. Let's keep on it."

"While we're on Bakkour," said Melanie, "I'm getting a drip feed from the interviews. Our Julia is wiping the floor with Metcalfe's finest, very demanding, pushing really hard for Jibril's immediate release."

Justin gave a short laugh. "But Allenby's photograph shows him wearing a turban, beard, the full works."

"So her client had a make-over before he came to London, says Julia. None of it's enough to keep him banged up without charge. I can't get hold of the actual interview transcripts, which is no great loss because Jibril isn't saying a word, apparently."

"It's not all bad," Fargo's Cornish voice drifted into the silence. "I've got some info about Jibril's flat. Justin, there were two numbers on the Sim card you lifted. Could be London contacts."

"Addresses?" asked Kerr.

"Working on them now. Hold on." Fargo disappeared from view for a couple of seconds to make a call, leaving them with voices off and a blurred, broken view of St James's Park through the venetian blinds. "No, still waiting on the specifics," he said, when he reappeared.

202

"Soon as you can," said Langton. "We need to watch these people from right now, whoever they are."

"Does that cover it from your end, Al?" said Kerr.

"No. I saved the best till last. We're starting to join the dots. The guys here just came back with a terrorist finance connection. Jibril's flat in Lambeth is one of nine flats in a run-down Victorian house, yeah? And remember I told you Julia Bakkour's firm does conveyancing? Well, they go back a long way. TF tell me they acted for the purchaser of the lease on that house in 1986."

"So her firm buys the property more than two decades ago and represents the occupier today at Paddington Green," said Kerr. "That's neat. Who owns the lease?"

"It's a company. Falcon Properties. Probably a shell but we're checking it out. And get this. The house also has mentions re Syrian-state-sponsored terrorism around that time. The Hindawi case."

"Proxy bomb on El Al flight via innocent Irish nurse?"

"That's the one," said Fargo.

"Say again?" frowned Justin.

"Look it up," said Kerr. "Op Derwent."

"Yeah, but I'm wondering whether we should be sharing this with Metcalfe," said Justin. "You know, the numbers, previous intelligence links?"

"You're joking, right?" said Melanie. They sat in silence, absorbing the news. A key turned in the front door and Kerr felt their eyes on him as he glanced at his watch again in sudden realisation.

"Didn't tell me you were having a party, Dad." They looked up to see Gabriella, Kerr's daughter, standing in the hallway in jeans, sweater and windcheater. She was just in from a couple of days at her mother's place in Rome. A violin post-grad at the Royal College of Music, Gabi shared a flat in the shadow of the Royal Albert Hall. She stayed over with Kerr from time to time, but only to please her mother. She was pulling a suitcase with one hand and holding two pizza boxes in the other. "Found him on the landing," she said, as the delivery biker appeared behind her in the doorway. "He wants paying."

"Hey, you're early," said Kerr, and then, to the screen, "Hold on, Al." He padded over to the door, kissed Gabi and paid the biker. He dumped the pizzas on the sideboard to hug her properly, but she was already dragging her suitcase across the room. "Didn't even remember I was coming, did he?" They all laughed, but Gabi looked serious. She managed a thin smile and made a face into the camera for Fargo.

"Come and join us," said Kerr.

"No," she said shortly, shaking off her coat. It was the monosyllable of a petulant child, and grabbed everyone's attention. "I have to practise and get ready. It's the Bruch Concerto tonight, remember?"

"Sure," said Kerr, glancing past her at the clock on the fireplace. "Looking forward to it."

"Good."

Kerr guessed everyone had seen Gabi's reaction when he tried to hug her. She had introduced tension into the room and it made them look away, pretending to scribble notes. Melanie and Langton had met Gabi during her teens, and Kerr knew this was not how they would remember the relationship.

Melanie filled the void. "I'll get the plates," she said, heading for the kitchen.

Kerr felt awkward. "And we need to leave here around six, right?"

"No, Dad," said Gabi, raising her eyebrows at Melanie. "Four-fifteen latest to make the rehearsal. Like we agreed last night, remember?" Gabi flung open her door and checked the bedside clock. "That's forty minutes from now, tops. Concert's at seven."

"No problem. We're almost done."

Kerr sensed their discomfort at seeing him wrongfooted. He knew they were vaguely aware that his personal history was complicated, affected by his job. With her parents in different countries, Gabi's upbringing had been difficult, but her coldness in front of his team had embarrassed him, especially since everyone was being nice to her. She was behaving like a bitch, and that was not how Kerr had raised her. He noticed Melanie squeeze Gabi's arm as she returned from the kitchen with the plates. Perhaps she thought Gabi was nervous about the concert, or she and Kerr were getting over a row. He hoped so. That would be better. An argument between father and daughter was nothing, a mere flash in the pan.

"Shall I update you on the visa?" said Melanie, as Gabi's door closed and Justin ripped into the pizza, waving a slice on camera to provoke Fargo. "I had a return call from Yemen. Remember the alcoholic from

King Charles Street nicked last year for drunk and diss? The whole criminal-record stroke security issue they dumped on us? Well, guess what, Foreign Office reviewed our wino's vetting and posted him to the embassy in Sana'a. Visa section. My contact got him out to the ex-pats' club last night, poured a gallon of wife-beater down his throat. Nothing official, but the rumour is Ahmed Jibril was fast-tracked for a student visa authorised from London. The duty logs show no record of Jibril even being interviewed. Looks like he simply showed up at the embassy and got his passport stamped."

"So who authorised it?"

"Couldn't say for sure. Fatso believes it originated with the Foreign Office counter-terrorism section in London. That's where they sent the paperwork. But no names."

They paused again to eat their pizza and figure out the implications. Gentle sounds from Gabi's violin began to drift through the door and the beautiful poignancy of her playing, so at odds with her behaviour only moments earlier, distracted them all.

They looked at Kerr. "She's good," said Justin, speaking for them all.

"Cheers," said Kerr, with a quick smile, then returned to Fargo. "And that would be unusual, presumably?"

"Our government gave special entry privileges to a terrorist?" Fargo laughed. "Yes, John. You could say that."

"We need to find out what makes Jibril so special that he couldn't join the no-hopers' queue like the rest," continued Melanie. "And the name of the official who authorised it."

Melanie's mobile vibrated as they listened to the music again. "She is seriously brilliant, boss," repeated Justin. "I think we should all come along tonight."

"No," said Melanie, with a hand up, reading the text and checking the time. "This is from my contact at Paddington Green. Finch just announced he's going to release Ahmed Jibril in forty minutes."

Everyone stared at her as if she was speaking a different language. Even Kerr was stunned by her bombshell. They sat, mute with shock, as the truth sank in. The only sound in the room was from Gabi's violin. She was rehearsing a lament now, and her playing matched the message.

"But why the hell . . .? They've got fourteen days," said Langton. He seemed to be thinking aloud for them all: people in their own organisation were about to let a *jihadi* back onto the street. It was seismic, incomprehensible.

Justin was the first to recover. "Shit," he said, sitting bolt upright. "The Sim card. Jibril's gonna go home to Lambeth, isn't he?"

"That's where his stuff is," said Melanie, "or was."

Kerr felt their eyes on him again, anxious, uncertain, but he stayed ice cool. "So, better make sure you get there first," he said to Justin, handing him the last slice of pizza.

Langton collected his things together. "You are going to ring Bill Ritchie about this, John, yeah?" he said, but it didn't come out as a question. He sounded threatening, as if he wanted to fight someone. "And the commander?"

"Not now, Jack."

"What, then? We put Jibril's property back and drop him?" Langton snatched his mobile from the table, as if he might just ring Paula Weatherall himself. It was rare for him to show emotion, but when he was worked up, the Geordie accent laced his anger with acid. He jabbed a finger at the screen, causing Fargo instinctively to push back in his chair. "Is that what Al's hard work comes down to? Was all that shit we took on the street for nothing?"

Kerr looked at him. "I'm not saying that."

"What, then? For fuck's sake, since when did we start letting terrorists off the hook? That bastard was heading for a bomb factory, and we were right behind him."

"Yes, you were." Kerr caught Fargo's eye down the wire, as if checking something with him first. "And from now on you're going to be all over him."

Langton gave a harsh laugh. "Against a man they just set free?" For the second time Kerr's number two seemed to be speaking for everyone. "How the hell do we keep that from the bosses?"

"It's a game-changer." Kerr looked each of them in the face, then flashed a glance at the screen again. "So we fly a little lower and a lot quieter."

208

★ ★ ★

They were out of Kerr's apartment in less than a minute. On the sprint across London, Justin rode pillion with Langton to recover the Sim card from Fargo at the Yard and return it to Jibril's safe-house before he got there.

Kerr gave Gabi money for a taxi and promised to reach the Royal College of Music in time for the concert. Then he and Melanie dived down to the garage for the Alfa and charged to Paddington Green high-security police station. They parked in a side-street next to Edgware Road Underground station just as Jibril appeared with a woman at the top of the steps. She was olive-skinned and dressed for business, even though it was Sunday, but Jibril was instantly recognisable in the clothes he had been wearing when he was arrested. On the other side of Edgware Road Kerr and Melanie watched Jibril and the woman talk for a few moments, then shake hands. She walked swiftly down the steps and headed north.

"That must be Julia Bakkour," said Kerr. "I need a photograph." Before Melanie could say anything he dived out of the car and jogged north, overtaking Bakkour and continuing until he was about twenty metres in front. Then he wove across the traffic to Bakkour's side of Edgware Road and doubled back towards her, pretending to text on his BlackBerry as he snatched a couple of rough stills. He walked past her without hesitating, then crossed the road again back to the car.

As Kerr sent the photographs of Bakkour to 1830, Jibril lingered on the steps to the police station. He was looking around him, as if undecided where to go.

"He can't make up his mind whether to take a bus or the train," said Melanie.

"Or he's scanning for surveillance." Then Jibril came down the steps and turned right, heading for the nearest Underground sign.

"It's the Tube," said Melanie, opening the door. "Want me to take him?"

"Too risky. He'll recognise you. Let Jack know. We have to assume he's coming their way. Best we can do."

"Sure," said Melanie, checking her watch. "And you'd better shoot."

Kerr raced home, changed into a linen jacket and fresh shirt and reached the Royal College of Music in Knightsbridge with time to spare. He found Gabi mingling in the foyer with the other players. She looked beautiful in her black dress and patent heels, blonde hair piled high to accentuate her long neck. He gave an embarrassed shrug. "Sorry about the rush earlier. Bit of a panic."

"Another."

"But I hadn't forgotten. And I made it. Which is good, yeah?"

"I just texted Mum. Let's just say she'd have killed you if you hadn't."

Gabi was first violin in the front row of the orchestra and Kerr sat at the end of a row near the back with a clear view of her. He had his BlackBerry on silent mode in the palm of his hand, waiting for Fargo's call. The screen lit up near the start of the second movement and he caught Gabi's glare as he slipped out into the foyer.

"Sounds nice," said Fargo.

"What's Jibril been doing?"

"No movement since he got back to number nine, and no visitors."

"Can we use that council block for the OP again?"

"The Reds are already back inside."

"So let's stay with him twenty-four seven till I give the word. Thanks, Al. Better get back."

"Hang on. That's not why I called. I've got the readout from Jibril's Sim card. There are two numbers. One outgoing, timed nineteen-fifty-three two days earlier, last Tuesday. Comes back to a Samir Khan at an address in East Ham. Hold on a sec." Kerr heard a shuffling of papers. "No record on Excalibur, but I turned up a trace in 1830 linking him to the Al Qaeda airline conspiracy in 2006."

"Great. So let's deploy surveillance from now."

"Jack's already on it, but keeping it tight within the Reds. Looking for an OP as we speak."

"Al, you just made my evening."

"It gets even better. Jibril also took an incoming call. From the same number Julia Bakkour had in her diary."

"Omar Taleb?"

"The attorney with the business card, correct. I'm a bit knackered so it didn't click till now."

"Don't worry about it, Al. It's fine, and you've been working non-stop. Go home and get some rest. We'll find this guy tomorrow when you've . . ."

"No, that's not it. Listen to me. Taleb's call to Jibril was very brief, six seconds. And guess when?"

On high alert, Kerr instinctively moved to the edge of the foyer. "Just tell me."

"Thursday morning, the thirteenth, at eight-oh-seven."

"Jesus," said Kerr, his mind racing back to the surveillance logs. "When did we first have sight of Jibril?"

"Steve Gibb has him leaving the safe-house at eight-twelve. Five minutes later. Jibril must have been sitting inside ready to roll, waiting for the call. Taleb was giving him the off, John. The same guy set Jibril loose *and* instructed his defence brief a couple of hours later. How's that for command and control?"

"Better than Al Qaeda. We're up against a professional operator here. So who's controlling him?"

"Exactly," said Fargo. "John, this has to be state sponsored. Back to the eighties."

Kerr was staring through the main doors onto the street. "And now you've got me wondering who else knows about it."

"Good question. And Finch just released the man."

"So let's move fast and tread carefully."

CHAPTER
TWENTY-THREE

Monday, 17 September, 08.32, Hammersmith

Naked in Olga's bathroom with his mobile clamped to his ear, Karl Sergeyev remonstrated with Nancy, his estranged wife, and watched his marriage swirl down the toilet with the used condom. Behind him, Olga waited with the patience of the professional while, in his ear, Nancy took him to task. Karl stood impotent, hands occupied.

"It's five-thirty on Wednesday or nothing. You're in no position to set the pace here, Karl." When they had met almost nine years earlier Nancy had worked in Special Branch Registry. Logical, thorough and modest, she had fallen for him completely, overpowered by the charm that was to prove equally seductive outside their marriage.

"Nancy, you know I have a lot on. All I want is you to cut me some slack."

"Don't make me laugh," she said, as the cistern filled with a noisy clunk, "and what the hell was that? Why aren't you at the office?"

This reminded Karl that Nancy's working Monday had started two hours earlier. She would have been getting their two children washed, fed and ready while Karl and Olga were having early-bird sex. She was on the school run, speaking on the hands-free. Karl could hear the indicator and the acceleration into the turn, and was calculating exactly where she would be. Before he had walked out on her a month earlier, he had always driven on the morning stint, Nancy taking over when they dropped him at the station.

"You're angry, Nancy. I can understand that, but you shouldn't make these calls in the car. It's dangerous for you and the kids."

"Oh, wonderful. You walk out on me to fuck your latest tart and still think you can slag off my driving. Pathetic." There was the sound of a car horn followed by Nancy's high-pitched "Go screw yourself!" and he imagined the raised finger.

His wife had never handled traffic congestion well. Karl reflected how their roles had been reversed: throughout their married life, the calming influence had always been Nancy, not the hot-headed Karl. "I mean in front of the children," he said. "They shouldn't be hearing this."

"You really are something else. You think they don't know?"

In the mirror, Karl watched Olga advance on him. "OK, calm down, say hello to them for me." Then Olga almost disappeared from view, her breasts softly pressing into his back. "Tell them I'll take them for a burger on Wednesday."

"Tell them yourself," snapped Nancy. Olga's laughing eyes appeared over his shoulder and he suppressed a gasp as she gently cupped his balls. "Hi, Amy, hi, Tom."

Two small voices pulled at his heartstrings. "When are you coming home, Daddy?"

He covered Olga's hand with his, checking her, but stayed locked into her reflection. "Are they all right, Nancy?"

"Ecstatic. Look, we're nearly at school. Don't be late on Wednesday. Try and do something right for once."

"I'll call you tonight."

"Don't bother." There was another horn, and Nancy disconnected.

Olga took the phone and led him back into the bedroom. "They all right, yes, the children? What did she want, this early?" She sat beside him on the bed and eased him back against the pillows.

"They're fine," he said, glancing at the clock, "and she's right. I'd better get to the office."

Olga lay beside him and stroked his brow. "You poor baby, your wife put you on the guilt trip, yes?"

It was Karl's third morning in Olga's bed and he had not been back to his rented flat for the whole weekend, even for a change of clothes. Now he could feel himself hardening again, after less than an hour. He had called Olga from the Dorchester's lift lobby in the early hours of Saturday, moments after shaking hands with a bruised, chastened Boris and escorting Rigov to his room. When he saw her again she was standing on the Welcome mat, naked under her robe and still towelling her hair. Forgetting the vodka, they had launched themselves onto her canopied bed. He had entered her modest apartment in Hammersmith within thirty-five minutes of leaving the hotel and penetrated her sweet-smelling body inside fifty. "Karl, my darling Tartar," she had laughed afterwards, admiring his sweating body, "you really are a gift from God."

Flattered, Karl had given his most modest smile. Now Olga raised herself on her elbow as Karl's eyes moved over her breasts. "You love my bosom, no? Can't take your eyes off it." Olga was nothing if not classy. She told him her breasts had served her well because they were natural, her own divine gift. Silicone was for tramps, she said. True men preferred the real thing.

Karl Sergeyev could tell she fancied him as a soul mate and potential partner. As the weekend drew on she told him she wanted to resume the studies she had abandoned at eighteen and swore to reserve her assets for his exclusive use. They talked about it over shared vodka and, because Karl was such a jealous boy, she promised to tell the escort agency next week, or the week after at the latest.

His mobile rang just as things were getting interesting again. He saw Donna's number on the screen and pushed himself up against the pillows. "It's the commander's PA," he told her. "I have to take this."

"It's no problem," said Olga, kicking the duvet down the bed as she worked her magic. "Tell her you can work from home."

"Hi, Donna." The message was brief. Karl listened carefully, thanked her and cut the call. "I have to get going," he said, glancing at the clock. "Commander wants to see me at ten-fifteen and I need a change of clothes."

Olga continued arousing him. "Ah, yes, to chide you about your life of immorality."

"It's no joke, Olga. Not from what Donna says."

"All these women against you. But will you ask your friends about Tania today?" she said, disappearing again down his body.

"If I get the chance."

He felt her lips pull away from him and her face reappeared above his, eyes on fire. "But you promised!" she said, brushing her hair back and taking his head in her hands. Olga had been fretting about Tania all weekend, ever since her first call had gone to voicemail early on Saturday morning. Karl remembered her as the shy teenage girl perching on the staircase waiting for Olga to return with the champagne. Her disappearance was the only cloud over their otherwise perfect three nights and two days together. Olga told Karl she shared with three other girls in a small flat in Barons Court. She kept ringing every couple of hours, and with each failed call became more anxious.

This had never happened before, and she insisted something was wrong. Ever since Olga had befriended her, Tania would always text her to say she had reached home safely. That was the arrangement. She felt guilty about rushing off to have sex with Karl without first seeing Tania into a taxi: if anything bad had happened it would be her fault. And Karl's too, partly, she added through her tears. The least he could do was use his contacts at Scotland Yard to help find Tania.

"Look, I may not even see John today," said Karl. "He does a lot of work away from the office."

"No more excuses," she cried, dissolving into tears. "Bastard! You swear you love me and then you do nothing."

His lover's abrupt changes of gear were becoming a source of erotic fascination to Karl — he never knew where she would take him next. After two days and three nights of frenetic love-making, despite intervals of weeping about Tania, this was the first time she had actually applied the brakes. But with Olga, even restraint was arousing. "Tania will turn up, you'll see. Don't stop now," he moaned, gently pressing her head back down his body. "We've just got time."

"No! Something bad has happened," she shouted, banging his chest, "and you have to call your friends today." She got off the bed and picked up her robe. "Why will you not do this one thing for me?"

"And what am I supposed to do with this?" said Karl, staring down at his erection.

"You really want me to tell you?" she screamed, slamming the bathroom door.

CHAPTER
TWENTY-FOUR

Monday, 17 September, 10.33, the Fishbowl

Tieless, sipping in-house black coffee from a paper cup, Kerr watched Karl through the blinds as he made his way down the open-plan office towards the Fishbowl. Word had already reached him through the grapevine about the latest love of Karl's life. Minutes earlier Donna, always ahead of the game, had warned Kerr that Karl needed to see him and the news was not good. A few of Karl's friends called to him, throwing around the usual banter. Karl, elegant in navy single-breasted suit, crisp white shirt and yellow tie, was smiling and courteous to the end, but hardly broke step.

Kerr waited for the knock on the door, then had to call twice before Karl's head appeared, leaving the rest of him on the wrong side of the threshold. "You must be busy, boss. Shall I come back later?"

"No, of course not." In fact, Kerr had been working non-stop since arriving in the office just after seven. Langton's surveillance teams were in constant demand to monitor suspected terrorist targets, often operating beyond the capital, and Dodge would speak with him several times a day about complex undercover or agent operations. This morning he had drafted a statement for Kerr to sign about the siege in Hackney, in which Melanie was referred to as "Officer A".

Monday morning was the busiest time for administration, which he hated. There were the previous week's overtime claims to approve and the security authorisations for all covert operations to check, including Jack Langton's late-night callout by MI5 on Saturday. In addition, he had to disguise his officers' work against Ahmed Jibril by showing them assigned to other surveillance targets.

He gestured Karl to a seat, shrugging an apology as he speed-dialled Kestrel, his MI5 insider, and left his third message. "I need an urgent meet with you, as in crash, so ring me back as soon as you get this." That would be the final call. In the past, Kestrel had ignored Kerr in order to assert the fiction that he was a volunteer, a free agent. But, as Kerr had made clear when he'd had Kestrel lifted off the street and brought to him, nothing could have been further from the truth. On this occasion, Kerr found himself wondering if the MI5 man's reluctance was connected in some way to the suspicious things Kerr's team was uncovering.

Kerr swung back to his desktop. "Just let me do this." When he had finished he locked his email, squeezed round the desk and dropped into the other chair. "What's up?"

"It's bad, John. Commander's withdrawn my security vetting."

"You what?" Kerr stared at him in surprise. Removal of the vetting status was effectively "game over" for an officer on Weatherall's side of SO15 because every intelligence post required national security clearance.

"She's going to transfer me to uniform. She gave me the kiss of death, John. I'm on gardening leave from now. Official. She told me I'm not to come anywhere near the Yard."

"And why do you think she's done that?"

Uncomfortable, Karl shifted in his chair, looking for inspiration through the glass. "Well, to punish me, I suppose."

"For not keeping your dick in your trousers."

"It's not like that. Her name is Olga. Christ, all I did was to fall in love and the commander practically gave me a bloody ASBO."

"You're another victim in her drive for ethical correctness, I'm afraid. Conduct above reproach and all that."

"But I'm already separated from Nancy."

Karl and Olga had collided in the early hours of Saturday; today was Monday morning, and it was a safe bet that Weatherall had none of Kerr's informal channels of insider info — Kerr had picked up a rumour about Karl and an escort girl from another protection officer late on Saturday afternoon. As he spoke, Kerr was wondering how she could have got to hear about Karl's indiscretion so quickly. "How did she find out about it? Who told her?"

"Search me," said Karl, "but I'm not waiting around to find out."

Kerr shrugged in sympathy. "Look, it's not the end of the world. I know what she's like. This is only temporary, till you move back home. Do yourself a favour, Karl. Live like a normal husband and father and she'll change her mind."

"Like you?"

"I mean it, Karl." Kerr's landline buzzed, then his BlackBerry, but he ignored them both.

Karl was staring gloomily through the glass at his disappearing world. "She's firing me but it's none of their bloody business. It's domestic."

Kerr's mobile beeped again. "No, it's political, and I'm very sorry about it."

"Do you know the last time I was in uniform? Sixteen years ago. No way am I going back to that."

"You're being hasty, Karl. We all need you here. Place wouldn't be the same without you." Unable to resist any longer, Kerr picked up his BlackBerry, glanced at the screen and put it down. "Just hold on for a few weeks and everything will be fine."

"Too late. I just called Olga back. She's really upset for me. Been making some calls since I left for the office. Says I can work for a friend of hers till things settle down."

"What sort of friend?"

"He was at the party on Friday. A real high roller."

"A client, you mean."

"No way," said Karl, looking awkward. "An associate."

"What's his name?"

"Yuri Goschenko. I'm going to do some driving for him, starting this afternoon."

"Hang on, Karl. What do you know about this guy?"

"He has his own company. Eagle Security Services. Protection, bodyguarding, home alarms, that sort of thing. It's just part-time."

"Moonlighting, you mean."

"Chauffeur to start, while I work my notice and get my life sorted. Better than doing nothing, John."

"I'm just saying don't burn your bridges. We want you back here some day, so make sure you do some more checks on this guy before you get in too deep."

"You don't have to worry about me. This is one Russian helping another, that's all. Just like the English do."

"What's Goschenko's politics?"

"Making money." Karl was beginning to sound irritated.

"Both of us know he might be a hood, Karl, so watch your back."

Alan Fargo was loitering outside the door with the padlocked canvas bag 1830 used to transfer top-secret documents between offices. Kerr gave him a thumbs-up and hauled himself to his feet. "Look, is there anything you need right now?"

"I will be fine," said Karl, wearing his lopsided smile that said things would not be so bad, "and it's been very good to work with you. I'd like to buy you a beer some time. Perhaps with Nancy. I know she'd like to see you again."

"Send her my best. Take care of yourself and let's catch up soon," said Kerr, shaking hands. "And don't be frightened to dish the dirt on this guy."

As soon as Fargo had brought him up to speed Kerr hurried to his regular takeout, an Italian sandwich bar at the top of Strutton Ground. Because he ordered the same thing, a tuna Siciliana baguette, and paid with the right money, the owner's daughter often quietly served him before the rest of the queue.

"There is one more thing, John, a last favour." Karl had been stalking Kerr from the safety of the street market and almost collided with him outside the door.

"You've changed your mind," said Kerr, recovering quickly, "come to your senses, decided to go home to Nancy and the kids so we can rehabilitate you to the fold." He began walking at speed, heading back to Victoria Street and the office. "Walk with me."

Karl took Kerr's arm as they wove through the crowded market. He was taller and heavier set than Kerr and had to stoop to make himself heard. "John, it's about Olga."

"Don't tell me. She's married with kids and her old man has a contract out on you."

There was desperation in Karl's face. Kerr stopped in the middle of the thoroughfare. "You said it yourself, Karl," he said, as office workers threaded past them. "I'm up to my eyes."

"Two minutes, John," pleaded Karl, tugging at his arm like the biggest kid in the playground. They were in the firing line of a market trader hollering the price of

224

tomatoes. "Please, this is very personal. Unofficial, not for the office."

"No secrets in our team," said Kerr, turning back the way they had come. They found a bench opposite the fire station in Horseferry Road. Kerr opened his sandwich bag, tore the roll in two and handed one half to Karl. "So what's on your mind?"

"Olga has a friend, Tania, quite young, very presentable. Even beautiful, when she grows up."

"Don't tell me you've been shagging her as well," said Kerr, through a mouthful of tuna.

"Well, she's been missing since last Friday. The agency sent her to the same party where I met Olga. She never got home."

Kerr laughed. "And what kind of agency would that be, exactly? Friday to Monday? Get real, she's a hooker and he's fallen in love. It happens. Christ, Karl, you're living proof."

"No, you don't understand. Olga says Tania is special, like the kid sister she never had. They speak every day."

"Sister? How old?" Kerr was already checking his watch, chewing quickly.

"Quite young. Below twenty."

Kerr's mobile was ringing. "She went clubbing, buggered off to Romania."

"No. She's not from Romania, John. I saw her at the party. With Olga."

"Hold on a second, Mel," said Kerr, into the BlackBerry. He abruptly stopped chewing and swung round to Karl. "This was in Knightsbridge, yeah?"

"Flash house opposite the church."

Siren blaring, a fire engine pulled out of the station. Kerr had an eye on Karl's half of the baguette. Karl shook his head so he grabbed it back, took a bite and spoke into the mobile in one movement. "Mel, is Jack still there with you? . . . Tell him I need to see him this evening. I'll come out to the plot around nine . . . Fine. So, what's occurring?"

Karl held out his hand again but Kerr was engrossed in his phone call. The sandwich wrapper was about to blow from Kerr's lap so Karl screwed it up and tossed it into the waste bin. "Thanks for lunch," he mouthed, touching Kerr's arm and standing to leave.

Kerr gave him the thumbs-up.

As Melanie briefed him on the surveillance against Jibril's mobile phone contact in East Ham, Kerr watched his friend walk back through the market. In the past hour he had grown increasingly anxious about Karl. Fargo had just searched Yuri Goschenko for him in 1830, and the results were not reassuring. Karl's potential employer was on record as a Russian businessman-playboy, one of many post-Cold War millionaires with interests in steel and gas production. Moving to London in the late nineties, he had used a fraction of his wealth to start up a security company, offering bodyguard services and office and home protection to the capital's wealthy élite. There were yawning gaps in his business profile, and even the parts he could nail down were peppered with allegations of fraud, extortion and theft. Yuri Goschenko would not be receiving an Entrepreneur of the Year award any time soon.

Kerr badly wanted Karl back in SO15, and employment with a potential gangster would not help his rehabilitation. Olga's involvement also filled him with misgivings. Had Karl asked her to find him a job, or was this all her idea? Karl had joined Special Branch when he was only twenty-one and, once Kerr had worked on Weatherall and Ritchie, still had a bright career ahead of him. Could a professional escort really persuade him to throw everything away?

Karl was turning the corner into Strutton Ground when Kerr hailed him, shouting above the traffic. "Karl!" He turned as Kerr trotted up to him, still taking Melanie's update.

"Hang on, Mel," Kerr said, covering the mouthpiece. "Sorry, Karl. Things are crazy these past few days. Look, this isn't a good way to say thanks. Let's have that drink tonight. Late — say around eleven? And I want to meet your new girlfriend. You guys choose the venue and text me." Then Kerr was off, swerving through the market throng, taking his briefing from Melanie in the middle of lunchtime shoppers who carried on with their lives as if nothing bad was happening.

CHAPTER
TWENTY-FIVE

Monday, 17 September, 21.41, observation post, East Ham

For the Met's breed of health and safety fascists the observation post would have been a wet dream. To offer the best possible view of their targets, Jack Langton's sourcing officer had chosen the deserted roof space above a run-down row of shops in East Ham, just over a mile from Julia Bakkour's office on the other side of Wanstead Flats. It was cold, draughty, very damp and, at nine-thirty in the evening, almost pitch dark. It had been raining the whole evening and a steady stream of traffic swished along the soaking street below. The roof leaked and most of the floorboards were rotten or missing, so that hopping to the cameras by the window was like negotiating a minefield. Pinned to the wall was a mugshot of Samir Khan, code name Bravo, whose mobile number had been found on Jibril's Sim card. Beside it was a photograph of a second, unidentified man, code name Charlie. The Red team watchers had had to use extra staples to prevent the photographs curling away from the dripping plaster. In the farthest corner, where the floorboards were relatively safe, they had set up a camping table, two folding canvas chairs, flasks of coffee, a coolbox and a weak desk light. A ten-pound note lay on the table, weighed down by three pound coins.

As he climbed the back stairs John Kerr could smell the damp, mixed with aromas from the curry house beneath. Forcing the crooked door with his shoulder, he found Jack Langton and Melanie in sweaters and waterproofs. Perched high on bar stools, they operated three cameras on tripods. A heavy net curtain, stained and carefully torn to allow maximum lateral vision, was draped over the cracked window and, because the day's rain was still dripping through the roof, Langton had covered the gear with sheets of plastic. Kerr found him speaking into the electronic log as he worked the night-vision video. He turned to give Kerr a wave.

"Charlie returns carrying two orange plastic shopping bags. Bravo opens the front door. They're talking. Charlie goes inside with Bravo and the bags. Bravo out of the house and turns left. Can you take it, Mel? At . . . twenty-one-forty-two."

"Check." Melanie was already standing beside him, snapping rapid action stills, and acknowledged Kerr without losing pace. Langton left the video running, lit his pencil torch, skipped over the joists to one of the canvas chairs and reached for a flask. "Watch your step, John. Floor's a death trap."

Kerr tiptoed over to the window and looked through the viewfinder. The street opposite was a crowded terrace of small Victorian houses, some divided into ground-floor and first-floor flats. The few that had been carefully tended stood out from the rest, with freshly painted front doors, double-glazing, stone window ledges painted white and flowerpots in the lit porches. But most were dilapidated rented properties with tiles missing, flaking wall paint and collapsed fences. Khan's house was among the neglected. A cracked grey wheelie bin and discarded sofa filled the tiny front yard, cramped against a black 125cc Cobra scooter, and the black wrought-iron front gate had come off its bottom hinge. A couple of double-decker buses eased past each other in the narrow thoroughfare, obscuring Kerr's view for a few seconds. "Are they doing anything?" he asked. Charlie had disappeared inside and closed the battered front door, so he watched Samir Khan walk down the street.

"Looks like regular domestic stuff. Most of the people who drop by are young men. A couple we identified have cons for street robbery, theft and assault. Charlie got done last year for sexual assault. Three of them use the scooter, so probably uninsured. I'd say we're generally talking low-life criminality, John, not extremism. But Khan's in a different league. Very surveillance-conscious. Eyes everywhere, just like Jibril."

Kerr heard Melanie rattle off four shots and kept Khan in view. He was mid-twenties, wearing jeans, trainers and a black sweater. "What was Khan's connection to the airline conspiracy?" he asked.

"Email," said Langton, pouring coffee.

"Wrong," said Melanie, rattling off a couple more shots. "Facebook."

230

"So remind me why this guy isn't in jail," said Kerr, still tracking the target.

"Samir Khan wasn't a player, apparently. Just an online friend of a contact of an associate of the main man. Something like that. MI5 said they had to concentrate on crocodiles closer to the boat."

"Speaking of which I rang Kestrel again this morning and he's still taking the piss. Can you give him a pull for me tomorrow, Mel?"

"No problem."

Kerr watched Khan until he moved out of shot, then edged across to Langton, stepping over his motorcycle helmet. Langton had poured him some coffee in a plastic cup. Kerr sat in the other canvas chair and swung round to Melanie. "Want some?"

"She's gone herbal," said Langton, as Melanie shook her head. He leant back, stretched, and watched Kerr take a sip and wince.

"Jack, it's about the surveillance you did with MI5 Saturday night. In Knightsbridge?"

"Sure. What about it?"

"I was checking the authorisation this morning. What was the job about?"

"Well, it was totally their op," said Langton, and swigged some coffee. "A4 surveillance eyes only, as it turned out."

"Who were the targets?"

"No names given out. At least, not for me."

"So were they friend or foe?"

"Hard to say. We were covering two men in a bog-standard Ford Thames van. But it was definitely a babysitting job. Bit weird, actually, all very last minute. A4 were there to watch over them. I did the operational security."

"Where did it kick off?"

"Clapham. Why?" As Langton frowned, Kerr could almost hear his mind rewinding the event, self-protection instinct kicking in. "I know you didn't come to this hole just to look through a viewfinder, John. Who screwed up?"

"No one. It's just something Karl Sergeyev said this morning.

"Who was the desk officer, the sponsor?"

"No one showed. Trust me, the whole night was bloody strange."

Kerr gave the coffee another try. "What was your role, Jack?"

"The usual, stay well back with an ear on the comms and deter any overactive uniforms. Just as well, actually, cos one of their cars got a pull on the way to the plot."

"What was weird about it?"

"I got the call at home from their night-duty officer just after zero-two-thirty. By the time I bowled up around three they were already on their second cup of coffee, briefing done and dusted. The curtains were drawn tight over the picture boards but they'd obviously been looking at stills or video because the screen was up. And they'd definitely been given photos to take away. I clocked the master copy on the lectern. Two men, mid-thirties, Turkish appearance. One slim, prematurely receding hair, round glasses, intellectual type. The other guy looked a real gangster."

"Perhaps they're agents, doing some business. Maybe A4 were protecting them."

"Whatever, no way were they going to fill me in. Thing is, there was less than half a team, so this was not your regular A4 job. I mean, they can't have been expecting trouble because there were only four. Anorak geek who does their signals stuff, the bloke who works the covert rural observations with us now and again, and a couple of others," he said, lowering his voice. "Who's the girl with the big tits Justin was shagging last year? Bev or Jan or something? She put in a complaint."

"Sam," called Melanie, from the window.

"Her. Sorry. Plus a school-leaver type I hadn't seen before. Looked more like a desk officer than a watcher."

Someone was knocking gently at the door. Kerr swung round but Langton was already on the move, picking the money off the table. "Grub time." When he wrenched open the door, an Indian girl was standing there with two plastic bags. "Thanks, Safira, keep the change." He pushed the door closed with his hip and made his way back to the table. "It's no problem. Her old man thinks we're Drugs Squad watching the house two doors up." He opened a carton of onion bhajis.

"What else?"

"A4 picked their van up around oh-three-fifty, just off Clapham High Street. No address given. They led us to a six-, seven-bedroom place in Knightsbridge, collected some gear in cardboard boxes and left." He offered the carton to Kerr. "Help yourself."

Kerr shook his head. "Marston Street, yeah? Any counter-surveillance?"

"Nothing, and they seemed totally relaxed. Said thanks very much and stood me down. Would have earlier if I hadn't saved them from the cops. Home in bed by five, nappy detail at seven, totally knackered by eight, on the pitch at ten. Then the afternoon at your place."

"Who owns the house?"

"No idea, but whoever it was has moved on. I rode by earlier today. Shutters closed, no furniture and obviously unoccupied."

"Thanks, Jack. I'd better get going." Kerr stood up. "But keep me up to speed, yeah?"

"Sure. Like I say, most of the stuff was in cardboard boxes. But then these two guys backed the van up at right angles to the railings and brought something up from the basement."

"What was it?"

"Couldn't see. Like I say, they parked right across the pavement."

"Bloody hell, Jack. Why didn't you say?"

"I just thought . . . I dunno. It did seem a bit odd. But, like I say, the whole night was surreal."

Kerr was already pulling at the door. "Have you got your entry kit with you?"

Langton nodded at his bag. "Of course. What's up?"

"We need to take a look at that place right now." Kerr turned to the window. "Can you cover for an hour, Mel?"

"No problem, they're settling down for the night. Go. Just leave me the samosas."

CHAPTER
TWENTY-SIX

Monday, 17 September, 22.27, 36 Marston Street, Knightsbridge

Although it was Monday night, the streets were busy with cabs and limousines carrying high rollers to the clubs in Mayfair, and it was almost ten-thirty when they reached Marston Street. The house was empty, as Langton had already noted. Langton parked the team's four-year-old VW Golf between a Bentley and a Jaguar.

By Kerr's logic, a burglary in late evening was more defensible than in the middle of the night. Langton had seen the targets reverse the van to remove something from the basement, to the left of the entrance, so that was where he had decided they should make their entry. Langton opened the heavy-duty padlock to the iron gate in seconds and, once down the steps, they were hidden from the street. With Kerr directing the pencil torch, Langton quickly disabled the security system and went to work on the three locks.

"Come on, Jack," said Kerr, with a glance up to street level, "you told me three minutes tops."

"So shine it on the lock, not the back of my hand." Langton defeated the locks in just over two. They stepped inside and closed the door behind them. Langton's flashlight picked out a double sink to their left and a wrought-iron spiral staircase with brass handrail diagonally opposite the door. They climbed the stairs to check out the two ground-floor rooms. "See? Deserted, just like I told you," said Langton, impatient. "So can we go right now, before we both drop in the shit?"

Kerr knelt and examined a couple of severed video cables snaking up from the floor, then shone his torch at two brackets on the wall of the reception room. "What kind of host wants to spy on the guests?" Back in the hallway, Kerr nodded up the wide staircase and reached for Langton's bag. "Take a quick look upstairs, Jack. I'll hang onto this."

"What am I looking for?" Langton's beam was already bouncing up the staircase.

"Signs of past life."

Kerr spiralled back down to the old kitchen. Apart from an American fridge to the left of the staircase, in the corner nearest the door, the room was empty. He ran his finger at random along the tiled floors and walls, checking for dust and grease. The surfaces were completely clean, and the floor smelt of disinfectant.

He switched off his torch and took out one of Langton's infrared lamps. In the ultraviolet light a narrow smear of blood glowed on the floor. With a swab kit from Langton's bag he took a sample, just as Langton padded down the staircase. "Anything?"

236

"Zilch, but there's a chill all the way through." Langton sniffed. "They've used a lot of antiseptic upstairs, too."

"This whole area has been completely scrubbed out."

Langton shone his torch at the walls. "Looks cleaner than an operating theatre."

"Except they missed a blood trace on the floor," said Kerr, handing Langton the swabs. He checked his watch: 22:43. "I have to shoot. Close it down yourself, will you, Jack?" He was already heading for the door. "I have to be somewhere else." ·

Kerr took a cab from Marston Street to the smart wine bar Olga had chosen for their meeting in a quiet mews behind Knightsbridge, within walking distance of Harrods. Karl was nowhere to be seen but he found Olga perched on a bar stool sipping a double vodka and tonic. They had never met, but Kerr recognised her straight away. She was just as he had imagined her, fabulous in navy mini skirt, tight silk blouse and exotic earrings. He held out his hand, but Olga slipped from the stool and kissed him on both cheeks, as if they were already lifelong friends.

Despite the late hour she smelt of fresh flowers, as if she had just stepped out of the shower. She asked what he would like and ordered him a gin and tonic. The barman called her Olga and put the drink on her tab. She had saved Kerr a stool by the bar, but he wanted their meeting to be private.

"Let's grab a table," he said, picking up their drinks.

"Sure, if you like." Olga spoke as if she would have preferred to remain on display.

For the cop to observe, and the working girl to be seen, both professionals prefer a clear view of the entrance. Kerr got there first because a red-faced toff in striped shirt, expensive jeans and brown suede loafers intercepted Olga to offer her a drink. She kissed him, too, called him Henry, and wafted over to join Kerr.

Seeing Kerr's expression, she flicked back her hair and laughed. "He's fine. Everybody knows me in here." She clinked glasses and pulled a third chair up to the table. "Anyway, Karl will be here in a minute."

"Tell me how you two met."

"There was a private party for a lot of big cheeses. Karl was bodyguard to one of them. Lucky me."

"And you were looking after Yuri Goschenko."

"He's an admirer who likes to be seen with me. Nothing more. It happens a lot."

"I bet."

"Enough to give Karl a job as a favour to me. Is that so bad?"

"Where was the party?"

"Close to here, off Wilton Crescent, not far from the embassies." Karl had appeared from nowhere and sat down beside them. He kissed Olga and shook hands with Kerr, who felt vaguely surprised he had missed Karl's entrance. "The guests were screened off. But noisy," said Karl. "No, I didn't get any names," he said, seeing Kerr's questioning look, "but one of the royals was there."

"Really? You sure about that?"

238

"Audi with the special marker parked down the street."

Kerr turned to Olga. "Did you see who it was?"

"Olga wouldn't know any of those people," said Karl, before she could answer.

Kerr looked between them. "So how about you two? Who went for who?"

"Whom," said Karl, instinctively, always the linguist, then gave an embarrassed laugh. "Look, it was magnetic, John," he said, hand moving to his breast pocket as a mobile rang, "and there's no need to take the piss."

"Relax, darling, it's for me," purred Olga, reaching into her handbag and checking the screen. "I have to take this, so sorry." She kissed Karl and moved back to the bar.

"We share the same ring tone," said Karl, embarrassed.

"Could be awkward." Kerr detected a spark of irritation in Karl. He seemed to have changed even in the twelve hours since they had parted in the market. Perhaps it was his escape into a place where no one could tell him what to do. He wore the same suit but seemed more assertive, as if he had already adjusted to his new world.

"Look, John, this happens. She is impossible to resist, my woman."

Kerr looked across to the bar, where Olga was still on the phone, laughing and flicking her hair. "And still working, I take it?"

"Look, are you going to help us find Tania or not?" said Karl, staring him down.

Kerr's BlackBerry vibrated before he could reply, breaking the tension. Although it was more than a year since their last meeting, the text from Robyn, Gabriella's mother, was as economical as ever: "In town till fri eve worried abt g we need to talk can u make 7 wed."

"I need to deal with this," he said, and typed, "8 is better," hoping she would not see it as another round in their domestic conflict.

"Trouble is, John, what I told you this morning was not quite correct," he said, as Kerr locked the BlackBerry and drained his glass. "Olga tells me she thinks Tania is about fourteen."

Kerr was angry now. "A child?"

"That's why she's so worried."

"For God's sake, Karl."

"The girl is Turkish. To me she looked older. The makeup, the clothes."

"Do you have any idea what you're getting yourself into here?"

"I swear I didn't know this when I saw you this morning."

The place was filling rapidly with Henry lookalikes, who crowded against their table. Kerr found himself and Karl standing-room deeper inside the bar as Robyn buzzed back, "ok usual place", but he still had to raise his voice to be heard. "I'll need a sample of her DNA. Hairbrush will do. And a photograph."

"Sure. I'll see what I can find."

"Tomorrow morning, first thing. I'll text the time and place."

Olga appeared with another gin and tonic, and vodka for Karl. "I have champagne at the bar, of course," she said, draping her arm round Karl's neck and kissing him full on the lips. "You're not telling John bad things about me, are you, darling?" She pouted, then wove back through the punters. Karl wiped lipstick from his mouth with the back of his hand.

"Olga put Tania up for this, didn't she?" said Kerr, moving in close. "And now she's shit scared because she knows the type of games these people play." A couple of blondes in little black dresses were picking up on Kerr's anger, so he spoke directly into Karl's ear. "How could she send a fourteen-year-old kid to mix with people like that?"

"Tania had the body of a young woman, and Olga didn't know it would be like that. Look at her, she's too beautiful to do anything bad."

"Yeah, sure. A real pro." The words hit home, and Karl bowed his head. "Who is she working for, Karl?" Kerr stepped back and idly stirred his drink, waiting for an answer while the women looked across at them, timing their move.

"Why should she be working for anyone? John, why are you so cynical? Look, this is a closing chapter in her life. She's a young woman who wants to go to college and study. I'm going to help her. What's wrong with that?"

"Whatever you say." Kerr slid his glass aside. "Now let me tell you how I see it. You're an intelligence

241

officer, Karl. Found yourself at a party involving prostitutes and an underage girl, attended by an official from a foreign government and probably a few Brits with high-security clearance. Classic targets for blackmail, but you didn't make any effort to get the idents. This was a potential breach of national security, my friend, and you should have reported it. End of."

Before Kerr could reach for his drink Karl grabbed at his forearm. "But I did, John," he shot back, eyes blazing, "and all Rigov's calls, too. I copied the whole fucking log. Gave it all to Mr Ritchie. And how do they thank me? By sacking me!"

CHAPTER
TWENTY-SEVEN

Several metres out of her depth, Commander Paula Weatherall shifted uncomfortably, cleared her throat and tried to sound authoritative. She had developed a cold over the weekend and it was making her feel vulnerable. "Philippa, I really need help here." She had chosen to wear full uniform to meet Philippa Harrington, director-general of MI5, soon to be Dame, but was already regretting it. At Thames House, the display of rank actually seemed to diminish her. Weatherall fidgeted as Harrington frowned at her across her slim-line desk. She knew she must sound like a woman sinking fast.

Three chairs were set in a semicircle facing the desk, each lower than the DG's own executive model in soft brown leather. Harrington was well known for her manipulation of partners and allies. For civil-service equals and American intelligence officials she offered a clear view of the Thames from one of the comfortable armchairs. For discussion with MI5 staff she used the conference table. But the lower orders she corralled at

243

her desk, just as her headmistress had done at Roedean. This morning she had directed SO15's overdressed head of intelligence to the junior seat with her back to the private office door.

Her desk was clear, except for a document marked "UK EYES ONLY" with the Security Service crest and motto, "Regnum Defende". While Weatherall waited for an answer, Harrington checked her email on one of the three desktop screens, presumably to demonstrate she had more important things to attend to. Eventually she looked across the desk again. "As you already acknowledged, this was an operational decision, a matter for the police. For you," she sighed, "in this unfortunate case."

Weatherall sniffed and dabbed her nose with the damp tissue. She was feeling increasingly isolated. Jibril's release on Sunday afternoon had done nothing to allay her feeling that John Kerr had been right all along. Had she taken his advice and let Jibril run, he might have led them to the bomb factory, in which case they could have captured the terrorists before they could make their bombs lethal. The thought that she was partly responsible for such terrible loss of life troubled her almost as much as the need to save her own skin. And with the inevitable inquiry looming into the manner of Jibril's arrest at Vauxhall station, she needed to demonstrate that her judgement on the day had been reasonable.

This morning she was looking to Harrington for backup and was about to be sorely disappointed. "With respect, Philippa," she continued, "all I want is a public display of partnership. We're in this together, after all."

The director-general winced visibly at the use of her first name without invitation. "Absolutely not. You started this operation without any reference to us. You believed Ahmed Jibril was a suicide bomber . . ."

"Acting on SIS intelligence from Yemen."

". . . and apparently gave the go-ahead to shoot him," the DG said, ignoring the interjection. "But it transpired that he wasn't. He was unarmed. The only certainty is that your Mr Jibril was about to catch a Tube or overground train."

"To the bomb factory, possibly."

Harrington gave a thin smile. "Which we will never know because you arrested him prematurely. Anyway, the others in the hideout most certainly were suicide bombers. You elected to stop Mr Jibril instead. Ironic, but *che sarà*." She slid the dossier across the desk. "Clearly, your operation had nothing to do with the Service. How could it, since no one had the courtesy to notify us? The Note in there sets out our general position. Very much *post hoc*, of course, in view of your failure to consult. Want me to run through it with you?"

"That won't be necessary, thank you," said Weatherall, tightly. The room fell silent while she tried to absorb the three pages of densely worded text and the DG looked busy again at her computer screens. Weatherall always found intelligence documents difficult to unravel. The Note included a couple of bog-standard intelligence assessments from the Joint Terrorism Analysis Centre, based at Thames House, and a paragraph from MI5's G Branch, which dealt with the threat from international terrorism. This offered a guesstimate of the number of radicalised Muslims, trained *jihadis* and bomb factories in the UK, and a summary of its efforts to "drain the swamp" of terrorists.

There was no mention of Ahmed Jibril until the top of page three, where the Service opted for neutrality, neither fingering him as a terrorist nor excusing him as an innocent. After several briefings from 1830 since her arrival in SO15, even Weatherall knew enough to expect details of Jibril's entry documentation and a financial profile. But this morning she could not pin down a single shred of quality subject analysis.

She ploughed through to the end with growing dismay. Philippa Harrington's people had used hundreds of words to say nothing until the final paragraph, where there was "disappointment" about the failure to consult MI5 from the start and the usual cop-out that operational matters were "solely a matter for the police". She sighed as she realised the Note amounted to a long-winded indictment with a single charge: Commander Paula Weatherall had screwed up. It heightened her sense of loneliness. Dismayed, she closed the dossier and slid it back across the desk.

"Make sense?" demanded the DG, impatiently.

"Seems a little thin on the personal profiling. I'd like my officers to do some work on Jibril's financial profile."

"Absolutely not," said Harrington, her head jolting up. "My Service will sponsor any new leads on Ahmed Jibril."

Weatherall looked across in surprise. "So you have people working on this case?"

"That's an assumption," said Harrington, swatting her again. "Always unreliable in our kind of work."

"Are you suggesting you want me to clear everything with you first?"

"I'm saying we have the lead and require you to do nothing. Frankly, I advise you to lay off the man you almost shot dead," said Harrington, looking over Weatherall's uniform. "And if you value our partnership so highly, perhaps you should have restrained your Mr Kerr from breaching every protocol in the book. Our joint group is there for a purpose, after all. To agree surveillance targets. This is what happens when one of your senior officers goes off on a jaunt of his own."

"Senior?" said Weatherall, blowing her nose again.

Harrington had acquired a pair of bifocals and shot Weatherall a look of mock surprise. "He's been in this game a lot longer than you, if you don't mind me saying so, and in my book that spells senior and potential trouble."

"I've already spoken to him."

"That may not be enough." Before Weatherall could collect herself, Harrington opened her desk drawer and removed a single sheet of paper. "While we're on the matter of the troublesome Mr Kerr," she said, scanning the text, "I'm told he was interfering in one of our technical operations last night. A bit of overactive, unauthorised snooping. Freelance again, I presume, paddling his own canoe." She paused, and Weatherall felt crushed under her scrutiny. "Would you like to know what it says?"

"Are you going to tell me?"

Instead of answering, Harrington removed her glasses, pressed a button under her desk and stood up to indicate the interview was over. "He triggered one of our remote counter-intrusion devices." As she walked Weatherall to the door the PA entered.

"Intrusion?"

"It happens," the DG looked Weatherall up and down, "and I'm assuming from your reaction you know nothing about it. But your tits are in the mangle, sister. You urgently need to get Kerr back on the leash, restore trust between us, if we're to be serious about saving your skin."

Weatherall knew it was an orchestrated move to inflict maximum humiliation in front of a junior member of staff. She flushed as the PA looked away in embarrassment. "Which operation are we talking about?"

"Alison here can give you the background," the DG said, "but I'd appreciate a call once you've spoken to him. There's no place for mavericks in this line of work, trespassing, crashing around on our patch. What we need from the police is a sharper effort to prevent the next attack. High-visibility patrols, stops and searches in the street, that sort of thing."

"That's very much a uniform responsibility." Weatherall sniffed.

"And the kind of partnership we need, these days, as I know the commissioner agrees. Leave the intelligence aspects to us and our international allies."

248

Weatherall half-heartedly offered her hand as the PA held the door, but Harrington was already turning back to her desk.

Because mobile phones and pagers were prohibited inside Thames House, Weatherall had to wait a couple of minutes before they located hers from the rack behind the reception desk. She called up Barry, her civilian driver, and saw the Toyota turning into the Embankment as she walked down the steps. She was speed-dialling Donna from the rear seat as soon as they pulled away from the kerb.

"I need to speak with DCI Kerr in my office now."

"He's on the plot in Kentish Town," lied Donna, who had no idea where Kerr was.

"So get him back to the Yard. I'll be at the office in ten minutes."

Glimpsing the driver's reproachful eyes in the rear-view mirror, Weatherall turned to the Thames. Since she had told him he was to be replaced by a woman from the government car service, Barry had worn the saggy look of a man whose days were numbered. Weatherall sneezed, resigning herself to another bad day at the office.

CHAPTER
TWENTY-EIGHT

Tuesday, 18 September, 10.23, Lambeth

Kerr was less than a mile away when he took Donna's call, greeting forensic scientist Anne Harris with a kiss on the cheek. For Kerr's special requests, they always met under the gloomy Victorian railway arches on the opposite side of Lambeth Bridge from Thames House, with the lab practically in view. She glanced at his Italian raincoat with the collar up and told him he looked furtive.

Kerr took out his BlackBerry and shrugged an apology as he received Donna's summons. "I'm in Lambeth."

"Wrong, you're racing back from Kentish Town."

Kerr cut the call and handed Harris a plastic exhibits envelope. Earlier that morning he had walked to the end of Strutton Ground, at a safe distance from the Yard, where Karl was waiting to slip him Tania's hairbrush and a photograph. The exhibits envelope contained the brush and the swabs from Marston Street. "Just the basic DNA for now, Anne, if you get the chance. But there may be a follow-up." Harris had just sent him an invitation to her post-divorce celebration. At the wrong side of fifty, he thought she looked good in her raincoat and waterproof hat, curvy and fresh-faced. "You sure this is OK? I mean, it won't drop you in it?"

Anne Harris was one of the country's foremost authorities on the forensic interpretation of petechiae, the tiny specks of blood that may prove a victim has been strangled. She had spent all her working life in the Met's forensic laboratory, before its absorption into the Forensic Science Service. "Poor girl. Is she alive or dead?"

"Yeah."

"You really love this 'need to know' stuff, don't you?" Harris was famous in her modest way. Every unofficial meeting with Kerr was a risk to her career. But the cause was good, and she could be sure Kerr would have all the bases covered. "And you know I'll have to give some sort of reason."

"You'll think of something. It's an HCR, Anne, you told me yourself."

Kerr's requests, though rare, required complete secrecy and use of expensive laboratory resources without trace. He described them as favours, but she rationalised them to herself as hot-case reviews, carried out in the national interest.

"I'll call you in a couple of days."

"Perfect," said Kerr, pushing the rain hat to one side and kissing her cheek again. "Have a great party."

He reached the Yard in seven minutes and tossed his raincoat at Donna's coat-stand. "Smartarse," she murmured, waving him into Weatherall's office.

There were no pleasantries. "I understand you made a covert search of a house in Knightsbridge without authorisation," Weatherall said accusingly, even before he had sat down. Without being invited Kerr took the chair nearest her desk, thinking fast. While she checked her notes he glanced at a flip chart in the corner of the room, covered with scrawled speaking notes in green felt-tip. The title was "Heraclitus and the State of Permanent Flux: My Champion of Change Management".

"Marston Street," she said. "What the hell were you doing there?"

He knew Weatherall had just returned from Thames House, and assumed she must have learnt about his trespass from Philippa Harrington. That meant either someone had told MI5 about him and Jack Langton, or else they had a remote technical operation running. He dismissed the first, because he and Jack had told no one about their clandestine visit.

His mind was racing back over the blood traces and the MI5 surveillance team watching a couple of thugs remove something from the same house in the darkest hours of Sunday morning. Watching or protecting? And what was so secret that they'd had to reverse their van right up to the railings? Weatherall's outburst had just made things even more complicated: as he considered his reply, he now had to figure out why his illicit search had excited the interest of the director-general herself. On the flip chart he noticed Weatherall had misspelt "Heraclitus" with a K and a Y.

252

Weatherall poured some water and drank it in one gulp, her eyes flickering to the spot where Kerr's tie should have been. The desk was covered with thick brown policy files and she looked stressed out. Kerr noticed she was already more than halfway through the litre bottle, and wondered if it was the first of the day.

"I was following up on some info from Karl Sergeyev," replied Kerr, calmly. "He found himself at a dodgy party attended by a Russian principal called Anatoli Rigov, a handful of Britain's great and good and a couple of hookers. Always an interesting combination. Sex, drugs and probably video, for all we know." Weatherall was making notes, so he paused to let her catch up, like a barrister watching the judge's hand. "It was a national security issue and he says he reported it. Didn't Bill Ritchie brief you?"

She looked up in surprise. "And what has that got to do with you?"

Kerr shrugged. "No one else wants to run with it."

"How the hell do you know?"

"Am I wrong?"

"Assumptions are always unreliable in our kind of work," she said, repeating Harrington's phrase. "Who did you take with you?"

"Rolled up on my own," he bluffed.

"Are you sure about that?" she demanded, scribbling again. Since returning from Thames House Weatherall had changed out of her uniform into a faded dark green tartan suit. Waiting for Kerr to reply, she squeezed out of her jacket, revealing an overwashed Met-issue shirt with epaulettes. One of the buttons came undone in the

253

exertion, revealing a flash of bra. It had lost its whiteness, as washed-out as its owner. He stayed silent while she checked her notes. "Who signed the authorisation?"

"It wasn't intrusive. And whoever organised it has gone, probably taking their blackmail material with them." He paused again while Weatherall twisted to drape the jacket over her chair, like an old-style detective out of the movies. Christ, she'd be turning up in braces next. "Anyway, the estate agent let me borrow the keys," he lied again, wondering how much detail Harrington had given her.

As Weatherall swung in her chair to reach a box of tissues, a shoulder of the jacket slipped free. "Who else have you spoken to about this?"

"No one. Why would I? I'm just wondering, you know. There's a potential security breach here, surely. Shouldn't we be notifying Cabinet Office?"

"Mind your own damned business."

"I'll take that as a 'No', then," murmured Kerr, as Weatherall sneezed heavily into a single inadequate tissue, flashing more bra. She dropped the Kleenex on her desk, surreptitiously wiped her hand on her skirt and picked up her pen.

"I employ you to run my covert policing unit, and you acted way outside your brief. For the second time in less than a week. This is none of your business."

"I think it is, ma'am, because of what Karl Sergeyev reported. Anything to do with national security is exactly our business. It's what we used to do in Special Branch. What SO15 should be doing now."

"Let me be the judge of that," said Weatherall, grabbing more tissues. She dropped the used one into the bin. "I trust you're not pursuing any other private adventures, Mr Ritchie, that I know absolutely nothing about?" To give herself more space she pushed aside a couple of files, inadvertently knocking over the family photograph. Her jacket slipped to the floor. "Do you have any idea how close I came to disciplining you again today?" she snapped, disappearing for a moment behind the desk.

Kerr leant over to rescue the photograph and caught a glimpse of Weatherall, her partner and teenage daughter in their Sunday best, as flushed as if they had been at the communion wine. "Can I ask, ma'am, what it is about me you don't like?"

"You need to become integrated," she said, as she reappeared with the jacket, red-faced and nodding at the flip chart, "to embrace change. You're too set on doing your own thing, taking the law into your own hands, as with the whole Jibril thing and now this ridiculous unauthorised search."

With the mention of Jibril, Kerr guessed Philippa Harrington had also been giving her a hard time about his unauthorised surveillance without putting MI5 on notice. Harrington was notorious for her weaponry of put-downs, condescension and threats veiled as advice. Wondering how many she had brought to bear this morning, he spoke out, undeterred: "But we still believe Ahmed Jibril is a terrorist."

"We?"

"I," he corrected. Kerr's priority now was to conceal his team's secret investigation into Jibril. In the Fishbowl on Friday afternoon they had stepped up to the plate to take risks on his behalf. His duty was to protect them by keeping everything secret, strictly "need to know". If Weatherall could be as worked up as she was over his look inside an empty house, how violently would she react if she knew about Justin's burglaries over the weekend?

Until he reached the truth Kerr would operate with his team beneath the wire, out of sight of Weatherall and Ritchie.

"Ma'am," he continued, "MI6 gave Jibril to us for a reason and I'm still convinced this man is a *jihadi*. And I believe you feel uneasy about his release, deep down."

"Drop it," snapped Weatherall. "This is for MI5. You do nothing more on this man without clearance and a specific request from Philippa's people."

"I understand," he said.

Weatherall tried to replace the jacket but gave up and laid it untidily on the air-conditioning vent. Beneath all the bluster she looked chastened, like a victim of bullying. "From now on you work only on targets agreed with MI5," she said. "Nothing else."

"Right." Yes, he thought, Harrington had been applying serious pressure.

"So take this as a final warning. We're a team in SO15. Individualists have no place here, and your corporate profile is practically non-existent," she said emphatically, as her shirt gaped open even farther. This time she spotted Kerr's glance and fastened the button.

256

As she dismissed him she was already reaching for a blue ring binder marked "Institute of Management". "Make sure you learn something from this. And on your way out tell Donna to find Mr Ritchie for me."

Weatherall's PA was already dialling as Kerr grabbed his raincoat in the outer office. "She wants to see . . ."

"Bill Ritchie. Yes, I know."

"You got this place bugged, Donna?" smiled Kerr. "And can you ask Alan Fargo to drop by?"

"I already did that, too," she joked, looking past him.

"You're kidding," he said, as Fargo appeared in the doorway.

She put her hand over the mouthpiece. "And Sir Theo Canning rang. National Crime Agency. Asking me for your number. He wants you to call him *tout de suite*." She held out a piece of paper. "Says he'll make it worth your while."

CHAPTER
TWENTY-NINE

Tuesday, 18 September, 11.17, Farnborough airfield

To bring Anatoli Rigov home, Moscow provided a private jet to fly him from Farnborough airfield in Hampshire, southwest of London. In Karl's absence, the Yard found another liaison officer to escort him from the embassy, a deferential, pinstriped spare from the Royalty Protection Squad with muscle but no background in intelligence work. At the VIP reception desk, Rigov clapped him on the back and sent him away with his deepest respects to all at Buckingham Palace.

Rigov's Bombardier Learjet 40XR waited among seven others on the tarmac, but he had one more appointment before he could sink into its plush leather seats for the journey home. As Boris disappeared with his escort, Rigov slipped away from the reception area and into another vehicle waiting for him outside, a four-year-old silver Peugeot. The driver was a Russian in his thirties, harder than Boris and twice as sharp, who only addressed Rigov when he was spoken to. They rejoined the M25, then raced west along the M40,

Rigov staying silent until they reached the outskirts of Stratford-upon-Avon.

The driver dropped him ten metres from an Italian restaurant off Church Street, within a short walk of the Royal Shakespeare Theatre. He handed Rigov an unsealed white envelope and a ballpoint pen, then drove away to wait for him by the cricket ground on the other side of the river. The restaurant was in an ancient building with its original oak beams and uneven doors and windows, a private place with subdued lighting, the tables separated by thick black oak pillars supporting the low ceilings. Rigov's lunch guest was waiting for him in the corner farthest from any natural light and opposite the staircase leading below ground to the cloakrooms. They had arrived before the lunchtime rush, with only three of the twenty or so tables occupied.

Rigov had chosen the location because it was close to the motorway, where he could quickly lose himself in the traffic, and far enough from Cheltenham, where his secret agent lived and worked. They had met here once before, in the winter of 2007, shortly after Rigov had recruited him; both had enjoyed the risotto.

The agent stayed seated as Rigov joined him and shook his hand. In these public surroundings, both men remained nameless and chose their words with care. The agent was in his late forties, short and paunchy, with lank hair dyed a gingery brown, and stained, roll-your-own-tobacco fingers. He wore the faded jeans, black T-shirt and baseball shoes of a man in midlife crisis. For eighteen years he had been employed as a low-paid technical officer at GCHQ, the British government's gigantic listening station in Cheltenham. For the past three of these he had also worked for Anatoli Rigov, passing information on logistical planning, strategic priorities and, in two especially bountiful years, passwords and an encryption key.

To the FSB, successor to the KGB and equally deadly, he was the most satisfactory of espionage recruits, a volunteer motivated solely by greed. Their prime asset, born and brought up in Gloucester, displayed none of the politics, ideology or fear that made other cases so demanding. This relationship required nothing more than the occasional heavy drink and regular payments from Moscow into a secret account in Grand Cayman.

No one in the restaurant would hear Rigov's foreign accent. At his bidding, the agent ordered for them both, risotto and large glasses of red wine. Rigov had already decided this would be their final lunch and the last time they would see each other. The signs that all was not well had been evident to him since May: within a month of being arrested for driving under the influence, his sole intelligence asset in this quiet corner of the world had deserted his wife for a local barmaid twenty years younger, then promptly been accused of drunkenness and sexual harassment at work. He swore on his mother's life that the allegation was rubbish, but Rigov recognised the crumbling life of a stressed agent in middle age and sensed danger. In the FSB man's long experience, one indiscretion so easily led to another. Left unattended, the dominoes might collapse all the way to his office in Moscow.

They talked for a while, inconsequential chatter about anything but drink and sex, until the risotto arrived. Rigov waited for his agent to order more wine and offer his *mea culpa*.

The man picked up his fork. "Look, I'm sorry about this. Really." The voice was West Country, slow and soft, but Rigov picked up the hint of desperation, the plea of a failure needing money for a new life with a younger woman.

Rigov gave him the smile he had used against Karl Sergeyev. "No hard feelings. As I always said, we met as friends and that is how we will part."

"This stuff in the office is all bollocks." He leant forward, invading the Russian's personal space, his gaze intense. "Honestly. It'll blow over. I can handle it."

Rigov slowly shook his head. "But they may review your security clearance," he said quietly, holding his ground, "which eliminates your usefulness to me."

"No. I'll dig myself out of this shit. Promise."

"And in the meantime you need money. I understand completely." The smile was still there as the envelope appeared in Rigov's hand. He slid the agent's plate to one side as he handed it across the table. "Which is why we are continuing the transfer for two more months, as a goodwill gesture. We wait until things settle, then we meet again." He pressed the envelope into the man's hand. "But you have to sign on the dotted line."

Rigov had remembered his agent wore glasses for reading. As he nervously pulled the single sheet of paper from its envelope and fumbled with the spectacles case, Rigov held the pen directly over his agent's food and clicked the end twice, squirting two streams of clear liquid into the risotto. "These days, we all have to satisfy the bean counters," he said. Rigov scribbled on the envelope to demonstrate the pen did not work, then produced another from his jacket and handed it across the table. "With a pen that writes." He smiled.

The signing was a charade, for the account was already closed and the agent doomed the moment he swallowed his food and settled their bill in cash. The phial in Rigov's magic pen contained a new poison developed by the FSB, whose scientists had exploited the European *E. coli* epidemic in 2011 to develop an even more aggressive variant, resistant to every known treatment. In the days to come the bacterium would quietly embed itself in the agent's gut. Within a week he would suffer stomach cramps, quickly followed by diarrhoea, vomiting, collapse of the nervous system, kidney failure and death.

CHAPTER
THIRTY

Tuesday, 18 September, 13.47, River Thames

Because it was closest to the station exit, Kestrel, John Kerr's mole within MI5, always travelled to work in the third carriage of his Jubilee Line train from Stanmore to Westminster. Whenever possible he stood by the second set of double doors, so that he could be first onto the escalator for the brisk ten-minute walk to "Toad Hall", the fun name by which MI5 employees referred to Thames House, their headquarters.

For the journey home, around five-forty-five every weekday evening, Kestrel always boarded the fifth carriage. His routine breached the first principle of tradecraft, which required intelligence officers to avoid regular patterns of behaviour. It was a curious lapse from a man whose job was to deal with security breaches.

This morning he was much later than usual, close to lunchtime. Waiting to join Kestrel's train at Baker Street, Melanie spotted him in the crowded carriage exactly where he was supposed to be, complete with shabby blue raincoat and copy of the *Financial Times*. He was shorter than most other men in the carriage and appeared to be experimenting with a comb-over. He evidently clocked her the moment she boarded the train. This morning she guessed his reliance on the second law of deceit; no overt recognition of people you knew was for personal, not professional, reasons.

As Melanie moved up the carriage towards him, he turned away and buried himself in the newspaper. "You didn't return John's calls," she said quietly, squeezing in close between a couple of rucksacks, "and he needs to have a chat today. Right now, in fact."

They were slowing on the approach to Westminster. Kestrel looked around and tried to appear cool, but Melanie saw panic in his eyes. "I'm due in the office, for God's sake," he hissed. "I've got meetings."

Melanie's hand came over the top of the paper. "So throw a sickie." The train stopped and the doors whooshed open. "You know where to go."

She followed him out of the station and watched him turn left, calling the office with his excuses as he crossed the Embankment towards Westminster Bridge. Then she hurried back down into tunnel, taking the Tube to Tower Hill.

Kerr was loitering by Westminster Pier. He watched Kestrel purchase two boat tickets to Tower Bridge and waited for him to board first.

Kestrel's real name was Jeremy Thompson, and he was a middle-ranking officer in MI5. Because he doubled as John Kerr's agent of duress, discretion was vital. They had used this method twice before, and today the river was perfect for their meeting, visibility reduced by grey cloud and drizzle.

Kerr waited for the crew to cast off before joining him in the open by the small deck on the stern, separated from the saloon by toilets and a storage cabin, where the engines would camouflage their voices. The boat was empty, apart from a German family in waterproofs being blown about on the foredeck and a scattering of French retirees in the saloon buying drinks and crisps from the female deckhand. Without any prospect of tips, the coxswain had abandoned his running commentary on famous sights.

Kerr had originally phoned Kestrel early on Friday morning because he needed the inside story on Ahmed Jibril. But things had moved on in the intervening four days: right now he was preoccupied with the heat coming from Philippa Harrington about his illicit search in Knightsbridge. Complaints from MI5's lower orders were routine: why should Kerr's misbehaviour be attracting the anger of the DG herself?

Kestrel looked gloomy as Kerr gave his account, fixing his eyes on their soapy wake as they sailed downstream towards Waterloo. When he had finished, Kerr tapped him on the shoulder. "So how did they get to me, Jerry?" At their very first meeting Kestrel had told Kerr he hated any shortening of his name; Kerr used it the whole time. "Must have been from an OP or remote camera."

"Or cell site on your mobile," said Kestrel, looking away to the riverbank.

"No chance," said Kerr. "So why would they keep CCTV on an empty house? And, more to the point, why didn't you tell me?"

"I'm in vetting, for Christ's sake," said Kestrel, in exasperation, "not in the loop any more."

This was true, to an extent. When they had first met, Kestrel had been working as a liaison officer. But he was being disingenuous, for Kerr knew that his current job was in the policy secretariat, with access to the director-general's private office, and chapter and verse on MI5's strategic planning. In some respects Kerr judged him to be better placed than before.

"Don't try that 'need to know' crap on me again. I'm telling you, Jerry, I believe they took away a body that night. Possibly a fourteen-year-old girl's. I'll know for sure very soon. The place was deep cleaned like you never saw in your life but I still found traces of blood on the floor. And brackets inside for some kind of video loop. What's that all about? And why would your engineers want to cover it outside by remote cameras? That's even weirder. I need to see the paperwork on this, and I know you guys don't fart without creating a record, so have another think."

Jeremy Thompson was forty-two, married with three children. Kerr had recruited him four years earlier after a fundamentalist-Christian PC had arrested him with another man on Hampstead Heath for committing what he insisted on describing as a "lewd act", then becoming involved in a brawl. The moment they found Thompson's government pass, the local uniform boss had called John Kerr, his contact in SO15. Kerr had made the deal with the duty inspector in three minutes; his pitch to Thompson in the stinking police cell had taken four hours.

266

Over the years, Kestrel had veered between co-operation and resentment. On dark days, when he was fractious after a risky cruising adventure the night before, Kerr would calmly remind him he had saved his job and his marriage, but Kestrel often responded badly. "What you do to me is straightforward fucking blackmail," he had once shouted into the mobile Kerr had given him, "and all for sticking my cock in a chartered accountant's gob." Kestrel's offence, of course, lay not in the bisexuality but the subterfuge. Both men knew Kerr's leverage would evaporate the day Kestrel came out to his wife and put his hands up to his vetting officer.

"I can't call up the file," he said eventually, "because there almost certainly isn't one." The two German kids ran through the saloon onto their deck, caught Kestrel's grim look and retreated. As she turned, the little girl tripped on his shoe and burst into tears.

"Wrong answer. And do you know what, Jerry? I might have let this go if Philippa hadn't been so enthusiastic about slagging me off to my boss," Kerr yelled, above the child's screams. They watched her run back past the wheelhouse to her parents. "We're talking a life here, Jerry, so don't blank me."

Kestrel sighed heavily and his body actually seemed to deflate. "Look, this all goes back a long way. It started overseas. A small circle in MI6. Totally in-house. No one outside the family. Queen and country offered exotic postings in those days, alternative lifestyles. Boys, girls, discretion assured, especially if you were married. Anything to keep the pecker up and all totally unofficial."

"Honey traps, you mean?"

"No way. House parties among consenting adults."

"So, a bunch of immoral bastards screwed around to liven up the spying and took it up the arse from time to time. What's new in the higher gene pool?"

"MI6 saw no reason to change just because they got transferred back to Century House."

The German parents were in the saloon now, buying drinks from the bar. The boy was pointing at Kestrel, and the mother, little girl in her arms, glared at him.

"Then, in the nineties, the management introduced lie-detector tests and some got out PDQ. A few took their chances and winged it, and a handful were protected. After a while they introduced a few key players in my Service. Things sort of carried on as normal, but on a much smaller scale."

"So how do you know about this?" Kerr's question echoed back at them as they steamed under Waterloo Bridge.

Kestrel looked back through the saloon, then turned to face aft, as if the tourists might read his lips. "One of our leavers told me. A regular desk officer, nothing flash."

"Which branch?"

"G. International extremism. Officially she resigned to retrain as a teacher, but that wasn't the real reason. She knew what was happening."

"She was involved in it, you mean," said Kerr.

"Everything changed. They started to introduce girls from outside the circle. Sometimes boys, too."

"Hookers, you mean? Rent boys?"

"Kids. Children were being kidnapped off the street."

"Where? Here in London? Don't go all coy on me, Jerry."

"Not London. Abroad. I don't know. Turkey, I think. She just said it had all gone horribly wrong."

"Because they were compromised, you mean? Who found out about it?"

"No one. It's a total secret."

"So give me some names. Spit it out, Jerry. You're used to that."

"I don't have any detail. It's never talked about in the office."

"Well, MI5 didn't follow those two men to Marston Street by accident, so someone in your Service is aware. And if they're not part of whatever this is, who are they protecting?"

"I don't know. I swear."

"So I'll give their boss a pull and ask him."

"Jesus Christ." Kestrel looked close to tears. "Please don't do that."

They stood in silence, watching the Houses of Parliament recede as the boat rounded the wide bend towards Southwark. "How did your friend find out?" asked Kerr, eventually.

"She wasn't a friend, exactly. I hardly knew her." Kerr's agent moved to the port side of the boat and stood watching HMS *President*, the old naval training ship. "She signed the Official Secrets clause promising to keep schtum for life, got pissed, took me home and shagged me. Blurted it out over a post-coital ciggy. Followed by a surprisingly efficient blow-job." Kestrel took a deep breath. "They were being trafficked to order. I think she said they were being smuggled into the UK for sex and never heard of again."

Kerr was incredulous. "You think?"

"I'm not sure. Like I said, she was drunk. We were both the worse for wear."

"So let me get this straight. HMG employees were actually conniving in the importation of these kids, right? And still are, for all we know."

"A tiny circle. A rogue element."

"Great. That makes me feel a lot better. Arranging to have them trafficked to order. Kidnapped, abused and murdered. I'd say this is a real show-stopper, Jerry, wouldn't you? Pushes torturing AQ suspects right to the back of the queue. And what did your friend do about it?"

"What could she do?"

"How about blow the fucking whistle?"

"I dunno, by the time she 'fessed to me she was well out of it. And when you leave the Service the shutters come crashing down."

"So why would she tell all to a relative stranger?"

"It's what people do under stress, John," Kestrel suddenly snapped back, "or duress. Christ, you should know."

"Or maybe she thought you had the guts to follow it through." Kerr watched Kestrel's eyes slip downstream

270

to his right and knew he was looking out for the City of London School, his old school. "But you didn't, did you? You did sweet FA," he said, turning his agent to face him, "and now you're going to tell me who she is, so you won't feel quite so bloody guilty once I know for certain they removed a young girl's body that night, with MI5 watching and protecting them."

Kestrel stood silently by the rail, looking out at St Paul's. "She's a teacher at a girls' private school near Windsor," he said, watching the happy part of his life drift away. "But I'm telling you she won't want to get involved. She'll deny everything."

"I need to speak with her anyway. Name, Jerry."

"Pamela Masters."

"That wasn't so difficult, was it?" said Kerr, squeezing his agent's arm. "Doing the right thing at last?"

"What? Betraying the Service to you?"

"Thought we were on the same side."

"Don't kid yourself," said Kestrel, with a harsh laugh. "This is blatant fucking coercion, not patriotism."

They paused, both looking up at Tower Bridge. "So while you're on a roll, Jerry, what's happening with Ahmed Jibril over at your place?" said Kerr, evenly.

Kestrel immediately looked away. "John, let's not go there."

"I'm already too far down the track. And don't tell me you haven't got a file on him."

They were almost at their destination, slowing on the approach to St Katharine's Dock in front of the Tower

Hotel. "There is, but it's under double cover. Never leaves Philippa's office."

"What does it say? Tell me, Jerry."

The crewman had come aft to take charge of disembarkation now, followed by the German family. On the pontoon, another hand waited with the gangway on wheels. Releasing the guardrail, the crewman held the mooring line ready to cast to his mate on the dock.

"I don't know."

"So why the nervous breakdown all of a sudden?" Kerr could see his agent growing increasingly agitated with talk of Ahmed Jibril. He was like a trapped animal, eyes flitting everywhere, looking desperately for an escape. "Philippa tells my boss to do nothing more on Jibril and everyone's even more pissed off with me than usual. Where did I go wrong, Jerry? What makes this target so special?"

"That's all I can tell you."

"Is MI5 protecting him?" Kerr silently regarded his agent for a few moments. "Did I screw up an agent operation or something, Jerry? What the hell's going on here?"

"I swear," said Kestrel, close to tears.

"Because if Mr Jibril is a good guy on a nice little earner, that's absolutely fine. I'll say sorry, buy you lunch and back off. But I've been lifting a lot of stones these past few days. And the vermin underneath all tell me he's a *jihadi* working for Al Qaeda."

"What stones?"

"Now, if that's true, and I find you people are shielding a bad bastard who's not under control, then we're in a completely new ball game and I'm going to be coming to you with a lot more questions. Day or night."

"You didn't answer."

"So you need to get your sticky fingers inside that double cover for me. And if I find you're bullshitting, I'll do your fucking legs."

"What stones?" said Kestrel, turning to face Kerr.

Kerr laughed. "You don't seriously think I'm going to show my hand to you?"

"Perhaps you're the one who's bluffing," said Kestrel. He was trying to be combative, but his voice had risen a pitch. "Could you really burn me to Philippa now, after all I've been through? I don't think so."

Kerr was already walking through into the saloon, ready to disembark. "Try me," he said, over his shoulder.

They were six or seven feet from the dock when Kestrel made his move, suddenly swinging back to the stern deck. By the time Kerr became aware, the agent was already clambering over the port rail and balancing on the gunwale. The boat was still a couple of metres from the dock but closing fast against a strong tide.

"Jerry, stop!" As Kerr yelled, Kestrel bent his knees and launched himself into the air, scrabbling for the ropes on the dockside. But he lost height so quickly that he only managed to grab one of the protective tyres lining the pontoon. He hung, suspended with his feet and lower legs beneath the water just as the boat was being sucked against the dock. Everyone was shouting now as the crewman on the pontoon rushed to save him. Before they could reach him, Kestrel hauled himself, with a show of strength that surprised Kerr, onto the pontoon. A split second later the boat would have come alongside and crushed him.

The crewman and a couple of astonished passengers waiting to embark tried to hold onto him, but Kestrel shoved them away, ran up the ramp and escaped onto the Embankment. Kerr was already speed-dialling Melanie as Kestrel sprinted towards the street.

Out of sight by the hotel, Melanie clocked Kestrel as soon as he made his astonishing run from the dock. She followed him but did not attempt to intervene. At this moment of crisis and high agitation, she wanted to see what he would do next. His pace reducing to a fast walk, Kestrel could have turned right and reached Tower Hill Underground station by walking up the slope to Tower Hill. Instead, to her surprise, he took the longer route, turning left through the giant studded gates along the cobbled lane leading to the Tower, losing himself among clumps of pedestrians. She followed him past the souvenir shop towards the station. Distracted by the squelching of his bulky shoes, tourists gawped at the eccentric figure hurrying past in his flapping raincoat and soaked trousers.

Descending into the Tube, Melanie followed him to the westbound platform and kept her distance, unseen, as he sat on a bench. It was mid-afternoon, passenger traffic was light, and down there in the gloom he could be anonymous again. He stayed there for several minutes, head in his hands, unnoticed except by Melanie, and let two trains go past. With the sound of the third approaching he abruptly stood up, walked forward to the edge of the platform and stood motionless, hands at his sides. With thin strands of hair blowing in the draught, his eyes seemed glued to a poster on the curved wall across the track as the train whooshed out of the tunnel mouth.

Five metres away, Melanie realised she was too far from him to intervene as their agent prepared to kill himself. Kestrel was standing in the middle of a thin line of people waiting to board. In horror, as the train lumbered down the platform, she saw him take his penultimate step past the yellow line until his feet were right on the platform edge.

A young woman, immaculately groomed in a smart business suit, was first to realise the danger. Melanie saw her hand on his arm and her head rapidly moving as she shouted something in his ear. The driver must have seen him, too, because the train whistled, a sharp, piercing scream. The combined effect seemed to drive Kestrel back from the edge, to bring him to his senses. Melanie watched him walk along the platform, away from the attention, and board the fourth carriage. She watched him go, then dashed to the surface to ring Kerr.

She had expected Kerr to be on his way back to the Yard, but he was waiting for her just outside the station, on a bench beneath a tree overlooking the Tower, as if he had guessed she would return. The last time he and Kestrel had disembarked there they had shared a drink at one of the bars behind St Katharine's Dock: perhaps, she thought, Kerr had hoped she might persuade Kestrel to return with her.

Kerr listened in silence while Melanie described Kestrel's attempt to kill himself. She was genuinely concerned about his fragile state of mind: was it fear that Kerr would expose his double life, or the burden of some terrible knowledge he was carrying around with him? She tried to give her boss some notion of the stress Kestrel was under, to make him acknowledge the danger signals. "I'm saying we have to step back, John," she concluded, "give him space to collect himself."

"Oh, really? Is that so?" When Kerr switched his gaze from the Tower to look at her, his face was set. "There's only one thing we have to do, Melanie, and that's to stay on MI5's inside track. We agreed the priority, didn't we?"

"The truth."

"It's what we all signed up for. Do you believe our man can take us there?"

Melanie began to speak, then realised he wasn't expecting an answer.

"No way am I going to let Jerry Thompson hold out on me, Mel. We crack on at him. Nothing else matters."

CHAPTER
THIRTY-ONE

After their debrief at Tower Hill, Melanie left for the Lambeth plot and Kerr took the Tube back to St James's Park. He grabbed a sandwich at Strutton Ground and caught up on his emails in the Fishbowl. As the weather was reasonable, he left the Alfa in the underground garage and walked to the headquarters of the National Crime Agency. It was quicker, gave him time to think and, because parking at the Yard was first come, first served, prevented anyone snatching his space while he was away.

Kerr was intrigued by his invitation to call. Officers from the agency were drawn from HM Revenue and Customs, and Immigration, as well as the police. Its national law-enforcement remit was to bring to justice major criminal targets across police boundaries, and it regularly carried out joint operations with the Yard.

Bill Ritchie called him bang in the middle of Vauxhall Bridge to summon him to his office. He sounded buttoned up, so Kerr put him off, pretending he was in Chiswick supporting Dodge on a non-existent agent

277

pitch. It was a nifty piece of footwork until a couple of seagulls squawked loudly overhead and blew his cover. Eventually they settled on a meeting at seven, after close of play.

Theo Canning was already bounding to the door like a man half his age as the PA showed Kerr in. The two men had collaborated on more dodgy operations than Kerr cared to remember, so there was genuine warmth in the welcome.

Canning had built a reputation as an exceptional field officer in a long career with MI6. He had begun his career thirty-seven years earlier at Century House, near Southwark, the old MI6 headquarters, a grim tower block with a petrol station in the forecourt, and completed it at Vauxhall Cross, the futuristic green glass monster right on the riverside. For nearly four decades he had spied in the world's most hazardous countries, sometimes buried in the Diplomatic List as a third secretary, often undeclared. His reward was to be promoted to director of global operations and close confidant of C, as the director-general of MI6 had signed himself since the days of Sir Mansfield Smith-Cumming nearly a century before.

He had been within seven months of retirement when the government had brought him back to take over its high-profile agency. His brief was to co-ordinate the nation's war against organised crime although, unofficially, ministers wanted him to "knock heads together" and stamp out the turf wars that had plagued his predecessors. Canning and Mary, his wife of thirty years and former MI6 signals clerk at the station in Moscow, had just purchased their first real married home in England, a converted farmhouse near Trowbridge in Wiltshire.

Kerr knew from the grapevine that Canning had been undergoing medical treatment. They had not seen each other for a couple of years, and he was thinner than Kerr remembered him.

But the handshake was still bone-crushing. "Great to see you again." He beamed, steering Kerr to an armchair with a panoramic view of the Thames. "Thanks for dropping by."

"Very swish," said Kerr, looking admiringly around him. "Better than you're used to."

"Nairobi was always great fun but a bit of a khazi." Canning dropped into the chair opposite and crossed his legs. Dapper in light grey pinstripe suit and powder blue tie, he still favoured the timeless brown suede shoes Kerr remembered so well. "And as for dear old Geneva. Let's just say v. cushy indeed but bored the pants off me."

The PA asked if they wanted tea. Kerr said he was OK but Canning told her to bring some anyway, then glanced at his watch. "Unless you'd like something stronger, old chap?" Kerr laughed as the PA left. "Old chap." He had lost none of his style.

"No, suppose not. We're all too fucking sensible these days."

"I heard you were unwell."

"Touch of the Big C, but nothing fatal, all perfectly curable these days. Regular check-ups, and the medics

279

insist on shooting some magic bloody potion into me every couple of weeks," he said, shaking a hand in the air. "Feel like a bloody junkie, but it seems to be doing the trick. Mary wanted me to retire but they shooed me in here last year as chairman. Sorry, person. PM's special appointment. How come you're still DCI?"

"Is it starting to work yet?" said Kerr.

Kerr had been surprised when Canning had accepted what most in the business regarded as a poisoned chalice. In the early days the jealousies, hostility and outdated working practices among the various parties had proved corrosive. Each organisation had brought its own agenda and carried on as if nothing had changed, as did the gangs of serious and organised criminals. Now there were real signs of improvement, driven by the unequivocal message from Whitehall that the National Crime Agency had to work. They had appointed a chief constable as front man, but no one was in any doubt that real power lay in the hands of Theo Canning.

"You know the score, my friend," laughed Canning. "Bollocks to the turf wars. Things are getting better. Drugs, guns and gangs. Money-laundering, of course. And more cybercrime than we can handle. A lot of confiscations. We're kicking some multi-millionaires where it hurts most. The judge sends them down and we lift the yacht, which is nice. Contract's for two days a week, but I always end up doing four. Keep a handle on all the dodgy operational stuff for obvious reasons. Am I succeeding? Fuck knows."

280

"Doing a great job from what we hear," said Kerr, smiling to himself. Canning made even foul language sound elegant.

"Let's say I'm searching for some fresh blood." He stopped, looking Kerr in the eye.

"And?"

"I want you to help me."

"Beg your pardon?"

"Come and join me in some dirty work again. Like the good old days."

"Jesus, Theo," exhaled Kerr, "didn't see that one coming."

"You can guess what I'm up against here, John," he said. "There's still a heady mix of Spanish practices and good old 1990s corruption." He arched his fingers. "Last thing I need right now is a government inquiry or a press scandal. Shall I tell you who I want alongside me? Someone honest and competent from outside this monastic circle of doom and fucking gloom. And at the higher grade you richly deserve."

They fell silent as the PA served tea, with china crockery and silver spoons. The two friends were more accustomed to drinking from cracked glasses at the top of Century House, and Canning winked as she offered milk and sugar.

"Not exactly like the good old days, is it?" Kerr smiled.

"Look, I want you to run the intelligence side of the business on the ground," Canning continued, the moment they were alone again, "manage the undercover officers and oversee the surveillance, with a promotion to detective superintendent as soon as I've squared the wankers in HR."

"My boss hasn't been speaking with you by any chance?" asked Kerr, taken aback by Canning's directness.

"No, but I want to give her a call, if that's all right?" He sat back in his chair, waiting for a response, but Kerr simply shrugged. "Look, John," he continued calmly, "I know what you guys in the Met are going through. Political correctness gone mad, cult of the clitorati and all that. And I know they don't take to you over there, the new breed. The SO15 CT fucking Directorate or whatever has pushed the Special Branch operators into the cold. Am I right? Well, I need you here right now."

He paused for a moment, letting his words sink in. "I also gather you're suffering with this Jibril nonsense. What the hell was Finch thinking of to let that boy run again? He had fourteen days, why not use them?"

"It's certainly made life difficult."

"And goes against the grain. Do you want to talk about it?"

He listened without interruption as Kerr told him everything about the flawed arrest of Ahmed Jibril, the devastation of the explosions that had almost killed him and his team, the loss of his friend Jim Gallagher, and the obstructiveness of Jim Metcalfe and his crew.

"So why not tell them to bloody well poke it?" he said, when Kerr had finished. "You'll get no aggravation here. Run your own show from day one. Don't tell me you're not tempted."

Kerr laughed. Offloading to Theo Canning had been cathartic, and he suddenly felt a huge sense of relief. Paula Weatherall clearly believed there was no place for him in SO15, and his prospects were diminishing as even Bill Ritchie turned against him. If half of what Kestrel had told him about high-level corruption was true, he was about to upset some very senior people. Nothing he uncovered was likely to prove career-enhancing.

With such powerful forces opposing him, the prospect of joining the man he admired most in the intelligence community became more attractive. Theo Canning was a top-flight field operator and agent handler of complete integrity and incredible connections. It would be inspiring to work alongside his friend again. "Actually, Theo, the most difficult thing is, we acted on intelligence from your old Service."

"Go on."

"Well, the original info came from head of station in Sana'a."

"Joe Allenby."

"You know him?"

"Top man." Canning was nodding vigorously. "Old school."

"Yeah. He was returning a favour. Sent me a photograph and everything beneath the radar. Sunday afternoon, you know, sod-all happening back at Vauxhall Cross. Jibril had traces on Excalibur. Then we found someone had removed the lot and Joe seems to have disappeared. We're getting a complete blank on the normal liaison channels. I don't suppose . . ."

"You're wondering if I can do anything unofficially, you mean?"

"That would be fantastic."

"Tell you what," he said, "I'll stroll over to Vauxhall Cross to do some proper searching unmolested, meet up with a few conspirators of my own. So long as you promise me you'll think about my proposal."

Kerr smiled again. "Are you leaving me any option?"

Kerr knew something was not right the moment he stepped into Vauxhall Bridge Road. Even before he had buttoned up his jacket his sixth sense told him he was being followed. He picked out the black Nissan saloon in the line of slow-moving traffic, clocked the registration number and occupants, and requested an immediate "lost or stolen" check on the Police National Computer.

CHAPTER
THIRTY-TWO

Tuesday, 18 September, 17.36, Lambeth

It was only the second time Ahmed Jibril had left the crumbling Victorian house since his release from Paddington Green high-security police station. Apart from a brief excursion to the convenience store an hour after his return to his safe-house on Sunday evening, he had stayed invisible.

From the observation post in the council flat across the street, Justin activated the video and rattled off a couple of stills. He had taken over from Steve Gibb, the SAS secondee, at five o'clock and felt refreshed after a day with his girlfriend and another road run.

He was more fortunate than Gibb had been when Jibril had appeared the previous Thursday because his bladder was empty and the target, jacketless this time, in jeans and a thin sweater with his hands in his pockets, was walking slowly. He was alert, but the body language was that of a man out for an evening stroll, not a bombing mission. "Mel from Justin, subject on the move."

Melanie's voice bounced straight back. "Thanks. We have him."

The Red surveillance team was fully stretched, with most operatives secretly deployed on Kerr's orders against Samir Khan, Jibril's contact in East Ham. Melanie was left to cover Jibril's Lambeth address with Red Four, the young linguist who had forced his way onto the bus as Jibril headed for Vauxhall station. Justin heard the clunk of the car door as they got out of the dark green Honda and separated to take him on foot.

He sat back and relaxed, imagining Jibril would make his usual tour of the area and return within thirty minutes. A couple of people he recognised entered the main door of Jibril's house, and he contemplated crossing the floor to boil the kettle. Had he been near the end of his shift, more bored, tired or thirsty, he might have missed Julia Bakkour; if Alan Fargo had not been diligent in circulating the stills Kerr had snatched outside Paddington Green police station on Sunday afternoon, he might not have realised the significance. But because Justin was good at his job, sensitive to the rhythm of the area and alert to the unusual, he spotted Jibril's lawyer as soon as she turned into the street.

He captured four shots of her as she approached the house and started on the path. She was wearing a business suit and overcoat, carrying a thin attaché case, and Justin guessed she had come straight from her office in Wanstead.

"Urgent, Mel. I have Julia Bakkour, repeat Bakkour, on foot towards the address. Where is your man now?"

"South Lambeth Road. Up and down the shops, criss-crossing the street, eyes all over the place. The usual."

"She must have come to see him. Stand by."

Through the magnified viewfinder Justin watched Bakkour turn into the path, search the lopsided intercom plate for number nine and press the buzzer. While she waited, she looked around, uneasy in unfamiliar surroundings. When there was no answer he expected her to call Jibril, but no mobile phone appeared. She buzzed again, hesitated, then walked back down the path.

"Mel, she's leaving," said Justin. "No telephone contact. Watch in case she bumps into him."

"Roger that."

Justin tracked Bakkour down the path and into the street as she retraced her steps to the corner with South Lambeth Road.

"Coming your way, Mel." As he spoke she stopped again, half turning back, undecided. She opened her case, rummaged inside, then withdrew a sheet of paper and a ballpoint pen.

"Cancel that. She's going to leave him a note."

"Roger."

"Where is Jibril?"

"Buying vegetables at a street stall. Not hurried. He'll probably wander around for a while. Usual dry-cleaning game, so we're keeping back."

Justin watched the lawyer look around for somewhere to write. She settled for the bus shelter a couple of metres away from the entrance to the path. She wrote rapidly, and before she had finished, Justin had pulled on his jacket and grabbed a bodyset. "What's he doing, Mel?"

"This is about as far as he normally goes."

"They've screwed up. This is an opportunity."

"Repeat?"

"I'm going to get the note."

"Negative that. It's probably nothing. Outstanding crap about his detention at Paddington Green. Stay back."

"I know the layout, Mel. She'll leave it in his pigeonhole. No worries. Just give me a heads-up when he's on the way back."

Melanie bounced something back to him, but Justin was already on the move, pulling his woollen hat over his eyes. From his bag he grabbed the Pentax and stuffed it into his pocket. Activating the video, he locked the door behind him and dashed down three flights of stairs.

He had sight of Bakkour as soon as he regained the street. One of the residents was walking up the path and she hurried to catch him up.

"Justin from Mel. Target has turned back. Repeat, subject is returning to the address."

"Received." Justin watched the tenant unlock the front door as Bakkour flashed the note and tailgated him into the house.

"How long have I got?" shot back Justin, as he dashed across the street.

"Five mins max. Where are you?"

Ten seconds after Bakkour had entered the house Justin was already halfway up the path. He reached the front door as she opened it to leave. Because he was on the move, holding his keys ready as if arriving home, she instinctively held the door for him. "Ta," he mumbled, head down as he slipped past her.

The note was inside an envelope simply marked "9" and he immediately checked the seal. Bakkour had obviously licked it inside the lobby, for the saliva was still wet. Watching her through the frosted-glass door panel until she disappeared up the street, he eased it open and removed the note.

Melanie was sounding anxious. "Where the hell are you, Justin?"

"Lobby. I've got it. Stand by."

"He's three minutes away. Less. We can see her, too. They'll probably meet."

"Is she using a phone? Is she calling him, Mel?"

"Negative."

"So this is all we have," he said, unfolding the piece of paper.

"Just leave it and get out of there."

"I can do this. Keep it coming, Mel."

The note was in Arabic. Justin rapidly checked the staircase and path, listened for signs of life and stretched the note on the ledge in front of the post boxes.

"Justin, they've met up," said Melanie, urgently. "She's coming back to the house with him and they're in a hurry. Get out now."

"Roger."

The Pentax was the same camera he had used to photograph Bakkour's diary and business cards. He took it out again now and grabbed three shots of the note.

"They've turned into the street. Thirty seconds."

"Roger." He put the camera in his pocket, folded the note and carefully replaced it. He spat on his fingers, spread the saliva on the flap and pressed it until the remaining glue bonded.

"You've left it too late, Justin." Melanie's voice was urgent. "They're at the path. You're gonna have to wing it."

"No problem." Through the frosted glass he glimpsed the figures of Jibril and Bakkour. "Stand by but stay offline till I get back to you, yeah?" On the first and second landings, Justin remembered, there was a communal bathroom. He would hide himself in the lower one until they had gone past. Sliding the envelope back into the pigeonhole exactly as he had found it, he raced up the stairs to the first floor. The bathroom was occupied. He heard the front door open and low voices in the lobby as he climbed to Jibril's landing. The upper bathroom was to the right, to the side of the house, and it was free. He bolted the door, pulled the blind over the frosted panel and switched on the light, which also activated a noisy, old-fashioned extractor unit.

He heard them reach the landing, speaking Arabic. There was the clink of Jibril's keys and Justin pictured him opening the Yale, then the Chubb, just as he had done three days earlier. He kept his hand on the bolt, ready for his escape.

Then there was only Julia Bakkour's voice, and footsteps on the landing towards him. The door handle rotated and he turned the cold tap on full power until her footsteps receded, then switched it off to listen for Jibril's door closing.

When he calculated he was clear he silently drew back the bolt, twisted round to flush the toilet, and padded down the landing, covered by the noisy cistern and rattling of the extractor fan. He was cautious on the way down, remembering the creaking stairs to avoid, and checked Jibril's pigeon hole was empty.

He was back on the street within twenty seconds and reached the safety of the observation post in another minute. He checked the video and called up Melanie. "I'm back on line in the OP, Mel. No compromise."

"You sure about that, Justin, over?"

"I've got it on stills," he said, plugging the Pentax into his laptop.

"Nice one."

"I'm emailing it to 1830 for translation." He pressed "Send" and speed-dialled Alan Fargo.

Fargo got back to him in less than ten minutes, as Justin was filming Bakkour leaving the house. "Are you ready for this?" he said. "She wrote: 'Suit delivery 4.30 on day instructed. Fitting in Afghan shop not Saudi. Await confirm call.'"

"What the hell does that mean?"

"John Kerr just asked me the same thing."

"Incomprehensible. Typical bloody lawyer."

CHAPTER
THIRTY-THREE

Tuesday, 18 September, 18.56, Bill Ritchie's office, New Scotland Yard

Drinking Diet Coke and checking messages on the move, Kerr bumped into Ritchie in the lift lobby on the ground floor. "Any probs?" he asked as he followed Ritchie into the lift, trying to keep it light.

"Later," grunted Ritchie, punching a button. He fixed his eyes on the floor indicator, acting as if Kerr was a stranger. At the eighteenth floor he ignored Kerr as he walked swiftly down the corridor to his office. He unlocked the door and switched on the main lights. "Have a seat."

"What's up?"

Ritchie slumped heavily behind his desk and adjusted the armrest, a sure sign he was annoyed. He launched straight in. "What are you and your teams up to?"

Kerr gave a short laugh. "We're into day five after a bombing. Everyone's working their nuts off."

"I've seen the tasking schedules," Ritchie said, shuffling through his papers, "and some of the diary sheets don't tally with the team surveillance logs."

"You've dragged me up here to talk admin?"

Ritchie sifted through the forms. "I think you know what I'm getting at. Melanie Fleming. Justin Hine. Alan Fargo. Shown on duty all weekend without a break, overtime through the roof. Jack Langton's doing all hours, too. What have you got them working on?"

"I manage a lot of operators, Bill. Surveillance plots all over the place. Jack was working most of Saturday night for MI5." Kerr drained his Coke. "Look, those officers were almost killed less than a week ago and still want to work for us. To protect the public. They're dealing with trauma in their own way and for now that means staying on duty. Working. It's what they want. So where's the problem?"

"This isn't about the paperwork. We both know that." The armrest shifted again. Ritchie exhaled heavily and Kerr waited for another of his boss's in-sorrow-rather-than-anger routines. "John, the commander's on your case and I can't defend someone who refuses to listen." Kerr had been right. Since the arrival of Paula Weatherall in the office next door it was a performance Ritchie delivered with increasing frequency. "The Jibril cock-up, then the illegal search in Marston Street. Harrington gave her a very tough time because of you."

"And Derek Finch humiliated her in front of me. Is that my fault, too?"

"Don't push it," said Ritchie. "She was going to suspend you until I stepped in, remember? And she's still thinking about it."

Kerr crushed the empty Coke can. He looked around him. "There really isn't room to swing a cat in here, is there?" he said, tapping the plasterboard partition wall. "I mean, how do you stick it?"

It was a delaying tactic, a distraction while he decided how to play his boss, whether to confront him or test the extent of his knowledge. Ritchie's office was next to Weatherall's, and less than half the size. She had recently had it partitioned to accommodate a "leadership and management" consultant on an expensive short-term contract. Everyone knew it was a sore point with Ritchie. There was standing-room only at the many urgent operational meetings in his office, while Weatherall's prime real estate next door often lay empty.

"Don't change the subject."

Kerr went for option two. "Come off it, Bill. Finch's lot were holding back from day one. Whoever heard of the Bellies soft-pedalling? I mean, what the fuck is going on here?"

"MI5 have the lead."

"The man is a *jihadi*, Bill. Finch released a terrorist onto the streets. We both know that."

"This is not our business. End of."

"Which is so unlike you," said Kerr, looking hard at his boss, "totally out of sync with the guy who always demanded every sodding detail. It's also why I don't believe you."

"So get over it."

"Why are you holding out on me, Bill?"

"Ahmed Jibril is a free man," said Ritchie. "Game over."

"Or is MI5 working him up as a source? Is that why they let him out, and you can't bring yourself to tell me? Are they trying to recruit him?" Kerr gave a sardonic laugh. "Brilliant. How soon before that spark of genius sets the whole fucking city on fire again? I'd better tell the troops to keep standing by."

"If you go on like this you risk getting yourself disciplined. I'm telling you, John."

"For doing my job?"

"For insubordination. Is that clear enough?"

They looked at each other in silence, Kerr trying to read the expression of the man he had known for most of his career. He made him wait for an answer, staring across St James's Park to the Post Office Tower and the lights of north London. Thinking rapidly, Kerr settled for deception. "All right, I'll let it go," he said eventually. He tossed the can into Ritchie's waste bin. "And you can tell Ma'am I consider myself well and truly bollocked."

"You just don't get it, do you?" Ritchie sighed and leant forward. He was clearly exasperated. "John, you need to be very careful, or I won't be able to protect you."

"What the hell does that mean?" asked Kerr, quietly, wondering if Ritchie knew he had spooked a surveillance team outside Theo Canning's office just a few hours earlier. "Protect me? From what?" Red flags were popping up in Kerr's brain. For a second he flashed back to his undercover assignment so many years ago, when for half a decade he had trusted Ritchie with his life. It was inconceivable that his protector would now leave him vulnerable. "Come on, Bill. You're the guy who watched my back day and night for years. What's different all of a sudden? Jesus, you've changed so much."

"No. Time has moved on . . ."

"Did someone slice your balls off when they made you chief? You're not the same man. Ask anyone who knows you . . ."

". . . but you don't seem to have bloody noticed," continued Ritchie, his voice rising.

"Is that why Karl Sergeyev had to go?"

Ritchie suddenly looked wrong-footed. "DS Sergeyev had his vetting removed because of his relationship with a prostitute," he said evenly, as if reciting the party line.

"This happened late Friday night. Early hours of Saturday, in fact. Weatherall's not on the grapevine. And I know you're not, either, these days. So how did she find out about it so quickly?"

"Phone call."

"Bollocks. Karl was in the sack all weekend."

"From the Foreign Office. A formal complaint about his conduct from the Russian Embassy."

Kerr looked incredulous. "What — for shagging?"

"For being obstructive. Exceeding his brief."

"Well, that's not the story Weatherall gave Karl," retorted Kerr. "Karl told you what he saw that night in Marston Street, didn't he?"

"None of your business," said Ritchie, looking away.

"He gave you his principal's call log, didn't he? The Russian minister, Anatoli Rigov? Told you that place was a security risk? He did everything a good protection officer should do and you still let Weatherall stab him in the back."

"John, I'm telling you for the last time. Go and do your job. Keep away from things that don't concern you."

Was it a warning or a tip-off? Or was his one-time mentor issuing a threat? Ritchie looked tired, a man who carried too many secrets. The voice had suddenly lost its edge, making it impossible to decide whether he was speaking as senior officer or friend. But Kerr's inner voice told him to keep it light and move on, so he stood and stretched his arms wide. "Blimey, you can practically touch the walls on either side. Tell me, Bill, how the hell do you get anything done in here?"

"What about doing some work in your own office for a change," Ritchie said, shuffling the papers again, "clearing this mess up?"

"No chance of that tonight," smiled Kerr. "I've got choir practice."

As Kerr wrestled with his boss, Anatoli Rigov arrived back at Farnborough airfield and boarded his luxurious Learjet. He already felt relaxed, reclining his seat as the attractive flight attendant poured a generous tumbler of his favourite vodka. There was another vacancy to fill in the British signals organisation, but otherwise he felt at ease with the world as the plane taxied down the runway. Rigov had delivered a more powerful strain of an existing *E.coli* bacterium, and his victim was a British traitor, not a Russian dissident. He had done nothing to arouse suspicion; neither poison nor victim would point an accusing finger at Moscow. The attendant returned his smile and strapped herself into her jump seat. The engines roared as Rigov downed his vodka in one. His lunch would attract none of the attention surrounding other murdered enemies of the Russian state, and now he could look forward to dinner. Problem solved, he thought as the Bombardier streaked into the sky. Mission accomplished.

CHAPTER
THIRTY-FOUR

Tuesday, 18 September, 20.23, Dolphin Square, Victoria

Every Tuesday evening, between seven and eight-thirty exactly, the combined choir of MI5 and MI6 practised in a church close to Dolphin Square in Victoria. The choir held concerts for Service families, friends and other trusted insiders at Easter and Christmas. It also sang at occasional special events, such as memorial services for heads of both agencies, normally in the privacy of the Guards Chapel in Wellington Barracks.

Kerr knew this because Willie Duncan had told him at one of the surveillance tasking and co-ordinating meetings at Thames House. Duncan managed a couple of surveillance teams in A4, the MI5 surveillance unit, the people Jack Langton had been called out to assist the previous Saturday night. The operators in A Branch watched, listened and engineered. But they never commissioned a job of their own accord. They were the MI5 underclass, the blue-collar guys, B-list techies with A-class skills, who did exactly as they were tasked. Duncan went along to choir practice because it was a welcome break, he said, from the fatigue and monotony of shift work, and raised the spirits from the daily grind of watching and listening.

Employees in A Branch had their own civil-service career structure, quite separate from other MI5 units, with less scope for promotion. Often ex-military, like Duncan, their job was to act in support of the officers who set the operational priorities. A few managed the transition to mainstream work, but it was rare for a watcher to climb MI5's greasy pole, and Kerr suspected this was another reason Duncan enjoyed the choir. If his work excluded him from the professional heights, his voice was as acceptable as that of any rising star. No one ever discriminated against his singing. The choir, Kerr guessed, was the only part of MI5 to which Willie Duncan truly belonged.

Walking across from the Yard, Kerr edged the door open as they were reaching the end of a piece he did not recognise. The choir stood at the front of the church just below the nave, facing the middle-aged conductor, spindly and hyperactive, whom Kerr recognised as a one-time MI6 deputy director of training. There were eighteen singers, including nine women sopranos of various ages in the front row. He recognised an analyst, three or four desk officers, a couple of agent handlers from way back and a signals clerk. It was cool in the church and some of the women had kept their coats on.

From his bulk Duncan should have been a baritone or bass, but Kerr located him in the row of tenors, hair prematurely grey with an untidy moustache covering his upper lip, his face bright red from exertion. Kerr slipped into a pew at the very back of the church, concealed by a pillar, and waited in the gloom for the singers to disperse. Most of them left by the vestry door, which shortened the walk to the pub in the side-street, but Duncan spotted Kerr straight away. Music under his arm, he trotted down the nave and eased into the pew in front of Kerr, concealing him from view. Duncan was wearing heavy cords, polished brown boots and his usual heavy coat complete with hood and winter lining. He had to twist round to reach Kerr's outstretched hand, which made him look uncomfortable. "Christmas programme. Bit rough and ready but it's early days."

"Very nice," said Kerr. "Fancy a pint?"

"Business or pleasure?" asked Duncan, his face clouding.

"Depends."

Duncan's cheeks were still red, but from awkwardness now. "You're a bit *persona non grata* at the moment, John. No offence."

Kerr knew Duncan had served in Saudi and wanted to use his knowledge of Arabic and intelligence-gathering skills in G Branch, the MI5 section that dealt with the international terrorist threat. But when he had applied for a desk officer's job they had rejected him for a London University post-grad in Oriental studies. Duncan had reached his MI5 career ceiling at thirty-nine, destined to spend the rest of his life working for the fresh-faced novices of the professional grades, and Kerr always felt a little sorry for his surveillance counterpart.

"None taken," said Kerr. "Because I had a look at that house, you mean? In Marston Street?"

"And the job last Thursday," said Duncan, quickly. "Jibril. He wasn't on the target list. You should have consulted us." He glanced back up the aisle. A clutch of singers was still gathered round the piano, and one of the men was pointing his thumb to the door. "Be right there," his voice echoed to them, as he held up five fingers. "Now is not a good time," he said quietly. "Looks a bit odd. Can't it wait till next week?"

Kerr sat forward, head lowered, hands between his knees as if in prayer.

"No need to involve anyone else, my friend. We can sort it right here. What was Marston Street about? I mean, who was the sponsor?"

"You don't need to know that, John."

"Willie, you can drop the holier-than-thou routine. Jack Langton assisted you at very short notice on Saturday night, so I think you should level with me."

For a moment Duncan looked as if he was about to cross himself. Instead, he clapped his hands on his knees. "I have to go."

"What did they take out of the house that night, Willie? Just tell me that."

"Leave it, John. I just organise the watchers, do what I'm told. We can talk about it at the tasking meeting." Duncan began to stand. "That and the Jibril mess-up. You caused me a lot of grief there."

"Jibril can't wait till next week. I'm going to deploy surveillance on him from tomorrow," lied Kerr.

"No." Duncan sank down to the pew. "We're already covering him."

"Since when?"

"Since he was released."

"Really? So what about associates? We can take them off your hands."

"There aren't any."

"You sure about that? Don't fuck me around, Willie."

"You shouldn't swear in church, John. It's offensive."

Kerr was already walking away. "So is lying."

He had his BlackBerry ready even before he reached the street. Ritchie's coded warning plus Duncan's evasiveness had triggered his instinct for self-preservation.

Stark naked, Justin Hine was lying in bed while his girlfriend gently massaged oil into his back.

"Justin, you OK to talk?"

"No worries, boss." They were listening to Michael Bublé, who always turned her on, and Kerr had rung just as he was about to flip over and invite treatment to his uninjured front.

"I think I need some extra security at my place."

"I agree."

"Can we install it tonight?"

Justin glanced at the bedside clock as she gently worked on his shoulders. "Bit tucked up at the moment, actually, boss. Physio session. But if it's really, you know . . ."

"No, tomorrow evening will be good," said Kerr. "If I'm not there I'll tell the concierge to let you in. And thanks for what you did today, back at the safe-house. You took a chance and it was smart work."

"No problem at all, boss. Leave it with me." Justin turned over.

"Hey, sorry to ruin whatever it is I'm interrupting. This was a bad call."

"No, not at all." The massage had stopped abruptly, the atmosphere broken. Justin watched his girl sashay into the bathroom, her job done. "It's fine, boss, honestly. I'll see you in the morning."

Much later that night, a couple of miles upstream at Hammersmith, in her modest flat marketed as within easy reach of the river, Olga emerged from the shower and defended herself to her lover. She had not dropped the blinds, and the lights of a houseboat moored upstream from Hammersmith Bridge punctuated the blackness. Wrapping the towel around her, she shook her damp hair. "Darling, it was one evening. Some trade thing in the City, completely boring," she said, in Russian, almost their first words since his phone call.

Karl emerged from the kitchen with scalding black coffee. Half drunk and suffering, he sat on the sofa and took off his shoes. At short notice his friends had insisted on taking him for a few beers at a pub only a stone's throw from the Yard. "What time did you get home?"

"Karl Sergeyev, you are pissed, you can hardly see straight, and you look and sound ridiculous." Olga stood in front of him, drying her breasts and underarms. "And you think I want to screw your new boss, is that it? You think I am that crazy?"

"It's possible," said Karl, rubbing his temples in pain. A couple of the older guys from Special Branch days with grown-up kids and tolerant wives had stayed till chucking-out time. He had bought double shots of vodka for two of the locals from Ashburn House round the corner and then, from habit, almost caught the last train to the home he had shared with Nancy.

"Don't be such a big cry-baby," said Olga, vigorously towelling her hair. She walked away and he heard her flick the kettle on. "And don't forget who got you your stupid job."

The little man in Karl's head went to work with a hammer again as he bent to put his shoes back on. There was a dried spattering of something on the toecaps: why did vomit always look like tomato skins? He downed the last of his coffee and whipped his jacket off the back of the chair. "Go fuck yourself."

"Go find Tania," came the shout from the kitchen, like a bullet. The door slammed as she switched the hairdryer to top speed.

CHAPTER
THIRTY-FIVE

Wednesday, 19 September, 11.34, Berkeley Square, Mayfair

Three days after the Sunday-afternoon meeting at his apartment, Kerr summoned the team for another secret update away from the Yard. One thing was certain: as he moved against the establishment, association with John Kerr would become toxic. It made him acutely conscious of the need to protect his gifted officers, who were laying their ambitions on the line.

Six days after the bombings the media were still cranked into Doomsday mode. Spurred on by Finch and off-the-record MI5 briefings, reporters were speculating that the explosions were the first in a new series of planned Al Qaeda attacks by terrorists embedded in the UK. And because a climate of fear was good for security budgets, the message ringing out from New Scotland Yard and Thames House was not if, but when.

Everything Kerr's team was unearthing convinced him that Ahmed Jibril, the man Finch had released as an innocent, was one of those embedded, perhaps the prime suspect, with the suicide bombers disposable cannon fodder. The energy Philippa Harrington and his own bosses used to condemn him only served to strengthen that belief. And the cryptic note left for Jibril by Julia Bakkour propelled suspicion into conviction: "Suit delivery 4.30 on day instructed. Fitting in Afghan shop not Saudi. Await confirm call."

To Kerr and Alan Fargo, unravelling this message took absolute priority with the first code recovered from the water heater in Jibril's tiny kitchen: "13 + ED-TA − 4". They shared the same conviction: Justin had recovered two linked operational instructions giving notice of another pre-planned terrorist attack. And they assumed that the trigger for this attack would be Omar Taleb, the man who had called Jibril minutes before he left the safe-house on the day of the suicide bombings.

Fargo had secretly circulated Taleb's name to contacts in intelligence agencies throughout Europe, but with no result. He had searched every legal directory he could lay his hands on in Europe and the Middle East, but nowhere did the name of attorney Omar Taleb appear. Gaps in knowledge were anathema to the head of Room 1830. They always increased his anxiety, and he knew the time remaining to prevent more bloodshed might be very short. Fargo had already circulated the note to each of his team individually, asking for urgent ideas, to see if they came up with the same possibilities. There was one common thread in their feedback: "suit fitting" was the type of code terrorists often used to trigger attacks.

One of Kerr's neighbours in his Islington apartment block was head of business-space investment at a classy property company in Mayfair. It took a single call that morning for him to make one of his ground-floor meeting rooms available to Kerr, no questions asked. The company was based in Curzon Street, less than twenty metres from the old MI5 headquarters, and the contrast to the Yard could not have been starker. The complex was low-build, clean, modern and minimalist, all glass, stainless steel and black wood, with fresh coffee, sparkling water and Diet Coke laid on in meeting room G3.

Reception had five visitor passes made out for them in false names invented by Kerr. They arrived separately. Melanie was first, businesslike in a charcoal grey suit and white blouse, ready for another meeting that afternoon. Justin turned up five minutes later in his customary denims, trainers and woollen ski hat: even pulled low over his ears, it did not quite cover the plaster protecting his head wound. Langton came straight from the surveillance plot in East Ham and sat in his motorcycle leathers with the helmet on the ash-wood table, the unzipped top spilling down over his waist.

Kerr was late. Since spotting the surveillance outside Theo Canning's headquarters, he had slipped back into the dry-cleaning methods he had routinely deployed as an undercover officer years before, taking a circuitous route from the Yard. He spotted nothing suspicious, but was not reassured. The surveillance was either very good, or the watchers knew he had checked their vehicle on the Police National Computer and were holding back. Either would be bad news.

The only absentee was Alan Fargo, who rang Kerr from 1830 when they were already assembled. Kerr thought he sounded anxious, or just excited. He told Kerr he had just taken a call from Islamabad and was awaiting results on a couple of important leads, but would definitely be along. He wanted Kerr to keep everyone there until he arrived.

Langton reacted instantly when Kerr reported Willie Duncan's claim the previous evening that A4 surveillance were covering Jibril. "That's bullshit, John," he said, his leathers squeaking and farting on the chair as he leant forward. "Jibril's only left that safe-house twice since release. If Willie's A4 teams were anywhere near we'd have flushed them. So why is Willie standing in that church lying to you?"

"Perhaps I took him by surprise. Maybe he got the MI5 spin all wrong. Whatever, we stay with it, Jack."

"Sure." Jack looked at the others. "And now we're all dying to hear about your river trip."

Kerr popped a Diet Coke and shot a glance at Melanie. "Guys, you're not gonna believe it."

The Foreign and Commonwealth Office in King Charles Street stretches from St James's Park to Whitehall, a fading white monument to an era when Britain ruled the world and international borders were decided over whisky in Pall Mall clubs only a stroll away. As John Kerr walked the team through his meeting with Kestrel on the Thames, culminating in his agent's bizarre escape, Alan Fargo was hurrying there across St James's Park, in hot pursuit of his best lead yet.

The previous winter Fargo had spent a month assisting the Foreign and Commonwealth Office Counter-terrorism Policy Unit, omitting to hand in his photo-pass when he returned to 1830. Fargo was acquainted with the warren of haphazard offices, staircases and corridors converted into open-plan offices, and friendly with the custodians who protected them. As he reached the top of Clive Steps he took the laminated pass from his pocket and looped the distinctive blue ribbon around his neck. The pass bounced off his stomach as he hurried through the arch into the inner courtyard, originally designed to accommodate horse-drawn carriages but now abused as a car park for the privileged. The custodian by Reception told him it was long time no see, and flashed him through.

Fargo checked his watch: 12.03. The policy unit held a weekly meeting at eleven-thirty each Wednesday in one of the conference rooms, lasting exactly one hour. This gave him a window of twenty minutes tops.

The department had about eight staff spread out in a jumble of disconnected offices on the second floor. Fargo's objective was tucked away in a separate room in the roof, reached by its own staircase. Access was through a heavy oak door with its original brass handle, protected by an old-fashioned four-button coded lock. Fargo was banking that no one would have thought to change it.

310

To reach his old office Fargo had to walk to the other end of the building nearest the park, then climb two flights to reach a landing almost two metres wide. It would take him six minutes, which left him only fourteen to find what he needed and get away.

The corridor to the right of the staircase led to the department's small conference room, where Fargo was relieved to see the "Engaged" sign on the door. Beside it, a short staircase led to a kind of attic, which housed the document room; once committed, there was no other way out. The staircase took one turn back on itself, concealing Fargo from the main corridor, and the locked door was less than a metre from the top step. The combination was 5231. Puffing from the climb, he had to make two attempts because the buttons were so worn, and the door handle had lost traction through a century of use.

Inside, six desks were crammed into an office large enough for two, built into the sloping roof. It was even more claustrophobic than he remembered. The stale air, desktops with locked screens, jackets on the backs of chairs, rucksacks and scattered papers were signs of very recent occupancy. At the farthest end, in a section beyond the far wall where Fargo had based himself, three secure steel cabinets with combination locks shared space with a photocopier and a shredder. The doors were closed, but Fargo guessed the locks would have been left "on the click", a lazy habit that enabled the next user to open each safe with a single half-turn anti-clockwise.

The cabinet Fargo needed stood in the left corner, marked "UK Entry Documentation". He switched the photocopier on, carefully turned the combination dial until he heard a satisfying click, and pulled open both doors. It was stacked with box files and loose folders, a memorial to the pre-computer age, with no reference to global region or date.

The photocopier was warming up noisily, masking any signs of activity from the staircase. He moved the boxes around until he found a ring binder marked "Yemen and Ethiopia" hidden on the bottom shelf. The file was overfull, the rings forced apart so that a few papers became dislodged as he lifted it onto the nearest desk and riffled through. Fargo knew these were the papers flown back to London by diplomatic bag. Each document contained original handwritten notes of the entry-control officers at the embassies in Sana'a and Addis Ababa, with the visa decision marked at the foot. Batches of documents had been inserted in rough date order, with no alphabetical index. Fargo sprang the ring lever, removed some papers and worked back ten days.

He found what he wanted in less than thirty seconds. The document relating to his target was buried in a clump of regular applications and confirmed everything his contact in Islamabad had told him. It was a photocopied letter occupying three paragraphs on Home Office notepaper, initials only. Headed "Special Access Visa Authorisation (SAVA)", it was a requirement for the issue of a student visa to Ahmed Mohammed Jibril, who would attend the embassy with his passport on Thursday, 6 September. There were unreadable initials where the authorising signature should have been.

The photocopier was ready. Fargo placed the letter on the glass, whipped it away as soon as the light went out and replaced it in the file. He stuffed the copy into his jacket and checked his watch: 12:19. He replaced the papers in the ring binder, squeezed it back into the bottom shelf and closed the doors, locking the combination with a gentle half-turn to the right.

There was laughter on the other side of the "Engaged" sign as he hurried down the stairs, a warning that the meeting was breaking up early. The door flew open as he turned away down the corridor, releasing a swell of voices. He waited for someone to recognise him from the back and call his name, but instead the voices receded up the stairs.

In the broadest stretch of corridor, by the gallery bordering the Locarno Room, he speed-dialled Kerr. "John, I'm ten minutes away."

"Where are you?"

"Can you hold onto them till I get there? Everyone needs to see this."

While they waited for Fargo, Kerr asked Melanie what she had managed to find out about Pamela Masters, Kestrel's former associate at MI5.

Melanie remembered everything by heart. Masters was in her late forties and single. Graduating in 1979 from Sussex University with a BA Honours in English, she had worked for a charity in Kenya for a couple of years before being recruited to the Security Service.

After a period in F Branch, the MI5 section dealing with domestic subversion, in 1988 she had won a secondment to a newly formed joint team within MI6, then returned to Thames House for the rest of her career. Melanie confirmed she had resigned eighteen months ago to become a teacher at St Benedict's Independent School for Girls, ten miles west of Windsor. Her recent appointment as head of English entitled her to occupy a flat in the school grounds.

"What was the reaction when you rang her?" asked Kerr.

"Aggressive, refused to meet point-blank, told me to bloody piss off, her words not mine, and cut the call. So Justin and I are driving out to see her straight from here. Car's parked outside. Oh, and she had a child, by the way. Lucy Ann, born 1991."

"Father?"

"Not shown. She died in infancy," said Melanie, checking her watch. She collected her things together, tapped Justin on the knee and stood up. "And we have to get going. Can you tell Alan we'll touch base with him later?"

They collided with Fargo at the smoked-glass door. He was in a rush, wearing a green ribbon this time, the visitor pass facing the wrong way, shirt front damp with sweat. "You have to hear this, guys," he said, corralling them back into the room. "Two minutes, then I'll let you go."

"Want some coffee?" said Kerr, shifting up to make room. But Fargo seemed not to have heard, apparently unaware of his posh new surroundings as he pulled a

314

bundle of dog-eared notes from his jacket and dropped them onto the table. He was still breathing hard, but Kerr could tell this was from excitement as much as exertion.

Langton poured him a glass of water. "How did you get here?" he asked.

"Legged it across the park. Thanks. Listen up, everyone. Hot intel about Jibril's visa." Fargo gulped some water and tried to smooth his papers. "There's definitely something special about Ahmed Jibril."

"Such as?" said Kerr.

Fargo reached for the copy letter and passed it around. "I just found this lying about in the Foreign Office. See for yourselves. It was authorised by the Home Office. And it applies only to this one category." Fargo jabbed a stubby finger at the letterhead. "Special Access Visa Authorisation. The SAVA programme. I checked with 1830 on the way over. It applies to a government agent tasked to operate within UK borders, either potential or already under recruitment. If Jibril is a spy working for our side, it counts as national security and the home sec can clear him direct."

"But we had him under surveillance as a hostile the moment he arrived at Heathrow," said Langton.

"Bypassing normal tasking and co-ordinating channels," said Kerr. "So is Ahmed Jibril one of the good guys, after all? Alan, are you telling me I made a gigantic cock-up?"

Fargo shrugged. "All we can say for sure is that the Home Office brought him into the country and someone suppressed damaging intelligence about him. We weren't supposed to get anywhere near him, basically. For whatever reason. Which is probably why the bosses are giving you such a hard time."

"No signature," said Kerr, staring at the letter.

"Initials only, and unreadable. But I'm checking out the hierarchy in that unit," said Fargo. "We really need to stay with this, John. They're protecting him. Look, he's either a good guy or a terrorist. If he's an asset, why is no one being upfront with us? Why was Joe Allenby kept in the dark? And if he's the terrorist we think he is, then we're facing some kind of grotesque cover-up. I'm just saying we have to stay with it until we bottom this out one way or the other."

Kerr looked round the room and exhaled heavily. "OK. So we don't let Ahmed Jibril out of our sight until I find out what the hell's going on here." He nodded at Justin and Melanie. "On your way, guys."

"Two ticks," said Fargo, revealing a couple of inches of bum cleavage as he stooped to tie his shoelace. They waited while he shuffled through his pile of notes. "I've got the traces back on thirty-six Marston Street. I already told you the lease on Jibril's Lambeth safe-house is owned by Falcon Properties, remember? Well, get this. Falcon also owns the Marston Street address."

"Jesus." Kerr frowned hard. "You sure about that?"

"One of my terrorist finance guys just confirmed it. I dunno how, but the whole thing around Jibril is linked to what happened in that house, the stuff Jack witnessed Saturday night."

"No wonder everyone's blanking us," murmured Langton.

Suddenly Fargo's mobile was ringing deep inside his trouser pocket. He held up a hand for silence as he took the call. He listened intently. "You certain about that? . . . Spell it for me." Fargo clamped the phone against his ear as he patted himself down in vain for a pen. Justin was the first to respond, producing an elegant hotel ballpoint from nowhere. "That's absolutely bloody brilliant," said Fargo, taking dictation. "I'm on the way back."

When he rang off he looked elated. "That's what I've been waiting for," he said, beaming round the table. "We've been trawling back through the papers on Operation Derwent, the Hindawi case. We kept a hard copy in 1830 because the case is technically still open. Thousands of pages in the files. Were getting nowhere all last night and again this morning. Then, bingo, up pops Omar Taleb. It's an alias."

"And?" they all said in unison.

Fargo looked at his note. "His real name is Rashid Hussain. He's Syrian Secret Service. We have him on record as an undeclared Al Mukhabarat officer in London, May 1986, working out of the Syrian Embassy. The man whose number appeared on Jibril's Sim card, who activated Jibril on the day of the bombings and instructed Julia Bakkour to represent him, is your classic fifteen-carat hood."

"What was his role?" said Langton.

"Syrian agent Nezar Hindawi seduces an innocent Irish nurse and makes her pregnant, right? Buys her a

317

one-way ticket from Heathrow to Tel Aviv and gets her to take his transistor radio for him. Promises to join her on a later flight. Just before boarding El Al find a bomb concealed in the radio. Well, get this. Hussain was Hindawi's case officer and fled to Damascus before we could reach him. This guy is hardcore. We haven't heard from him in at least twenty years, but you can bet he's still seriously active. He'd be late forties now. John, this fits with the stuff about the safe-house used by Ahmed Jibril. Like we said on Sunday, it all connects to Syrian-sponsored terrorism in the eighties."

"Anything else?" said Kerr.

"You bet. There's nothing about Taleb on the electronic database because someone wiped it. But they forgot about the paper records. And here's what makes this a stone bonker. Julia Bakkour and Taleb both appear on the lease for thirty-six Marston Street."

"Nice work." Kerr exhaled, his mind racing. "So get all the traces together and nail him for me." Kerr was already thinking about Bill Ritchie's obstructiveness the previous evening. "And, hey, while we're on Marston Street, what's the score with that Russian's call log?"

"Anatoli Rigov. I was about to mention it. Telephone Intel in 1830 know nothing about it. They still haven't received anything from Mr Ritchie."

Justin groaned. "What the hell's going on here?"

"Are they sure?" said Kerr.

"I rang Karl. He kept the info on his mobile, so I asked him to forward the log to me direct," said Fargo. "We'll handle it from 1830."

318

Kerr looked at Fargo. "So where is Mr Taleb slash Hussain right now?"

"Turkey."

"Where, exactly?"

"We need to involve GCHQ for that."

"No. We can't risk it. Think of another way." Kerr looked across at Melanie and Justin, waiting by the door. "On your way, guys. I want you to wind our Pamela up, see where she takes us."

CHAPTER
THIRTY-SIX

Wednesday, 19 September, 13.53, St Benedict's Independent School for Girls, Berkshire

It took Melanie and Justin nearly an hour to reach St Benedict's, then another twenty minutes to find Pamela Masters.

The neo-classical buildings and grounds occupied fifteen acres of Berkshire countryside. The receptionist was Mrs Balderstone, a bulky spinster in her late fifties with her name on a brass doorplate. As her pretext, Melanie said Pamela was a friend from her previous job and she wanted to catch up.

"I'm afraid that will not be possible," said Mrs Balderstone, immediately suspicious. She had long ago formed the view that young women were not to be trusted, especially when they turned up without an appointment. "Miss Masters is still in class."

"I'm sure she'll want to see me," said Melanie, with a smile. "We spoke on the phone earlier. Please tell her I bring warm greetings from the Office." The receptionist's knowledge of Miss Masters's service to the nation was sketchy, because the lady herself gave little away, but

320

she knew enough from watching *Spooks* to guess the dangers faced by their head of English in an earlier life.

As she dialled, Mrs Balderstone kept Melanie standing. It was not the job of the receptionist to make cold callers welcome. She was always protective of Miss Masters. There was an enigmatic quality about her, but the receptionist felt privileged that the former huntress of Osama bin Laden had settled for Wordsworth, hair in a bun and a challenging sixth form.

The school bell clanged as she passed the message, so she had to repeat Melanie's name three times. Melanie could guess the teacher's reaction to mention of the "Office". She would be calculating the odds of Melanie declaring herself if she refused the meeting. "Miss Masters is busy with her marking but has a ten-minute window," conceded the receptionist, as the corridor erupted, "so you need to go back through the main entrance, then to the new block on your right and you'll find her in Seven C."

A few minutes later Melanie peered through the glazed classroom door to check for stray English students, but Pamela Masters was alone. The matching green woollen skirt with jumper and comfortable flat shoes made her look ten years older, and her hair was turning grey unchecked. She was making a show of marking the pile of books on the table beside her but clocked Melanie straight away. As Masters reluctantly took her hand, Melanie couldn't decide whether she was angry or just anxious. Her voice sounded less strident than it had on the phone and, face to face, she seemed to have lost her authority. Melanie spotted her mobile on the desk beside her bag.

"You shouldn't be here," Masters said, closing the door behind them. "This is my place of work, for God's sake." She retreated behind the table and took her seat, leaving Melanie to perch on the front-row desk.

"You hung up on me, Pamela. Gave me no choice."

She must have been attractive once, but now she was too thin and her head darted nervously, like a bird's. "I told you, the door on that part of my life is closed."

"As I explained, we're investigating a possible murder," replied Melanie, deadpan, "so I'm afraid I have to prise it open." She took a small notebook from her handbag and used her teeth to remove the top from her pen. "The Service may be connected in some way."

"Who the hell told you about me, and how dare you intrude into my private space?"

"You should have invited me to your flat when you had the chance," said Melanie, evenly. "Why did you leave the Security Service so suddenly?"

"Mind your own bloody business."

"Did MI5 begin to offend your newly discovered civil-libertarian instincts?" Melanie looked her straight in the eye. "Did you leave of your own free will, Pamela, or were you pushed?"

Girls' laughter swirled around the corridor outside but, in the classroom, there was only the ticking of the clock as they stared each other down. Masters blinked first. "Do you mind?" she said, picking up books from the top of the pile. "I have work to do."

"No, I don't mind your hostility at all, Pamela. It's what I expected. All that illicit screwing around was bound to leave a lot of guilty memories," said Melanie, as Masters began loading the books into a soft leather shoulder bag. "There are things you can't bring yourself to speak about, even now, aren't there? And that's fine. I understand."

Masters let the bag fall to the floor, evidently stunned by the realisation of how much Melanie knew, then dropped her head into her hands, as if all the breath was leaking from her. "Why don't you just leave me alone?" she said, almost inaudibly. "Please, let me be."

Melanie went to her and gently touched her shoulder. "What are you frightened of, Pamela?"

"Bloody piss off," Masters hissed, jerking herself upright as if suddenly conscious of her weakness. "Just who the hell do you think you are?"

Melanie looked at her for a moment, picked up her bag and walked away, discreetly sending Justin a draft text. By the door she turned. "I'm the person you should keep in touch with." She took a scrap of paper from her bag, scribbled her mobile number and left it on the nearest desk. "You can't hide out here in the sticks for ever, Pamela. Things are going to get bad, and I'm the detective who can look after you," she said, and quietly closed the door behind her.

Justin had parked well away from the school gates because Melanie had kidded him he would frighten the girls. She sprinted down the lane alongside a row of shiny black SUVs and clambered, breathless, into the passenger seat. "Anything?"

The cell-site scanner in Justin's lap was already activating. "You are so out of condition," he chided, as numbers rolled onto the screen. "And scary. What the hell did you say to her?"

"Just get your foot down," she panted, reaching for the seatbelt and checking the time. "How soon can you get the readout?"

Alan Fargo called them with the mobile result as they were speeding along the elevated section of the M4, near the junction with the North Circular Road. Melanie scribbled the details down and speed-dialled Kerr.

"How was she?" asked Kerr, the second he picked up.

"Tore into me like I hadn't learnt my Wordsworth."

"Did she ask how we got to her?"

"No. Kestrel's dirty little secret is safe for the time being," said Melanie. "She called two mobiles, one UK, the other international. Justin says speed-dialling, so they were in her contacts list. Must have been calling the moment I walked out the door. No names yet. Al says they're both blocked."

"So let's unscramble them."

CHAPTER
THIRTY-SEVEN

Karl Sergeyev was trying to persuade his new boss to back away from the most recent love of his life. It was only his third day of gardening leave but he was already fully occupied with driving assignments for Yuri Goschenko. Mostly, Karl was annoyed with himself. Olga had persuaded Goschenko to employ him and he should have been expressing gratitude, not the adolescent sexual jealousy that had pulsed through him since he'd stumbled back to Hammersmith from the pub the night before. Never before afflicted by self-doubt, Karl was feeling more stressed with each passing day. In less than five weeks he had sacrificed his family, his job and, with that, his many friendships at the Yard. Of all the women in his life, none had moved him so violently as Olga, and jealousy only seemed to stoke his passion. He also knew he was drinking too much: the vodka that had fired his weekend in Olga's bed was starting to become a crutch.

"This is difficult for me, Yuri. I thought Olga had told you. We are both moving on and she wants to study." Karl winced inwardly. It made him sound needy, and Karl Sergeyev had never wanted for anything in his entire life. The more he pleaded, the less he liked himself.

"Relax, Karl. Last night was no big deal, believe me. A boring trade delegation in Highgate, for God's sake, not your bloody Baftas. A reception afterwards, a few drinks. You know how it is. I was seen, and so was Olga. She makes me look good. You can understand this is important for me, yes? Great for business?"

Goschenko sat back in his chair and looked at Karl, conversation over. He was very broad-shouldered, with close-cropped hair, a wide, grey face, and eyes that narrowed whenever he spoke. In a long and colourful career he had grown accustomed to acquiescence. He was shorter than Karl, yet his body and personality exuded power. For a Russian millionaire eager to integrate within the City's corporate élite, Goschenko maintained a curiously old-fashioned office. He described it as the "global headquarters" of the innocuous-sounding Eagle Security Services, even though most of the company's major clients were wealthy Russian *émigrés* within Europe and the Middle East. His clothes, car and lifestyle choices were thoroughly Westernised, and the tabloids sometimes described him as a playboy; yet the business setting just off Belgrave Square seemed vaguely Soviet.

The heavy curtains were permanently drawn, requiring the giant crystal chandelier to be lit whenever the maestro was in residence, and a heavy oak desk was kept clear except for his computer and telephone.

Visitors were confronted by ornate carvings and then by the great man himself, seated in a heavily upholstered chair like a bishop's throne, with the apex rising a full three feet above his head. The conference table could easily accommodate eight, and Goschenko regularly invited special guests to join him on the dark leather suite and enjoy a glass of vodka from the richly decorated drinks cabinet.

Olga told Karl it was all an act, designed to impress Westerners brought up on stainless steel. But whatever the City thought of Goschenko, the guests Karl had chauffeured away earlier that afternoon from his comfortable sofa seemed full of admiration.

Goschenko had insisted Karl take an armchair. He perched uncomfortably on the edge, knowing Goschenko was deliberately confusing the master-and-servant relationship in order to win the argument. "It was escort only," Goschenko smiled, slapping Karl's knee, "with a couple of drinks afterwards. And she told you I delivered her safely back to you? Like I say, Karl, this is business, not pleasure."

After he had stormed away from Olga's apartment, Karl had spent two hours wandering by the Thames in Hammersmith before skulking back to her well after three. His late night of drink and high emotion had left him feeling shattered. This was one of the rare occasions when his appearance was actually working against him, and he guessed Goschenko knew it. "But she doesn't want to do this any more, Yuri."

"Well, I asked her and she said yes straight away," laughed Goschenko. "Come on, Karl, you know all beautiful girls love being seen. Let's hear no more about it. You look tired. A lot of things are happening to you all at once. Go and be kind to your family. Have fun, and I will see you tomorrow."

"Thing is, Yuri, Olga and I, well, I don't know if she told you yet but we're kind of an item. She's going back to college. Ealing, to study psychology. Enrols tonight."

"Karl, let me come to the point." Goschenko was no longer smiling. The new look dispelled any ambiguity about their relationship. He spoke softly, gliding straight to the bottom line: "You look like shit, and I cannot employ a man who drinks and drives. You need this job, my friend. Don't tell me you are going to leave so soon over a hooker?"

Karl wanted to hit Goschenko but left without another word, his boss's ultimatum ringing in his ears. He knew the insult was aimed at him as much as Olga: what man could hope to share his life with a woman who used her body in that way? Swamped by his obsession with his beautiful lover, Karl felt his self-respect ebbing away. And Yuri Goschenko, who was supposed to be his saviour, was simply compounding his sense of failure.

Karl left the office immediately and went to his old home to play Dad to his children, just as he had promised Nancy. They were looking out for him from the living-room window when he drew up outside the house shortly before five-thirty. As soon as they clambered into the car they asked him again why he and Mummy were not friends any more. He drove them to a local burger bar and was halfway through his double cheese-burger and fries before he realised he had left his phone in the office. When he took the children home he asked Nancy if he could come in to talk things over, but she made him stay in the car and slammed the door on him as soon as they were safely inside.

He found his mobile in the cramped space Goschenko had set aside for him at the far end of the carpeted corridor, with a text message from Olga, in Russian. "Hi babe c u around 10 all good for psych course lol xxxxx." He smiled to himself and switched off the light.

As he was leaving, he heard noises coming from Goschenko's office. The door was ajar, so he crept along the corridor to check it out. As he drew closer, the sound acquired the quickening, instantly recognisable rhythm of wood on wood and flesh on flesh. He peered through the doorway, transfixed by his boss's thrusting backside and Olga's half-naked body arched on Goschenko's desk.

Karl could have killed them both there and then. After all, he had committed his future to the two players who now grunted and moaned their betrayal at him, and everything about his new life of work and love lay in their hands. He watched with cold intensity as Goschenko ejaculated into her.

Perhaps he did not have enough love for Olga, or hatred for Goschenko; perhaps his senses had become paralysed, or he feared for his pathetic new part-time job. Maybe it was poetic justice for deserting his wife. The scene was a challenge, a threat to his whole life, yet the fight-or-flight moment sent him slinking back down the corridor the way he had come, isolated, leaving them to their pleasure. By the time he found himself again he was out in the street, searching for his car keys. He would always remember it as the most cowardly act in his entire life.

CHAPTER
THIRTY-EIGHT

As misgivings flooded Karl about his future with Olga, John Kerr was having another of the regular confrontations with his past. The subterranean wine bar just off Trafalgar Square was close to the Amnesty offices in Covent Garden so he usually met Robyn, Gabriella's mother, there. The place was actually a cellar divided into gloomy, low-ceilinged arches stained with the soot of a million candles and cigarettes, but the wine was excellent. It was as if the owner had locked the doors during the Blitz and reopened without a clean-up. Old photographs clung to the peeling walls, with posters advertising Ovaltine and Woodbines, and Robyn always mocked the portrait of a bullish Winston Churchill hanging near the entrance.

The bar offered privacy, which they both needed for different reasons. Arriving late was her counter-attack to Kerr's brush-off, so by the time she turned up he was already sitting at a table in the darkest corner with a bottle of Italian red. She was a couple of years older than Kerr, with brown hair in a bob and clear skin free

331

of makeup and undamaged by the sun. She looked neat in blue jeans, sweatshirt and trainers. "Hiya. Sorry."

"No, you're not," said Kerr, sliding her a glass. She leant forward so he could kiss her on both cheeks.

"Lots to talk about at the office." Although Robyn had lived in Rome for nearly two decades, her accent still belonged to Glasgow.

"So much injustice in the world."

"And how many people have you betrayed today, Signor Kerr?" she asked, sniffing her wine. "Or whoever you are this year."

Their encounters always began like this. When they had met in 1990 Kerr was in the second year of his undercover mission, using the name John Corley, with Bill Ritchie as his controller. Robyn Callaghan was on secret record as a Scottish nurse with links to Brigate Rosse, the Red Brigades, in Italy. Their lives had converged at a meeting in Brighton organised by a radical left-wing group called International Prisoners' Aid. Kerr had studied Robyn's secret Special Branch file and targeted her from the first day.

On the final evening they had spent four hours getting drunk and fifteen minutes having sex in the back of his van. By the time Robyn tracked John Corley down she was five months pregnant with Gabi. He had spotted her walking into the yard behind the car-spares shop in Southall, where he'd had his cover employment, and his blood had frozen.

"Congratulations," he had said, leaping out of the delivery van and forcing himself to think. "Who's the father?"

332

"Do fuck off."

He had taken her to the pub across the road, draining half his first lager in one swallow. "What are you going to do?" he had asked, brain in overdrive, wondering if she could hear his heart trying to jump out of his chest.

"Obviously we'll have to get married," she had said, drinking her Diet Coke without ice. "I thought you ought to know, yeah? And I do want it, in case you're wondering."

"Absolutely," he had said, trying to figure out what she would expect him to say, "but this can't disrupt our civil-rights work."

"Don't you think our baby has rights?"

"How did you find me?"

"Listen, I want you to be involved with this child," she had said, as if reading Kerr's mind, "so don't think you can just bloody disappear."

"This is really going to fuck me up." Another flash of reality.

Much later, when he had finally revealed his true identity, Robyn never admitted to her comrades she had been duped, and Kerr never told Bill Ritchie or anyone else in the Branch about his indiscretion. Robyn had had their daughter in Italy and named her Gabriella after the mother of a Brigate Rosse activist. She had set up shop with a couple of radical street lawyers off Via Giuseppe Rosaccio, in the northern industrial suburbs of Rome, and immersed herself in a network of human-rights campaigns across Europe.

"You look utterly shagged," she said, but made it sound an accusation. "Still fucking for Queen and country?"

"Thanks," said Kerr, clinking glasses, "nice to see you, too."

"Anyway, I enjoyed Gabi staying over," said Robyn, handing Kerr an Italian supermarket bag, "and she left her sweater behind."

"She did a great concert Sunday night. Brilliant."

"She told me you missed most of it."

"I was there. It was only one call. And you know we're full on with the bombing. Her playing seems great."

"Well, it's not. She isn't practising as much as she needs to. To be successful she needs to be full on, John. You know that. We agreed it when we funded her."

"We did."

"She's getting very active politically. Do you know what she's been up to in London?"

"I think she's been on a few demos," said Kerr. "Labour Party stuff. Student protests, that sort of thing. Who hasn't?"

"And the pro-Palestinian marches. Did she tell you about that?"

"You should be proud of her."

"So you didn't know. She's active in a couple of splinter groups in Rome, too. Got herself bloody arrested last time she was over for assaulting a copper. Not good. I don't like it."

Kerr laughed. "Spoken like a true radical."

Robyn was not smiling. "Don't take the piss." She stared at him. "Doesn't she tell you *anything*?"

"She holds out on me." Kerr looked away. "I'm the last person she'll take advice from. You know that."

"So work on your relationship. You can't turn your back on this, John. Christ, I'm supposed to be the leftie, but you're the one who politicised her. This is down to you. You killed that boy with your bare hands. You're not the father she thought you were." Robyn gave a short laugh. "And I should know exactly how she feels."

"So she cares about what's happening in the world. What's wrong with that? It's tough for this generation. Don't be so hard on her."

"You're missing the point, John. She's mixing with some really heavy-duty people here in London. You should see her stuff on Facebook. And some of the tweets."

Kerr looked at her in mock surprise. "You're reading her messages?"

"She bloody shows me. She's proud if it."

"She's compassionate, Robyn. She cares about stuff. It's the way we brought her up."

"Don't be naïve. I'm not talking non-violent direct action here, John. She's putting herself out to some bad people. Some of it's anti-police. She talks about her dad being a cop."

"Not my name?"

"No. But it's unsafe all round, and you should know about it. I want you to talk to her."

"And I will." Kerr sipped some wine. "So what were you talking about over the road? Still involved in the campaign against the sex trade?"

"You already asked me that on the phone, so cut the bullshit."

Kerr had called Robyn within minutes of Kestrel leaping from the boat, telling her as much as he could without disclosing the scale of the scandal. "This is important. Like I said, I'm not talking about your regular sex workers. This is kids taken off the street, with Turkey as the point of origin."

"Who are the end users?"

"Can't say."

"Well, it's the London end you should be worried about," Robyn said, then seemed to check herself. "But fuck off trying to change the subject. We're here to talk about Gabi. Promise me you'll speak to her."

"Next time she drops by."

"No. Call her. Be a father. Take the initiative."

"I promise. And I mean it, Robyn, it really is good to see you."

"Is that it?"

"Well, I haven't come here to shag you, if that's what you mean."

"Can we talk sex trafficking again for a minute?"

"Seriously?" Robyn laughed.

"Everything you've got."

"You don't stop, do you?" Then she slid her glass aside and frowned, gently chopping the table top with both hands while collecting her thoughts. "For starters, you need to read the report we did for the EU. But there are several routes into the UK, as you probably know." She waited for Kerr to reply but he was studying his shoes. "A couple of weeks back we had a tip-off from a Dutch drugs trafficker who said a British police officer services one of the London connections, drives the truck himself."

Kerr's head shot up. "What sort of police officer?"

"A corrupt one, stupid," she said, with a lopsided look. "Why is your profession so full of deceit?"

Flashbacks to the siege in Hackney seared his brain. The rubber-heelers had tasked Melanie against a corrupt undercover officer. The mission to identify and trap this individual could so easily have resulted in her death. Suddenly Kerr was back in the stronghold again, ice cold, wanting to kill Melanie's captors. He tried to keep the urgency from his voice. "I mean, is he in the Met?"

"No, and for once just listen. This particular trade route originates in Turkey, with girls snatched from the street to be sex workers in London. He's absolutely specific about that. The cop makes the pick-up in Holland, hides them in metal coffins beneath the truck for the ferry trip to England and gets a free pass through Customs. The girls must be half dead by the time they get here."

"Why would a drugs trafficker tell Amnesty this?"

"Because he deals drugs with the cop on the side but draws the line at this kind of abuse."

"What kind of drugs?"

"High-quality cocaine, mainly," Robyn said.

"What did Amnesty do with this? Who did they tell?"

"Above my pay grade. One of our workers has a friend she calls a rubber-heeler, whatever that is."

"Anti-corruption Unit. Jesus, this is important, Robyn."

"Said she was going to call him off the record."

"Did she? Do you know if she made the call? Can you get me a name?" pressed Kerr, sitting forward.

Robyn exhaled. "All I know is that the bad guy is unusual because he's got a licence to drive those massive bloody beasts that shouldn't be allowed on the roads."

"So, probably HGV-qualified to drive thirty-two-tonners," said Kerr. "Which narrows the field. Anything else?"

"She thinks he works in some sort of crime-fighting unit, one of those useless bureaucratic monsters they refer to by its letters."

Kerr's jacket pocket was buzzing.

Robyn scowled. "Don't you ever turn that bloody thing off?"

"Doesn't matter. Go on."

"Cosa something, as in Cosa Nostra."

"SOCA? Does that sound right?"

"Yes," she said softly. "Yeah, it does. Whatever it stands for."

"Serious Organised Crime Agency. It's the old name for the National Crime Agency. Their boss just offered me a job to investigate this kind of shit. He's a good man, a friend, and I want to look out for him. Can you get me some more, Robyn? It's really important."

"So you keep saying. I'll see what I can do."

"You're a one-off," said Kerr, kissing her on the cheek and checking his BlackBerry in a single movement, "and I have to make a call."

"Another woman?"

"It is, actually," he chuckled, reading Melanie's surveillance update, "but it's just work."

Robyn laughed, almost choking on her wine. "Yeah, just like me."

CHAPTER
THIRTY-NINE

Wednesday, 19 September, 21.53, Kerr's apartment

Kerr arrived home to find Justin high up in the hallway on his step-ladder. "Help yourself from the fridge," he said, flicking on the kettle.

"Already did."

Kerr saw the three miniature microphones as soon as he returned to the living room. "Where the hell did these come from?" They were lying on the sofa, where Justin had lined them up like exhibits.

"Telephone, table lamp and TV. Usual places," said Justin, scampering down the ladder. "I'm sorry, boss. They got here first, but I'm installing the camera anyway."

"Jesus. When did you find them?"

"The scanner was beeping like crazy as soon as I walked into the room. They weren't hard to track."

Without touching it, Kerr bent down to examine the nearest device.

"They're not your bog-standard Met issue," said Justin, apparently reading Kerr's thoughts, "but not hard to find."

"Jack and I searched Marston Street Monday night," said Kerr. "So let's assume they're bugging me because of that. Which means they broke in during the last forty-eight hours. I've hardly been home. Made no calls from here. All they'll have is me snoring."

"Let's not assume anything, boss. We had the meeting here Sunday, remember? That was a pretty free and easy discussion, as I recall. No holds barred. Including my ducking and diving inside Jibril's safe-house and Julia Bakkour's office."

"Which gives them what? The fact we know about Omar Taleb calling Julia on the day of the bombings."

"Plus the code — you know, the ED dash TA stuff — and the fact I found Jibril's Sim card."

"Right," said Kerr, frowning as he rewound Sunday afternoon's get-together. "And the dodgy history of that safe-house linked to Syrian terrorism in London."

"If the bugs were in here on Sunday they'll have the lot, for sure," said Justin. "And there's something else you have to think about as well, boss."

Kerr was looking around, as if he might find another microphone Justin had missed. "Go on."

"Your daughter. They'll know Gabi stays here."

"Yeah, of course." Kerr sounded as if he had already considered that possibility, but his eyes were still scanning the room. "I'll give that some thought. So you think I'm clear now?"

"As of this moment completely sterile. I'll do another sweep in a couple of days."

"And they'll know we found them."

"Yeah," said Justin. "Looks like we just upped the ante."

Kerr showered, changed into jeans and a white T-shirt and made mugs of ginger and lemon tea. He handed one up to Justin and padded, barefoot, into the living room, checking the late headlines on Sky.

The frenetic pace since the bombings meant Kerr had a late night of catching up ahead of him. Now he set his laptop on the dining-table, with papers and other surveillance photographs scattered around it. Alan Fargo had been examining every detail he could steal about the bombing investigation and checking every hour of the surveillance logs. Kerr would work late into the night, going over the data, checking for anything 1830 might have missed and hunting for new leads.

After a few minutes he heard Justin packing away his tools. "All done, boss," he called, folding the step-ladder.

"Cheers, Justin," said Kerr, walking over to give him a hand. "I owe you a pint."

Justin pointed up at the camera, buried deep in the plaster cornice. "Tape's on a thirty-six-hour loop," he said, picking up his toolbox, "and I left a couple of spares in the kitchen. If they risk a return visit we'll have them."

When Kerr sat down again there was a message in his inbox with an attachment. The sender was simply "A Friend", the subject "VERITAS VOS LIBERAVIT". Kerr opened the envelope. The attachment was a single colour photograph of a man raping a young woman on a couch. Both bodies were naked, with the man on top holding onto the arm and back of the chair. The attacker was heavily built, in his late forties, and visible only from behind and the left side. The girl, in her mid-teens, was arching her head back in a scream, and tears poured down her face.

In the background, almost out of the picture, there was a narrow black iron fireplace, the type that belonged in a bedroom. The mantelpiece was plain but there were tiles down each side in the shape of a trailing plant Kerr did not recognise, edged in small red diamond shapes.

Searching for identifying marks, Kerr spotted a gold signet ring on the man's left hand, reflected in a mirror on the facing wall. He zoomed in on the image and could just make out some italicised letters. Squinting at the screen he immediately called Fargo in 1830 and put him on the speaker while he forwarded the email and talked through options around researching names of the great and the bad. "I have to know who this guy is, Alan."

"I'm looking at it now," said Fargo, and Kerr could hear him cursing under his breath. "And we need to find out who the hell sent it. I'll get it out to Justin."

"He just left here," said Kerr, "so he'll still be on the road back to the workshop."

Waiting for Fargo to get back to him, Kerr played with the laptop, fruitlessly trying to identify the originator, before conceding it was a job for Justin's team. Then he wasted fifteen minutes zooming into every fragment of the image, studying each detail of the bodies and surroundings, before the solution hit him like a train and sent him speed-dialling Jack Langton.

Langton was with Melanie in the OP in East Ham. "Jack, cast your mind back to our visit to Marston Street, when you had a look upstairs."

"What's up?"

"I'm trying to place a photograph. Go to the smallest room."

"I'm there. And it's creepy."

"Was there an old sofa-bed?"

"No. Completely empty, like I said."

"How about a fireplace?" He could almost hear Langton's brain whirring and, in the background, Melanie's voice as she spoke quietly into the electronic surveillance log.

"Yup. With honeysuckle painted on square tiles. They stood out because the room was so bare. There was a mirror too."

"That's my next question."

"Fixed to the wall. I remember that because the actual glass was in rubbish condition, you know, kind of mottled with the silver backing coming through. But the frame was ornate, all swirly gold, looked like it deserved better. Oh, and there was a crack in the glass, bottom right, I think. How's that?"

Kerr studied the photograph again, confirming the detail he had already memorised. "Spoken like a true surveillance professional."

"So what's the story?"

"I think we just found our victim." Kerr's BlackBerry showed an incoming call from Alan Fargo. "Let me get back to you."

"John, I think we're onto something here," said Fargo, straight away. "The marking on the ring was a set of initials: 'RGA'. I tried Googling it, then gave up and got into the commissioner's library for the old copies of *Who's Who*. Had to go back a few years but there's a Ralph Godfrey Attwell QC, born 1929."

"Too old . . ."

". . . and very dead," said Fargo, "but he has a son, Robert James, under-secretary of state in the Foreign Office."

Kerr was suddenly alert. "Who wears his father's signet ring?"

"I reckon so. Hang on a sec." Kerr could hear Fargo shuffling books on his desk. "I've borrowed the lawyers' list. Robert James Attwell is also a barrister, left Gray's Inn on secondment to the Civil Service and stayed. And listen to this, he was in the Ministry of Defence for a while but made his name in the Foreign Office. The man's a specialist in international law, John."

CHAPTER
FORTY

Friday, 21 September, 10.43, New Scotland Yard

On Friday morning, Paula Weatherall sat at her desk behind a thick blue ring binder stuffed with briefing papers. Meetings of the Terrorism Committee of the Association of Chief Police Officers, known as ACPO, took place quarterly, each UK region hosting the meetings in rotation. For Weatherall, the expensive dinner in a local hotel the evening before the meeting, usually after a long drive from London, was always a drag. The toasts, vacuous speeches and male pecking order gave it a cliquey, quasi-Freemasonry feel. A glance at the seating plan warned her to expect an evening of sly politicking and red-faced your-room-or-mine sexual harassment.

Next Wednesday's meeting in Birmingham, she could tell from the agenda, would be even longer than the dinner. She was less than a third of the way through the papers when Donna buzzed. "I said no calls."

In the outer office Donna had Weatherall on the speaker. She raised her eyebrows and winked at Kerr, on his way to see Bill Ritchie next door. "It's the chairman of the National Crime Agency," she replied, as Kerr disappeared into Ritchie's office. "Shall I say you're too busy?"

Weatherall could tell from the echo that Donna was up to her usual games. "Of course not. I'll take it now . . . Sir Theo. Good morning."

"Ms Weatherall, hope you're well? I'm afraid I'm calling for a favour. You have a chap called John Kerr on your books, a career Special Branch detective chief inspector. Expert in highly sensitive investigations, from what I hear."

Weatherall shifted in her seat. "We're the SO15 Intelligence Unit now."

"Of course," said Theo Canning, his voice smooth as velvet. "I was wondering if you could bear to lose him to me for a couple of months?"

"A secondment, you mean?"

"An integrity issue has raised its delicate head in my Agency and I need a trusted specialist from outside to help me nip it in the bud."

"That's out of the question, I'm afraid."

"Just the month, then? Paula, isn't it?"

"Sorry, Sir Theo, but I can't help. I've just assigned him to a new position within SO15."

"Really? Something more important than our collective fight against corruption?"

Weatherall could feel her face reddening. She imagined Donna outside, listening to every word. "Not exactly, but I have to consider what is right for his career development."

"Difficult for an officer who punches so far above his weight, and for that alone I believe this would be a great opportunity all round. He'd be acting superintendent over here, so you could make him substantive on return, if you wanted to. Isn't that right?"

"It's not quite as easy as that," Weatherall replied defensively. "There are processes, Sir Theo, as I'm sure you appreciate. Dotted-line responsibilities to reassign. Our modernised counter-terrorism arrangements are really quite complex."

"But this is an issue you might feel able to revisit?"

"I'll give it some thought," Weatherall said, cursing herself for sounding so flustered and browbeaten. "I'll speak with HR and get back to you."

"That's really decent of you," said Canning, as if giving his consent. "Any chance of a decision by close of play today?"

Weatherall heard herself mumble something about not being able to give guarantees, but by now Canning was talking as if it was a done deal. "Paula, that's terrific," he said. "We'll all be very much in your debt. Have a lovely weekend. Hope to catch up soon." By the time Weatherall had marshalled her thoughts to recover lost ground the line was already dead.

In the adjacent office Kerr's eyes widened in disbelief. "Policy Unit? You've gotta be kidding me. I mean, you are joking, aren't you?"

Ritchie leant forward. He had his shirtsleeves rolled up in combative mode, anticipating Kerr's reaction. "I tried to warn you but you never switch to 'Receive', do you?"

"Powerpoints, organograms and Excel bloody spreadsheets? Bill, when was I ever Mr Pie Chart? This is a fucking punishment posting."

"You said it."

"I've always been operational, you know that. Front line. Up to my neck in muck and bullets."

"And often charging down some dead end of your own making."

Speechless, Kerr shook his head at the absurdity of what he had just heard. He swallowed hard to control his anger and keep his voice calm and controlled. "Meaning Ahmed Jibril?"

"You've caused everyone a massive amount of grief."

"Eleven people are dead, Bill, including three of our own. Don't talk to me about grief until you've been to visit the families."

"You really are so far up yourself," said Ritchie, kicking a chair over towards Kerr. "And sit down when I tell you to. You told us you returned Jim Metcalfe's Dragstone database intact. But you opened it, didn't you? Copied the info?"

"Of course I did," said Kerr, rapidly calculating how Ritchie knew this and whether he needed to protect Alan Fargo. "Collecting relevant intelligence was always our job as Special Branch officers, Bill, or have you forgotten?" He reversed the chair and sat down, leaning on the backrest. "But now you mention it, why the hell were MI5 tasking the Bellies at Paddington Green? Metcalfe couldn't wait to tell me."

"MI5 have the lead and choose the targets. You know that as well as I do."

Kerr's BlackBerry buzzed and he quickly checked the text while speaking. It was a meeting request in his calendar from Theo Canning for two o'clock, "Somewhere neutral. Please call."

"So who gave the order to release Jibril so soon?"

"I don't know. But you should never have taken Jibril on," said Ritchie, reaching for his pile of paperwork. "Discussion over."

"Well, that's where you're wrong, actually," said Kerr, pressing "Accept". He hesitated, still unsure how much to reveal. "I believe another attack is already planned, and letting Ahmed Jibril loose was a monumental screw-up." He searched for some understanding in his boss's face, but saw only anger. "You've got to place him under surveillance."

"No," said Ritchie. "I have to follow the rules. Jibril is a free man. Finch let him go."

"With MI5 all over him, which stinks."

"But is nothing to do with us. And I'm certainly not going head to head with Derek Finch."

"Jobsworth bullshit."

"Like it or lump it," said Ritchie. "Finch is head honcho and you're a chief inspector who needs to wind his neck back in. Paula thinks you're a maverick and she wants you here where she can keep an eye on you."

"Paula?" asked Kerr, looking quizzical. "Very cosy. Do you know what they called her in her last job?"

"Be very careful . . ."

" 'Tsunami'. Arrived without warning, fucked everything up and disappeared. Oh, and I've been burgled, by the way," he said, before Ritchie could react. "Followed as

350

well, but not very professionally. Trace comes back to the Anti-corruption Unit. Now why would the rubber-heelers be interested in me?" Kerr waited a moment, but Ritchie's expression was unreadable. Reaching into his pocket, he threw one of the microphones on the table. "Let's try this, then. It's more sophisticated than your standard Metcrap anti-corruption issue, so who else has me in the frame?" He paused again, watching for Ritchie's reaction. "Is that a look of surprise or guilt, Bill? Why don't we go and see the commander now, ask 'Paula' if she can enlighten both of us? Why can't you be honest with me?"

Ritchie sat back in his chair and folded his arms. "Collect your things. You'll be working three doors away."

Kerr regarded Ritchie levelly for a few seconds. "I don't think so."

"It's an order."

"You going to discipline me?" said Kerr, standing to retrieve the bug and holding it in Ritchie's face. "No, of course not. So tell Paula thanks for the thought but I need to get this sorted first. Seeing as my own boss isn't interested."

CHAPTER
FORTY-ONE

Friday, 21 September, 13.51, Victoria Embankment Gardens

When Kerr called back to arrange their meeting away from the office, Theo Canning suggested Victoria Embankment Gardens, a quiet stretch of green alongside the Thames. He returned a missed call from Melanie as soon as he surfaced from the Tube. "Anne Harris just rang me from the lab because she couldn't get hold of you. The DNA trace from Marston Street is Tania's. Will you let Karl know or do you want me to?"

"I'll handle it," said Kerr, checking up and down the Strand for surveillance, "and I'm telling you to go home. Have a long weekend."

"I'm taking Justin to have another crack at Pamela Masters tomorrow, remember?"

"Jack can do that. Stay home and play with the kids. Rob must be worried about you."

"Rob doesn't know, and don't you breathe a word."

To reach the gardens, Kerr took a short-cut past the old Water Gate, built in 1626 as a triumphal entrance to the Thames but now a long way from the river's edge. He found Theo Canning sitting alone beneath a statue of William Tyndale, most workers having returned to the office after their lunch break. The gardens lay within striding distance of the Inns of Court and a pinstriped barrister was studying a brief, absently twining the red tape around his fingers, robe bag on the bench beside him.

Canning stood as Kerr reached him, eager to be on the move. "You look knackered," he said, as they strolled around the path. "Been overdoing it?"

"Only at work, unfortunately," laughed Kerr.

"We both need to get out more, my friend," said Canning, "and you know why I wanted to see you."

"Yes, and with all the shit I'm taking, your offer is becoming irresistible." Kerr made it sound light, but meant every word. Theo Canning was the only senior person Kerr trusted, and the man with the authority and the desire to re-energise his career. He was transforming the National Crime Agency into a new, level playing field, offering real opportunities to someone untainted by the stale politics and infighting that had mired the early years of its predecessor, the Serious Organised Crime Agency. Who knew what they might be capable of achieving? "Also, I believe you have some problems in-house."

Canning's eyebrows shot up. "Really? So let's have it. Tell me all."

Kerr had already briefed his team about Robyn's sex-trafficking allegations. Now he broke the news to Canning, without disclosing her identity. But it was her claim that a corrupt undercover officer was infiltrating girls into the UK under the cover of his Agency that

353

stopped Canning in his tracks. "HMG conniving in the trafficking of sex workers? Aided and abetted by someone in my own organisation?" he said. "Jesus Christ, it beggars belief."

They had reached the east gate alongside the Savoy, where a woman in a *burkha* and stilettos watched over her two children circling the path on plastic tricycles. They stood aside as the kids careered past their ankles. "We have to close this down quickly, Theo, no matter who's involved."

From the safety of his plinth, the statue of Robbie Burns glared down on a rough sleeper. "This is another hangover from the past. The sort of thing I was telling you about. Fuck, it's all I need on top of everything else," said Canning as they accelerated through the tramp's stench, "but I'm going to investigate it." Angry eyes fuelled by heavy-duty lager, the wino was shouting after them now, calling them a pair of bastards. Canning ignored the ranting and stopped to face Kerr. "You've just told me I may have another big corruption problem inside my organisation. If this story has legs, John, I need you more than ever. I called Paula What's-her-name to ask if she would release you but she hasn't rung back yet."

The children had run back to their mother and Kerr watched the tramp struggle to focus on them. "Like I say, Theo, I'm giving it serious thought. Let's wait and see what she says first."

"Of course. But in the meantime I really need to progress this." They wandered back towards the Water Gate and Embankment station. "I checked on Joe

Allenby over at Vauxhall Cross, by the way, as promised. Turns out he's resigned. Very sudden, but it happens over there a lot, these days. They're all very tight-lipped about it. Perhaps they bollocked him for passing you the Jibril stuff on the side and he told them to poke it. I'll try and get some more out of them."

"That would be great."

They continued a few steps in silence. "Look, John, I appreciate this other thing is highly confidential and all that. Is there anything you can tell me about your source?"

Instinctively Kerr checked behind him and saw the mother ushering her children through the gate to the safety of the Savoy. "Sorry, Theo, I gave my word."

"All understood, my friend," said Canning, holding his hands up. "Third-party rules and all that. Forget I ever spoke." He slid Kerr a mischievous glance. "But you don't mind me trying, do you?"

"What — to bend the rules?" Kerr laughed. "I think we both know the answer to that."

CHAPTER
FORTY-TWO

Saturday, 22 September, 15.07, St Benedict's Independent School for Girls, Berkshire

Mid-afternoon on Saturday, Pamela Masters sat in Classroom 7C tutoring four of St Benedict's brightest for the Oxbridge entrance examinations. They were working through Chaucer for the specialist paper, and Masters was content to sacrifice her weekend because the pursuit of excellence in her students was the most important part of her role as head of department. Diligence had characterised her professional life and she wanted to give the girls the opportunities Fate had denied her.

She still wondered how life might have turned out had her own application to St Hilda's College, Oxford, been successful twenty years ago. She could have pursued a career in the private sector, perhaps, or one of the more respectable civil-service departments, with marriage and family life displacing a thankless existence in the shadows.

With knowledge came power, the MI5 training officer had cautioned her on her first day at Gower Street, but with power came the prospect of corruption.

In her first years with the Security Service she had relished the adrenaline rush that accompanied secrets, but by the time she had left, she hated the terrible knowledge they gave her. St Benedict's had released her to share her love of literature and lap up her pupils' hopes as if they were her own. And in the quiet times she was happy to settle for her books, *University Challenge* on BBC2, and generous glasses of Tuscan red.

Her living quarters in the school grounds lay within a five-minute stroll around the perimeter of the netball courts. She had a one-bedroom flat at the top of the West Tower with panoramic views of the countryside, and on a good day she could just see Windsor Castle. Searching for her keys, she almost bumped into Melanie and Justin waiting for her outside the main door.

"What the hell are you doing here?" she exclaimed, appraising Justin's woollen hat, sweatshirt and jeans as if he were a truant fifth-former. "I've already told you I can't be of any help."

"Are you going to invite us in, Pamela?" asked Melanie.

Unsure what to do, Masters fiddled with her keys and fell back on a lie. "I can't talk now. I have coursework to prepare."

They had made their visit outside office hours to avoid a counter-attack from the receptionist, and Justin had driven the BMW right up to the building. "This has to be cleared up now," said Melanie, nodding at the car, "so we can either talk here or invite you back to London for the afternoon."

"Arrest me, you mean?" Masters laughed at Melanie. "I don't think so."

"Try us," said Justin, quietly, suddenly looking grown-up as he absently rubbed his neck.

Reached by two narrow flights of uneven stairs, Masters's flat was Spartan and impersonal. The living room had a single armchair, cramped sofa, drop-leaf dining-table, 1930s oak sideboard and a television. In places the plaster had blown from the walls and, before the gas fire warmed the room, there was a faint smell of damp. The low ceiling, creaking floorboards and gurgling pipes recalled the decrepit safe-houses Kerr's team used for agent debriefings. There was not a single photograph in the room to suggest a life outside. The only personal touch lay in the poetry and literary novels crammed into floor-to-ceiling bookcases on the opposite wall, and there was nothing on politics or current affairs.

Worn with schoolteacher's flat, lace-up shoes and thick black tights, Masters's maroon raincoat looked too long as she hooked her bag on a door-handle and flopped into the armchair. "Well, can we get on with it?" she said, slightly breathless, "and to save time, anything to do with my career in MI5 is off limits."

"You may just have to rethink that," said Melanie, squashing against Justin on the clapped-out sofa. He had kept his hat on and drew another look of distaste from Masters.

358

"You said you had something specific to clear up about a murder," she said, eyes flitting around the room again. "Or was that a lie?"

"I want you to tell us why you left the Security Service," said Melanie.

"I repeat, I absolutely will not talk about my time in MI5," Masters said, with finality, ostentatiously checking her watch.

"Can we stop playing games, Pamela?"

Strands of greying hair had become detached from Masters's bun and distorted her face, tightening the look of pinched anger. "Who told you all this nonsense, anyway?"

Melanie put down her pen and sighed. "Remember those comprehensive enquiries we used to do for the Service?" she said drily. "All those extremists, subversives and future government ministers? Well, now we've done a job on you, so let's cut the crap, shall we? Who did you call when we left on Wednesday?"

"Haven't got a clue who you're talking about."

"We know you rang a mobile phone the minute we left. Whose was it? I'm asking you to tell us."

Abruptly Masters stood up to switch on the standard lamp. On the court below they could hear a group of girls beginning netball practice. When Masters sat down again she played with the stray hair, as if Melanie was not worthy of an answer. The girls' laughter wafted through the window.

"Are you tapping my phone?" Masters demanded.

Melanie ignored her. "We know you made a second call, too. Somewhere outside the UK. Both numbers are blocked, so we're assuming these are friends from the old days. We'll find out anyway, whether you co-operate or not. But I'm inviting you to tell us now. We're getting information about a sting operation, Pamela. Against someone significant."

"Really? Well, if you're so bloody clever you obviously don't need me to help you."

"Using a young girl, probably trafficked from Europe. We already have evidence. A photograph. We'll piece this together, however long it takes. Is that why you left MI5 in disgust? Because you learnt how depraved things had become?"

"That's enough rhetorical clap-trap for one afternoon," said Masters.

"Did you tell your reporting officer?" said Melanie.

"How much more of this shit do I have to take before you get out of my home?"

"Or the Service ombudsperson? Whistleblowers get a promise on non-retaliation these days, don't they? Since the cock-up over David Shayler? So why didn't you report the terrible things you were uncovering, as you were morally bound to do?"

"This is absurd." Masters drew her knees together and shifted to the edge of the chair, getting ready to stand and see them off the premises. "You're here under false pretences."

Melanie's voice was kind. "And you're a decent person, Pamela. You must have been horrified at what was going on. What's still happening today, because you chose to do nothing."

360

Masters walked to the door and held it open. "Arrest me if you like. Otherwise I want you both to leave immediately."

Melanie got to her feet. "Have you ever had dealings with a government lawyer called Robert Attwell?" Silence hung in the air, broken only by the laughter of the girls below calling for the ball. "Is there anything at all you want to tell us?"

Holding the door handle, the other hand thrust into her raincoat pocket, Masters looked away. Suddenly she seemed deflated by the extent of their knowledge. "It's none of your business," she said quietly, close to tears now. "I've moved on and don't want to go back."

On cue, Justin slipped between them and disappeared down the stairs. "Pamela," said Melanie, gently, when they were alone, "I'm sorry to intrude in your life. Truly. But you know we won't let you hide away for ever." When she touched her arm, Masters did not pull away. "And I know you're troubled because you have so much to tell me. When your conscience is ready you must call me any time, day or night."

CHAPTER
FORTY-THREE

Saturday, 22 September, 19.54, Kerr's apartment

Because he waited until Melanie and Justin had returned from Berkshire to brief him on the meeting with Pamela Masters, Kerr did not arrive home until shortly before eight, immediately checking Justin's security tape.

He had spent his second Saturday in the office, catching up on paperwork and trying to make sense of the pieces of intelligence springing up all around him. There were myriad operational demands in addition to the secret work against Jibril, a pile of regular political and security briefings and assessments of terrorist threats to Europe and around the globe that cascaded over his desk, waiting to be read.

From habit, he switched the TV to Sky News for the headlines on the hour. He caught the report about the missing girl while he was mixing a long gin and tonic.

"Police in Hampshire are investigating the disappearance of Sara Danbury, the eleven-year-old daughter of shadow justice minister Michael Danbury, whom they believe was kidnapped as she left a dance class at Lyndhurst in the New Forest in Hampshire earlier today. Officers are keeping an open mind, but say there is no indication at this stage of any connection to her father's politics. Michael Danbury came to prominence earlier this year with controversial demands for a further tightening of the government's immigration policies. Police are seeking witnesses and collecting CCTV footage from cameras in the surrounding area. A friend of the family, says the parents are distraught and appeal to the kidnappers to return their daughter unharmed."

Searching the fridge in vain for anything edible, Kerr ordered an Indian takeaway, then took a shower. As he came back into the living room his BlackBerry was vibrating with a text from Robyn: "nice to c u I herd the bent guy drives the beast thru hull but that's yr lot u owe me big time. TALK TO GABI."

He fired back a *"Grazie"* and was through to Jack Langton's home number when the lamb Madras arrived. He could hear a baby screaming in the background. "Hope I didn't do that," he apologised unconvincingly to Langton, as he opened the front door, slipped the delivery rider a tenner and refused the change. "What is it? Teething?"

Langton told him he was changing his daughter's nappy before the last feed of the day. "She's eight months. It's what babies do, John, remember? And shouldn't you be getting your head down?"

"You know that info I gave you earlier? About a corrupt undercover officer?"

"Go on," said Langton.

"How long would it take you to bike it to Hull?"

"Depends on the traffic and whether I'm ignoring the speed cameras." Langton had dropped his voice to a whisper, so Kerr guessed his new wife was nearby. He had met Katy once, and liked her. She was a sports teacher, also a Geordie, and Langton had met her on a return home to watch Newcastle United. "And I'm assuming you mean late tonight, so I'd say a couple of hours, give or take. Hold on." There was suddenly a lot of murmuring in the background. Kerr imagined Langton breaking the news to his wife with his trademark nothing-I-can-do-about-it shrug and overactive eyebrows. "No problem," he lied when he came back on the line.

"Jack, that would be great," said Kerr, pouring the curry onto a plate. "Latest info is this guy has been driving the girls in through Hull. I need you to get into the Customs office and check the port warnings."

"How far back?"

"Two, three months, as far as you can without pissing off the Cuzzies. Our boy will be marked up in the protected caveat list. Not sure what colour they use these days."

"It's a blue flag for undercover officers and agents under control."

"Theo Canning is going to check things out this end. Thanks, mate. Apologise to Katy for me and call if you get anything, yeah?"

By nine o'clock Kerr was ready to hit the sack. He dumped the takeaway packaging in the rubbish-chute on the landing, double-bolted the front door, locked the door onto the balcony and checked his emails.

Wandering through into the bedroom he vaguely heard a second report about the disappearance of a young girl, but it would be many hours before his exhausted brain registered its true significance.

Langton snatched a couple of hours' sleep and was on the road just after midnight. The baby was stirring as he left and burped when he winded her, leaving a rancid gobbet of sick on his shoulder. To avoid waking his wife, he free-wheeled the Suzuki away from the house, as he did on his early-morning ops, and started the engine up when he reached the park.

The Langtons lived in Mill Hill, north-west London, in easy reach of the start of the M1. Kingston-upon-Hull lay almost two hundred miles away, but Langton's surveillance teams regularly travelled there to pick up targets who believed security was less rigorous outside London. Monitoring police messages on the multi-channel radio as he flashed through each force area, Langton cruised at a steady hundred and ten and reached the city outskirts in one hour fifty-seven minutes.

By twenty past two he was strolling up to the deserted security checkpoint, crash helmet under his arm. The police and immigration posts were unmanned, as expected, but there was a light in the Customs office, where a middle-aged Jamaican woman in a blue overall and name-tag was vacuuming the heavily stained carpet. She did not hear his knock, so he had to distract her through the window. As soon as she unlocked the door he was inside, ID at the ready with a glance at her tag. "Hi, Celia, DI Jack Langton, remember? Nice to see you again," he lied, face in a reassuring smile. "Just need to collect something. They're expecting me."

The woman's tired face clouded as she studied his ID. "I'm not supposed to let anyone in," she said, uncertain, but Langton was already sitting at the desk nearest the checkpoint, riffling through the rubbish left there by the late shift. "I know, but no worries, I'll only be a few secs." He walked over to the kitchen area and filled the kettle to make her think he was familiar with the place. "Give them a call if you like," he said, flicking the switch, "while I make us a nice cup of tea." Langton sat at the desk again, making unnecessary notes, wondering if she would know who "they" were and getting ready to escape the moment she picked up the phone. Instead, the vacuum cleaner started up again.

Customs messages requiring attention to particular vehicles or travellers, known as "all ports warnings", were forwarded electronically from London, but the two computer terminals were obviously broken with their plugs dangling from the desks. Hard pressed customs officers at the port of Kingston-upon-Hull, it appeared, were expected to secure the border with clipboards and sheets of A4.

There were three drawers on each side of the desk, but only the middle right was locked. Langton jiggled it as soon as Celia's back was turned, before the kettle came to the boil. Inside there were disordered bundles of routine copy search forms, a couple of condoms and a Rolling Stones CD, but nothing connected to special warnings. On the adjacent wall there was a grey metal security cabinet with a special lock that Langton cracked

366

in two minutes while Celia finished the hoovering. The cupboard contained rows of outdated spiral binders bulging with a forest of directives, regulations and PR rubbish reaching back nearly a decade. But there was nothing of the remotest operational interest.

He found the confidential information he was looking for in the bottom drawer on the other side of the desk. It was a lined, red hardback document known as a "Book 40", a survivor of hi-tech law enforcement favoured by generations of police and Customs officers. The dog-eared pages were full of scrawled notes made on the hoof but, from the back, roughly pasted to each page, were copy printouts of outdated port warnings in sequence. The format was instantly recognisable to Langton, with a different-coloured flag against each name or vehicle number. For satellite offices without a colour printer they included a letter beside each flag: R for red, B for blue, and so on.

As he flicked back, Langton found only a few blue flags. Against each was the vehicle registration number and the coded reference to the source, two letters and a four-digit number: PI for an agent, short for "Participating Informant", and MI for an undercover officer, a reference to the "Main Index", the definitive national list of undercover officers retained by the National Crime Agency. Celia had disappeared into the washrooms and Langton heard water running as he primed one of Justin's Pentax cameras and switched on the desk lamp. By the time she returned with her mop and bucket, Langton had captured each of the twenty-three pages and isolated three references to MI/2403.

"So what's happened to me cup of tea?" she laughed.

"Coming right up, Celia," Langton said, slipping the camera into his pocket and squeezing past her through a haze of disinfectant, "and I think we both deserve it."

He was back home just after five-thirty. Katy was feeding the baby again, so he prepared breakfast while he made his checks. By seven his exhausted wife was in bed again and he was in the living room, on the phone to Kerr. "John, I tracked the Customs warnings back over three months. There are plenty on the list but only one possible undercover officer if you're definitely linking this to recent Crime Agency operations. He's on the national register for trained undercovers, and I cross-checked him with a mate in the Serious Crime UC Unit. He appears three times on the warnings, different truck each time."

"So what have we got?"

"Ex-Met guy, borough CID at Stoke Newington, then did a lot of UC drugs and firearms work. No one in the Met shed any tears when he jumped ship for the Agency. My contact reckons he was bent then, so he's odds on favourite now."

"What's his name?"

"Mickey Baines. Detective constable, HGV-qualified up to thirty-two-tonners. At least four work names for his sets of duff papers. I've put the three vehicles on the magic box with a warning flag to Alan Fargo, so we may get a sighting if they use any of them in the future."

"Nice one, Jack," said Kerr. "I'll let Theo Canning know."

CHAPTER
FORTY-FOUR

Monday, 24 September, 08.46, Home Office

Claire Grant MP, minister of state at the Home Office, was late for work. On Mondays, she normally reached the glassy new building in Marsham Street by eight o'clock for a team meeting with the home secretary. Today, in view of Saturday's news, she had taken a detour to visit Michael Danbury in his Battersea mansion flat.

Grant hated her right honourable friend with a vengeance. But for his vicious party politicking, her rise would have been unstoppable. A Cambridge economics graduate, she had been an international aid worker, supply lecturer and councillor before entering Parliament. Carefully airbrushed photographs of Grant's student partying cemented her reputation as an approachable, right-on woman of the people, and six years of assiduous manoeuvring had delivered her first Home Office ministerial appointment with responsibility for immigration, nationality and citizenship.

Grant was married to a corporate lawyer, who lived with their two children in an expensive farmhouse ten miles from Manchester. When Parliament was sitting she stayed during the week at their second home, a one-bedroom flat in Southwark, within easy reach of Westminster, arriving by train late on Sunday evening.

Michael Danbury was her parliamentary shadow and had been identifying the thousands of dodgy asylum applicants spirited into the UK on Grant's watch. He had timed his attack to coincide with a media bombardment about knife, gun and gang crime, prostitution, organised criminality, theft of British jobs and the failure of multiculturalism.

The campaign generated a resentment of migrants that surpassed even the climate of fear against terrorism. Every time he accused her of incompetence, Grant played the race and tolerance cards. But then a number of things happened in quick succession. A tabloid published actual numbers of rapists, drugs traffickers, quasi-terrorists and sociopaths "ripping the heart out of Britain", and a bad-tempered debate with Danbury on *Newsnight* had exposed Grant's manipulation of the statistics. The next day the home secretary expressed complete confidence in his favourite Home Office minister; by breakfast the morning after, Claire Grant was toast.

Grant was the exception to the belief that the House of Commons club transcended party divides. Even a recall to government on promotion years later did nothing to soften her visceral loathing of Michael Danbury. Yet when he opened the front door, pale and watery-eyed, she embraced him as she would a brother. It was a gesture, though her skin was so thick that his peck on her cheek scarcely registered. "Crises like this

370

have nothing to do with political differences," she had said to him, on the phone the night before.

Grant sat with Danbury for a few minutes in his living room, politely refusing his offer of tea, observing his suffering at first hand. "I know we've had our battles in the House," he said, close to tears.

"Nonsense, Michael, that's all in the past. This is parent stuff," she said, vaguely thinking of the adult son from her first marriage she never saw, "me to you, nothing to do with politics. Now," she said, sitting forward in her chair, "I want to know what the police have been like."

"Chief constable came to see me last night. Seemed a bit of a prat, actually. Had the head of CID in tow and asked if there could be any connection to my political work in the Northern Ireland office. You know, revenge attack, kidnap for ransom, that sort of thing."

"What do you think?"

"Absolute garbage, as I told him to his face. That was a lifetime ago and I asked if he'd heard of the Good Friday Agreement, so then he droned on about the threat from AQ."

"Well, you have made some pretty trenchant remarks about Islamic terrorists."

"Kidnapping's not their style in the UK," said Danbury, shaking his head. "Different MO." He sighed and looked Grant in the eye. "But since you've taken the trouble, Claire, I just want to make sure, you know . . ."

". . . that they're doing everything possible? Of course, I understand."

"It would be enormously comforting if you could give Hampshire Plod a kicking."

"Go home and spend time with Selina. And don't worry, I'll drag the chief constable up to brief me personally, make sure he pulls out all the stops."

"Thanks, Claire, truly. From both of us."

Her work done, Grant stood to go. "I'll keep in touch, and let's speak again soon."

By the time she swept into the Home Office with her red box she was forty minutes behind schedule. She was renowned for her unpredictability and love of status. While other ministers mingled with their civil servants in the lift lobby, Grant's driver ensured a lift was held for her exclusive use whenever she was on the move, leaving the infantry to take the stairs. In the outer office her diary secretary was hovering with the list of rescheduled meetings, but the three other staff kept their heads down, gauging her mood. They had only seconds to wait. "Get me the chief constable of Hampshire," Grant ordered no one in particular, "and coffee, now."

"Number Ten would like you to call as soon as . . ." said Susan, the senior private secretary, as Grant bustled into her office and slammed the door. In addition to her own lift, the minister required fresh coffee all day, served black with sugar. There was a high turnover in the private office.

Susan buzzed through to Grant's desk. "I have Chief Constable Clark. He's on his carphone."

"First name?" demanded Grant, wriggling out of her jacket.

"Gordon."

She used the speaker, scrolling through her emails as she spoke. "Gordon, I've had Michael Danbury onto me. What progress?"

"Sara Danbury is a core priority investigation. Scores high on the matrix."

Clark had a high, reedy voice, and spoke like a statistician. "We're resourcing it as a kidnap, with the potential to develop into a murder scenario."

"Obviously," replied Grant, shaking her head in irritation. Clark's face suddenly came to her. Somebody had introduced him to her at Bramshill Police College, a blond schoolboy, with fluff on his top lip and coloured pens in his shirt pocket, who still believed in mind maps. "But what information do you have for me now?"

"Early days, Minister. The victim was snatched outside her dance class."

"We've all seen the news."

"We're still doing house-to-house and forensicating the scene, checking CCTV and trying to keep it high on the national bulletins."

"Your signal keeps breaking. What leads do you have, witnesses, et cetera?" Grant demanded, ignoring Susan as she entered with her coffee.

"The investigation is building steadily," said Clark, to the sound of papers being shuffled. "Three witnesses mention a grey Ford Transit van, sliding side door, no windows, and one says it was a long wheelbase. Male behind the wheel, dark complexion. Are you sure you want this much detail, Minister?"

"Everything you have," she snapped.

"Slim build, wearing round glasses. Wire-rimmed. A second male grabbed her. This one was also dark but heavy-set, wearing jeans and sweatshirt. I went to see Mr Danbury personally last night."

"I heard. Listen, Michael Danbury is a parliamentary colleague and friend, so I want to know every detail about progress. If you get anything at all, you come through to me, understood?"

"Certainly, Minister, if you feel it's necessary."

"I do, and let me know if I need to bring in the Met." Grant cut the call and buzzed the office. "What's happened to the call into Number Ten?"

CHAPTER
FORTY-FIVE

As soon as he received Kerr's tip-off about the corrupt Mickey Baines, Sir Theo Canning acted with the decisiveness that had served him so well as an undeclared MI6 field officer. Kerr had rung his office mid-morning while he was at the leadership meeting he chaired every Monday. As he had left instructions that he was not to be pulled out of it, he did not return Kerr's call until lunchtime, losing two precious hours for damage limitation.

Kerr laid out the child-trafficking allegation exactly as Robyn had told him, including the use of Hull to smuggle, and this time mentioning that the originating source was a dealer to whom Baines was selling cocaine. "Sorry to be first to piss you off at the start of the week, Theo," Kerr had said. "Must be a bit of a shock."

That was an understatement. Canning tried to keep himself in check as he absorbed the scale of the undercover officer's betrayal. The gross breach of operational security went against everything he had worked for in his own long and distinguished career, and Baines's sheer greed left him practically speechless. His professional instincts kicked in to cover his anger with coolness and gratitude, but he guessed John Kerr knew him well enough to sense his true feelings.

He kept the conversation with Kerr short, less than two minutes, while a deeper part of his brain worked out a game plan. By the time he buzzed his PA he already had a strategy mapped out. "Dorothy, I need to see Mickey Baines now. I'll hold."

She was obviously eating something. There was an audible gulp, and the chewing started as she dialled.

"No reply," she said. "I'm getting his voicemail."

"So try his mobile." Canning took a deep breath. Whatever his PA's failings, he was invariably courteous and patient. "Quick as you can, please, Dorothy."

Canning silently locked his main office door, removed a laptop from his safe and set it on the coffee-table. From a small inner drawer in the safe he withdrew a palm-sized transmitter and plugged it into the laptop. He took an electronic token from a locked drawer in his desk, waited for the number to change and typed the numerals into the laptop. He skim-read the decoded message, closed the laptop down, replaced it in the safe and unlocked the door as Dorothy buzzed him.

Mickey Baines was waiting in the outer office and jumped to his feet the second Canning appeared. As usual, he was dressed for action in baseball pumps, narrow jeans and torso-hugging red T-shirt, a Secret Squirrel always ready to deploy at a moment's notice.

376

Canning groaned inwardly as he led the way into his office.

Canning sat at the head of the conference table overlooking the Thames. His old office was less than half a mile away, concealed by a bend in the river. "I have an emergency special assignment, Mickey," he said gravely, "which I need you to carry out tonight." He was finding it difficult to conceal his true feelings. Having placed such trust in Baines, he took the man's treachery as a deep personal affront. He now viewed Baines as a double agent working for two masters: Theo Canning, and naked self-interest. He had ordered the execution of several doubles in his long career, and Baines would be no exception.

Baines already looked pumped up. "No worries, Sir Theo," he said, running a hand through his shoulder-length hair. "I'm ready to roll. Totally."

Canning fought to conceal his distaste. He had always held misgivings about the rough and ready Baines. Successful undercover officers exuded confidence, and the tiny minority who were corrupt often exhibited charm bordering on the charismatic. But this designer-stubbled insubordinate oaf had never progressed beyond a coarse extrovertism.

Canning outlined the emergency special assignment he needed Baines to carry out that night. The information was short and explicit. When he had finished, he sat back in his chair. "So, is that all right, Mickey? Can you do it?"

"Of course. No probs at all."

"Usual sensitivities apply, Mickey, naturally," murmured Canning, inclining his head to emphasise the gravity of the mission. "Can you make an excuse to your wife at such short notice?"

"Totally, Sir Theo." Canning sensed a physical expansion in Baines as he absorbed the importance of his role: he actually seemed to be flexing his biceps. Canning sensed he was the worst kind of police braggart, for whom secrets and indiscreet whispers lurked cheek by jowl. Stories about his vanity and sexual harassment of young female analysts over rum and Coke in the Thames Barge were legion.

"I want you to drive your own car and travel out through Dover," the chairman continued, "returning with the truck through Hull. Under no circumstances are you to call this office. For cover I want you to register three days' leave, in case anyone is foolish enough to ask. Understood?"

"Crystal."

"Thank you again, Mickey," said Canning, knowing he was seeing Baines for the last time. "This will not go unrecognised."

Canning left the office as soon as Baines had gone. It looked like rain, so he took his umbrella. For crash calls Canning used Hyde Park because its openness made close-quarters surveillance impossible, and there were so many options for the approach. He took the Tube from Pimlico to Green Park, changing to the Piccadilly Line for the one stop to Hyde Park Corner. He entered the park, walked briskly west along Serpentine Road and carried on under the bridge, tracing the northern perimeter of Long Water. It was a tried and tested route. He timed things to reach his destination at 14.07 exactly.

"Sorry, boss, hot intel," said Fargo, bowling into the Fishbowl with a glance at Kerr's regular Monday pile of duty sheets and a wink at Melanie, "but I think you're going to find this interesting."

Kerr felt refreshed, having snatched a few hours on Sunday to rest and recover. As he had promised Robyn, he had called Gabi to invite her for lunch at one of the many pasta restaurants near the market. It was mid-morning but she sounded sleepy and began to gabble excuses about having other plans. He made it easy for her, apologising for the short notice.

Kerr had spotted Fargo out of the corner of his eye at the entrance to the main office, tieless with his sleeves untidily rolled up, hurrying along from 1830 with the padlocked security envelope he used for transporting secret documents around the office. "More paperwork. Nice," said Kerr, drily, as Fargo squeezed into the spare seat.

"You heard about the missing child?" said Fargo. "Eleven-year-old Sara Danbury, politician's daughter, snatched after a dance class?"

"I caught the headline," said Kerr, with a glance at Melanie.

"Home Office is stirring the shit. Claire Grant's been kicking the chief constable, demanding personal updates."

"So why should that have you sprinting out of 1830?"

"You're being a bit slow today, guys," said Fargo, nodding at Kerr's desk again, "but I'll let you off because it's admin day. Grant is police and security, right? So what other office would that make her minister for?"

Melanie got there a second before Kerr. "Not counter-terrorism?"

"The ultimate authority for Jibril's entry visa," said Kerr.

Kerr had the blinds up today, so they sat in silence for a few moments watching the activity on the other side of the glass wall, assimilating what Fargo was saying. "OK, so Claire Grant's been making herself busy," said Kerr, eventually, "and her name pops up twice on our radar . . ."

". . . the same day . . ."

". . . in different contexts. So what you're giving me, Al, is what we call a coincidence."

"A linkage, which is what you pay me to make."

"But still conjecture, not fact. I mean, what are you saying here?"

"I've been kicking things around and I'm still not absolutely sure," said Fargo. "But I suppose I'm asking you both to look at what we have." He stared at his hands for a moment, collecting his thoughts. "We have all this weird cover-up stuff around Ahmed Jibril, with a special UK entry visa authorised by one of Claire Grant's offices. And you're investigating the disappearance of a young girl from that house in Marston Street.

380

Jibril's flat and the house have a connection to Syrian extremism going back years. Now another girl goes missing and who do we find sniffing around the crime scene?"

"Yeah, but that's because the victim is a prominent MP's daughter and Grant's expressing, I dunno, parliamentary solidarity," said Melanie.

"Or Grant is involved in everything. She's the link." Reddening, Fargo stood up to go, tucking his shirt into his trousers. "I'm just trying to put the jigsaw together," he said defensively. "Tell me, boss, do you have anything better?"

All three were relieved when Kerr's phone broke the silence. He picked up on the first ring. "Kerr . . . He's here with me." Kerr handed the phone to Fargo. "Islamabad."

Fargo listened intently, pausing occasionally to scribble something on the corner of Kerr's yellow notepad. "Thanks for letting me know . . . Yes . . . Cheers."

He handed the phone back to Kerr and exhaled. Fargo's body was beginning to warm the air in the cubbyhole, reminding Kerr of the moments in the bus just before the terrorist bombs had exploded. "Theo Canning told you Joe Allenby resigned, right? Well, someone gave him duff info. Joe is dead. A gardener found him in his car, parked in a lock-up with a hosepipe from the exhaust. Poor sod never even got out of Yemen."

CHAPTER
FORTY-SIX

Tuesday, 25 September, 09.16, Kentish Town

On Tuesdays, operations permitting, Kerr would take work away from the Yard in a secure briefcase to concentrate on a particular case without interruption, sneaking to one of Dodge's safe-houses. That morning he needed a couple of hours to review the intelligence from Room 1830 in peace and unearth any clues about Ahmed Jibril that Fargo might have overlooked.

For additional reading Fargo had brought him the current *BG*, or *Blue Global*, a monthly bulletin produced by the Joint Intelligence Committee. Classified "Secret" and printed on light blue paper, the *BG* laid out British security assessments on key countries worldwide. Membership was restricted to a numbered circulation list headed by the Queen and the Prime Minister. Weatherall's SO15 Intelligence Unit received two copies, both addressed to Room 1830.

Kerr spooked the surveillance around ten-fifteen, as he was driving along Eversholt Street, just north of Euston station. A dark blue Nissan Almeira had been with him at least since Trafalgar Square, and each time he made a dry-cleaning deviation, the car was there when he rejoined the main drag. It was driver-only, and Kerr could see him speaking into a mike on the hands-free.

This time Kerr would not need a computer check to tell him the watchers belonged to the Anti-corruption Unit. As he anticipated, the traffic came to a standstill along Kentish Town Road, with cars parked each side of the roadway and buses scarcely able to pass each other. In the tailback from the red light just before Fortess Road he cut the engine, ran back two cars to the Nissan, and climbed into the passenger seat before the driver could react.

"Shouldn't you be out chasing criminals," asked Kerr mildly, "and keeping your doors locked?"

The driver was in his mid-twenties, dressed in jeans and black leather jacket, frantically checking his mirrors as he snapped the glove compartment shut to hide a miniature tracking screen. "What the hell? Piss off."

"DCI John Kerr," Kerr said, flashing his ID, "but you know that, don't you?" He pretended not to have noticed the screen, which told him they must have attached a tracker to the underside of his Alfa.

"Get out of the car. Now!"

The driver looked vaguely familiar, but Kerr was searching for definitive evidence of police involvement. He spotted a Met Police time sheet, a mainset with a bog-standard serial number, and a chequered baseball cap for emergency ID tucked down the side of the seat. He checked the wing mirror. "Why is Anti-corruption following me?" he demanded, watching a young woman in standard plain-clothes jeans and sweatshirt get out of

383

a green VW Passat three cars back and begin urgently speaking to herself. "You and your lovely assistant, the one calling you up on her throat mike?"

The rubber-heeler tried to sound hard. "I'm telling you, leave now or you're nicked."

"I don't think your commander would want that," said Kerr, noticing the traffic ahead begin to free up, "not after all we've done for you." He got out of the car and ran round to the driver's window. "But here's something you can tell your bosses," he said to the startled surveillance officer, reaching in to remove the keys from the ignition. "Either put up, or get off my back."

As the driver hesitated, Kerr dropped the keys into the nearest drain, trotted back to the Alfa and drove off. Horns surged and lights flashed behind the surveillance vehicle as Kerr accelerated into the clear road.

He turned into a side-street, parked behind an unattended truck with Newcastle registration plates, and checked the underside of his car. He found the tracker within seconds, exactly where he had expected it to be. It was a magnetic device known as a "lump", the type Jack Langton and Justin had consigned to the crusher years ago. Kerr couldn't believe the officers' stupidity in following him so closely when they could have relied on the signal from the tracker. He quickly removed the device, clamped it to the underside of the truck and drove off, doubling back around Parliament Hill Fields towards Kentish Town Road.

The safe-house was in the roof of a three-storey villa just off the high street. It had a small living room and bedroom with tiny kitchen and bathroom, but it was cleaned regularly and there was enough frozen food to last a couple of days.

Kerr unlocked the briefcase, set his laptop on the living-room table, made a mug of black coffee and organised his papers to the cooing of the pigeons on the roof.

He worked on the time-specific operational material first, then picked up the *Blue Global*. He scanned the key political judgements about the countries most susceptible to terrorism, particularly from Al Qaeda, and depressing summaries of reverses in the Middle East. In the Appendix there was a Foreign and Commonwealth Office summary of live political issues under consideration by its Europe Department. There was a paragraph on the state of the euro and farming subsidies, an assessment of continuing economic instability in Greece, and a section on what officials judged might be a crucial milestone in Turkey's long, faltering journey towards full EU membership.

He spent the next forty minutes skimming the regular batch of routine confidential threat assessments, circulars and intelligence briefings. There was a critical status review of Contest, the British government's international counter-terrorism strategy, and a domestic security paper from MI5.

It was only when he broke off to make more coffee that bells started ringing in his head. Had he been in his office at the Yard, swamped by the daily frenetic email and telephone traffic, it was unlikely he would ever have made the connections. He flicked off the kettle and raced back to the table, riffling through the *Blue Global* Appendix until he found the section on Turkey. Marked "Secret — UK Eyes Only", it was a single paragraph disclosing discussions scheduled for Monday, 1 October, in London between British ministers and senior EU officials to assess Turkey's political and economic prospects within the enlarged European Union. But it was the heading that really grabbed Kerr's attention: "Europe Department — Turkey Assimilation", followed by a bracketed FCO link "ED-TA".

He needed Fargo to help him make sense of things. His friend picked up on the first ring. "Al, I think I just unravelled ED — TA," said Kerr. "Check out your *BG*, page fifty-three in the Appendix. Look at the header."

He heard rustling, then a low whistle as Fargo skimmed the text. "And Jibril's code is 'ED — TA minus four'. If that's an operational order, four days back from the first of October sets the next attack next Thursday. Is this all about scuppering Turkey in Europe?"

"An attack linked to Turkey gives the press all weekend to sabotage any EU aspirations. If we're right about this, we have less than forty-eight hours," said Kerr.

"And these talks are secret," said Fargo. "So, are we saying they blackmailed Attwell for the date?"

"I think it's likely, yes."

"Right."

Kerr heard Fargo take a deep breath. Then there was silence as both men absorbed the implications. Kerr's mind was suddenly a kaleidoscope of competing thoughts. They whirled him from his rescue of Melanie at Hackney, through Robyn's information about children trafficked for sex and the terrible image of child rape in Knightsbridge. And when those images faded he found himself wrestling to explain why a Home Office minister should show such personal interest in the kidnap of a young British girl. Every lead, from Jibril's safe-house to the fate of several young girls, to the compromise and blackmail of Robert Attwell, took him back to Marston Street. And when the churning stopped and his mind settled, he realised there was a gap.

"While you're on, Al, did you get the readout on that Russian's call log?"

"Yeah, an hour ago but I didn't want to disturb you. Most of it confirms what we already knew from Karl. Calls into the Russian trade delegation in Highgate, a couple to the London embassy, one incoming from Moscow while he was resting up at the Dorchester. Sorry to disappoint you, John, but there's nothing startling about Anatoli Rigov."

"Except he was a guest at that weird party," said Kerr, shuffling the papers back into the briefcase. "A murder scene. I need to speak with Karl again. Can you fix it for me, Al? And tell him to bring Olga along."

"I already tried and he's not picking up," said Fargo.

"OK, let's get hold of Olga. If Karl gets back in touch in the meantime, don't tell him. Make it

387

somewhere neutral — say, Starbucks in Kensington High Street."

"No problem."

"I'm on my way back. Look, this Rigov guy's job is to build UK trade links, right? How long was he in London?"

"Karl picked him up from Heathrow a week ago last Friday. He flew out from Farnborough by private jet on Tuesday. Back to Moscow."

"So, less than five days, with a weekend in between. Who did he see?"

"No one, apparently. I checked with my contact in Foreign Office Protocol. Her office has no record of any meetings with ministers or officials. Rigov seems to have spent his time holed up in the Dorchester and the Russian Embassy."

"Except for that party when Karl tracked him down," said Kerr. "Which makes me think the trade thing is a cover. I think Mr Rigov is in a completely different line of business. There has to be much more to this guy than we're seeing right now."

"If there is we don't have access," said Fargo.

"Which makes me doubly suspicious. So let's open another channel. Who's our friendliest European ally, these days?"

"I'll try the French."

"You're kidding."

"Dodge's team pitched an agent for them on Eurostar last month."

"I won't hold my breath."

Fargo came back to Kerr while he was still on the road back to the Yard. "Olga can meet you tomorrow morning, ten o'clock in Starbucks. Turn left out of Kensington High Street station and it's on the corner of Allen Street. And she asked me to give you a message. Yuri Goschenko is taking her to another of his special parties this Thursday evening."

"Where?"

"She says he won't tell her."

CHAPTER
FORTY-SEVEN

Tuesday, 25 September, 18.47, Chiswick

The fall-back house for the blackmail operation after the compromise of Marston Street was in Chiswick. Detached, on three storeys, it lay unobtrusively halfway down a quiet crescent lined with cherry trees, not far from the cricket ground and within a ten-minute walk of the Thames. Despite the wide black double doors topped with a semicircle of painted glass, it was less grand than the Knightsbridge address, with smaller rooms, lower ceilings and comparatively modest furnishings.

By the time Claire Grant arrived early on Tuesday evening Harold was already waiting in the sitting room with a tumbler of neat whisky. The room was cosy, about fifteen feet square and wood-panelled, with a landscape above the marble fireplace, dusty glass chandelier and threadbare rug over polished floorboards. There were two deep leather armchairs, each with its wine table, and a matching sofa. A decanter of malt whisky and two crystal glasses stood on an oak table in the far corner.

The minister had come straight from the Home Office and threw her coat on the sofa. Harold stood and kissed her on both cheeks. She let him ease her into the adjacent armchair facing the door. "You look ready for a drink," he said.

"Harold, what the hell is this all about?" She had to wait while he refilled his glass and poured one for her. "Not too much," she cautioned. "I have to vote tonight. Where is everyone?"

"It's just us." Harold laid a line of cocaine on her wine table and dropped into his armchair. "They want us to have a chat. They're so pleased with the public display of support for Michael Danbury. Delighted. Really. And as for the TV appearance, very impressive. Top notch, actually."

"Bollocks. Danbury's a complete dickhead." Grant leant over to snort her coke.

"Believe me, Claire, they know how difficult this is for you."

"So what the hell have they done with her?" demanded Grant. She stared at Harold, calmly sipping his malt. "Come on, what's the deal? Get to the point, Harold. This is dangerous territory."

"It's a little late to worry about that, my dear." Harold laughed and made a face. "We do what is required. And I'm afraid we have some more business to conduct."

"We?"

Harold was already reaching into his jacket pocket. He produced a folded sheet of paper and waved it in small circles as he spoke. She wished he had allowed time for the drug to kick in. He infuriated her when he was in this mood, making coercion sound like an enticement. "You, actually. Sorry," he said, sounding like a man put upon.

Seeing that Harold was waiting for her to take the note from him, she sat back in the armchair and crossed her legs. "No more, Harold. It's too fucking risky."

"A most urgent requirement for the London end," he said, still waving the note in the air. "A final call upon your services, apparently."

"You promised that last time."

She gave in, sliding forward for the paper. There were two names, with the precise details necessary for the visa applications. When she had read them she looked sharply across at Harold. "These are extremists like Ahmed Jibril, yes?"

"Students like him. Travelling from Islamabad," said Harold, soothingly. "Their presence is required here imminently for special duties."

"For terrorism."

"For a purpose devised by our masters, my dear."

"They're forcing me to connive in extremism."

"They have not said that, so how are we to make such a judgement? You authorise it as a special-category approval again, prepared and recommended by the appropriate civil servant, just as before."

"But it's too soon after Jibril. If this gets out . . ."

"Any review will show the background papers to have been recommended by your trusted official, just like his, and we both know how vague these intelligence assessments can be. A terrorist or agent out of control, who can tell, these days?"

"Well, I can't bloody well do it."

"As I remind you every time," said Harold, with another short laugh, "we respond to direct orders, not indirect consequences."

"Jesus Christ." The minister gulped at her drink, close to panic. "I can't take any more dead bodies, Harold. It's too much."

"And when did you discover your shiny new scruples, exactly?" Harold was looking down at his hands, his voice low. "Our masters' friends call the Danbury girl English Rose. God alone knows what they've planned for her, but she's tied inextricably to you." When he looked up, she saw menace in his face. "So, come, my dear, no more hypocrisy. Of course you can. And will."

"No. They have to let me go, Harold." Grant was pleading now. "You have to make them."

"Try to relax." Harold took his empty glass to the drinks table. "Perform this one more duty and your precious skin is saved. I promise."

"Then they leave me alone, yes?"

"Trust me." Harold turned with his whisky. "Look, I'm chained to them for life, but for you it's different. The night after tomorrow they will release you from any further obligation. On Thursday you will drink champagne, part as friends, and watch your career soar to the heavens." He put the glass down and removed his jacket. Grant let him take her hand, lean over and kiss her on the lips. "Everything all right at home?"

393

"Christ, Harold, you could fuck me to within an inch of my life before David noticed anything."

Harold pressed a button on the wall and smiled. "Would you like me to?"

Before she could react the door opened and a woman stood before them. She was heavily built, in baggy black trousers and a short-sleeved white blouse stretched over her bloated stomach. The minister had seen her before and glared nastily. "What the hell do you want?"

The woman spoke directly to Harold. "Are you ready?"

"Yes, please," said Harold, lightly clasping Grant's hand. "I think now would be a good time."

The woman looked down the hallway and reached out her plump arm in a beckoning gesture. They heard a faint voice, little more than a whimper, then Sara Danbury was standing in the doorway, red-eyed and weeping. They had dressed her in a plain cotton shift and her ballet shoes. She wore a woman's bright red lipstick and rouge, but looked tiny against the woman's bulk.

Grant recoiled in her chair against Harold's arm, as if the child was about to attack her. "Oh, no, Harold. Don't let them do this to me," she wailed, as the awful realisation struck her. "Please. I'm begging you."

Harold was stroking her hand now and making shushing sounds as the woman led the child to the drinks table. "She is here to serve you, my dear," he whispered soothingly, "so you must sit still and enjoy."

Grant froze as the woman awkwardly closed Sara's fingers around the whisky decanter.

"I have to work tonight," was all Grant could say. Then she managed another glare at the woman. "Don't you listen? I said I don't want any more, you fat bitch."

Ignoring her again, the woman positioned Sara by Grant's wine table. Her mind already blurred by whisky and cocaine, Grant tried to get up, but Harold's restraining hand rested on her shoulder as Sara began to pour into the empty glass.

The terrified child splashed whisky onto the table, but neither Harold nor the woman checked her. Grant was aware of Harold taking a couple of steps backwards. Then a video camera appeared in the woman's hands and she began filming her. "Say 'cheese'," she mocked, as she trapped the government minister being served whisky by the kidnapped child.

The woman led Sara from the room as quickly as they had come, leaving Grant alone with Harold again. She lurched forward in the armchair, face in her hands, distraught.

Harold moved in close, stroking the nape of her neck. "It's just their little piece of insurance," he murmured, "and you know how to make things right."

Grant was quietly sobbing, her head rising and falling in her lap. "I'm finished."

"Nonsense." The piece of paper Harold had given her lay in the fold of the armchair where she had left it. He reached down and gently pressed it into her hand. "Two more students, my dear," he breathed, "then both of us can have her and everything will be normal again. I promise."

CHAPTER
FORTY-EIGHT

Tuesday, 25 September, 19.38, Bill Ritchie's house

Kerr intended to drive straight home from the Fishbowl. Cruising down Finchley Road while Melanie trailed behind, watching his back for any new surveillance, he tried to relax with Magic FM, but the anxiety that had been washing over him since the *Blue Global* revelation would not let go.

He pulled in on a double red outside a kebab takeaway near Seven Sisters and switched off the radio. The road was broad, straight and well lit, so he waved Melanie past, confident of spooking any suspicious vehicles. Couples were already queuing outside the cinema farther up the road, tailing back almost level with his car. In his mirror a bus in the designated lane was flashing him as the stationary Alfa forced it into the main carriageway. The driver honked and gave him the finger but Kerr, deep in thought, kept his eyes straight ahead.

The interpretation of the message Justin had stolen from inside Jibril's water heater changed everything. He and Alan Fargo now understood the code "13 + ED-TA − 4". The key, buried in the *Blue Global*, had converted suspicion about another attack involving Ahmed Jibril into a conviction. Every hour counted.

Three youths were leaving the shop with kebabs, attracted by the noise from the bus and eyeing up Kerr's illegally parked car. One picked out a soggy piece of tomato and tossed it at the Alfa. They laughed and jeered as it hit with a faint splat and drifted down the windscreen, but Kerr was so absorbed that this, too, scarcely registered.

He had to balance the protection of his team as they developed their secret investigation with his duty to protect the public from another bombing. If more *jihadis* attacked before they reached the truth, all his work would count for nothing. Knowing he could have prevented an atrocity, he would carry another burden of guilt for the rest of his life.

The discovery that morning in the peace and quiet of Dodge's safe-house also left Kerr feeling even more isolated. He knew his team trusted his judgement; they depended on him, and he had never let them down. Now, sitting quietly in the Alfa, anxiety stirred deep in the pit of his stomach. With every danger sign his team uncovered, he had never been in greater need of someone in authority he could trust. But for him there was no back-up, no higher level of support.

Through the smeared windscreen Kerr saw that the youths had given up on him, distracted by some shivering jailbait outside the cinema. Suddenly, he knew what he had to do. His sense of duty left him no choice. The kids looked round again, startled, as he gunned the engine and squealed a U-turn.

Bill and Lyn Ritchie lived in Margaret Thatcher's old constituency of Finchley, north London. Their spacious four-bedroom 1930s semi was in a quiet, tree-lined cul-de-sac opposite a well-maintained park. The last time Kerr had been there, Ritchie had organised a party for the Special Branch Irish Squad after another Real IRA defeat in London, and the same ancient Merc had been parked on the drive.

Kerr looked apologetic as Lyn Ritchie opened the door, but her face lit up. "John, what a nice surprise. Come in," she said, as he kissed her on both cheeks.

He could hear the TV from the living room. "Sorry, Lyn. Is he around?" he asked, glancing past her down the hall.

"Of course. Bill!" she called, pushing open the door. "It's John — John Kerr."

In baggy green cords, open-necked check shirt and slippers, Ritchie was relaxing in his armchair with a glass of red wine. The decoration was tasteful and contemporary, with fresh wallpaper, a clutch of original watercolours and the kind of cream carpet parents daren't risk until the kids have moved out. Lyn's white wine was on a table beside the double sofa and, as Ritchie stood up, Kerr found himself wondering whether they spoke to each other or left it all to the TV.

There was an awkward moment as Ritchie flicked the mute button and pointed Kerr into Lyn's place. "What's up?" he asked.

The cushion was still warm as Lyn picked up her own glass and offered him a drink. "Red, thanks," he said, with a brief smile.

"What's on your mind?" said Ritchie, as soon as they were alone.

"Sorry to mess up your evening."

"You haven't," said Ritchie, taking a sip of wine.

"I'm going to. If I'm right, something terrible is about to kick off."

"What?"

"I don't know. But what I have to say can't wait any longer." Kerr leant forward and placed his own glass carefully on the coffee table. "I've had my team working on Jibril. Seeing as no one else is."

Ritchie flushed. "Against my direct order. And your assurance."

"So I lied. But there's too much at stake here. We've been working non-stop on him. And turning up some other things you really need to know about."

Lyn returned with a glass of red for Kerr and a refill for Ritchie. "I'll leave you to it," she said, sensing the atmosphere and closing the door on them.

"Look, what we're uncovering goes way beyond Ahmed Jibril. What would you say if I told you a clique of our great and good are getting their rocks off at sex parties where they rape girls trafficked from Turkey? Boys, too, probably."

"I'd say produce your sources."

"I'm already halfway there," he said, driving forward on a roll. "They've murdered at least one of their victims."

"Prove it."

"I intend to."

Ritchie punched straight back. "You need to get back in line, Chief Inspector."

"Have this for starters." Kerr reached into his jacket pocket and held up a copy of the photograph sent to his inbox at home six days earlier. "The rapist is a Foreign Office lawyer called Robert Attwell. Alan Fargo identified him for me. He's a specialist in international law. These days he works directly to the Europe minister. I believe Attwell is being blackmailed."

"Where did you get it?" said Ritchie, reaching out.

Kerr slipped the photograph back into his pocket. "Someone sent it to me. Anonymously. Would you have believed me if I hadn't shown you? No?" He slowly shook his head in dismay. "Bill, if you're holding the lid down on any of this, you have blood on your hands . . ."

"That's complete crap."

". . . you and whoever's pulling your strings."

Kerr expected another verbal punch, but Ritchie seemed to have run out of things to say. An outsider would have said he looked deflated, anxious and tired, but Kerr knew he was still capable of deception, his features honed to a blank canvas by decades of intelligence work. The phone broke into the silence from the hallway as Kerr tried again.

"I have to know what turned you against me, Bill? Or who? Why did Weatherall set the dogs on me?" He paused, but Ritchie's expression was unreadable, eyes darting away to the TV screen. "Is it Philippa Harrington? She's been raving to get me pulled back into line, which I presume you know about." They stared at each other in silence, the air filled with mistrust. "Look, some bad people are doing a number on me. I need back-up."

"So back *off*. Do something sensible for a change."

"Why the great cover-up, Bill?" Outside in the hallway they heard Lyn laugh as she took the call.

"When I last checked you were my guy running Covert Ops," said Ritchie, his eyes drifting to the silent screen again. "Why don't you just get on with the job we pay you for?"

Kerr's sixth sense began whispering to him again, so he reached for his wine to break the rhythm and slow things down. The visit to his boss's house had been impetuous and now he was playing catch-up, calculating how much it was safe to reveal. He took a deep breath. "So, have some more. Ahmed Jibril's safe-house comes up in connection with Syrian state-sponsored terrorism in the eighties. Remember the Hindawi case?"

"What the hell are you getting yourself into?"

Kerr carefully revealed the linkages his team had made between Jibril's safe-house and the house in Marston Street, and the role of Julia Bakkour's law firm in drawing up the leases for both. He explained Alan Fargo's clever identification of Omar Taleb, whose number had been found on Jibril's Sim card, as Syrian Secret Service officer Rashid Hussain. "Who buried the microphones in my flat, Bill? If any of this leads back to Hussain, I'm under threat from the hostile agent of a foreign power."

"I don't deal in speculation, or have you forgotten everything I ever taught you? How about some concrete evidence?"

"What — so you can check how much I know?" Kerr sat back in the armchair, crossed his legs and drank his wine, weighing the risk. "All right," he said, taking a step into the unknown, "here's a name you'll recognise. How about Claire Grant, Home Office minister? Ahmed Jibril's visa was signed off in her name, under Home Office cover."

This time Ritchie's reaction was unambiguous. He jolted forward in his armchair. "How the hell did you find that out?"

"So it's true? I've touched a nerve, haven't I, Bill?" snapped Kerr. "Is that expression anger or surprise? Are you furious because I know?"

"Do you have any idea what you're doing?"

"Or shocked because you don't? If Jibril is a terrorist, why did he receive the kid-glove treatment? Oh, and you know about the kidnap of the politician's daughter?"

"I read the paper."

"Grant is screaming for updates on Sara Danbury every two minutes. But I suppose that's just another coincidence in your book."

Ritchie was wearing his belligerent look, but even if it was genuine it gave away nothing about the extent of his own knowledge. In the hallway outside Kerr heard Lyn finish her call, then clattering in the kitchen as she emptied the dishwasher. Ritchie's body language left Kerr mystified, the eyes betraying nothing about the

402

clever brain whirring behind them. Was it controlled anger at being confronted in his home, or genuine sorrow at Kerr's career suicide?

It was the latter. Ritchie folded his arms. "All right. I was going to tell you tomorrow, but you might as well know now. Paula's offered you up to the National Crime Agency for a month, starting Monday. You report to Theo Canning for a briefing at five tomorrow."

"A month. Then what?" Kerr's BlackBerry was vibrating with Robyn's name on the screen.

"Do you need to answer that?" said Ritchie.

Kerr pressed "Ignore". "I said, what happens to me then, Bill?"

Ritchie sat in silence for a moment. His eyes were flickering to the TV again. "Don't say I didn't warn you," he said eventually.

"I'm not coming back? Sacked? Is that what you're telling me?"

"Commander's on her way to Birmingham. It's out of my hands. She's transferring you out of SO15."

"For doing my job? I don't believe I'm hearing this. Especially from you." Kerr's phone was buzzing again, this time with voicemail and text. He read Robyn's message: "Can't raise Gabi. Very worried. CALL NOW."

Ritchie must have seen the anxiety in Kerr's face. "What's up?"

"It's personal," said Kerr, already heading for the door. "Why should you give a toss?"

CHAPTER
FORTY-NINE

Wednesday, 26 September, 13.11, St Benedict's Independent School for Girls, Berkshire

When she had first joined St Benedict's, Pamela Masters would spend the lunch hour overseeing the girls in the refectory, then snatch half an hour in the staff-room before the afternoon bell. When they had given her the home over the shop she had begun to sneak back to the flat for a sandwich and a bowl of soup while glancing at the lunchtime news. Wednesdays were special because she had no afternoon classes. She might drive into Windsor to watch a movie, or spend the extra time preparing something exotic for her evening meal.

She was still breathless from the climb up the narrow stairs when she flicked on the TV. She froze with shock, but recovered in time to press "Record" on the video. She had caught the end of a news item about the disappearance of Sara Danbury.

The Home Office minister for police and security was making a statement on behalf of the child's parents, according to the on-screen text. Eyes glued to the TV, Pamela felt behind her for the footstool and perched on the edge, transfixed by the voice and face of the woman she hated more than anyone in the world. "As I have already made clear, the loss of any child is a terrible thing," Claire Grant was saying, "and each new day Sara is missing brings unimaginable torture for the family. Michael and Selina Danbury will not be giving interviews at this time and are waiting at home for news. As a parliamentary colleague for many years, and as the minister responsible for keeping our communities safe, I want to make it absolutely clear that the police are doing everything possible to return Sara to her family safe and well. You people in the media always deride the so-called Westminster Village," she concluded, with a thin smile and a tilt of the head, "but at times like this, I like to think it comes into its own."

Masters played the video over and over. With each repeat the truth dawned more starkly. "You cow," she murmured to herself, "you perverted fucking murderous bitch." She knelt on the floor inches from the screen to examine every tic in Grant's face, each nuance in the voice. Eventually she hauled herself to her feet, turned off the TV and stared at her shaking hands. She needed a drink. She rushed into the kitchen, but the cupboard was bare. Grabbing her coat and keys, she hurried downstairs.

She kept her car, a maroon Nissan Micra, in an old stable block across the yard from the netball court. She had bought it from the local showroom when she had joined St Benedict's, a new car for a fresh start in life. It was her pride and joy and she drove it into town every

Sunday morning to be handwashed and valeted in the supermarket car park.

The town was three miles to the east, reached by a pleasant drive through woodland. It was a bright autumn day and normally Pamela Masters loved the changes that accompanied each season. But today, speeding at a steady fifty-five because she was so agitated, she hardly noticed the leaves starting to turn on the horse chestnuts. The town was little more than a high street of shops and two petrol stations, with a church at one end and a couple of pubs at the other, just before the supermarket. Because it lay on the route to Windsor, traffic was always heavy, and there was a more or less permanent campaign for a bypass.

Parking bays were set diagonally to the street and she veered into the one remaining space on her side. She locked the car and hurried into the off-licence, only a few paces away. As the air was warm the shopkeeper had wedged the door open, and the explosion hit her as she paid for her litre of vodka. There was a massive bang, which shook the whole shop, then a whistling punctuated by loud cracks, like a giant firework going off. She saw the shopkeeper duck behind the counter, then a flash, and a heatwave blasted straight through the shop. She dashed to the doorway and looked out. Her beloved car was a cube of orange metal engulfed in fire. The upper branches of an adjacent ash tree were alight, and acrid black smoke billowed from the flaming tyres. The fire inside the car was intensifying into a fierce burn as it consumed the velour upholstery and the last of the petrol. People young and old were running to escape the danger, some screaming, all of them terrified.

Farther up the street she saw lunchtime drinkers drift out of the pub with their pints to enjoy the spectacle in the sunshine. Fucking rubberneckers, she thought. Someone's just tried to kill me and all you can do is laugh. But then, even as the shopkeeper dialled 999, the rational side of her brain took over. Carrying her vodka in its plastic bag, she walked calmly away from her car to the taxi rank on the other side of the street, next to the bookmaker's, for a lift back to school. By the time the fire crew arrived from the next town and directed the first hose onto her wreck of a car she was climbing the stairs to her flat again.

Masters acted quickly. She kept her coat on and rang the receptionist to ask if she could borrow her car for the afternoon, lying that the Micra was being serviced. She took a slug of vodka straight from the bottle and tipped the contents of her handbag over the floor in search of Melanie's scribbled mobile number. "I have to see you today," she demanded, after the beep on Melanie's voicemail. "It's two-fifteen and I'm driving to Scotland Yard now because this can't wait a moment longer so you have to be there."

Locked into her desk drawer, a brown A4 envelope contained such a terrible reminder of her past that she could not bear to open it. She made a brief second call on her mobile, unlocked the drawer, seized the envelope, and dashed down the stairs to collect the keys to the receptionist's ancient Ford Fiesta.

It was her first trip to London by car for years. She had to stop for fuel and forgot about the congestion charge. It took her twenty minutes to find a parking space in Buckingham Gate, and by the time she reached the Yard she was in a permanent hot flush.

Unkempt in jeans and sweatshirt, hair tied back, Melanie was also under pressure in East Ham, watching for signs of increased activity, a precursor to the second attack the team feared was imminent. Just before Pamela Masters had called, she had been on the phone with Kerr, who had wanted to update her on Gabi. Unable to contact his daughter the previous night, Kerr said he had spent part of the morning tracking down her flatmates. Neither could shed any light on her whereabouts. She often disappeared for a few days, they said, sometimes telling them she was going to his place for a stopover. Neither seemed alarmed, and both assured Kerr she would just turn up. So far as they knew, Gabi had no current boyfriend and was cool about everything.

Kerr told Melanie he was troubled by the possibility his apartment might have been bugged before his team meeting the Sunday after the bombings. If it had been, the eavesdroppers would know Gabi was his daughter and stayed with him. He told her he had kept this fear from Robyn, but was pressing her to remember any Facebook and Twitter messages Gabi had shown her.

When Melanie rang him back, Kerr told her to bring Masters up to the Fishbowl. She should conduct the interview, he said, as the officer who already knew her.

He wanted her to get inside the woman's head, exploit the weakness that had made her pick up the phone, cultivate her sense of dependency until she reached the point of no return. "You won't even know I'm there," he said.

When Melanie arrived, she saw that Kerr had pulled the blinds and was already sitting on the wrong side of his desk. "Thanks for coming in," was all he said, as she introduced Masters, then sat back in the corner, as promised.

"You sounded anxious, Pamela, like it was urgent," said Melanie, from Kerr's chair. She wanted to avoid speaking to her across the barrier of the desk, so had squeezed in another chair beside her.

"You said I could call you at any time," said Masters, looking between them.

"When your conscience was ready, that's right," said Melanie, pouring dusty water from Kerr's chipped jug into paper cups, "and you can tell I've come straight from the plot to meet you, so let's have it."

The Fishbowl was warm but Masters had kept her coat on and was fiddling with the buttons. Her silk scarf was tied unusually high on her throat. "Someone has just tried to kill me," she said.

"You what?"

"Say again?" said Kerr, unable to contain himself.

"No need to look at me as if I'm completely bonkers," she said, glancing at Kerr across the desk. She was twisting the ends of the scarf now. "They blew up my car. Torched it, whatever. I'd just parked it to go shopping. Booby-trap on a timer or something. Another

409

minute and I'd have been burnt alive. They must have found out you came to question me."

"Who?" said Melanie.

"They also sent me some pictures to frighten me off. But they obviously realised that hadn't done the trick because you came back on Saturday. Must have thought I was co-operating, you know, telling you things."

"What kind of images?"

Masters threw Kerr an embarrassed glance, but he had already dropped his eyes. "Pictures. Filthy, disgusting photographs that made me throw up."

"Showing what?" said Melanie.

"Do I need to spell it out to you?" She lowered her eyes to her lap.

"You need to show me, so I know you're telling the truth," said Melanie, calmly, pointing at the envelope in the woman's bag. "May I?"

There were three enlarged colour photographs of a much younger, naked Pamela Masters having sex with multiple partners. While Masters looked away, Melanie gave each no more than a glance, just long enough to register the other faces, then returned them to the envelope without showing Kerr and handed them back. "Thanks. I'm sorry. Who sent them to you?"

"A man called Harold. It was a threat to shut me up, before they tried to kill me."

"Harold who?" said Kerr.

"We just knew him as that."

Melanie shot Kerr a glance to back off. The invective streamed across the desk as if Melanie had suddenly

410

released a dam. "He's a child abuser. A bugger who likes little boys, but little girls will do," she said, voice rising. "He's a shit, a fucking bastard."

"Pamela, you need to calm down," said Melanie. "But this is your chance to tell me everything you know."

"He takes everybody in, then charms the pants off them. But Harold is a beast, a rapist."

"So you have to tell us who he is," said Kerr.

"I can't."

"Or won't?"

"It's simply not possible."

Melanie threw another warning look at Kerr. "Because you're frightened of him. Is that right?"

Her voice was scarcely audible. "Bloody terrified."

"But you still choose to shield him," said Kerr.

"I'm protecting myself!"

"We'll do that."

"Oh, bloody marvellous." She turned red-rimmed eyes on him. "Next time they burn me out you'll come running, yeah?"

"If you give him up now we won't need to."

"With me as your star witness? No way." Masters burst into tears. "I'm trying . . . doing my best here. Do you people have any idea how ashamed I feel?"

Melanie wanted to respond but Kerr got there first. "Pamela, no one's ever going to know, but for once in your life you have to be upfront." He leant forward. "I need this man's name right now, so stop pissing about."

"And you need to stop bullying me." In an instant her mood had swung from tearful to aggressive, reminding Melanie of their first meeting in the classroom. She wrapped her coat around her, picked up her bag and glared at Melanie. "If he keeps this up I swear I'll walk. Just try and stop me."

"No one's going to force you to do anything, Pamela," said Melanie, gently, pressing a tissue into the woman's hand to defuse the tension. She frowned at Kerr, trying to slow things down. "Why don't you take your time and tell us how you know this man?"

Masters dropped her bag to the floor, wiped her eyes and took a deep breath. "Joint MI5 and MI6 section over at Century House. I was a young desk officer, green as grass but actually quite tasty in those days, believe it or not. He was already a rising star. And he overwhelmed me."

"You mean he raped you?" said Melanie, quietly.

She wept softly, her head lowered again. "He introduced me to sex and I was willing. All of us were, you know, enthusiastically consenting adults. It was exciting, as much dope and as many partners as you could handle. Party-time every night, boy on boy, girl on girl, everyone doing as they pleased in the days when being gay would cost your vetting. No one raped anyone and no one ever knew because it was the best-kept secret. Christ, I can't tell you how cheap this makes me feel."

Melanie reached for her hand. "I know you had a child, Pamela."

"Lucy Ann. She died at ten months." She was quietly weeping now. "It's the worst thing that ever happened to me."

412

"Was Harold the father?"

"He was a charismatic man who picked me out from the crowd, simple as that. He finds a weakness and makes you believe it's a strength."

"The mark of a good intelligence officer," said Melanie.

"Don't make excuses for him. He had massive sexual energy, and the capacity to inflict pain. Then everything changed in 1993 when I got pregnant. Suddenly I wasn't family any more and he dumped me for a grasping, low-grade bitch."

"What did you do?"

"Mourned for Lucy and picked up the threads of my life back in the Service. Never saw him again, but I was hearing bad things."

"From friends in MI5, yeah?"

"They were making it all very organised," Masters continued, ignoring Melanie's question, "and Harold was introducing people from outside the circle, you understand? It was an incredible security risk. I'm amazed they got away with it for so long before it went tits up."

"What do you mean?" said Melanie.

"They were targeted and compromised. The penetrators well and truly shafted. What a joke."

"Who by?" said Melanie.

"They introduced blackmail, with everything secretly on film."

"When are we talking about here?" asked Kerr.

"I don't know exactly."

"But while you were still in MI5?"

"Yes. Five, six years ago."

"Pamela, who were the blackmailers?" said Melanie.

"Harold had several postings in post-colonial Africa. Kenya, I think, mainly. But his early speciality was Eastern Europe. In 1989 the Bulgarian Secret Service caught him buggering a nine-year-old boy in the middle of downtown Sofia. A classic sting operation. I found this out much later. They ran him against the West until the collapse of the Soviet Bloc, then handed him over to the Russians, who have controlled him ever since."

"How many victims?" said Kerr. "Do you have names?"

Masters shook her head. "But I know it goes on. The whole thing is disgusting. It's the reason I resigned."

Kerr was on a roll again, sounding more assertive with each demand. "How did you find out?"

"I can't say."

"So why didn't you report it?"

"Work it out for yourself. Harold was fucking me and his country at the same time. Imagine what they would do to his spurned lover."

There was silence for a moment as Melanie's "shut up" look pushed Kerr back in his chair. "It's all right, Pamela. I understand," she said, trying to slow the tempo again. "But if you can't bring yourself to name him, why have you driven all this way to see me?"

"I saw something on television when I came home for lunch. Just before I got in the car and . . . you know," she said, faltering. "Anyway, it gave me the most dreadful realisation."

"Go on."

414

"Claire Grant was on TV talking about that missing girl. But she must be involved in the kidnap, don't you see? Danbury got her sacked. He's her main political enemy. This is her revenge, to torture the parents by appearing to empathise with them."

Melanie made a face. "How can you know that?"

"She's the bitch Harold dumped me for. I just know something terrible is happening here."

"Pamela, do you have any idea what you're saying?" Melanie sat back in her chair and shot Kerr another glance. "I mean, do you have any proof?"

"Please don't stare at me as if I'm a complete lunatic. All that about getting the chief constable to brief her every day, it's so she can monitor what they're doing. Claire Grant is crazy. A complete pervert. I know her. I can read her body language, every fake expression. She hasn't changed one bit in all the years since Harold betrayed me."

"How did they meet?"

"Africa, I think. She had a job in international development after uni. These people are cunning in their madness. It's what they do, Melanie. It's what Harold has done all his professional life. Bring your enemies in close so you can watch them, don't you see?"

Kerr was already by the door, back in charge again. "I need to check something out in 1830. I'll be five minutes max. Pamela, this is only a pause. When I get back, you're going to give me the name."

CHAPTER
FIFTY

Melanie and Kerr had conducted countless interviews together. Like her, he would have preferred to maintain the flow of the interview, but Melanie guessed he wanted to brief Alan Fargo and initiate searches to identify "Harold". Who knew what 1830 might unearth while they continued coaxing information from Pamela Masters? She knew Kerr would also be telling Fargo he had been right to suspect Grant all along, sticking by his hunch in the face of their initial doubts.

Making coffee in the main office, Melanie kept an eye on Masters through the open door. She believed she understood her reticence better than Kerr did because she viewed the situation in the same light as other abusive relationships. The man Pamela Masters was unable to name had exercised total control since her early twenties. He had dominated her, shamed her, filled her with guilt and paralysed her with fear. She had protected secrets all her professional life, and her torment by this man inside her tiny, enclosed circle would be the heaviest of them all.

416

After the break, Masters seemed visibly to withdraw into herself again, staring into her lap and nervously fiddling with her coat and scarf. But Melanie was unperturbed. She had no shred of doubt that, before Masters left the Yard, they would have the man's true name, either by her own admission in the Fishbowl or Alan Fargo's deduction in 1830.

She offered her milk and sugar, then squeezed back in beside her with her own mug of coffee, deliberately pushing in so close that Masters had to shift in her chair. The scarf slipped, revealing a glimpse of her neck. While people went about their business on the other side of the glass, she behaved as if she and Melanie were strangers brought together in the same empty waiting room. It was an odd atmosphere, but Melanie let the silence hang in the air while they waited for Kerr to return. She studied Masters carefully, but the scarf was in place again. They sipped coffee until Melanie could resist no longer. "Pamela, you told us you never saw Harold again. But that's a lie, isn't it?"

"He dropped me years ago."

Her bag was lying between them, so Melanie retrieved the envelope. She studied both sides, which were blank. "You said these were sent to you. But there's no name and address, no postmark. Nothing."

"I put them in a different envelope."

"What did you do with the original? So we can do the forensics? And this isn't a new envelope. You have to level with me, Pamela. I think Harold delivered these in person. Or someone working with him."

"That's rubbish."

"Is that why you're so afraid?" Melanie gently lowered the woman's scarf to reveal red blotches and weals around her throat. "Did he still want to play games with you?"

Masters tried to outstare Melanie, then broke down and wept again. "He came to my flat on Saturday night, after your second visit with that young man. And, no, he doesn't want to have sex with me any more, if that's what you're thinking. Just to hurt me."

She stopped speaking as Kerr reappeared and slipped into his chair. Melanie readjusted the scarf to demonstrate that had been between the two of them. "Go on."

"He brought the photographs and warned me against speaking out of turn. He threatened me and I told him to fuck off, I really did. So today they tried to kill me."

Kerr was looking quizzical. "Later," mouthed Melanie. "You mentioned you still have friends in MI5, Pamela," she said. "And now that we've come this far, I want you to tell me who you called from the classroom immediately after I left you last Wednesday."

This time there was no hesitation. "Jeremy Thompson."

"And where does he fit into this?" asked Kerr, mildly.

Masters looked at him and gave a short laugh. "I think you know the answer perfectly well. Do you really think I'm stupid? I know it was Jeremy who put you onto me because he admitted it."

"That's not what I asked you."

She stayed silent for a moment. "Jeremy and I became friendly in the office because we were the only ones to have studied Latin at school. Ridiculous, isn't it, the things that bring you together? It was a bit of a standing joke between us, really, and to the others. But there you are."

"And he was a party animal, too?"

"Let's say he knows about what I've been telling you," Masters said carefully. "We both felt disgusted. I left the office but he stayed on. Married with kids, too much to lose. He believes the terrible bombing in Walthamstow is somehow connected to all this."

"What makes him think that?"

"I only know it's something connected to that man Jibril they just released. There's a special file under double cover, apparently. It never leaves Philippa's office. He must have got hold of it. And now the knowledge is destroying him."

"Jerry told me about the file," said Kerr. "So why did he deny everything when I saw him? Why the hell couldn't he tell me this himself?"

"He says you've been putting him under the most terrible pressure. Threatening him. He wanted it to come from me because he thinks you won't protect him."

"Bollocks. The coward's cop-out."

"No. You mustn't blame Jeremy for this. He has discovered far more dreadful things than I ever realised. He believed you would uncover this for yourselves once you'd met me. You wouldn't be able to damage me. No

419

one would. But I was wrong, wasn't I? Others can and will."

"I think Jerry's been spinning both of us a different line."

"I've talked to him a lot over the past week, believe me. Persuaded him to do the right thing. Jeremy will deal with this . . . in his own way. He has to protect himself, don't you see? The poor man truly thinks he's going mad. How could a few years of partying end in all those innocent people blown to bits? That's what he thinks. You have to promise not to harass him any more."

Kerr threw Melanie a glance. "Show her," he said.

Melanie scrolled through Kerr's emails until she found the photograph of Robert Attwell sent to Kerr the previous Wednesday evening, only hours after Melanie's first brief meeting with Masters.

They waited while she studied the date and time. "Yes, Jeremy must have sent you this. I spoke to him after you left, as I said. Then I called him again later the same day. He told me the guilt was driving him crazy, but I calmed him down, told him he could put things right. He called me again in the evening, when he'd had time to think things through. Promised me he was going to send your boss something. Look at the heading. '*Veritas vos liberavit.*'"

"'The truth shall set you free,'" said Kerr.

But Masters was looking directly at Melanie, as if Kerr wasn't in the room. "He called it his suicide note. He told me that as soon as he revealed this MI5 would find out and destroy him."

420

"It's not true. We can protect him."

"It's what he believes."

As soon as Melanie closed the photograph another email pinged into Kerr's inbox. The sender was simply "A Friend" and the subject "*Ultima voluntas*". "Hold on a minute, Pamela." She beckoned to Kerr and shifted her chair sideways.

Kerr came round Melanie's end of the desk and leant between them. "Open it."

All three of them stared speechless at the screen. The attachment was a good-quality colour video with sound showing a teenage girl being raped on a couch. She had her face turned to the camera, and Melanie recognised her instantly. "Tania," was all she could murmur.

The child's attacker was naked except for his face, head and shoulders, which were concealed by a black hood; he also wore black cotton gloves. From inside the hood came a muffled crescendo of groaning and snorting.

"Meet Harold," said Pamela, flatly.

"What?"

"He always grunts like that when he's in sex-attack mode," she said. "It means he's going to kill her and he won't let himself come till the victim's dead. There. I told you he was a beast, didn't I?"

The video lasted a couple of minutes. When it ended they sat in stunned silence for a few moments. "Now will you give this bastard up?" said Kerr, eventually. When Masters looked away he reached across her to his middle drawer, banging it open against her knees without apology. She had to push back as he shuffled through his papers until he reached an enlarged photograph of Tania. He dropped it on the desk in front of her. "You're a teacher, Pamela," he said angrily. "Now you see what happens when good people do nothing."

"You heard the woman's voice goading him on from behind the camera?" said Masters, stony-faced. "That's Claire Grant. She's the one filming it, I'm telling you. She often used to do that. She loves it. To film and be filmed."

Kerr took his chair again. "And I take it Jerry sent this too?"

"I called him just before I left, told him I was coming to see Melanie. '*Ultima voluntas*' means 'last will'. I really fear for him."

"So are you going to carry on playing the Queen of Dumb," said Kerr, "or help us put a stop to this?"

"Go and arrest Claire bloody Grant. As soon as I saw that bitch on the lunchtime news I guessed what she was up to. That's why I'm here. I have spoken out."

Kerr was looking her straight in the eye. "But that's not the only reason you came forward now, is it?" he said. "It wasn't only Jerry Thompson who made the connection between in-house shagging and outright slaughter, was it?"

Masters lowered her head. "Jeremy called me on Monday night." She took a deep breath. "Told me Joe Allenby had been murdered for sending you that stuff about Ahmed Jibril. You can see why he's so terrified for himself."

"So that's what drove you here, is it?" said Kerr. "Guilt for a good man you didn't even know?"

"But I did." Head lowered, Masters was quietly weeping again, her voice scarcely audible. "Joe knew about everything."

Melanie touched her arm. "He was the other person you phoned, wasn't he, Pamela? That day we first met? The international call? You rang Joe, didn't you?"

"I loved him." She looked up at Melanie, tears running down her cheeks. "Joe Allenby was the father of my baby."

While Melanie took Masters back to Reception, Kerr watched the video again, examining every detail. "Did you spot it?" he said, the moment she returned and took Masters's chair beside him.

"What?"

"I know who 'Harold' is." Kerr muted the sound and froze the video. He clicked through a series of frames. "Look at the bastard's left hand against Tania's leg, as he really gets worked up. Watch the glove. It slips . . . just . . . here. See that dark mark on the back of his hand? Who did I tell you had been having chemo?"

"Jesus."

"She mentioned Africa, right? I remembered he served two tours in Nairobi. Alan Fargo just confirmed he was in Bulgaria before that."

"So why didn't you . . .?"

"Because I wanted to hear the bastard's name from her own lips."

"What are you going to do?"

Kerr checked his watch, locked the screen and grabbed his jacket. "I'm going to see him, of course. And while I'm gone I want you to get hold of Kestrel. Wherever you catch up with him, I'll be there."

Perplexed, Melanie ran after Kerr and caught him by the lift lobby. "Look, I think Pamela may be right. Don't you think we should lay off Kestrel for a while? I mean, what he tried to do on the Tube. He knows what happened to Joe for speaking out. The guy's on the edge, John. Depressed. I think he needs help."

"Find him," Kerr shot back, as he stepped into the lift.

"John, I'm really not comfortable with this."

"Today," he said, as the doors closed on them.

CHAPTER
FIFTY-ONE

Jacketless and relaxed, cuffs turned back, Theo
Canning bounded across the carpet to greet Kerr,
pumping his hand and leading him into the room.

"John, welcome aboard at long last," he said,
ushering him to an armchair. "Make yourself at home."

Kerr had never known a senior official capable of
disarming people as expertly as Canning. "So the magic
touch finally worked, Theo." He smiled.

"Your commander Paula Whatever totally blanked
me, then called out of the blue last night to offer you up
immediately. Can't wait to hear what you did to annoy
her." He chuckled. "Anyway, you were spot on about
Mickey Baines. But I want us to keep this as close as
possible, obviously. Things turned out very badly for
this chap. For your ears only, John."

Over the next five minutes Canning described the
discovery of the murdered Mickey Baines just outside
Amsterdam. He had been found with his throat cut and
a kilo of heroin stuffed inside his jacket. Early
conclusions from Dutch police were that he had been

425

murdered in the course of an illegal drugs transaction. "Bastard was on leave driving his own car. Absolutely no official business in Holland, but loaded with Class A in a city he knew like the back of his hand. The Dutch have promised a thorough investigation but don't hold your breath. Now you see why I need you alongside."

Kerr kept himself as relaxed as Canning, mirroring the other man's deception. "Hope I can make it worth your while."

"You can help me start cutting out the cancer straight away." He sat forward in his chair, elbows on his knees, fingers in a steeple, and dropped his voice. Kerr had to drag his eyes from the bruising on the back of Canning's left hand. "Now for the difficult part, which I'm telling you in absolute confidence. I've had suspicions about Baines for several months. Already asked others to take a look at him, people from my old firm, and your information confirmed the dirt they managed to dig up. Now here's the urgency. Baines was due to receive a payment late tonight from a major target in our Operation Pyramid. It's a bog-standard sting. Because Baines went AWOL we set up the transaction through a third party, another corrupt officer within this organisation. We arrested him this morning. He's rolled over, admitted everything, but I very much want this handover to go ahead."

"Using me as the decoy," said Kerr, every nerve on high alert.

"Got it in one." He looked apologetic. "I know you don't start officially till Monday."

"It's not a problem."

426

"Time's pressing. And I'm having to keep this so tight within the Agency."

It was Kerr's turn to lean forward now, his smile even broader than Canning's. "Theo, I don't need persuading. We're on the same side."

"Spoken like a true gent." Canning chuckled again. "The cut-out is unknown to the target. You say the code word, they hand over the loot. Risk is negligible, John. Armed cover and arrest teams on the plot, and we'll pick up any counter-surveillance. Just receive the money, keep the evidential chain intact."

"Where's the meet?" Kerr's voice was so light he could have been arranging a social get-together.

"Wapping. So, will you do it, my friend?"

"I've got masses of loose ends back at the office," said Kerr, standing, "but sure, of course I will. What time is the handover?"

Canning glanced at the clock. "Twenty-three-thirty. Gives us about six hours. Leave me your mobile number so I can brief you later this evening. And again, everything's strictly *entre nous*, John," he said, as Kerr scribbled his number. "Dirty linen and all that."

"Of course," said Kerr, and edged towards Canning's private bathroom. Do you mind?"

Kerr locked the door and retrieved a couple of tissues with a few strands of Canning's hair from the waste bin. The toilet was unflushed, so he dipped a handful of toilet paper in the urine, enclosed it in some paper towels and stuffed it into his jacket pocket. He flushed the toilet and washed his hands.

Opening the door to his outer office, Canning shook his hand and clapped him on the shoulder. "I'll set things up and give you a bell," he said, as Kerr memorised Canning's mobile number from the whiteboard behind Dorothy's head.

"Great to be on board, Theo." He smiled broadly again, searching the other man's face. "And I won't let you down."

CHAPTER
FIFTY-TWO

Karl Sergeyev was waiting in his tiny office for an evening driving assignment when Yuri Goschenko rang for him. The call came thirty minutes early, leaving him no time to freshen up and snatch some food. Behind with his laundry, he had worn the same shirt for two days, which he would never have contemplated in his previous life. There was a stain on his pale blue silk tie and his suit trousers were creased from hours spent sitting in Goschenko's limousine.

He had just taken a call from Nancy, the third that day, and her mood had graduated from upset through anxiety to screaming fury. Karl had missed two of the money transfers he had promised her since leaving home. The previous day he had defaulted on a mortgage repayment. The children needed new uniform and shoes for school, and trainers for home. When Nancy said she was desperately short of money Karl knew she was telling the truth, for his own situation had lurched rapidly from tricky to dire. In a week he would receive his final full pay cheque from the

Met, a realisation that had already sent Nancy scouring the sits-vac columns. Worse still, his remuneration from Goschenko, in terms of timing and amount, remained worryingly opaque.

A full week after he had watched Olga and Goschenko having sex, Karl still felt wrecked and deeply unhappy. He had not told Olga what he had seen, letting her false denial stand unchallenged. Although she was still angry with him, her sexual passion seemed as hot as ever, and she insisted she wanted to change her life so that they could be together. This confused Karl even more. Obsession, jealousy and humiliation joined forces with guilt over Nancy and the children. His emotions were tearing him apart.

Karl had always been known for his optimism, and now he told himself everything would be all right. He knew that, observing each chapter in his complicated love life, bemused work friends wryly referred to him as the "hope-over-experience guy". Karl had always taken this as a compliment, but his newest relationship was proving a lot more testing. This affair was making him recalibrate the balance with each day that passed. His heart longed for a future with Olga, but his head warned him to keep his rented flat.

Buttoning his jacket, Karl entered Goschenko's palatial office to find the throne occupied by Anatoli Rigov. Goschenko sat in a slightly more modest upholstered chair to one side of the vast desk, in clear deference to the Russian trade minister. Neither was smiling.

430

Goschenko spoke first, his hand outstretched. "Key," was all he said.

Mystified, Karl reached into his pocket for the Mercedes key and handed it over. "I warned you, Karl," said Goschenko. "I cannot employ a man who drinks and drives. Who takes so little pride in his appearance."

Everyone remained silent, until Rigov broke the atmosphere with a smile. "I would put it somewhat differently. For a mere chauffeur in London we have people like Boris. You have the skills to navigate a far more complex world, my friend."

"Not any more."

"For that I can only express my regret," said Rigov, with a sideways glance at Goschenko. "Which is why I wanted to see you. I believe you were disciplined because of . . . shall we say over-sensitivity by our embassy officials? I merely informed the ambassador you were being fastidious about your duties that evening. In any event, I apologise. That is what I am here to tell you. I feel responsible for what happened, Karl, and want to help you resume the profession for which you are so well suited."

Karl was astonished at Rigov's forwardness, which sent a pulse of excitement through him. His career had come to a shuddering halt just as his emotional life had shot into overdrive, and this work-life imbalance had been another cause of unhappiness. Somewhere deep inside him a gear changed up, but he put on his sceptical face. "Oh, yeah?"

"I have seen you work at first hand, Karl," Rigov continued. "It pains me to see a brother Russian treated with such disregard. I want to put things right between us."

Another pulse. Karl gave a short laugh as he briefly reached inside his jacket. "Not possible."

"People change their minds," said Goschenko.

"No chance."

"And people can be overruled," said Rigov, smoothly. "Yuri is concerned about you. He knows of your emotional ties to the girl and your problems at home. Your shortage of money, in particular."

Karl shot another look at Goschenko. "Did Olga tell you that? Have you been talking about me?"

"Of course not," said Rigov, all smiles again. "Your face is an open book to us, Karl. Right now we can both read the anxiety written there. It is natural. And I want to help you get your life back at Scotland Yard."

"Why?"

"We hold you in high regard, Karl, as a fellow Russian." The smile had not left Rigov's face. Even Goschenko was looking happy. "We have seen you with your family."

"You've been watching me?"

"And they deserve a secure future. So does Olga, would you not agree?"

"And in return?"

"I want our friendship to grow. You accept my invitation for a discreet drink from time to time to talk about matters of mutual interest."

432

Now Karl managed the flicker of a smile. "And who would I be talking *with*, Mr Rigov?"

"Come now, my friend." Rigov was regarding him like a long-suffering parent. "We both recognised each other the moment we met. Yuri will be here for you if I am away."

"And what if I choose not to?"

Rigov shrugged. "Then we part as we met, as friends. You owe us nothing," he said, with a glance at Goschenko. "But Yuri has yet to pay you." He paused as Goschenko placed a wad of new fifty-pound notes on the desk. "Five thousand pounds, on account. Whether you accept my offer or not, this is yours. Payment for the services you have already rendered Yuri. And a goodwill gift, compensation for the difficulty we have caused you."

Karl exhaled and sat back in his chair. He stayed silent for a few moments, looking between the two of them. "Does Olga know about this?"

Rigov shook his head. "No one outside this room. If you allow me to help you, I will arrange a less clumsy method of remuneration, of course."

Karl had been covering Russian targets long enough to know that "parting as friends" was an old KGB euphemism for murder, sometimes slow and agonising, often violent and bloody. He reached forward for the money and looked from one to the other. "What do you want me to do?"

Goschenko spoke first. "Just continue being a good intelligence officer at Scotland Yard, of course," he said.

Then he caught Rigov looking hard at him. "And a faithful Russian for us, naturally." The smile returned, but the voice did not sound friendly any more.

Melanie had to loiter around MI5 headquarters at Thames House for nearly two hours before Kestrel appeared. She waited out of sight in Victoria Tower Gardens, a precious stretch of green between Millbank and the river, the route Kerr's agent always took for the short walk to Westminster Underground. She sprawled with a paperback on a bench beneath overhanging trees looking across the grey, fast-moving Thames to the flashy glass apartments on the south side of Lambeth Bridge.

By the time Kestrel appeared, dusk was falling. Melanie had just climbed the steps beside the children's playground for another check of the Thames House entrance when she saw him. She watched him turn left outside the front arch and launch himself onto the pedestrian crossing in the busy Horseferry Road. Traffic was racing onto Lambeth Bridge and his sudden appearance forced everything to brake sharply. Melanie heard a screech of tyres, then White Van Man was shouting obscenities through the passenger window. But Kestrel seemed completely unaware, entering the gardens at a rush, raincoat flapping, his comb-over waving in the breeze from the river.

Melanie kept herself invisible as he hurried towards Parliament Square. She caught up with him by the Buxton Memorial, a fountain erected to celebrate the emancipation of slaves.

434

"We got it, Jeremy," was all she said, lightly taking his arm.

He swung round in a rush, evidently unaware she had been following him. He looked tortured, face sweaty and grey despite the fast walk, his whole body shaking.

"The video." Melanie spoke quietly. "Pamela told us everything and John needs to see you again right now."

Kestrel swung his arm away. "Well, he can bloody piss off."

"This is too serious to leave, Jeremy."

"And you, too."

Melanie kept her distance as Kestrel raced off towards the Tube without looking back, half running now. On the busy approach to Westminster Bridge he charged across the road without waiting for the lights to change, and Melanie almost lost him in the crowds converging on the station. She managed to get alongside him again as he went through the ticket barrier, following him onto the escalator and standing on the step above him. He was heading for the District and Circle Lines, rather than his normal Jubilee which would take him home. An alarm bell immediately rang in Melanie's head, for she knew that only Jubilee Line trains were separated from the platform by Perspex security screens, making it impossible to jump onto the line.

Kestrel seemed desperate now, looking about wildly for anyone who might recognise him as they descended into the depths. She spoke directly into his ear. "Jeremy, you have nothing to fear. We'll protect you. But we can't let this go. None of us."

When she touched his arm again he seemed to go crazy, yelling, "Thief! Thief! Leave me alone!" at the top of his voice and pushing her away from him. As they rumbled downwards the scene was unambiguous. Commuters saw a respectable man in a suit, just like them, being threatened by a woman from the underclass.

But it was not the suits who fought her off. At the bottom, a couple of workmen in fleeces and paint-spattered trackie bottoms grabbed Melanie and flung her to the ground, allowing Kestrel to lose himself in the crowd, pushing and shoving to reach the platform. One of the men kicked her and called her a lazy bitch, then both abandoned her to run for their train. Melanie suddenly felt sick, not from pain but from anticipation. She knew what Kestrel was about to do. She raced after him as warm air rushed into the tunnel, pushed ahead by the approaching train.

The curved platform was packed, a human mass taking a single step towards the edge, then becoming still again as the train lights appeared in the mouth of the tunnel. Then she locked onto Kestrel, just five metres away to her right. He was easy to spot, for his was the only body still moving on the entire platform. He was heading for the space nearest the tunnel mouth, the point of entry where the train would still be at its highest speed. The people surrounding him were mostly young women and she saw wisps of hair and his shoulders heaving as he pushed through them. Some turned their heads in irritation. Melanie saw one girl say something to him, then turn quickly away. She must have caught his look of fear, as if something in Kestrel's face signalled what he was about to do.

Melanie was shouting his name now, but her voice was drowned by the platform announcement. It warned customers to stay behind the yellow line, just as Kestrel reached the point of no return. She saw his body suddenly rise as he leapt from the platform, not simply to drop beneath the wheels but to leap at the cab in a kind of charge, as if taking on the whole train. There was the screech of the train's whistle, then the rush of air brakes and the crump of body versus metal as the train shuddered past her into the station.

The crowd that had been edging forward as one now uttered a single gasp. Silence filled the platform for several seconds, broken only by the grind of the escalators nearby, and Melanie saw the driver, ashen-faced, get out of his cab. Then came a crescendo of shouts and screams as people began to register what had happened. "Person under a train" was a concept they only heard about in the abstract, an irritation beneath someone else's transport. In a split second, that sense of remoteness had evaporated. The suicide, the selfish bastard who'd made them late for work or home, had chosen to end his life while moving among them.

The announcer was on full volume again, calling for calm. Shock, distress, fear and panic flooded the platform. Melanie had seen far worse things in her career, and felt none of these. Instead, quietly escaping to the surface, she found herself drowning in guilt and remorse.

CHAPTER
FIFTY-THREE

Wednesday, 26 September, 21.33, Paula Weatherall's office

Kerr knew Weatherall and Ritchie would be having a late-night catch-up after her return from the Birmingham conference because Donna had told him so. He decided to give them ten minutes before gatecrashing Weatherall's office, which was just as well because Robyn called from Rome. Unable to sleep, she wanted to know if he had any news about Gabi. Kerr tried to reassure her, saying Gabi's flatmates had promised to phone him immediately if they heard anything. But there was real anxiety in Robyn's voice. She recalled someone Gabi had met on Facebook, a guy called Sam. He was interested in what he called her "political integrity", and Gabi had thought it might be good to link in with Robyn's work in Rome.

Kerr, pumped up for his showdown, tried to reassure her as he strode down the corridor from the lift. "Robyn, I'm on a roll here. Gonna crack this thing wide open, one way or another. Everything will be all right. Gabi will be OK, promise. I'll hook up with her friends when I get a spare moment."

As soon as Robyn spoke, Kerr knew it had come out wrong. "This is your daughter," she snapped back at him, "so find yourself a moment tonight."

When he finally entered Weatherall's office the scene was not pleasant. Coat flung over the back of a chair, overnight bag abandoned near the door, Weatherall was sitting at the conference table gulping tap water from a chipped jug Donna kept in the fridge. The ceiling lights were weak for a room of that size and the whole place felt chilly. A shirt-sleeved Ritchie was sitting on the far side of the table. He looked as if he would rather be anywhere else.

Weatherall appeared tired and uncomfortable in the faded green tartan suit she must have been wearing all day at the conference. Tracking her whereabouts, Kerr knew that a West Midlands traffic officer had blue-lighted her to London: she had reached the Yard less than an hour after checking out of her hotel in central Birmingham.

Ritchie was the first to collect himself. "What the hell are you doing here?"

Without waiting for an invitation, Kerr took the chair opposite him, with Weatherall to his right, plonking his secure briefcase on her shiny table. "That's not very friendly, Bill." Anticipating a long night and gruelling next day, Kerr had dashed home for a shower and change of clothes as soon as Melanie had broken the news about Kestrel. In contrast to his bosses, he looked fresh in jeans, polo shirt and linen jacket.

Weatherall stared sourly at the case, as if sensing trouble. "You no longer have any business in SO15. Didn't Mr Ritchie tell you?"

"That you sacked me without having the courtesy to tell me yourself, you mean? Yes. And about the transfer to the National Crime Agency."

"Well?" she said, with a glare at Ritchie. "Did you meet with Sir Theo?"

"I did."

"So why this interruption? Do I have to spell it out for you? There's no place for you here, don't you understand?" Weatherall ran a hand through her hair. The race down the M1 seemed to have left her with serious car-sickness — she looked terrible. "I want you to get out and clear your desk tonight."

Unclipping her earrings, Weatherall started at the snap from the locks on Kerr's briefcase. "I think you need to see this first," said Kerr, quietly. He withdrew a DVD and a sheet of A4. "I had this downloaded from a video. It arrived just before I had my welcome chat with Theo Canning this afternoon." He slid the paper across the table. "This is a still that shows Canning raping and strangling a young girl. She was called Tania, surname unknown, and I can prove from DNA that her body was removed from Marston Street."

Kerr waited for a reaction, but Weatherall just gave an impatient nod. "The house you burgled," she said.

"The murder scene MI5 was protecting," he fired back, "which has links to Syrian state-sponsored terrorism, as I warned Bill. I'm checking now for a match with Canning's DNA. On the film you can hear the girl's dying cries." He paused to give them time to absorb the horror of the image. Weatherall appeared to be secretly testing her armpits for sweat while Ritchie looked down at some irrelevant notes. "Canning is a child abuser and a traitor. He has worked as a hostile agent against this country for at least two decades. His code name is Harold. He has directed me to meet him for a covert operation in just over two hours from now, when I believe he intends to have me killed. But I shan't be turning up for duty."

"How did you get this?" frowned Weatherall, her management liability kicking in.

"The man who gave it to me is dead."

"Name," demanded Ritchie.

Kerr shook his head. "He killed himself this afternoon because he couldn't face the horror of what I'm telling you now. And I hold myself partly responsible for his death because I should have helped him." Kerr delved into the briefcase again and passed Weatherall the earlier photograph. "Same source." He paused while they stared at the terrible images, their heads almost touching. "The rapist in this image is a government lawyer called Robert Attwell. This is a blackmail operation and they force the clients to become traitors like Canning."

Weatherall suddenly looked hot. She began to remove her jacket, then seemed to change her mind, gulping more water instead. "Really? You know that for a fact, do you?"

Kerr ignored the sarcasm. "Claire Grant was compelled to facilitate the entry of Ahmed Jibril into this country," he said carefully.

"John, you have to give us more evidence," said Ritchie, but his voice lacked heat.

"I can prove it with Foreign Office documents," Kerr fired back.

"So produce them," said Weatherall, unmoved.

"Claire Grant was coerced into authorising that visa," he said, ignoring her, "and the kidnap of Sara Danbury is part of the blackmail operation."

Weatherall glanced at Ritchie. "Who by?"

Kerr regarded his bosses for a few seconds, trying to read their faces in the gloom. "I think you really don't know," he said eventually, "which is something of a relief. So let me tell you this whole enterprise is controlled from Russia."

"Prove it," said Ritchie.

"Through a man called Anatoli Rigov. I believe Rigov has controlled Theo Canning for many years. Don't look so surprised, Bill. Nothing's changed. The targets are the same. Opinion formers, movers and shakers, anyone in the establishment they can compromise to fuck things up. These days they use Canning to identify them."

Ritchie still looked sceptical. "Where's your evidence?"

"It's the same iron fist, Bill. Different glove, that's all. But the grip got a lot tighter. I believe Rigov has subcontracted Canning to the Syrians. The Syrians use him to identify the blackmail targets and set up the stings."

"To do what?"

"Import *jihadis* into the UK to facilitate terrorist atrocities. That's where Claire Grant comes in. It's what I've been trying to tell you. Ahmed Jibril is living proof that the Syrian infiltration strategy is working just fine."

"I need more," said Ritchie.

"So pay a visit to the morgue," snapped Kerr.

"Enough," said Weatherall, angrily. "This is all hyper-speculation. Allegations incapable of proof. Photographs that may or may not be genuine. The real world is not one giant conspiracy, Chief Inspector. This obsession with Jibril has made you paranoid." She glared at Ritchie. "This is precisely the lack of balance I've been warning you about, Bill."

Kerr gave a harsh laugh. "Are you actually suggesting these are fakes?"

"I'm saying you may have been set up."

"John," said Ritchie, "I've checked. Rigov is a positive no-trace in every intelligence database. Including Excalibur. I saw the readout from his call log. There's nothing unusual here."

"Which shows how crap we've become at counter-espionage. Anatoli Rigov is KGB."

Weatherall was rolling her eyes. "That's not right, John," said Ritchie.

"FSB, actually. Son of KGB, but same difference. The people who poisoned Alexander Litvinenko in 2006."

Ritchie leant forward in his chair. He was still using his conciliatory voice, as if he wanted to protect Kerr from further humiliation. "John, can we just . . .?"

"An hour ago I took a call from Karl Sergeyev," said Kerr, staring him down. "Just before six o'clock this evening Anatoli Rigov pitched him."

"I beg your pardon?" said Weatherall.

"Recruited him. Tried to turn him. With his sidekick."

"Nonsense," she said, with another glance at Ritchie. "Is this Sergeyev trying to exact some kind of revenge?"

"No. Karl is totally loyal to us, despite the contemptible way you treated him," said Kerr, quietly. "And how do I know this? Because he recorded the whole conversation." He sat back as Weatherall and Ritchie stared at each other in silence, shocked by what he had just told them. "1830 is transcribing it now."

"I need to have that right away," said Weatherall.

"The curious thing is that Rigov claimed he could get Karl reinstated in SO15. Made it sound like a done deal." Kerr studied them both. "Why offer the promise if he can't deliver? Where does he exert his influence? That's what I'm asking myself. I'll let you hear it, ma'am," he said, "but I'll be holding onto the original and the transcription until I get the answer."

Kerr waited for their reaction. The room felt shivery, the bare windows casting a chill over the dimly lit room. Kerr could see Weatherall's side reflection in the black glass. She looked angry and lost, isolated in an office that was too big for her. "I'm still not happy about these photographs," she said eventually. "Bill, I want you to have them authenticated for me tomorrow before we take this any further."

444

"That's ridiculous," said Kerr. "Do you really think you can risk doing nothing?"

"If you satisfy me they're genuine I'll call a Gold group on Friday morning. Provided Mr Finch agrees."

Without another word Kerr grabbed the DVD and walked round the table to Weatherall's TV. She swung round as the sound from the video filled the office, to stare, spellbound, at the screen. The colour drained from her cheeks as she watched Sir Theo Canning rape and strangle Tania to death. The recording lasted three minutes. After thirty seconds she shouted at Kerr to switch it off, but instead he turned up the volume so they could hear the child's screams fade to a whimper as her head lolled to one side and the chairman of the National Crime Agency kicked her to the floor like a discarded toy.

"The person behind the camera is Claire Grant," said Kerr. "Your Home Office minister for police and security filming a rape and murder. Quite a headline."

They sat in stunned silence again as Kerr ejected the disk and faced them down. "The tiles on the kitchen floor were smeared with the child's blood. I believe they threw her dead body down a spiral staircase, which probably smashed her skull, then dragged her across the floor to get her out of the house and dump her body." Kerr locked the DVD and the photographs in his briefcase. "What did they tell you, ma'am?" he asked mildly. "Was it the old cliché about a cover-up being in the national interest?"

Kerr sat down again as silence covered the room with a heavy cloud, Ritchie looking down and Weatherall

445

close to tears. "Anyway, Friday morning will be too late. I'm afraid you don't have the luxury of a Gold group. And I don't recommend involving the Bull. We have significantly less than twenty-four hours."

"How do you know?"

"Karl tells me these people are planning a big event for tomorrow evening."

"Where?" said Ritchie.

"I don't know. But Karl says he'll be chauffeuring Goschenko and Olga to the venue. It's billed as a cocktail party involving 'a lot of major players plus a single minor royal'. Exact words as told to Karl."

"Christ. Which one?"

"No idea. Royalty Protection have nothing in the schedules to match this event, so it must be a seriously clandestine gig."

"Which we can't allow to go ahead," said Weatherall.

"You're going to tell them, are you, ma'am?" said Kerr, with a short laugh, nodding to the lights of Buckingham Palace far below to their left. "Anyway, whoever it is, this won't be the first snorting and shagging session out of the limelight. Karl spotted an Audi A5 with royalty coded markers the night this all kicked off at Marston Street."

"Are you saying this party could be the target?" said Weatherall.

"Blackmail, kidnap, *jihadi* attack, take your pick. They've shown they can do the first two anywhere, so I go with the third. I believe the party is being set up as the terrorist target. Gather their compromised movers and shakers together in one place and murder them. The political fallout will be massive."

"But you don't know where, when or who?" said Ritchie.

"I intend to find out. Ma'am, I want your authority for my team to tear the lid off this."

Weatherall looked at Ritchie. She seemed finally to be deferring to her head of operations. "What are you proposing?" said Ritchie.

"Everything possible. Anything necessary. You have to trust me. This is going to be fast-moving, so I need the freedom to make decisions on the ground as things unfold."

"You seem to have it all planned out," said Weatherall.

"Because I've known this was going to happen."

"Agreed," said Ritchie. "But we'll be in the ops room."

"Thank you," said Kerr. "I'll be using Olga as my source on the inside."

"How do you know she's not involved in this?" said Ritchie.

"Because I have Karl's assurance."

"The man who sleeps with her."

"Olga works for me now."

"Since when?"

"Since this morning when I bought her a coffee." With the prospect of an imminent crisis, Kerr was witnessing a dramatic transformation in Ritchie. As Weatherall sat in silence, his old boss seemed to come to life, sitting forward in his seat to throw questions at him. Bouncing his answers back across the table, Kerr saw flashes of his mentor's old self from a decade ago. "Olga is also talking tomorrow up as a big night," he continued. "That's what Goschenko has told her."

Ritchie's pen was poised. "Precise words, John."

" 'Big British establishment players attending. Surprise VIP guest.' That's it."

"Jesus, it's enough. If it's true. How do you know Goschenko isn't controlling her?"

"Because I've told her how Tania died and she blames Goschenko as much as Canning," said Kerr. "Hates him, says she wants to kill him."

His boss suddenly looked up from his scribbling. "Going to shag him to death, is she?" It was pure, unreconstructed Ritchie, and Kerr felt waves of disapproval from his right.

"Goschenko has hepatitis C," he said quietly, "and Olga has HIV."

Ritchie exhaled. "Has anyone told Karl Sergeyev?"

CHAPTER
FIFTY-FOUR

Thursday, 27 September, 14.12, St Pancras International

On the morning of the last day of his life Abdul Malik, director of the *jihadi* operation in Britain, arrived in London from Istanbul with a single item of baggage, an expensive soft brown leather holdall. Had he not spent the previous night in Paris for the purposes of cover, he could have disposed even of that. After a leisurely breakfast he caught the Eurostar from the Gare du Nord, travelling first class, and arrived unnoticed at St Pancras International in the early afternoon.

A couple of working girls accosted him on the walk from the station to St Chad's Street, reminding him of the humiliation he had endured as a student in this capital of depravity. Although it would not be required, he took a room for twenty-four hours in the first hotel with vacancies he came across. He paid in advance and told the receptionist his luggage was to follow. The deception was unnecessary, because hotel workers within a mile of King's Cross were used to businessmen looking for action away from home. From his room he made a brief mobile call to Rashid Hussain reporting his safe arrival, then prayed and lay in his suit on the narrow bed, eyes tightly shut as he tried to capture images of his wife and children.

Kerr rang Olga again around ten o'clock and she agreed to meet him at Hammersmith before leaving for college. Kerr drove there with Langton, and they parked up by a row of houseboats beneath Hammersmith Bridge.

"Yuri is picking me up in his limousine at six-thirty. Karl will be driving us."

Kerr glanced at Langton. "Did Goschenko ask him to?"

"Karl insisted. Made a big thing about it, I think," she said, from the back of the Alfa, shifting her bag of books to one side and leaning forward to bring her head level with theirs.

Kerr's BlackBerry rang. "What have you got, Al?" He listened intently for a few seconds. "Omar Taleb's number just activated again," he said to Langton, when he'd cut the call. "Taleb slash Rashid Hussain. He's giving the off to Ahmed Jibril."

Kerr reached into his jacket for a photograph of Sara Danbury and showed it to Olga. "Recognise her?" he asked.

"The girl in the newspapers, I know. She is killed, yes?"

"She could be at the place you're visiting tonight. They may be planning to hurt her, Olga. Just like Tania."

Olga nodded. "When I get inside I will find out everything. I will go to the bathroom and secretly text you."

450

Langton handed her a small cloth bag. "No need for that, Olga. Just wear these." They watched her take out a bracelet and tiny earpiece and examine them closely. "They're quite safe. Our surveillance officers wear them all the time and no one ever sees them. Bracelet's got a hidden microphone, but we'll bury it in some real diamonds by the time you get ready tonight."

"You just hold it to your mouth and whisper," said Kerr, "so you can tell Jack what you see."

"And where will you be, Mr Jack," she said, with a smile, "when I need you to protect me?"

"On the roof," replied Langton, deadpan.

"Listen up, Mel. Subject out of the address and off, off, off. Receiving, over?" Kerr and Langton were heading back along Cromwell Road when Steve Gibb's voice came over the mainset on Channel Five. The SAS secondee was speaking to Melanie from the observation post opposite Ahmed Jibril's bedsit, triggering the Red Team just as he had done exactly two weeks earlier.

Melanie's voice bounced back immediately. "Received. Thanks, Steve."

"Jeans, Puffa jacket, dark brown trainers," said Gibb.

"Yeah, I have him."

Kerr accelerated into Cromwell Road, splitting the pack of traffic even before Langton could stick the blue light on the dash. "This must be it, Jack," was all he said, but Langton was already reaching for the microphone.

He waited for three other units to acknowledge, then broke in: "All units from Jack, I'm with John in Earls

451

Court, ETA ten minutes. We need this one, guys, so keep the commentary going."

Kerr and Langton had ensured they were well prepared. With everything now centring on Ahmed Jibril, the stakes had never been higher. They had all memorised the curious note left for Jibril by Julia Bakkour: "Suit delivery 4.30 on day instructed. Fitting in Afghan shop not Saudi. Await confirm call." Still unexplained, it was enough to prove Jibril was the key player. The terrorist would lead them to the blackmailers. And because he was their only lead to another bomb factory, everyone was depending on the Reds to prevent another atrocity. Losing Ahmed Jibril was not an option.

Fargo's voice crackled into the Alfa. "Mel from Alan, I'm in the ops room now. Let us know what back-up you need."

"Roger that. He's on foot heading left down South Lambeth Road, towards Stockwell Tube. And our man is in a hell of a rush."

"Give us the formation, Mel," said Langton.

"Myself and Justin on foot. Red Four mobile. It's no problem."

"You have to be careful he doesn't recognise you, Mel," said Langton.

"Different clothes, but I'm dropping back while he crosses the road. Pull up, Justin."

"What's his demeanour?"

"This is Justin. I'm twenty metres back. He's relaxed. No glancing around, no deviation. This guy has stopped being nervous, and he's not looking for anyone. I'd say he gave up on us."

"Is he still heading for the station?" asked Kerr.

"Yes, gotta be the Tube," said Justin, "and at this pace, about seven minutes away."

Kerr broke in. "All Red units from Alpha. I'll be parked up on the north side of Vauxhall Bridge. Keep us posted. And stay back, Mel. No chances."

The air fell silent as the Reds followed Jibril down South Lambeth Road. Melanie had left her microphone open and Kerr heard her breath quickening as she and Justin advanced on the target.

"From Justin, he's at the station. Stand by."

Fargo came in again: "I need the destination so we can pick him up the other end."

In Scotland Yard, in Kerr's Alfa charging up Piccadilly and on the streets around Stockwell, they strained to hear Justin's voice. "Ticket machine, paying cash." It was less than a murmur. "Travelcard. Shit." This was bad news, for it would give no destination. "I'm on with him."

They could hear Justin hurrying down the escalator, then the whoosh of an arriving train. "Mel from Justin, he's taking the Victoria Line heading north. I'll go with him. Can you take the next carriage? Over."

Kerr heard running feet, the beeping as the train doors closed, and a murmur from Melanie: "I'm on."

A double-click from Justin, then radio silence.

Although it was mid-morning, the train was sufficiently crowded to give Justin and Melanie good cover. Jibril took a seat with his back to the platform, so Justin sat in the same row, three seats up, with a view of his target in the window's reflection. In the adjacent carriage he had Melanie in his line of sight, hidden from Jibril among shoppers. As the train slowed for the third station, Victoria, Jibril walked to the double doors, ready to get off. Justin eased his way to the single door at the end of the carriage. In his earpiece he heard Melanie above the squeal of brakes as she breathed the location to the units above ground.

As the doors opened, Jibril changed the game plan, standing aside to let other passengers leave, as if unsure of his whereabouts. Justin lingered by the door, too, allowing travellers to push past him into the train. Then Jibril stepped onto the platform and glanced up and down. When he looked the other way, Justin stepped off and sprinted for refuge in the tunnel walkway between the north and southbound platforms. The station announcer boomed that the train was being held for a moment to regulate the service. Justin could see Melanie meandering towards the exit, blending with a group of students and glancing at the giant platform posters.

Suddenly Jibril boarded the carriage.

Melanie reacted immediately. "He's seen us, Justin. Walk on."

"No, he's confused," said Justin. "Let's stay with him."

As Justin darted for the adjacent carriage, Jibril stepped off again and strolled for the exit. Justin and

Melanie followed, half concealed behind a group of stragglers.

Then, as the closing-doors signal beeped, Jibril hopped aboard again. With less than a second to react, Justin was not quick enough. It was a cruel break. The doors trapped him, then made him suffer excruciating seconds of exposure before swishing open again to let him inside.

As the train moved off he clocked Melanie stranded on the platform, then saw her break the cardinal rule of surveillance: never to make eye contact with the target. But Melanie was looking for Jibril as the carriage picked up speed. He read it clearly in her face.

And so did Ahmed Jibril. Reflected in the glass, Justin saw the terrorist raise his hand and smile at her.

Melanie's voice came straight back to him. "Justin, you have to abort at the next station. Get out of there. He's blown us."

"Not me. He hasn't sussed me," said Justin, hunkering down in his seat. "It's OK. I can do this."

He heard Melanie calling up Kerr: "Alpha from Melanie, did you receive that, over?"

Justin picked out Kerr and Langton speaking rapidly above the racing of the engine. Then there was just Langton's voice. "This is Jack. You have to stick with him, Justin. We're heading north again with a mobile unit. Keep it coming."

Then he could hear Melanie remonstrating again. "No, Jack," she said, "we need to arrest him right now. This is dangerous."

"Negative. He's our only lead. Justin, I want you to stay with him."

At the next station, Green Park, Jibril made it clear he knew exactly where he was going. He headed straight for the exit and took the stairs at a run. At the top of the long escalator, he wheeled right and raced down again to the platform. Then he turned and loped back to the surface.

In the heat of the moment, the mistakes rolled into one another. Justin should have followed his instincts into the safety of the street and disappeared. But he knew how vital the operation was to John Kerr. He had taken too many chances against Ahmed Jibril to be defeated now. And, most damaging of all, as he whipped his woollen hat off, removed his coat, changed his gait and blended with the students, shoppers and office workers, he was certain he could get away with it.

Thirty seconds later, Jibril was waiting at the moving rail with his back to the CCTV camera as Justin, trapped again and avoiding eye contact, slowly ascended to him. For the second time that morning the terrorist showed perfect timing as he vaulted on one arm and launched a mighty kick into Justin's lowered face.

Justin's unconscious body fell across the top of the escalator, obstructing the exit. Later, security footage would show several passengers, Oyster cards at the ready, stepping over him and walking away without a glance.

By the time anyone realised Justin was not just another daytime drunk, Ahmed Jibril had loped down the escalator for the last time.

CHAPTER
FIFTY-FIVE

Thursday, 27 September, 15.39, Kilburn

At the time appointed by Rashid Hussain, Abdul Malik took the Circle Line west from King's Cross, changing at Baker Street station for the five stops on the Jubilee Line to Kilburn in north-west London.

The object of his journey was what Hussain euphemistically called his "fitting", as if he were to visit a tailor. Hussain had arranged the logistics with great care. The people Malik was to meet, Walid and Fatima Ujama, were a married couple in their early twenties. They had arrived at Heathrow direct from Islamabad early the previous morning, courtesy of two special-access visas authorised on behalf of Claire Grant. Walid, a chemical engineer, was a highly valued bomb-maker within Al Qaeda. He had attended two terrorist training camps in Afghanistan as an instructor, and always travelled with his wife for cover.

The fitting of Abdul Malik was their first UK operation in a recruitment, training, support and quartermaster mission intended to last at least two years. As soon as their business was concluded they would take the train to Leeds, their planned centre of operations, and remain invisible, only returning to London for essential logistical requirements in advance of martyrdom attacks.

With the Lambeth safe-house effectively placed out of bounds since Jibril's arrest two weeeks earlier, finding a secure location even for a couple of hours had compelled the terrorists to fall back on their contingency plan. Years earlier, the Al Mukhabarat office in Damascus had acquired two other safe-houses in different parts of London for what its masters called "short-term critical deployments". Any Syrian agent tasked against the UK had to commit both addresses to memory, with bus and train routes from central London.

The first was a Saudi-owned two-bedroom terraced house in Hounslow let at low rent to Pakistani tenants, who could be displaced at short notice. The other was occupied by a half-blind Afghan veteran, who had occupied a flat near Finsbury Park mosque until 9/11 had brought the police to his door. His new home was a modest first-floor bedsit over a TV-repair shop in Kilburn. For the final chapter in this high-risk blackmail operation, Hussain had chosen the Afghan over the Saudi address. Hidden away in a quiet side-street twenty metres from Kilburn High Road, the bedsit was perfect for his requirements.

Jibril descended even farther into Green Park station after his assault on Justin. He took a Jubilee Line train north and, confident he had lost all surveillance, left the network at Willesden Green station. A light drizzle was falling as he walked down Walm Lane into Willesden High Road, continued past the church and turned right into a side-street alongside the police station. The houses each side were mostly modest 1930s terraces and semis, and parked cars lined the pavement. Some of the properties were well maintained, with neat front gardens or block paving for off-road parking, while others, probably rented, had been left in disrepair for many years.

Traffic was local and light in the cluster of streets contained between the High Road and the railway to which he was headed, and the young man passed unnoticed among mothers pushing buggies loaded with family shopping and kids bunking off school. He continued for a couple of hundred metres until the street swept to the left out of sight of the High Road, and then, with a quick look back, swung right into a much narrower turning.

This was little more than an access road of cracked concrete wide enough for only one row of parked cars. It separated a line of run-down 1950s maisonettes to the right from a decrepit block of flats four storeys high on the opposite side. The space for parked cars was on the maisonette side, while vehicles from the flats turned left halfway down the road to pass under an arch built into the block and park out of sight to the rear. Almost without exception, the cars were at least a decade old. Beyond the buildings there were railway tracks, servicing both main-line trains and the Tube. The road seemed to be a dead end, disappearing into overgrown bushes just short of the railway. In fact, it led to a sharp right turn just beyond the last maisonette, too small for anything larger than a hatchback to navigate without difficulty. The concrete, by this time even more potholed, then dropped into a dip at right angles to the maisonettes and ended in a row of twelve lock-up garages on the left, with the backs less than ten feet from the railway fencing.

The garages were brick-built with wooden double doors. They were small, constructed to accommodate cars from a much earlier era, but must have belonged to someone, for each was secured by a padlock. Rubbish blown against the doors and weeds growing through the concrete entrances showed that few, if any, were still used, and the curling felt on each roof and terrible condition of the door panels showed that all had been left to rot. The row was overrun by trees and vegetation, which masked it completely from the residential blocks and the railway. Apart from a few syringes and plastic bottles, there was no sign that anyone ever came here. The garages were invisible. It was as if their very isolation had protected them from the demolition men.

With another quick look behind him, Jibril followed the road into the dip and walked past the end garage to a clump of brambles. He reached beneath a rock concealed in the bush and removed a heavy-duty padlock key. He went to the third garage from the end, inserted his key, opened the left door a fraction and slipped inside.

The Turkish former Secret Service agents selected by Abdul Malik had constructed the bomb factory very quickly and with great skill. The decaying exterior bore no relation to the condition inside. They had fixed the ceiling and used a special sealant around the surfaces to make the garage dry, but without any visible sign of repair from the outside.

Along the left side there was a raised oak workbench with two high stools, good quality desk lamps, a toolbox, three soldering irons and a large reel of green twine. A metal box contained the copper tubing, nails, batteries and timers. The most recent target had been Pamela Masters: Malik's carbomb expert had made the device used to destroy her Nissan on this very bench.

Beyond it, by the far corner, there was a dirty electric stove with a large pan on the hob. Against the end wall a fridge was used to store fresh food and stabilise the explosive mix. A microwave oven stood on top of it. A futon with a pillow and a couple of blankets lay along the opposite wall. With the safe-house in Lambeth compromised, Jibril would hide here until his mission was accomplished. A specially made cloth vest, with pockets to contain the lethal mix that would convert it into a bomb, hung from a large wall hook. The string and toggle that would soon be used to detonate it draped innocently over the bench above a new sports bag. Jibril carefully opened the zip. Inside, exactly as Hussain had promised him, he found a vest identical to that hanging on the wall, except this was already lethal.

Jibril locked the garage factory, returned the key to its hiding place and retraced his steps with the bag as

461

far as the junction of the High Road with Walm Lane. He had memorised the Afghan address many weeks ago. Instead of returning to Willesden Green station he took a right fork into Willesden Lane, continuing for a quarter of a mile before turning left, following the sign for Brondesbury main-line station and Kilburn High Road, his mind a mirror of the street map he had studied and destroyed.

Abdul Malik arrived in Kilburn shortly after three. The Afghan had been sent away for the afternoon, so Fatima Ujama answered the door and, without a word, showed him into the tiny living quarters where her husband was waiting to reconcile his half of a ten-pound note with Malik's. The two men said nothing beyond a brotherly greeting in English, while Fatima made herself busy in the kitchen and brought them tea.

Walid Ujama knew nothing about Abdul Malik or his mission. Like Ahmed Jibril before him, his role was to survive, not immolate himself, and he had learnt never to be inquisitive unless it was for a specific operational purpose. And if he was intimidated or repelled by Malik's double-breasted black suit, expensive mid-length coat, highly polished shoes and general air of affluence, he did not show it.

The two men waited in silence while Fatima peered towards the street corner through a chink in the curtain. After a few minutes she shot her husband a glance. "Our brother is arriving now." She kept a sharp lookout for surveillance as Ahmed Jibril walked up the street, then hurried downstairs to let him in.

Entering the room, Jibril carefully laid the sports bag against the wall before allowing Walid to welcome him. There was warmth in the embrace, but respect, too, for the man who had just escaped imprisonment and interrogation in a British cell. In his turn, Jibril showed deference to Abdul Malik, who nodded but stood his ground by the table.

While Fatima brought refreshments and Malik looked on, Walid satisfied himself that the ingredients, components and detonating mechanism in Jibril's bag were of the highest quality, as directed by Rashid Hussain. He was so thorough and professional that he practically dismantled the device to ensure its fitness for purpose, while Jibril stood at his shoulder and studied every move.

After forty minutes, Walid nodded to the director that they were ready. Malik stood upright with arms outstretched as Walid gently fitted the bomb vest and fed the toggle through the sleeve of his expensive jacket. Fatima moved around helping him, subservient but skilled with experience, adjusting the length of the trigger line running along Malik's arm. When they were finished, Walid asked him when the vest would be needed. The question was out of operational necessity rather than idle curiosity.

"Tonight, brother," answered Jibril for him, without volunteering more.

"So I should wrap it in the bag for safety, yes?"

This time the reply came from the director himself. "No need for the bag," said Abdul Malik, casually, buttoning the jacket as if he had just bought a new suit and pulling on his overcoat. "I shall wear it now."

CHAPTER
FIFTY-SIX

Back at the Yard, Alan Fargo remained in the ops room after the catastrophic surveillance loss of Jibril, checking every piece of kit for the umpteenth time and keeping his comms specialists on red alert. Alice, his senior comms monitor, stayed in constant touch with Steve Gibb in the observation post opposite Jibril's safe-house, and everyone hoped against hope for their main target's reappearance on the plot.

When he recovered consciousness, Justin had refused to go to hospital. Kerr had him taken there anyway, as everyone regrouped around Whitehall. Then, by car, motorcycle and on foot, Jack Langton's Reds made their signal checks and prowled in wait for Robert Attwell and Claire Grant.

To the north, in the drab hotel room near King's Cross station, Abdul Malik rose from his bed and went to the bathroom to cleanse himself. He had returned from Kilburn around four and removed all his clothes, hanging his suit in the wardrobe and, like a modern

465

gunslinger, draping the bomb vest over the back of the chair.

When he was ready, he dressed again and carefully secured the explosives around his chest, feeding the trigger line through the sleeve of his jacket. He picked up his passport to make identification of his body easier and wandered to the corner of the street in sight of the station, where the hired limousine was parked, engine purring. His pair of ex-Turkish Secret Service hoods were waiting patiently for the leader they admired so completely.

The three men knew this was a special occasion, the last meeting in their lives. There were few pleasantries on the drive west along Euston Road to Chiswick, and neither felt in fear of the explosives wrapped around Malik's body.

Malik was quiet until they reached Knightsbridge, and the protectors had no wish to invade his thoughts. "At what time do you think I should act?" he asked.

"I advise you enter by eight o'clock," said the more intelligent of the two, polishing his glasses, "before the infidels disperse to the bedrooms. We will contain them in the reception room until you are ready."

"Rashid Hussain tells me the evening news is at ten o'clock, correct?"

"Yes. We have timed your holy mission to generate the fullest media coverage."

"And the building will be sealed, yes?"

"Tight as a vault."

* * *

To the west, in Hammersmith, Olga looked out for her limousine. Wearing a silk dress she hated because it was a gift from Yuri Goschenko, and the diamond bracelet she loved because it would bring her justice, she inserted the earpiece, checked in the mirror that it was hidden by her hair, and waited for Jack Langton's test call. His voice came to her immediately, as if he had been watching her. She breathed into the bracelet that she could hear him, and felt a childish pleasure when he praised her. "I am so nervous," she said.

Langton's voice came to her again as Goschenko's Mercedes swept up, with Karl behind the wheel. She found some of his words difficult to understand because of his Geordie accent, but he always sounded very calm. "Try to relax. John and I are parked very close by. We can see you. Just take your time and tell us whatever you can. Olga, we will never let you come to harm."

Robert Attwell gave the Reds the lead. They were waiting for him when he left the Foreign and Commonwealth Office in King Charles Street. He was carrying a black holdall and turned left, hurrying towards Whitehall. In a black cab, with Langton's surveillance operatives all over him like a rash, he went west through Hyde Park Corner, Gloucester Road and Kensington, passing within a stone's throw of Olga's street in Hammersmith on the journey to Chiswick. Dismissing the cab in Ellesmere Road, he walked through the park leading to a wide crescent and entered

467

a large Edwardian house. Fargo had left the channel open, so the team received everything. "Alan from Melanie, address is one five four Pentland Crescent, Chiswick."

"Received. Nice one, Mel," Fargo shot back.

"Property checks in quick time, please, Al," said Melanie, rapidly scanning the electronic map beside her. "All units from Melanie. Stay clear of the house. Rendezvous point is the cemetery car park off Old Station Road. Are you getting this, Jack?"

"Yes. Our subjects are just leaving for the address now. Olga with Goschenko. Karl driving. John and I are staying with them, approximately ten minutes away," came Langton's voice. "What's the roof like, Mel?"

When Attwell's taxi slowed, Melanie had pulled into the kerb, then skirted the park and stopped in the crescent. She had good cover, her vehicle concealed behind a row of parked cars. The target house was illuminated by streetlights, with an escape route down a side-road to the left. She was already out of the car when Langton called her, making a recce of the house on foot, a local jogger in trackie bottoms and grey hoodie, radio disguised as an iPod.

The house was double-fronted and painted white, on three storeys and set back about twenty paces from the crescent. The guests approached along a sweeping gravel drive leading to enormous black double doors wide enough to take a vehicle. Melanie immediately saw the fire escape on the right side and ran on the spot for a few seconds, catching her breath and surveying

468

the access. "Looks workable. I think we have a way into the top floor."

"Take a closer look and brief me at the rendezvous point," said Langton.

"Stand by," puffed Melanie, as the house came to life, "and we have more punters arriving. One by taxi, coming right up to the door, two on foot. Looks like the party starts at seven and no one wants to be late."

Behind Fargo the door opened quietly and he was suddenly aware of Weatherall at his right side. She slipped into the chair marked "Gold" but stayed silent, simply nodding to him. Seconds later Bill Ritchie followed. He was taking a call on his mobile phone, listening intently and scribbling notes as he sat down beside Weatherall.

"We have an address, ma'am," said Fargo.

"Good work."

"With TSG units *en route*, RV point in Old Station Road. Do you need a briefing?" he asked, as the messages flooded in.

"Is John Kerr aware?"

"On the scene, ma'am."

"And dealing, presumably," she said, folding her arms with a glance at Ritchie. "Just tell me what I need to know."

Fargo was taking another message. "Claire Grant on the move, ma'am. Just walked out of the Home Office. No car or driver, off towards Horseferry Road." He fired an acknowledgement, then turned to Ritchie. "She hailed our black cab, Red Seven. Asked for Waverley Road, which is adjacent to Pentland Crescent."

There was a tap on the window behind them and Ritchie turned to see Donna in the observation room with Philippa Harrington. The MI5 director-general looked angry as he slipped through the intercommunicating door, but he held out his hand anyway. "Philippa, what brings you here?"

"Why didn't you notify us of this operation?" she demanded, gesturing through the glass.

Ritchie had his notepad with him, checking something. "Why would you need to know?"

"I want to see your boss."

Ritchie perched on the desk and laughed. "Don't bullshit me, Philippa. We've known each other too long." He glanced at his pad. "The lease on the house we're looking at is assigned to Medlock Estates, which is part of the Rockville Group . . ."

"What the hell are you talking about?"

". . . which is wholly owned by Transcapital. That's the cover name for the business legends used by the National Crime Agency."

"So speak with Theo Canning."

"You can have a word with him yourself, if you like." He turned to see Weatherall looking for him. She tapped on the glass, ignoring Harrington. "He's about to get arrested."

CHAPTER
FIFTY-SEVEN

Thursday, 27 September, 18.58, 154 Pentland Crescent, Chiswick

Karl delivered Olga and Yuri Goschenko dead on time, but tension filled the Mercedes for the entire journey. Olga knew Goschenko was trying to keep things light, but he seemed nervous, as if this was to be his big night. He told Karl to take the rest of the night off, saying he would make "other arrangements" to deliver Olga home safely. "So tonight you can have a drink and no one will mind," he said, reaching forward to grip his shoulder. Olga wondered whether he was being generous or provocative. From Karl's hard look at her in the rear-view mirror, it was obvious what he was thinking. "No," he said. "I'll spend the evening with my family."

Karl accelerated away without another glance at Olga as soon as he had dropped them outside the house. Goschenko offered her his arm as they walked up the sweeping drive to the double front doors, which made her acutely conscious of Langton's magic bracelet against his sleeve. She resisted a look back, hoping Kerr and Jack would be watching every move.

The lobby was spacious, as large as a room. The broad staircase lay fifteen paces in front of them, and she saw a room to the left with the door closed. The two Turkish overseers Olga remembered from Marston Street welcomed Goschenko with deference, but ignored her. They were ushered through a set of double doors into the reception room to the right. With its armchairs and sofas removed for the occasion, the square room looked huge, with high ceilings and its original ornate fireplace, cornices and wooden floor. There were two giant chandeliers and the window onto the street, a sweeping bay, was covered with thick, purple velvet curtains.

Faces heavily made up, their bodies fattened up and dressed for sex, three young girls stood mutely by the door with trays of hors d'oeuvres and champagne. Olga watched them moving forward in turn to offer canapés and champagne to each arriving guest. Had she first seen them as the pinched, half-starved creatures smuggled across the North Sea in metal containers, she would never have recognised them now.

When they had met in Starbucks, Kerr had told Olga what she needed to know about Theo Canning, and shown her a photograph so that she could identify him. Scanning the room, she counted seven early arrivals, but immediately recognised Canning. He was unmistakable, the life and soul before the party had even begun.

More guests were arriving now, and the room buzzed with laughter and conversation. Another woman, a politician Olga recognised from TV, made a beeline for Canning, who greeted her with a peck. When Olga edged Goschenko alongside, Canning greeted him with a nod but kissed her warmly. She made her body exude warmth and sexual promise, but kept her mind ice cold and calculating. Within stabbing distance of Tania's murderer, she laughed and sparkled, made him smile at her, and silently vowed he would never leave the house alive.

When Goschenko said he had to speak with the Turks, Olga waited a few seconds, then wove out of the room behind him, intent on reconnoitring the house. The hallway was crowded now, with people arriving all at once. She saw one of the overseers leading Goschenko towards the kitchen at the rear, leaving the heavier man alone by the main doors.

There was a closed door adjacent to the reception room. Beneath the sweeping staircase was a cloakroom with the door ajar. Olga could see a desk and chair squeezed inside with a TV monitor. Sneaking inside, she silently pulled the door shut. When she rotated the monitor, she recognised the face that had smiled from millions of televisions and newspapers over the past five days. Dressed in school uniform, Sara Danbury was sitting on her bed, her face made up to look like a woman's, looking straight at the camera.

"Jack, Jack, are you there?" she murmured into the bracelet.

"I hear you, Olga."

"Sara is here, in one of the rooms upstairs. I am going to find her now." Langton said something urgent in reply, but she had already slipped back into the lobby, unnoticed. She wafted up the sweeping staircase as if she was looking for the bathroom, instincts driving her to the deserted landing. The first floor had a bathroom and four empty double bedrooms, all unlocked, so she kept climbing. On the top floor she found herself on another landing, long and narrow, with a couple of storerooms to one side under a sloping ceiling. But then she saw the door at the very end, crudely secured with a mortise lock and three heavy bolts. Jack's voice was in her earpiece again. "Olga. Can you speak?"

"All right. I am on the top floor and I think I have found her prison cell for you. Now I have to go back to the party this instant or they will be wondering."

"I'm outside on the roof. Listen, at the end of the landing is a door."

"No, there is nothing," she said.

"Olga, it must be the other end, the opposite end to the cell. It's bolted, so you have to come and let us in, otherwise it will be too noisy."

"I will try." Lifting her dress above her knees, Olga raced to the other end of the landing, which had a small wing to the left and a half-glazed door with a lock and three bolts. She could see Jack with Kerr and Melanie crouching outside in the darkness. The second she turned the key and unslid the bolts they slipped inside and, without a word, half carried her back down the landing, their movements smothered by the noise of laughter and excess two floors beneath them.

"She is here," she said, outside the locked door. "I saw her on the TV screen with my own eyes. They are going to kill her, I am telling you. Just like they did to Tania."

"What's happening downstairs?" asked Kerr.

"Still the champagne."

"How many?"

"Nearly twenty by now. Only one woman. They have girls serving drinks."

"What about the man in the photograph I showed you?" persisted Kerr. "Is Theo Canning there, Olga? We didn't see him arrive."

"I cannot be sure," she lied, ice cold again.

"What about Rigov?"

"No. Definitely not. Something bad is going to happen, I am telling you. These people are bastards, all of them."

"Olga, we're about to move against this place," said Kerr. "It's going to get very rough, so you need to get out now. We have another officer on the roof. He'll lead you to safety."

As Kerr spoke Olga was already heading for the staircase. "No. I stay here in the house. I can let you know what is happening, tell you the best time to break in. But do nothing until I tell you," she replied, her mind fixed on Canning. "This is your only chance."

"Olga, come back. You can't go down there again," said Melanie, but Olga was already out of their reach.

Three stairs down she paused and looked back at the three of them. "Everything will be all right. You must stay up here until I say."

As Olga scampered downstairs, Kerr quietly slid back the bolts while Langton took out his key kit. They could hear whimpering inside the room as Langton dealt with the lock. To avoid appearing on the CCTV they stayed by the door as Sara Danbury stared at them, stupefied.

"It's all right, Sara," said Melanie quietly, beckoning the child to her. "We're here to take you home. Bring your blanket and come to me."

"Please help me," she whispered when she reached the doorway, looking up at her.

Melanie wrapped her in the blanket. "It's all right. You're safe now." She lifted Sara in her arms and hurried back down the corridor with Kerr, while Langton resecured the door.

Melanie made it outside to the roof in less than three minutes. The night was cold and Sara seemed paralysed with fear as they edged along a drainage gully to the fire escape. Kerr went first, then Langton, with Melanie and Sara climbing last. On the ground, Melanie picked her up again and raced from the building to the safety of the Alfa. "All units, listen up," said Kerr, as he drove away, "we have Sara Danbury. Taking her to the RVP now. ETA three minutes for a briefing of raider units."

"All received," came Fargo's voice in acknowledgement. "And Gold is aware."

Inside the house, Olga knew she had to work quickly if she was to achieve justice before Kerr launched the raid.

476

Before rejoining the reception she slipped back into the cloakroom and pulled the plug from the TV monitor. She was taking a great risk, for she guessed the screen would be regularly checked. By the time she returned to the party the atmosphere had transformed. Another girl had been introduced into the room, but the canapés were forgotten. It was a scene Olga had witnessed countless times in her professional life. High on champagne and coke, inhibitions gone, the guests would soon be making their choices from the girls before drifting to the bedrooms. She had very little time.

From the other side of the room, Yuri Goschenko was beckoning her. Olga held up five fingers, mouthed something back to him and nodded across the room in the vague direction of Theo Canning. She eased off Langton's magic bracelet and hid it deep in her bag: for the next few minutes she had words only for one man. She took out a red silk scarf and moved across the room. With a deep smile at the woman standing beside him, she draped the scarf around Canning's neck. He gazed back at her, mystified.

"I am directed to entertain you as the special guest of honour," she said, leading him away by the scarf, "so you must follow."

"Starting early tonight," he said, with a backward glance at his companion. "Shan't be long."

With Langton in her ear, Olga took Canning to the first floor and entered the farthest bedroom. There was a kingsize bed with red silk sheets, a nightstand, and a couple of upholstered chairs. Locking the door, she moved in close, playing with the scarf, kissing his neck. She checked out his eyes and traced her hand around his erection. High on cocaine, hard on Viagra, she guessed. She slipped off his jacket and gently eased him backwards onto the bed. "Now you must lie down while we make you ready."

She kept her eyes fixed on his while she took a second scarf from her bag and loosely tied his hands together in a slip knot, a trick of the trade she had picked up early in her escort days, so casually that he scarcely noticed. "Tonight I give you something different, yes?" She smiled, loosening his shirt and trousers, but Canning simply nodded, his eyes wide, breathing rapidly in anticipation. "This will be a new treat," she said, loosely hanging the tied scarf over the iron headboard, "beyond your wildest dreams."

As Canning twisted his neck Olga suddenly reached over and pulled both ends of the scarf, jerking the knot tight and lifting his arms above him. Canning signalled alarm, but Olga was still smiling down on him, relaxed and reassuring. "Just another moment. Be absolutely still."

She casually unbuckled the belt, pulled down his trousers and then, in one practised move, secured it tightly around his ankles. Canning had no time to react and she saw fear in his eyes. "What the hell's going on?" he demanded.

Olga took a piece of gauze from her bag and tried to force it into Canning's mouth. "What are you playing at, you stupid bitch?" he blurted, but she calmly pinched his nose until he gasped for air, then stuffed

478

the gauze inside. Canning began to twist on the bed, pulling himself up on his arms and flailing his bound legs.

She moved fast. Canning was still hard from the effects of the Viagra, so she pulled his underpants around his ankles to mock him. The scarf she had draped around his neck was tied in a loop. Lifting her dress, she sat astride his chest and yanked it tight as Canning writhed beneath her, his face distorted with panic.

As his eyeballs bulged and the veins stood out from his forehead, she deftly removed a toughened hair clip and used it as a tourniquet, revolving it until he began to choke. She lowered her face close to his to be sure he could hear her. "I saw what you did to Tania, you disgusting pig. Now you know what it feels like to die, yes?" She spoke softly as she twisted the scarf. "It takes your breath away. Like I said, beyond your wildest dreams."

With Jack Langton's urgent voice in her ear calling her to the top floor, Olga stared into Canning's eyes until the blood vessels burst. She held the pressure even when it was no longer necessary, keeping a finger on his fading pulse. In the moments before he died she quickly disentangled the clip and, raising it in both hands above her head, plunged it deep into his heart.

Only when she was satisfied that he could never harm another human being did she climb from the bed and wipe the bloodied hair clip on his immaculate white shirt. Then she calmly freshened her makeup in the mirror, concealed the murder weapon in her hair, replaced Langton's microphone on her wrist and hurried down to join the party.

By the time she sashayed into the reception room, Yuri Goschenko had disappeared.

CHAPTER
FIFTY-EIGHT

Abdul Malik secretly made his farewells to the Turkish Secret Service agents in the deserted lobby. With enough explosives encircling his body to bring down half the crescent, he kissed them on both cheeks, dismissing them with a smile when they offered to remain by his side. It was their duty to escape, he told them. The work was not yet finished.

Unable to find Olga, Yuri Goschenko had already slipped away from the house through the kitchen. His instructions were to report to Rigov and Rashid Hussain with the names of the guests. The moment the Turks quietly locked and bolted the heavy double front doors, the house would become a tomb for Claire Grant, Robert Attwell and the other unwitting partygoers on the other side of the wall. It also sealed the fate of Harold and the innocent girls whose lives had already been diminished in freezing trucks driven across Europe. In completing his holy work, Abdul Malik was not selective. All were infidels, sunk in filth and depravity. Unworthy of salvation, they would perish with the rest.

Like Goschenko, the Turks were to escape into the safety of the back garden through the specially strengthened kitchen door at the rear of the house, double-locking it from the outside to block the escape of any survivors.

Before destroying himself, Abdul Malik needed somewhere to be quiet and pray. The Turks had invited him to prepare himself in the comfort of one of the first-floor bedrooms, but Malik chose the makeshift observation room beneath the staircase. The space would be convenient, he had said, for his final short walk across the hall. The blank TV monitor did not arouse his suspicion. There would be no further use for it, and he assumed it had been switched off. He sat carefully, removed his jacket and made a call to Rashid Hussain to co-ordinate the final phase. It was the last time they would speak, but there was no sentimentality as they said their goodbyes. Then Malik quietly swung to face the blank wall, committing himself to Allah.

With his eyes closed, deep in concentration, Malik never saw Olga as she silently eased the door open to restore the power.

"This is Olga and there is a man here wearing a bomb."

"Say again?" shot back Langton.

"He is in the room under the stairs, where they put the TV screen to watch Sara. You must be careful."

Lying prone on the landing, Kerr, Langton and Melanie watched Olga through the banisters as she hurried up the stairs towards them.

"Where is everybody?" said Kerr, as she lay beside them.

"You can hear the hubbub for yourself," panted Olga. "They are all in the main room, with the doors closed. They are being kept in there. I don't know why."

"How do you know the guy has a bomb?"

"I am telling you, there are explosives all round his body, in a kind of jacket." Olga could feel Kerr's eyes on her blood-stained dress. "You have no more time. John, it is too dangerous, we must get away."

"Olga, you're fantastic," said Kerr, with a nod at Melanie. "Get her away from here now, Mel. Keep her warm in my car but you must get the dress off her, understood?" he said. "Go to the rendezvous point. Tell the uniforms to stand off, but be ready to move on my command and prepare for heavy-duty entry. Tell them to drive the carrier into the fucking entrance if they have to."

"Gold control, urgent message from Alpha," said Kerr, as soon as Melanie had taken Olga's hand and rushed her away. "We have probable suicide bomber inside the premises, about twenty people in the main ground-floor room to the front of the house, right side. Am assessing with Jack Langton but request immediate invocation of Andromeda, over."

"All received, John." Kerr was relieved to hear Alan Fargo's soft Cornish accent. "Stand by."

Fargo must have been keeping Channel Five open, for they could hear Weatherall firing questions at him. "Where are the firearms teams?" she said.

"Trojans are five to seven minutes away, ma'am," said another voice.

"But the premises are sealed," interrupted Kerr, "so they won't be able to intervene in time."

"Well, I'm ordering you and Red One out of there now."

"That's not what we agreed, ma'am," said Kerr, with a glance at Langton.

"I don't care. We leave this to the Trojans."

"No time," said Kerr, quietly, reaching into the shoulder holster for his Glock as he and Langton edged down to the first floor. "I'm signing off till this is done." They crouched by the banisters again, switched off their radios and positioned themselves with a clear view of the reception-room doors and observation room.

On his last walk across the lobby, Abdul Malik was in Kerr's direct line of sight. His jacket was buttoned up and, as he turned to close the door to the observation room, there was no sign that he was carrying a bomb. He looked totally calm, carried along in a trance. Before Kerr could react there was a swell of loud conversation and laughter as Malik opened the heavy reception-room doors and walked inside, reducing quickly to the same blurred hubbub as he closed the doors behind him. Kerr cursed himself for not moving as soon as Olga had warned them. The bastard was thinking about maximum casualties, he thought, seeking to contain the bomb's explosive force in the

484

room. Kerr got to his feet. "Cover me as far as the hall," he whispered to Langton, "then run like fuck for the fire escape."

Kerr was halfway down the stairs, Glock at the ready, before Langton could hold him back. The second Kerr reached the ground floor the noise from the reception room was suddenly cut off, as if someone had thrown a switch. Kerr rapidly took in the bolted front entrance, looked up to wave Langton away, and silently eased open the double doors.

Kerr could scarcely believe his eyes. The guests had fanned into a perfect horseshoe. Not one seemed to notice him enter, but in the instant before he acted, he took in eight or nine faces he knew from television and the press, or had seen in person. There were a couple of senior politicians, a bureaucrat from the Cabinet Office current intelligence group, a general he recognised from the distant past and, almost hidden among them, a minor royal, his features locked in slack-jawed horror. Other faces, familiar but unplaceable in that split second, shuffled through his memory: an eminent barrister, a tanned business tycoon, a broadsheet journalist, even a senior diplomat he had bumped into at the Yard years ago. Champagne glasses in their hands, they formed a tableau, transfixed, faces stupefied from drink and drugs, eyes locked on the solitary figure who dominated the centre of the room, like some modern deity.

Abdul Malik was holding his jacket open as if to display the lining, drinking in the terror of the infidels he was about to destroy. In the moments before martyrdom, he seemed to enjoy watching their eyes flicker from the explosives and nails at his waist to the toggle he clenched in his right hand.

Kerr's mind turned to ice, just as it had when he had faced Melanie's kidnappers in Hackney. The man became a target, disembodied, no more human than the paper images on the firing range at Lippitts Hill. He stood five silent paces away from Kerr. Time to the target three seconds, provided Kerr remained unseen. The man had his back to the doors but was turning slowly clockwise, forcing every victim to stare death in the face. Weapon down by his side, Kerr took a single step into the room, eyes locked on the toggle. Then two more, which brought him within five feet of the target. Close, but still out of striking distance. If any of the victims gave him away, if the target spotted him, Kerr knew it would be too late. Letting his eyes dart upwards for an instant, Kerr saw the smile on the target's face, serene with anticipation, and the glaze in his eyes.

He covered the remaining ground in three more steps, not two, because he moved slightly to the left to bring himself directly behind the man's frame, the Glock held high. He got his right leg in front of the target and pushed him with all his strength, watching his arms instinctively stretch wide as he crashed to the floor. There was a crack of bones breaking as Kerr stamped on the man's trigger hand and rammed his knee into the centre of his back.

With panic exploding all around him, Kerr twisted the target's head to the right, held the Glock against his temple and fired a pair of shots, a double tap. Everyone was screaming as he rushed back to the double doors and yelled at them to lie on the floor, covering them in a wide arc and aiming at anyone who did not immediately comply. He clicked the radio live. "All units from Alpha, go, go, go!"

The Territorial Support Group had followed his advice. He heard an engine revving violently in low gear, then a deafening crash as the armoured carrier smashed into the hall. He rapidly holstered his weapon as the doors behind him burst open and officers in riot gear flooded the room, yelling at everyone to stay down as they checked the corpse.

Before they could register Kerr's presence, Jack Langton appeared out of nowhere and dragged him away from danger into the street. "You all right, John?"

"There's no sign of those two thugs," said Kerr, as they raced for the Alfa. "Or Goschenko. Wasn't anyone guarding the back of the house?"

"We told the uniforms to stand off."

"Well, they must have got away." Kerr started the engine.

"I think Ma'am would like a word, when you've got a moment."

"Well, I haven't," Kerr said, accelerating away up the street. "We need to get hold of Karl right now."

CHAPTER
FIFTY-NINE

Thursday, 27 September, 22.19 local time, Malik Holdings, Istanbul, Turkey

The offices of Malik Holdings were empty when Rashid Hussain had taken his final call from Abdul Malik. Malik's wife had encouraged him in his mission, giving her enthusiastic blessing, but the back-room staff knew nothing. Three days before he had left for London, Malik had redeployed them at his father-in law's business. It was part of the plan agreed with Hussain weeks before, to protect the innocents when the truth was revealed.

The two men had agreed everything together, right up to the moment Malik caught his taxi for Istanbul airport. But all Hussain's subsequent actions, even while his director waited calmly for the outward flight, were private, decided by him alone.

Three Al Mukhabarat agents had been flown in secretly from Damascus to Samandira Army Airbase just outside Istanbul the previous night. As soon as Hussain gave the order, they cleared the furniture from the deserted offices and obliterated every speck of evidence that could incriminate him or connect him to the site. As the final act, a technical engineer removed the secret server. Its hard drives were the heart of the operation, Malik had said, ready to pump the images of British decadence around the world as soon as his own had stopped.

Hussain had to lean against a wall for his last conversation with Malik in London. The telephone was the final trail to Malik Holdings, and the Al Mukhabarat engineer stood nearby, waiting to disconnect that, too. Hussain and Malik had planned their exposure of the scandal about Grant, Attwell and other, earlier, victims to coincide with Malik's martyrdom. But the moment after he had promised to reveal the images he had scrupulously helped create, Hussain stole them.

Preparing himself for death, Abdul Malik would never know that the man he trusted as his friend and mentor above all others had used him for his own purposes. But to Hussain it meant nothing, for betrayal came to him as readily as allegiance. Both were equally necessary to the skills set of the secret agent.

As the life-blood from Malik's head soaked into the carpet, Rashid Hussain watched the Syrian agents carry the server onto the military aircraft for the short flight back to Damascus.

Hussain did not follow them onto the aircraft immediately. He made a call on his encrypted mobile, listening intently for three minutes, interjecting twice to ask specific questions. Then he walked alone in the darkness to a Bombardier Learjet parked alongside. A bodyguard in a dark suit was waiting for him at the top of the aircraft steps. He gestured Hussain into the main cabin, then withdrew to the front of the aircraft, where the flight crew waited for the order to leave.

He found Anatoli Rigov alone, near the rear of the cabin, sunk deep into his leather seat drinking a large tumbler of vodka. Without being asked, Hussain perched on the opposite seat. On the walnut table there was a Diet Coke with ice, the drink Hussain always took at their meetings. There were no preliminaries and they spoke in English.

"You heard about Harold?" asked Hussain, awkwardly.

"Goschenko just called me."

"I apologise. He was supposed to escape with Yuri."

Rigov shrugged. "Harold never could resist his appetites."

"The girl wanted revenge."

"And now so do I. Yuri believes you were betrayed by this man Sergeyev."

"Can he be sure?"

"Are you telling me there are other people you distrust?"

"No. We are completely secure."

"Who else, then? Sergeyev drove Yuri and the girl to the house. Then he led the police to us. What other explanation can there be? We underestimated him. You must deal with it."

"The Turks are ordered to eliminate Sergeyev tonight."

Rigov sipped his vodka. "I need you to tell me this, Rashid," he said, unsmiling. "Is our mission to be judged a triumph or a failure?"

490

Hussain shifted in his seat. "Harold gave us what we both required."

"And paid with his life. You should never have allowed the Turk to end things in this way."

"Malik was a zealot."

"A narcissist."

"His martyrdom was the deal and I had to honour it."

"It was theatrical," said Rigov. "The British will cover it up."

Hussain picked up his Coke and Rigov could see that his hand was trembling. "My masters have what they need," said Hussain. "They are satisfied. And grateful to Moscow."

This was an understatement. In Damascus, awaiting Hussain's return, his superiors were already celebrating the victim database as an intelligence coup. Their plan had been decided many months before. Al Mukhabarat would not deploy the pornographic images against the British establishment blackmail victims in a single rush of sewage, as the naïve and obsessed Malik had intended, but gradually, drip by toxic drip, into the secret channels of diplomacy. For them, the fact that the victims had not been vaporised by Malik's bomb enriched the haul, for it strengthened the threat. The loss of the Golan Heights in 1967 remained a running sore, just one grievance they held against every ally of Israel. Applied with care, the poison of photographs, videos and profiles of the survivors would lubricate many years of leverage against the West.

"The people Malik wanted to destroy are base metal, Anatoli."

"And the jewels?"

"I protected them for you."

"All four?"

"Of course." Hussain reached into his bag and laid a DVD on the table. As he did so, Rigov clicked his fingers. Immediately, a slim man in his twenties in shirt sleeves appeared from the front of the aircraft, took the DVD and disappeared through a set of double doors at the rear of the plane.

"Reassure me I am not to be disappointed?" said Rigov, quietly.

"They are all there, as agreed. Our payment to you, with thanks. No one has approached them since their compromise."

The DVD contained sexual images of four victims selected by Rigov and Goschenko, targets they had been careful to exclude from Malik's final, murderous event. There was an encryption specialist employed by GCHQ, a Treasury expert in economic intelligence, a nuclear physicist compromised in a single night and a member of the Cabinet Office with regular and direct access to Number Ten. Unlike the high-level establishment figures, whose profiles would be analysed in Damascus, the targets selected by Rigov were present-day operators, who dealt constantly with top-secret intelligence, the hard currency of espionage. Al Mukhabarat would have no further contact with these targets. The jewels belonged to Anatoli Rigov. That was the deal. In the months to come, Rigov's agents would coerce them to betray their country to Moscow.

The technical expert returned the DVD with a nod to indicate everything was in order. "Tell them to start the engines," was all Rigov said, unsmiling.

Hussain stood to leave and board his own aircraft for Damascus. "Do I have your authority to continue with the final phase of the operation?"

"You still have control of Jibril?"

"He is in position, awaiting my final order."

"Then do whatever is necessary. No trail of blood must lead to my door."

"So let me ask you, Anatoli," said Hussain, tapping the DVD. "Do you count your operation as a success?"

Rigov did not move in his leather chair. "Time will tell." He clicked his fingers again, for more vodka this time, and looked Hussain in the eye. "You must hope on your life that I do."

CHAPTER
SIXTY

Kerr needed Langton and his team to be on high alert for the moment Jibril reappeared. Steve Gibb was covering the observation post opposite his safe-house in Lambeth and the Reds immediately redeployed there from Chiswick. Kerr caught up with Melanie on the other side of the park as he speed-dialled Karl Sergeyev. His mobile was busy, and Kerr's anxiety mounted with each attempt.

"He'll be speaking with Olga," said Melanie. "She rang him as soon as I got her clear of the house."

Finally, Karl picked up. Kerr put him on speaker. "Karl, are you all right?"

"Of course, but I should be asking after you. Olga just told me everything. You did great, John. And Jack, too. Wish I could have been there with you guys." He sounded as if he was in a bar, slightly drunk, but in a high-spirited, party kind of way.

"Look, Karl, I think you could be in danger."

"No way. I'm covered."

"Goschenko is missing. And those two hoods. What if they think you led us there?"

494

"Nah. I'm supposed to be on the payroll, remember?" Fearless at his betrayal of Rigov, he said it with a laugh, like a man back at the top of his game.

"And the driver," said Kerr. "Olga told us you were seeing Nancy and the kids this evening. Where are you?"

"Chalk Farm. Nancy blanked me so I'm buying Olga dinner instead."

"Where?"

"Dominika's. Russian restaurant off Regent's Park Road. I'm telling you, we're back on track and it's truly fantastic. If you get a chance come and join us for a drink."

"Karl, listen to me. Does Goschenko know you use it?"

"No one knows. It's below ground and dark. Very romantic. If anyone's looking, they're not going to find us."

"So do me a favour. Stay with Olga in a hotel tonight, yeah? Just until I get this sorted."

"Sure." Karl was distracted. Somebody in the bar was saying something to him in Russian, and it was making him laugh again. "And when you get me back on the team I'll be taking care of *you*, my friend."

"Just watch your back, Karl."

They met again around Paula Weatherall's conference table. Looking exhausted, she was trying to sip scalding black coffee. Ritchie was rumpled, but ready for another long night. Exactly two weeks after his rescue of Melanie in Hackney, there was blood on Kerr's clothes again. He had washed his hands twice, but they still smelt of the firing range. He had been bracing himself for another outburst of anger. Instead they got up to shake his hand and ask if he was OK. Then, to his surprise, they thanked him, as if it was all over.

They were on different cycles: Weatherall seemed to be suffering a chronic case of operational post-mortem, but all Kerr's instincts were telling him the terrorist plan still had life. "I believe this is only one part of it," he said. "That pair of Turkish gangsters escaped. Yuri Goschenko got out as well. And the most serious part? Ahmed Jibril evaded surveillance. I'm telling you, this is dangerous. Nothing's changed. There has to be another bomb factory out there for something big, like I've been saying all along." With adrenaline still coursing through him, it was all coming out in a rush. "This is not the end, Bill. The man I took out is just the start. We have to action things tonight so we can hunt down these bad bastards and neutralise them."

Ritchie seemed to absorb everything, but Weatherall was evidently regarding him with a mixture of pity and scepticism, as if he had suddenly become a victim of trauma. Her self-defence reflex was so obvious she might as well have had "management liability" scrawled across her forehead. She began to report back on the Chiswick situation, behaving as if Kerr had not spoken. The house was clear of bombs and corpses, and the TSG were busy identifying the guests. Very soon, she said, the commissioner would be fielding some interesting phone calls.

As she took refuge in her notes, the warning that had been tapping at Kerr ever since Karl had brushed off his safety concerns suddenly hit him like a sledgehammer. He was back in 1830, listening to Karl's recording of Anatoli Rigov's pitch. With Rigov's dark voice in his ear, the words from Fargo's transcript seared his brain: "We hold you in high regard, Karl, as a fellow Russian . . . we have seen you with your family . . . they deserve a secure future . . . would you not agree?"

We have seen you with your family. Kerr went cold. Rigov's men must have followed Karl when he had visited his children. They knew where he lived. Ritchie was saying something across him to Weatherall, but Kerr did not even register it. If Olga knew he had planned to spend the evening with his family, he would have told them in the car on the way to Chiswick, which meant Goschenko would know as well. If Karl had fallen under suspicion, Nancy and the children were in danger, too. He heard Weatherall's voice in his ear telling him it was late and they all needed to get some rest. Kerr was on his feet, but his mind was already sprinting away.

Ritchie was frowning. "You all right, John?"

"I just remembered something." He already had the door open. "Sorry. Need to check this out."

Kerr was already speed-dialling Karl as he waited for the lift, but got voicemail. "Shit." Underground restaurant, no signal.

Screeching up the ramp from the basement garage he barely waited for the security arm to clear the car's roof before activating the blue light and charging towards Marble Arch.

He knew Karl Sergeyev's family home was in Hornsey Vale, a few miles north of his own apartment in Islington, so he took that route because it was familiar to him. He pulled into the kerb to confirm the house number and check Nancy Sergeyev's phone number on his BlackBerry, then slipped the Alfa into drive and spun away.

The Sergeyevs' house was in darkness except for a night light on the landing for the children. Kerr tried Karl's mobile again before ringing the bell, but got the same voicemail. Nancy scampered downstairs in her dressing-gown and invited him in before he could apologise. "Is everything all right?" she asked, as if she had been expecting him, leading the way down the hall. "I saw on the news half of Chiswick's been evacuated, but no one seems to know why."

The house was a three-bedroom Victorian semi with the living room to the right and a long hallway running alongside the staircase to the kitchen and dining room at the rear. "Were you expecting Karl home tonight?" asked Kerr, hooking his jacket over a kitchen chair.

"You know Karl doesn't live with us any more, John," she said, filling the kettle and throwing him an amused look over her shoulder. "Have you come round to proposition me?" She stared in disbelief as he told her to pick up her children and leave home. "So it's not just Karl who could be at risk, it's me and the children too. Is that what you're telling me? Why would they follow him here?"

"It's a sensible precaution, Nancy. I should have thought of it before."

She frowned into the middle distance. "I suppose we could stay with my mother if we absolutely had to."

"It's just for a few days. I'll get someone round first thing to help you . . ."

They both heard the footsteps. Kerr grabbed her arm and flicked off the light as they tracked the sounds along the side of the house.

"You need to go back upstairs now," he whispered urgently. "Get the children and shut yourselves in your bedroom."

Kerr lay prone by the kitchen door as Nancy raced up the staircase, willing his eyes to adjust to the darkness. Raising himself on his elbows, he risked a snap look round the dining-room door. In that split second he caught the pencil light and the shapes of two men in black picking the lock on the French windows. Shuffling back into the kitchen he found the BlackBerry in his jacket and dialled 999 for police. "This is DCI John Kerr, SO15," he whispered. "Urgent assistance to one three six Highburn Road. Armed, repeat armed, suspects on premises now. Silent approach."

Upstairs in her bedroom, Nancy held the children close as she peered through a gap in the curtains at the intruders on her patio. She ran back to her bedside, pressed the panic alarm Karl had installed in guilt at deserting her and pulled the children into her bed.

Karl and Olga were climbing into a black cab for a modest hotel in Belsize Park when he caught the warning. Until that moment they had enjoyed a great evening, becoming reconciled over *khachapuri*, beetroot soup, chicken *satsivi* and a bottle of Georgian wine. They had each told only one lie: Olga that she had never had sex with Goschenko, and Karl that he believed her. After Karl had convinced her he would get his job back at the Yard, but not how, they spent the rest of the evening speaking about their future together.

The text was there, buzzing red for danger, "Intruder alarm operating". He had planned to leave his car in the street until the morning, but the message changed everything. He told Olga he had to deal with something urgent and sent her off to the hotel in the taxi, promising to join her later.

Adrenaline flushed his mind clean and sent him roaring through the black, familiar streets to rescue his family, dialling Nancy on the move and accelerating violently when the engaged signal convinced him someone had cut the line.

From the kitchen doorway less than twelve feet away, Kerr watched the intruders defeat the lock and enter the dining room. The men in black moved silently together as a pair, drawing nearer, sending a chill up Kerr's spine. These were no ordinary intruders. He was in no doubt about the quality of his opponents or the scale of the threat. He was edging back as far as he could into the kitchen, steeling himself for an unequal fight to the death, when the BlackBerry betrayed him. It was on "vibrate" mode, but shattered the stillness of the house like a volcano. He muffled it against his body, but the intruders, already by the kitchen door, were on him in a split second, drawn by the beacon of Bill Ritchie's caller ID lighting the screen.

With violent death looming over him, Kerr admired their speed and stealth, two executioners working in perfect harmony as the larger of the two men lifted him bodily from the floor while his comrade found the light switch and aimed his gun in a single co-ordinated movement. They acted according to a plan, but Kerr's reaction was instinctive. Yelling at the top of his voice, he jerked back his head into the mouth of the man who held his arms and heard the cracking of teeth as he kicked out wildly, elongating his body like an enraged child, desperately stretching for any contact to delay his assassination.

His shoe connected with the gun, and he watched it fly from his executioner's hand in a slow-motion arc, slithering up the hall carpet. As the man flinched in pain behind him, he wrenched himself free. In a co-ordinated movement of his own, he elbowed him in the ribs, then launched himself against the slimmer man facing him, smashing his BlackBerry into the hooded face, the crack of glass telling him he was wearing spectacles. Kerr was shouting at the top of his voice, but both his assailants stayed silent even when he hurt them, confident about the odds in their favour and driven by the sweet experience of killing.

They attacked him again, aiming for his arms and legs and neck as he strove to reach the gun. The three men merged into a rolling bundle of muscle and violence, the black of the assassins slashed by the cream of Kerr's fresh shirt, bouncing off the walls as he drove them back to the front door.

In their trial of strength the larger man reached the gun first. Senses smothered by the intensity of the struggle and the rush of breath inside the balaclavas, the Turks did not hear the front door opening as they prepared to murder their target at the foot of the stairs.

Karl Sergeyev demonstrated a murderous professionalism that matched their own. When he stealthily entered the house, only Kerr saw him draw the illegally retained Glock 19 from his waistband. And because they had worked together as neatly as the Turks, Kerr was already moving before Karl yelled at the top of his voice.

"Clear, John!"

As Kerr leapt back and his assassin turned to face the new threat, Karl fired a rapid pair of shots at the Turk's head. The action braked hard again, giving Kerr a micro-second to admire Karl's skill in placing one neat hole in the balaclava at the centre of the man's forehead and another in his throat. Then everything accelerated again as the Turk fell dead to the floor, sending the gun on the move for the second time, and his partner made the fatal mistake of grabbing it. There was another satisfying double pop as Karl executed him, too, although this time Kerr could not tell where the rounds had hit.

Apart from his shouted warning, Karl had been as mute as the assailants. Without a word, he stepped over his first victim to reach the second body with the gun. Closing his hand around the dead man's to avoid leaving his fingerprints, he carefully took aim and fired a shot at the wall above the front door to demonstrate that their assailant had fired first.

Nancy and the children appeared at the top of the stairs as sirens filled the air, and the street became alive with flashing blue lights and crackling radios. Karl stared silently from Kerr to Nancy and back again as his friend took the Glock from his hand.

"What the fuck are you still doing with this, Karl?" demanded Kerr, with a smile, checking the serial number.

Karl stared back at him, then raised his eyes accusingly to Nancy, perched on the top step in her nightdress, shielding his children. "What the hell are you doing in my house with him?"

CHAPTER
SIXTY-ONE

Friday, 28 September, noon, Paula Weatherall's office

Weatherall placed Kerr on sick leave by phone as soon as he was discharged from St Thomas's Accident & Emergency Department. With Langton prowling outside, the doctor examined the bruises on his arms and chest and stitched a cut above his left eye where the larger of the Turks had punched him. At three in the morning the medic sent him home with a stern warning to keep out of fights. Weatherall ordered him to stay there.

In his apartment he checked all the TV networks, which were reporting the miraculous reappearance of Sara Danbury, found wandering in Chiswick, and the fatal shooting of two armed robbers in north London. He woke before eight, showered and returned to the office. Weatherall tried to send him home again, then agreed to meet him with Bill Ritchie at noon.

In the meantime, he rang Justin from the Fishbowl to check his recovery and tell him the fate of the thugs who had probably attacked him, too, during his late-night run.

504

Justin sounded cheerful. "So you're telling me the streets are safe now, boss?" he joked. "Can I put my trackies on again?"

Kerr was not surprised to find Justin was already back in the Camberwell workshop with another dressing on his head. His youngest expert's enthusiasm to continue the job, no matter the cost, re-energised him. As he kicked his heels, waiting to see Weatherall and Ritchie, he felt restless. He had unfinished business, and was impatient to see things through to the end. But something else was unsettling Kerr that had nothing to do with his professional life.

The race against time of the previous days, culminating in last night's violence and fight for survival, had drained his energy, physical and mental. Only now, in the hours of calm before the storm he knew was coming, was there room for a single emotion to bubble to the surface. It made sense of everything else for which he had been fighting so relentlessly: the real victims at the heart of his secret operation were not the blackmailed adults but the abused children. He had found Tania's killer and rescued Sara; but he guessed there were many more young, defenceless victims he would never be able to identify. Deeply affecting, that single thought sent him hurrying down the spiral staircase to the underground car park.

Ignoring a call from Bill Ritchie, Kerr rang Sara Danbury's parents, then drove down to see their daughter in the expensive west London clinic where she was to receive specialist medical and psychiatric treatment. He found Sara hunched in a chair beside her bed, pale and traumatised, staring listlessly out of the window.

"She hasn't said a word," her mother, Selina, told Kerr outside in the corridor. "Doesn't even seem to know I'm here."

"How is your husband taking it?"

"He's not, Mr Kerr. You rescued her body, but Michael says they still have her mind."

"What's he going to do?"

"The government's working out some sort of deal with him."

Kerr looked at her in astonishment. "He's going to let them buy his silence, you mean? Spin the whole thing around his own daughter?"

"I know you're a Special Branch officer, Mr Kerr," she said, peering through the glass door at Sara, "so don't feign surprise at the great British hypocrisy. This is the way things have always worked." She turned to face Kerr, as if the solution was obvious. "Michael wants to be prime minister. Don't expect him to be any different."

Kerr had gone to visit Sara Danbury as a father showing compassion, not an intelligence officer harbouring secrets, but the mother's cynicism doused him in another hot rush of anger. "Will you tell Sara that one day?" he said, as he walked away, his mind made up.

Weatherall and Ritchie were already in conference when Kerr returned with his secure briefcase. In the outer office, Donna insisted on examining his eye.

506

"Watch yourself. They're in a real strop," she said, before taking him through.

The aircon was on the blink again, casting a chill to match the mood. He found Weatherall behind her desk, looking as if she had just retreated there, and Ritchie was sitting moodily at the conference table, ready to pounce. They were quiet when he entered, pretending to study their notes, but the body language told him they were taking time out from a bloody row.

Weatherall looked drained as she circled back to the conference table and gestured him to the chair beside Ritchie. "You really should be at home, John," she said, in a soft tone he had never heard before.

"And a lot of people should be in jail."

Kerr listened with mounting incredulity as she gave her account of the morning's developments, concluding with the schedule of what she called "outcomes". She explained that an official from the Cabinet Office in Whitehall had summoned her to a meeting at seven-thirty that morning. A group of bureaucrats she did not know had already assembled round the horseshoe table in the subterranean Briefing Room B by the time she arrived, and appeared to have a damage-limitation strategy already mapped out. The chairman had informed her they had shrouded the night's events, including the shootings at Karl's house, in a Defence Advisory Notice. Specifically it was a DA Five, which covered anything connected to UK security intelligence and special services, and prevented any reporting by the media until approved by the government. It was essential, he had said, straight-faced, to safeguard the public interest.

"And to protect their own official who was in that house last night. Which means never, a total cover-up," was all Kerr could manage when she had finished. "So we major on the blackmail."

"We'll see. Now I have to get on, and you should get some rest. You said you have something for us?" asked Weatherall.

Kerr slid a couple of dossiers across the table, a copy for each. "Alan Fargo prepared this overnight. They set out everything we have on these people. If you want the shorthand, it says we can show Claire Grant and Robert Attwell were targeted by a foreign power. And I want you to authorise me to work on the other blackmail victims."

Ritchie took a printed email from his notebook. "Blackmail may be difficult to prove without a lot more international assistance than we're likely to get," he said slowly. Then he made a show of putting on a pair of glasses he hardly ever wore. From experience, Kerr knew this was a delaying tactic, a precursor to unwelcome news. "Turkish National Police just got back to 1830 with preliminary findings on your bomber. Abdul Malik was a wealthy businessman based in Istanbul, a crazy, according to them, well known to their Secret Service. Radicalised in London as a student, he turned against the UK and his own country, blah blah. They claim the bombing was timed to inflict political damage on Turkey."

"I could have told them that."

"Scupper its chances with the EU. Mr Malik believed his government was betraying its Islamist roots, apparently," he said, looking at Kerr over his glasses. "Oh, and he had a couple of ex-Turkish Secret Service mavericks working for him in London. The people you met up with last night, presumably."

"So get them to check out his base. Capture his hard drives."

"They already did. The building was a shell. No computers, nothing."

"What about the Syrian, Hussain? A known terrorist still using Omar Taleb as his cover name after two decades? Come on, Bill, this has Damascus plastered all over it."

Weatherall frowned at Ritchie. "I thought the Syrians were supposed to be our friends, these days?"

"We're only as good as our last compromise," said Kerr, before Ritchie could react. "If we bottle it today we risk years of Syrian-sponsored subversion alongside terrorism. Don't you see that? Ahmed Jibril's still out there somewhere. And Julia Bakkour? Christ, we can show Taleb ordered her to defend Jibril. There's a clear connection," pleaded Kerr, in frustration. "For God's sake, it's a no-brainer. We should be nicking her right now."

The aircon coughed into action again, spewing more cold air through the vents and sounding as angry as Kerr. He looked from one boss to the other. "Look, this is no time for denial. Theo Canning was a long-term Russian agent and Claire Grant provided visas for terrorists. Those are the facts. I trusted Canning and the truth hurts, but we have to face up to it. They both betrayed our country."

"The Cabinet Office covered that element, too," said Weatherall, returning to the list of decisions. She read straight from the script. Claire Grant would resign the following morning, citing personal reasons in a letter drafted by the PM's private office. That evening, the National Crime Agency would announce the death of its chairman, Sir Theo Canning, from a heart attack.

"He was stabbed in the chest, for Christ's sake," exclaimed Kerr, in disbelief. His first call that morning had been to Pamela Masters. He had rung her early, well before class, because he needed to tell her Canning was no longer a threat. To Kerr this was a matter of duty, to lift the cloud under which she had spent most of her working life. Her star in MI5 had waned following Canning's rejection all those years ago and, in that sense, he and Melanie saw her as another victim. She should feel vindicated, he had said, ready to make a fresh start. Now he wondered how she would react when this news filtered through. Would she see the deceit about her tormentor's death as protection for her or simply another betrayal?

Weatherall was staring at him blankly, as if the facts had no place in this narrative, then carried on reading aloud. Robert Attwell would take a career break, from which he would never return.

"You're not serious?" Kerr was incredulous. "I mean, you're not going to allow government to protect these bastards just to save its own skin?"

Weatherall was pouring more water from Donna's jug. "The people who attacked us in this way wanted to destroy the government," she said, "and I don't want to be accused of doing the job for them."

"So you're going along with the cover-up, just like all the rest?" said Kerr. He looked across the table, but Ritchie's head was down. Suddenly he understood the root cause of their disagreement before he had walked in on them. "Don't you see what you're doing? Joe Allenby took a massive risk when he tipped me off about Jibril. Alone, in a hostile country, he refused to toe the line. He did the right thing and paid with his life. Are you telling me it was all for nothing?"

"You've done a fantastic job in saving dozens of lives, John," said Weatherall, evenly, "risking your own. That's something to be proud of. Let's just leave it at that."

"Really? So what about the bomb?"

"What bomb?"

Kerr's chair crashed back. "I should have let him blow the bastards up," he said, already on his feet.

Donna opened the door as he was turning, already wearing her I-did-warn-you look.

"Knock first," came Weatherall's angry voice from across the room.

Donna did not acknowledge her, speaking softly to Kerr and holding the door open for him. "Melanie's on the phone. It's about your daughter."

Kerr could tell Melanie was driving, but her voice on the hands-free was calm and rational. "John, I need you to sit in Donna's chair and just listen for a moment."

"Tell me."

"About twenty minutes ago I had a sighting of Jibril."

Kerr's stomach lurched as Donna wheeled her chair to him. "You're supposed to be in East Ham."

"I am, watching for Samir Khan. Everyone else is at Lambeth waiting for him to return to the safe-house, so I'm here on my own, covering from the car."

"You sure it's Jibril?"

"Positive. Khan's scooter was parked in the street, not the front yard by the wheelie bin. First time I've seen that. It's like they left it ready for a quick getaway. Jibril had the key. He just started up, helmet on and buzzed off."

"So what's he doing in East Ham?"

"He knows the safe-house is blown. Must have thought he'd be secure around Khan's place."

Kerr stayed on his feet. "And?"

"I think he's got Gabi with him."

"*What?*"

"I'm on the move here, John, so you have to listen hard. I followed him onto the North Circular Road, westbound. He went to a house near Brent Cross. Parked up, went inside, came back out with a young woman. White, early twenties, slim build, jeans et cetera. She was already wearing the helmet when she came out of the door. He had hold of her arm right up until she climbed on the pillion, like he was worried she might do a bunk."

"How did you know it was Gabi?"

"It was your daughter, John. I'm sure."

"How far away were you when you saw her?"

"About four cars down the street. But I recognised her, John. And I snatched a sideways look at a red light. She's terrified."

"OK." Kerr was already turning the Alfa key in his pocket. "Where are they now?"

"Just turned off the North Circ. I'm on that big interchange at Neasden. Hold on. Indicating left. Looks like they're heading down towards Willesden. Thing is, do you want me to intervene now, or do I wait for the cavalry?"

"Are you carrying?"

"No, I'm not, actually."

Kerr was thinking rapidly, weighing the odds of an unarmed Melanie rescuing his daughter from a terrorist who might be armed to the teeth. Kerr had been required to surrender his Glock after shooting Abdul Malik, but instinctively felt for it inside his jacket. "No. I'm coming to you now. Just stay with them, Mel. Keep the commentary going on Channel Five."

"Are we going to call the Trojans in?"

Bad possibilities were exploding in Kerr's brain like fireworks. Loudest among them, as operator and father, was the murder of his daughter if anyone acted recklessly. Just below that was the fear of a lengthy siege with Gabi as hostage and a violent outcome from a botched raid. He had no idea where this was leading, no clue what lay in store for all of them.

"Not now. We do this ourselves."

CHAPTER
SIXTY-TWO

Friday, 28 September, 12.46, bomb factory, Willesden

Kerr was through to Jack Langton and Justin even before he'd cleared the Yard. They told him they already had Melanie's commentary. "Shall we get up to Willesden?"

"Quick as you can."

The most direct route from the Yard was the Edgware Road, a major artery heavily regulated by traffic lights but running straight as a die north-west from Marble Arch. On siren and lights, braking hard at each red traffic light, then accelerating, Kerr reached seventy-five for short stretches through St John's Wood and Maida Vale. But his vision was not blurred by the red mist that afflicted the eyes of less experienced men. He drove with care, seeing only the road ahead and his daughter in jeopardy. He knew Gabi's life depended on him getting there.

Melanie's voice came on Channel Five. "Willesden High Road, John. You'll see the nick in front of you. Jibril's thrown a right into Stafford Street."

"I'm about five minutes away. Keep it coming."

There was the growl of Langton's motorcycle as he scorched a trail across the city from south to north. "Be with you guys in fifteen," said Justin, from the pillion. "We just crossed the river."

Overwhelming feelings of love and fear flooded the car as Kerr raced to the scene. But even more powerful was the cold rage that rushed in alongside. His daughter was the victim, but he was the intended target. It was obvious. Just as they had tried to reach Karl's family, now they intended to destroy his. Different perpetrators, same revenge. The realisation rolled through his mind with a terrible clarity. Gabi was the victim not just of the men who had taken her from him and Robyn but of his own stubbornness. Soon he would force them to confess exactly how they had got to her but, before that, Kerr had to admit something to himself: she had been taken because of his refusal to compromise in his determination to get at the truth. His obsession had exposed Gabi to a murderous threat. He had condemned his daughter to this fate. Remorse stabbed him in the pit of his stomach.

He cursed himself, then drove faster.

When he heard Melanie again she was obviously out of the car. "John, he's turned into a service road off Stafford. Just after the pillar box." Outside, on the street and running. "I can't drive in there without blowing it. I'm going to find another way. I'll talk you in."

"Two minutes." Kerr was already in Willesden High Road. He saw the police station and geared down for the right into Stafford Street. A patrol car was pulling out of the station yard so he braked sharply and let it go first. The last thing he needed now was to be pulled by the local uniforms.

He spotted Melanie's battered Honda by the pillar box straight away. "I'm here," said Kerr. "Do you still have them?" He saw that she had driven it nose in, abandoning it in too small a space, leaving the driver's door ajar in her rush to re-establish contact.

She was speaking to him again as he double-parked beside the Honda and leapt out. "Yes, I do. Into the service road, maisonettes on the right. There's an alley between the fourth and fifth leading to the gardens." She was breathing hard. "Wall at the end, then a fence. Watch your step. There's a drop the other side."

Kerr had difficulty locating Melanie as she was completely hidden from all sides, eventually finding her prone on a rough sleeper's patch of scrub in a space hollowed out from bramble bushes. Nearby were a couple of empty lager cans with plastic bags and strips of sacking beyond use. Relief surged through Kerr. She still had them in her sights. As he dropped down beside her she was pointing at a row of garages about thirty paces away, scarcely visible through the undergrowth. The left door to the third garage was ajar, and he could see the scooter parked outside.

"He just took her inside."

A man appeared briefly in the gap between the doors. He was head and shoulders only as he checked for intruders, and visible for less than three seconds, but it took them only a heartbeat to identify Ahmed Jibril.

"Let's go," said Kerr, clambering to his feet.

"No, John. Get a grip." Melanie had a restraining hand on his arm. "You're not thinking clearly. We're unarmed. Don't know how many are in there. Let Jack bring in the Trojans."

"What? Risk an armed siege against a *jihadi*? No way."

"It's your daughter in there, for God's sake. You can't risk just charging in."

"It's what I did for you at Hackney, Mel," he said, pulling his arm away. On impulse he stooped to pick up a length of fallen branch, weighing it in his hand. "Coming?"

Kerr skirted the bush to the right, then gently eased a passage for him and Melanie through a mass of softer vegetation until they reached the end garage in the row. The door of the target garage was still slightly ajar. There was a sliver of light, and as he edged down the row he imagined he could hear Jibril's voice, and Gabi weeping. He had no game plan, no idea of the situation he was about to face, or the odds of success. All he could be certain about was the limited area of the combat zone. He would act fast, with noise and violence, reacting to each movement in the few seconds he would have to eliminate the threat. Kerr had one advantage, which quelled any feelings of self-doubt: he was feeling murderous against those who threatened his daughter, and the surge of power from that raw hatred would only be stopped by a bullet to the head.

With Melanie right behind him, Kerr listened intently outside the garage. Then, abruptly, realising he would be covered by the noise from an approaching train on the main line, he stepped back and kicked the door wide open. At the same time he yelled, "Armed Police! Stand still!" before his eyes had registered anything, then charged inside, holding the branch in front of him with two hands like a firearm, Melanie shouting, too.

In an instant Kerr took in the confined space. He saw the bench with metal and tools, the fridge, microwave and futon. His mind was signalling "bomb factory" as it caught Gabi's open-mouthed terror and, close beside her, the startled face of Ahmed Jibril. The terrorist was only fooled by Kerr's stick for an instant, but it was enough for Kerr to throw it at his face, then charge him down with an attack yell that must have carried right to the street. Jibril was smaller and lighter than Kerr, and fell back easily against the bare brick wall. His head seemed to bounce back at Kerr, who punched him twice in the face and kicked him to the ground.

As Jibril fell, Kerr was aware that Gabi had circled round and now stood on the other side of the garage, by the bench. Melanie was holding her tightly, like a prisoner. Only then did Kerr see the main threat. His eyes first went to Gabi's ashen face, crumpled in tears, too frightened even to scream. He held his arms out, not to call her to him but for her to keep completely still. "Don't move, Gabi. Stay exactly where you are."

Over her shirt Gabi was wearing a black cotton vest. It had four pockets filled with material in clear plastic bags. Kerr had seen an identical item less than twenty-four hours earlier, around the body of Abdul Malik. Melanie was already kneeling down, examining every centimetre of the vest and its contents. "John, we've got a detonator and what looks like TATN. And nails. We need to get help here now."

Ignoring her, Kerr pulled Jibril to his feet and rammed him back against the stove. "Is it armed?"

"Go screw yourself," he said in broken English. Jibril's face was bruised but his eyes were bright. Kerr understood. The fanatic who had toyed with Finch's finest need show no fear: nothing in this country could do him harm. "I'll ask you once again. Is it ready to go?"

Jibril stared him down, eyes mocking, inviting Kerr to hit him again. Beside him, Gabi was sobbing and Melanie had both hands on her shoulders, to comfort her but mainly to keep her absolutely still.

"Where were you going to take her?"

"Why should we take her anywhere?" Jibril gave a harsh laugh. "No, we let the infidels come to her."

Kerr punched him hard in the face, and this time he fell unconscious. There was a coil of rope on a hook on the wall above the futon and Kerr used it to bind Jibril's hands in front of him. In the left pocket of Jibril's jeans his mobile was vibrating. Kerr carefully withdrew it and looked at the screen. It was a text from Samir Khan, the target in East Ham, with two words: "Send now?"

Kerr texted a one-word reply, "Now", and showed it to Melanie. She immediately covered his hand. "Be careful, John. The signal. You sure this can't detonate the bomb?"

"No. Everything will be all right." He pressed "Send". Seconds later, Kerr's BlackBerry vibrated. He had an email from an unidentified sender: "Your daughter will be waiting for you at two p.m. exactly. Brent Cross Shopping Centre, first floor by the main elevators. Come alone or you will never see her again."

Kerr knelt down with Melanie beside Gabi to examine the vest. It was fixed at the front by two metal clasps, with a narrow loop of fabric around Gabi's neck to support the weight of the detonator, explosives and shrapnel. A toggle identical to Malik's dropped by Gabi's right hand.

"It's hurting me, Dad." Gabi was shaking now, close to hysteria as the shock sank in. "Please help me."

"It's OK." Kerr took her hand. "We're going to get it off you. But you have to keep absolutely still." He glanced at Melanie, then carefully manipulated the clasps while Melanie pulled the vest tighter to ease the pressure. When it was released, the weight took her by surprise and she almost dropped it. She laid it gently on the concrete floor as Kerr took Gabi in his arms.

Melanie was already standing up and there was the glisten of sweat on her brow. "Job done," she said. "Please, let's get out of here."

Kerr gently pushed Gabi to her. "Take her to the car and tell Jack and Justin to stand off."

"John, this whole place could go up."

"I'm not finished here. I'll join you in a minute."

520

When they were gone, Kerr knelt down to study the vest again, then tested the hook from which he had taken the coil of rope. Jibril was groaning, beginning to come round. He tied a length of rope around Jibril's bound hands, dragged him across the floor until his body was directly beneath the hook, then looped the rope over it. He hauled Jibril to his feet and pulled on the rope until his arms were high above his head and he was almost on tiptoe. Jibril was awake now, but Kerr ignored him as he gingerly picked up the vest and secured it around Jibril's upper body.

"I'll ask you once again," said Kerr, looking directly into his eyes. "Is it live?"

Jibril's face looked different now. He was a *jihadi*, but suicide was not his favoured method of mass murder. Kerr understood perfectly. Suddenly, Jibril was betraying the fear of the ordinary man confronted with his mortality. His eyes showed surprise, too, perhaps because he believed he was destined for greater things than this.

"Were you really going to use my daughter as a bomb?" said Kerr, quietly.

Jibril was starting to say something, but Kerr suddenly realised the time for talking was over. Staring into Jibril's face, his mind reeled back to his Tube journey with Gabi so many years ago, and his execution of another bomber, which had caused so much damage to their relationship. A voice inside was telling him he could avoid making the same mistake again. This was his chance to walk away, it said. There would be no

521

cover-up this time. Jibril was going nowhere, except to jail for the rest of his life.

But even as these thoughts cascaded through Kerr's brain, his hands grabbed a roll of twine from the bench and tied the free end to the toggle. Without another look at Jibril he reeled out the twine, walked from the garage and closed the doors behind him, putting the padlock through the hasp.

Outside he moved quickly, carefully unravelling the twine as he crashed through the undergrowth. This time he travelled in a straight line, impervious to the twigs whipping his face and the brambles ripping his clothes. He was less than ten paces from the end garage when he stumbled on a fallen branch. His falling body yanked the twine hard. There was a loud crack followed by a roar and a rush of searing heat. Then he felt a sharp pain in his leg and head. It surprised him because it was such a different sensation from the tearing of the undergrowth. Then the same searing, roaring energy was ripping away his clothes and he was airborne, flying easily through the saplings and dense brambles, which, seconds earlier, had been so difficult to penetrate. Almost the last thing he heard was the deafening flapping sound of birds abandoning the trees and foliage, before something exploded inside his head in a final red-hot, searing meltdown, and he was wrapped in blackness.

CHAPTER
SIXTY-THREE

Melanie reached Kerr first, sprinting between the maisonettes with Jack Langton close behind. She found him, crumpled and unconscious, close to their original hiding place. His flying body had created a neat tunnel through the undergrowth and he must have bounced a couple of times to reach the higher ground, ending up hard against a beech tree. The explosion had ripped all his clothes and his skin was covered with weals and scratches. His upturned face was a swollen mass of red, almost unrecognisable, and Melanie immediately pressed her bare hand over a heavily bleeding wound on the left side of his skull. He lay like a discarded puppet, his limbs splayed at unnatural angles, and his broken lower left leg flopped haphazardly across his right shin. The shrapnel Melanie had been examining only a few moments earlier around Gabi's body had ripped into his legs, reducing his trousers to shreds, and his shoes were nowhere to be seen. As she searched for life signs, Langton was kneeling beside her, pressing a handkerchief to Kerr's head wound as he called for assistance on Channel Five, managing to give their precise location.

"Weak pulse," she said quietly to Langton. Melanie wanted to keep Gabi away. She shouted to Justin, but Gabi was already tearing into the bushes, kneeling down to cradle her father. Melanie checked his airway and immobilised his neck as best she could with a makeshift pillow of twigs and leaves. Justin covered him with his jacket, and everyone willed the competing sirens to reach them.

Melanie glanced at Langton and Justin, following their gaze to the bomb scene. The whole row of garages had disappeared, although the site itself was still burning fiercely. Melanie looked in vain for signs of Jibril's corpse: either the fire had consumed every trace, or his remains were covered with debris. The wind shifted as they stared, blowing dense black smoke in their direction. It made them cough, and Gabi tried to shield her father's face from the fumes as a huddle of onlookers from the maisonettes appeared at the end of the alleyway.

The first local uniforms on the scene were trying to clear the area. They sent the occupants back inside and came over to Kerr's team. The older of the two was brisk and professional as he tried to make sense of the situation and account for victims. "We need to clear the area. Paramedics are on their way." His glance at Kerr's body said they probably would not be necessary. He meant nothing by it. He was doing his job, trying to manage the crisis, but Langton flashed his ID and told them to piss off.

524

"How the fuck could this happen, Mel?" he said, when they had gone.

Without taking her finger from the pulse in Kerr's neck, Melanie pointed at the flames. "Jibril must have topped himself as John was getting clear."

Langton's body language was telling her he did not believe a word of it, so Melanie looked away and gave all her attention to Kerr. There was nothing else to say, so Melanie gently searched what remained of Kerr's clothes. She found his smashed BlackBerry in his jacket pocket, his car key and some cash in his trousers. She expected nothing more, for she knew Kerr always travelled light.

Everyone was relieved when the paramedics arrived. They needed space, so while they stabilised Kerr for the rush to hospital, Melanie put an arm round Gabi and slowly led her back to the car.

They took Kerr to Central Middlesex Hospital in Park Royal, about three miles away. Melanie followed with Gabi in Kerr's Alfa, while Jack and Justin roared ahead to clear the traffic. Gabi protested that she wanted to go with Kerr in the ambulance, but Melanie told her it was not possible. That was a lie, but Melanie needed space to get her talking. Gabi was in shock, crying that she was to blame for everything, so Melanie needed to extract as much information as possible before she closed down completely.

"Robyn told us a young man called Sam had been writing to you," said Melanie, as they pulled out behind the ambulance.

"He Facebooked me a couple of weeks ago. I should never have accepted. I'd been writing stuff about Palestine and he wanted to work with me. We were writing to each other for a couple of days, then I gave him my mobile number. He wanted to Skype me and he seemed such a nice guy. We chatted for ages." It was raining now and Gabi stalled for a moment at the memory, biting her lip and staring through the streaks of water on the passenger window. Then the words came in a rush. "His family in Pakistan had been through hell. Really suffered, you know? We met for a coffee near college. He wanted me to help him start a student group. Tuesday afternoon he picked me up on his bike and brought me out here."

Melanie slipstreamed the ambulance through a blot of heavy traffic in Craven Park Road. "To the house where he just collected you, yes?"

"There was another guy, too. They took my mobile and kept me upstairs in one of the bedrooms. Told me I could go in a couple of days."

"Did they harm, you, Gabi?"

"It wasn't like that. No one laid a finger on me. Just didn't want me to leave, that's all."

"It's kidnap, Gabi. Very serious."

"I feel a complete idiot. I was so scared, Melanie."

"There was nothing you could do. Try and think back. When did he contact you the first time? Exactly? It's important."

The ambulance had switched on the siren to negotiate a red traffic light and Gabi stared directly ahead. She was weeping again, as if she alone was responsible for everything.

Melanie reached for Gabi's hand. "Gabi. This is not down to you. We'll get you through it."

The ambulance eased its way across the junction followed by the Alfa, and then they were left with just the sway and swish of the windscreen wipers.

"It was the evening after the concert Dad came to," she whispered.

"Some people bugged John's flat. They must have found out about you that Sunday when we all came round, remember? When you got back from Rome?"

"So they were using me to get at Dad? How could I be so stupid?"

"This is so much not your fault, Gabi. Listen to me. You could never have known. This 'Sam' who contacted you. I think his real name is Samir Khan. He's a friend of the man who just killed himself and we're going to arrest him."

Gabi was crying again. "I've been so mean."

They were approaching the hospital. As the ambulance pulled into the emergency bay, Melanie could see Langton and Justin already waiting.

"He was going to blow me up," said Gabi in disbelief.

"We would never have let him."

"And now they've killed Dad instead."

"Don't say that." Melanie gripped her hand tightly. "Let's just hope for the best."

Melanie drove into the nearest waiting bay and switched off. She had the door open but Gabi was still sitting there, looking at the rain through the passenger window. "I can't go in," she wept.

Melanie pulled the door shut, scarcely able to hear her. "Of course you can. He needs you."

"I've been so mean to him, Melanie. A complete bitch for years." She swung round, her face wrecked and puffy. "It's just . . . he has such a weird life. You know, the thing with him and Mum. It's hard for me to get my head around."

"I can imagine."

"And no one else's dad does the things he does, none of my friends' dads. The things you all do. I didn't really get it till now. This is all down to me."

"No, it's not."

"I've been a complete and utter moron."

Melanie leant across Gabi and clicked her door open. "So let's start again."

In addition to the countless lacerations all over his face and body, and a badly gashed leg from where he had crashed into the tree, Kerr had serious shrapnel injuries to his head and back. Langton and Justin joined them in the A&E waiting room, where they hung around like caged animals, comforting Gabi and keeping in touch with Donna. When she was more composed, Gabi borrowed Melanie's phone to call Robyn, who told her she would catch the first flight the next day. When they sent Kerr up to the ward and settled him in the room closest to the nurses' station, the four of them went to the canteen for a break.

By the time they returned, Kerr's new doctor was using different language. She was young and looked tired, as if she had treated several Kerrs that day. She used different language to describe his condition. Things had moved on from unconsciousness, a temporary state they more or less understood. The word she used was "coma". At some time between being blasted against a tree and trolleyed up in the lift, the drip-fed, heavily bandaged figure they glimpsed through the screen had drifted to this other place. And that was a good sign, she said, because it gave his body space to recover.

"So what happens now?" said Langton.

"We wait and see."

"But what are you going to do?"

"I just told you."

Epilogue
The Great British Hypocrisy

Friday, 28 September, 20.42, the Fishbowl

Back at the Yard they took Gabi to the Fishbowl and brewed the decent coffee Kerr kept in his middle drawer. Jack Langton was already stepping up to the plate in Kerr's absence, briefing Ritchie to set things up for the surveillance and arrest of Samir Khan and his associates near Brent Cross. Melanie called home and asked her husband, Rob, to make up a spare bed for Gabi. Langton tried to send them home, but Fargo led everyone back into 1830.

While Gabi waited in the reading room, Fargo sat them down at two workstations and opened a Word document. "John and I have been working on this for ten days," he said, as they looked at each other in surprise. "It covers every detail."

"Great, Al," said Justin. "And?"

"We did it because John anticipated they'd try and conceal everything. Which is exactly what's happened."

Now they were all concentrating on Fargo in astonishment. "And?" said Justin again.

"I want you to read it now and tell me if I need to add anything. And if you agree with it."

530

"What are you going to do with it?"

"Just read."

It was a distillation of their investigation into a classic Special Branch comprehensive report headed simply: "Moscow's Hostile Operation against the UK". It ran to fourteen pages, together with an assessment, beginning with the hatred of Abdul Malik and his manipulation by Syrian secret-service agent Rashid Hussain. It described how Moscow had subcontracted their British spy to the Syrians and controlled the whole operation from day one through Anatoli Rigov.

And it named names, identifying Theo Canning as the agent Harold, the rapist who had made everything possible, and exposing Claire Grant as the government traitor addicted to sex and protector of Ahmed Jibril. Finally, it laid out the abuse of the girls smuggled into London by Canning's corrupt police officer. Attached to the main document were the dreadful photographs and video.

They absorbed the content in less than five minutes.

"Looks good to me," said Langton.

"What do we do with it?" said Melanie.

Fargo gestured them to his workstation. They huddled behind him and saw that the report was attached to an email ready to go. The title read: "Blackmail, Terrorism and Betrayal: Moscow and the Great British Cover-up".

"We blow this thing sky high," said Fargo slowly. "Provided we all agree?"

"You're sure this is untraceable?" asked Langton, when he saw the recipient address.

"Everything sender protected."

"What would John want us to do?" asked Langton, speaking their minds.

"He'd want us to add a sign-off," said Melanie.

"Fair enough." Fargo opened the document again and scrolled to the last page of text. "Go."

"For Joe, a loyal friend who loved his country," said Melanie. "And Kestrel, who led us to the truth. *In memoriam*."

"Check."

When he had finished, Fargo swung round in his chair to look them in the eye. "You sure?"

He was going to ask each of them by name, as if taking a vote, but the voices came in unison: "Send it."

In Sydney, Australia, Toni Miller, chief investigative reporter of the illustrious *Sydney Morning Herald*, saw the envelope pop up on her screen as she sat down with her coffee. She skimmed the text with growing astonishment, then opened the video of Theo Canning raping Tania. She grabbed the phone and dialled without taking her eyes from the screen.

"Harry? You need to get down here now."

ISIS publish a wide range of books in large print, from fiction to biography. Any suggestions for books you would like to see in large print or audio are always welcome. Please send to the Editorial Department at:

ISIS Publishing Limited
7 Centremead
Osney Mead
Oxford OX2 0ES

A full list of titles is available free of charge from:

Ulverscroft Large Print Books Limited

(UK)
The Green
Bradgate Road, Anstey
Leicester LE7 7FU
Tel: (0116) 236 4325

(Australia)
P.O. Box 314
St Leonards
NSW 1590
Tel: (02) 9436 2622

(USA)
P.O. Box 1230
West Seneca
N.Y. 14224-1230
Tel: (716) 674 4270

(Canada)
P.O. Box 80038
Burlington
Ontario L7L 6B1
Tel: (905) 637 8734

(New Zealand)
P.O. Box 456
Feilding
Tel: (06) 323 6828

Details of ISIS complete and unabridged audio books are also available from these offices. Alternatively, contact your local library for details of their collection of ISIS large print and unabridged audio books.